The World Traveler

Book 2 in the Clarence Duval Series

Also by Rob Bauer

Fiction

My Australian Adventure

The Buffalo Soldier

Darkness in Dixie

Nonfiction

Outside the Lines of Gilded Age Baseball: Alcohol, Fitness, and Cheating in 1880s Baseball

Outside the Lines of Gilded Age Baseball: Gambling, Umpires, and Racism in 1880s Baseball

Outside the Lines of Gilded Age Baseball: The Origins of the 1890 Players League

The World Traveler

Book 2 in the Clarence Duval Series

Rob Bauer

Although the people who participated in the Spalding Tour of 1888 and 1889 described in this book were real people, this is a work of fiction. My portrayal of each character is fictional, and so are many of the events of the tour I've written about. This story should not be interpreted as an accurate description of the Spalding Tour or its participants.

This is a work of historical fiction. Names, characters, places, and incidents are the product of the author's imagination or are used fictitiously. Use of actual historical events, authentic texts, and names is of public access and public domain.

For any inquiries regarding this book, please contact Rob at robbauerbooks@gmail.com.

No part of this book may be reproduced in any form or by any electronic or mechanical means, including information storage and retrieval systems, without written permission from the author, except for the use of brief quotations in a book review.

For David Mitchell

Our own baseball adventure wasn't quite this epic, but it remains one of the highlights of my life.

Author's Note on Language

One of the difficult things about writing historical fiction featuring African Americans is the use of racist language. Words that are painfully demeaning today were, sadly, commonplace usage in the era when this story is set. I've chosen to keep these words for the sake of historical accuracy. I mean no offense to any of my readers.

Contents

1. Ballarat, December 29   1

2. Melbourne, December 31   9

3. Great Australian Bight, January 9   23

4. Adelaide, January 10   37

5. Indian Ocean, January 15   46

6. Colombo, January 25   61

7. Colombo, January 25   71

8. Colombo, January 25   85

9. Arabian Sea, January 26   89

10. Cairo, February 7   104

11. Cairo, February 7   114

12. Giza, February 9   123

13. Naples, February 16   141

14. Naples, February 17   152

15. Pompeii, February 18   158

16. Rome, February 19   165

17. Rome, February 22   172

18. Rome, February 23   187

19. Nice, February 27   193

20. Paris, March 5   203

21. Paris, March 6   217

22. London, March 12   222

23. London, March 14   229

24. Liverpool, March 23   235

25. Dublin, March 26   246

26. Cork, March 28   256

27. New York City, April 6   260

28. New York City, April 8   265

29. Chicago, April 20   280

About the Author   288

Acknowledgments   289

Chapter 1

December 29, 1888
Ballarat, Victoria, British Empire

"Heeelp!" I shout while I topple over the edge of the pit and into the mineshaft, but no one can react fast enough to save me.

Clang!

The only thing that saves me from a long drop and certain death is that I fall inside the cage that lowers the miners down to the bottom and back up. My back hits the iron bars of its frame first, spurts of pain shooting through me as I bounce an inch or two off the iron rails. I roll onto my stomach and lie still, gripping the bottom of the cage.

I just stay like that for a moment, wondering if I've broken anything, but the pain starts to fade momentarily, so I don't think so.

The cage I've landed in is like a box with no lid. The frame of the cage features heavy iron rails, and more iron rails, a little thinner, lace between the frame to prevent people from falling through.

I'm safe here, I think to myself. I can even hear the babble of voices from the players up above. They'll get me out of here soon.

Although I try to breathe in and out a few times to calm down, my breath still comes in panting gasps. I look at my hands and realize I'm gripping the iron bars of the mining cage so tightly that not only are my fingers turning white, but also some blood trickles from where I've punctured my own skin. I uncurl my fingers and let go. Still, I'm safe. I just need to rest a moment, and someone will help get me out of here.

Creaaaaak!

The metal crane on the surface used to lower the cage lurches and crashes to the ground in a scream of tortured, twisting metal, and I realize how wrong I am.

Next, I hear two of the metal cables holding the cage in place start to whine. Normally, four stout metal cables keep the cage suspended in the mineshaft—one at each corner of the cage. The fall of the crane cut two of them, and now they're dropping into the pit. The half of the cage they held up drops, and I'm falling again.

There's no time but to reach out and hope I grab something as the gray walls of the mineshaft turn to gray streaks.

My fingers brush the iron bars but miss.

My body strikes what used to be the side rail of the cage but is now the bottom rail because the carriage dangles on its side by just two wires, and I bounce over the railing.

As I fall into the pit for the second time, again my hands reach for whatever they can grasp.

This time, my fingers curl around the railing, and I stop my fall with a sharp jerk.

"Someone help me!" I scream again in pain and terror.

For the second time in Australia, my shoulders feel the wrenching pain of having to stop my body while I plummet through the air. I manage to keep my grip, barely, but I'm hanging there, both hands on the cage's side rail, and I'm not strong enough to pull myself up, much less climb out of the mineshaft by one of the two metal cables keeping the cage suspended in air.

Desperately, I look up and see what happened. Two of the metal cables that support the cage slipped from their guides on the metal tower when it went down, which unbalanced the cage. The whole thing didn't fall to the bottom, but one side of it did, causing the cage to dangle from the remaining two support cables while I dangle from the side of the cage.

It now swings from side to side, which scares me. How long will the last two cables hold?

I hang there looking up because I'm afraid of what will happen if I look down. Finally, I see some faces appear over the side of the mineshaft.

"Clarence!" several of them yell down to me. "You're alive! Hold on, boy, we'll do something."

The faces disappear. I'm hanging there, and my arms and shoulders scream in pain before long. I see my fingers around the railing, the only thing preventing my death, tremble and shake with strain.

I look up. Nothing. No help.

I look back at my hands and realize both my arms are shaking from wrist to shoulder. My hands are sweating, too. I try to grip tighter, so I won't slip.

A scraping sound. I glance up and see John Healy, the pitcher for the All-America team, rope tied around his waist, making his way down the side of the mineshaft toward me. When he's level with me, he reaches out his arm and says, "Take my hand, lad. Careful now, not too quick."

I reach out my right arm to grab his, but my body drops a bit with only one arm holding on, and I miss Healy's hand. At the same time, I feel the little finger on my left hand slip off the railing. Then my ring finger.

Healy sees it, too. From the corner of my eye, I see him flex his knees, hear him grunt with effort, and push off from the side of the mineshaft and leap outward, toward me.

He grasps my right arm, just as my left hand lets go.

I'm dangling again, but this time, Healy has both his hands on my right arm.

"Pull us up!" he shouts, and I hear the grunting sounds of men heaving on the rope above us.

It seems like we're only moving inches at a time, but we're moving upward. "Don't worry, I've got a good grip, lad," Healy tells me.

Finally, with one final heave, we're up. Once we are, I just kneel for a moment, and then fall on my face and cry with my head down.

I'm dimly aware that a few of the players pat me on the back and mumble encouragement, but I don't look up to see who they are.

After a minute or two, however, I hear another sound. Stomping boots, getting closer. I decide I'd better look up.

When I do, I find that all kinds of guards and employees of the Barton Company have closed in around us, carrying guns of various types. In another moment, they begin hustling our party away from the pithead.

I feel a tug on my right arm once again. "Come on, Clarence my boy, we've got to go," Healy says to me, urgency in his voice.

Standing up to follow, I'm still so scared that my legs shake, and I fall back down. I get up and try again and keep my feet this time, even though my legs shake almost as much as my arms.

"Come on, lad, we've got to get out of danger. Follow old John."

I stumble after Healy, and, finally, we reach a place away from the pithead and damaged equipment, outside the fence enclosing the company's property. When we do, several of the baseball players come over to shake my hand and pat me on the back again for my escape, and they do the same to Healy. I still have trouble getting a breath.

I also notice how unlucky I was. A stout iron fence stands around the pit's entrance, so people won't fall in. I just happened to fall through the gap in the fence where the miners get in and out of the cage.

I hear Harry Palmer, the Chicago newspaperman, say, "John, that was capital of you, very brave. And you caught Clarence at just the right time. Whatever made you do it?"

"My brother Thomas is a miner in Montana Territory," Healy answers, his breath still a bit ragged, too. "He tells me about mining accidents there. They happen all the time, and they kill and injure the miners. I wasn't about to let an accident take away our lucky mascot."

"My readers in *The Sporting Life* and the *Chicago Daily Tribune* will hear of your bravery, John. You'll be a hero when we get back to America," Palmer tells him.

Finally, I have a chance to just sit on the ground, breathe easier, and gather my thoughts. I walk over to John Healy and give him a huge hug. My arms only go up to his waist because he's so tall. I start crying again when I do.

He just pats me on my head. "It's okay, laddie, no shame in crying."

That evening, we finish the tour of Ballarat we began earlier in the day, listen to more speeches, and enjoy more food and wine. The city officials are as apologetic as they can be about the incident at the gold mine. They tell us they believe that angry miners probably planned the bombing to strike back for the company firing some of them recently and cutting their wages. The officials also mention that the miners were talking about forming a vile union and that the gold mine would not tolerate such a thing. Finally, they mention that local authorities are already moving to find out what happened and arrest the criminals and that they have no reason to believe that the attacks were meant to target us. I look over and see John Ward, Ned Hanlon, and Jim Fogarty all scowl when the speaker uses the words "vile union."

While they tell us this, I stop for a moment and think about what the miner, Snelling, said about enjoying hospitality at the expense of the children of the miners. If the miners really did set off the explosions, they must be very upset to do something so drastic. I just wish they had done it some other day! Maybe the miners have a point, however. What people told me about children working in the mines and about how no miner lives to be forty frightens me. However, I also have my personal rule, about never turning down food if I don't have to pay for it, and decide today isn't the day to break my rule after everything that happened to me.

When it's time to leave the banquet, I'm walking down the hallway toward the front door of the banquet hall and my carriage back to our hotel, when, in a side hallway on my left, I hear the voices of Harry Palmer, the Chicago newspaper writer who came on our tour, and the Australian man who gave most of the speeches at the banquet tonight. I stop just around the corner from them and listen.

The Australian man speaks first. "Here, Mr. Palmer, take this and share it with your other reporter, Newton MacMillan. Ballarat cannot afford any more negative press regarding the conditions in our mines, here in Australia or in your country. This is the fifth incident we've had just in the past two years, and if word keeps getting out, we'll never get anyone to come work here."

"I appreciate your problem," Palmer says, "but still, I believe the public deserves to know of John Healy's heroism today. It will make quite a stirring story for my readers back in the States."

"Perhaps you can concoct an incident at the orphanage earlier today instead? Perhaps he saved a young child from drowning in the swimming pool or something of that nature?" the voice says.

"Yes, that could do. I may have to share a bit of the money with Healy, but he certainly deserves it after his work today. I'll tell my reading public that our trip to the mine went off without incident and that our boys all had a fine time while enjoying the hospitality of your company."

This is the second time on our trip I've overhead Harry Palmer talking to someone and taking money to change his version of the news that he reports. I know I can't trust him all the way, but I hope that if I'm nice to him, he will still help me and tell me information about what is going on. However, his agreement signals that his conversation with the Australian man is winding down, so to prevent them discovering me, I back up quietly, then walk forward again while whistling a tune, so that Palmer and the Australian will just think I'm wandering along, instead of listening to them.

When I pass the side corridor, I see Palmer emerge, although the Australian man is not there. He must have gone the other way.

"Greetings, Clarence," Palmer tells me. "That was quite an escape you had today. Your luck remains as strong as ever, it seems."

"Thank you, Mr. Palmer, that is nice of you to say. I think I've had enough of mines, though. They seem a bit dangerous for me."

"Yes, Newton tells me that, even before the drama at the pithead, you suffered from claustrophobia, or perhaps, to be more accurate, taphephobia."

"I don't know those words, Mr. Palmer." They are a little too long to be in any of the books I've practiced reading with Newton MacMillan, the other Chicago newspaper reporter. He's the one who agreed to teach me how to read.

"Claustrophobia is a fear of tight or enclosed places, while taphephobia is a more specific type of claustrophobia, which refers to a fear of getting buried alive or trapped underground. In either case, I am glad you are still with us and did not suffer any serious injuries."

"Thank you, Mr. Palmer. I guess we should go find our carriage to the hotel now, right?"

"Yes, I think you're correct, Clarence. They will probably depart soon, and we'd best be in one of them."

Once we arrive, I search out John Healy. "Thank you again, Mr. Healy, for saving me today."

"You needn't mention it again, Clarence. I wouldn't have thought of doing any differently."

"Can I ask you about something else, Mr. Healy?"

"Certainly."

"Does Mr. Palmer work for Mr. Spalding?"

"Not exactly. You know he writes for the newspapers in Chicago, right?"

"Yes."

"That means that he speaks with Spalding frequently, so he'll have information to put in his news articles. He doesn't just repeat everything Spalding tells him, but the two are on good terms, and he tries to help Spalding when he can."

"I think I see."

"It's just somethings reporters have to do sometimes, Clarence. Palmer needs to be on good terms with Spalding, so Spalding will tell him useful things to write about. Having access to inside information helps newspaper writers get ahead in their profession."

"Do that seem dishonest to you?"

"Yes and no. I consider their relationship a good reminder of how you should always consider the sources carefully when reading things in the papers. I don't know how often, or even if, Palmer lies about things in his articles, but he tries to put his stories about Spalding in their most favorable light."

While Healy tells me this, I wonder if Palmer's shared any money with him yet.

Chapter 2

December 31, 1888
Melbourne, Victoria, British Empire

We are back in Melbourne, and it's December 31st, the last day of 1888. The ballplayers came to Australia to show Australians what baseball is about, but today we're watching a new game that I've never seen played in America. A pair of teams, one from Carlton and one from St. Kilda, play a game the Australians call football. I'm watching them while sitting near Jimmy Ryan and Ned Williamson, who appear too fascinated by the game to take much notice of me.

Thinking back on what happened in Ballarat I realize how lucky I am to be here. I almost died twice within about three minutes, once from the mining cart flying toward me and once from falling into the mineshaft. Falling into the mineshaft was bad luck because someone else panicked and bumped me, but I'm worried because I panicked, too. When the mining cart came toward me, I just couldn't do anything. I froze. I also remember how badly I felt after going to the bottom of the mine. Palmer called it claustrophobia and some other word that I can't remember now. Whatever the word for how

I felt is, I felt so awful, so sick, that I know I shouldn't go into mines again.

While the football players run back and forth doing things with a ball that I don't understand, I look over at Williamson. He is, along with Ed Crane and Anson, the largest and most powerful man on our tour. A conversation I had a couple weeks ago about Williamson with Newton MacMillan comes to mind.

"Mr. MacMillan, how long has Mr. Williamson been with the White Stockings? He seems to be a friend to nearly all the players."

"Oh, some years now, Clarence. Since 1879, I believe, maybe even 1878. Longer than anyone but Anson, at any rate. It's true, Ned is an agreeable companion most of the time."

"Except when he joined the Howling Wolves," I say with a smile.

"Perhaps, but that is the type of man Ned is. He enjoys having a good time as much as anyone. When Mike Kelly was with the White Stockings, why, those two were a sight to see! The amount of beer they could drink was legendary. The only problem was it made Ned so fat he could barely play ball in 1886."

"Mr. Williamson used to be fat?"

"Like an alderman. Yes, he weighed nearly 270 pounds when the 1886 championship season ended and had but one hit in the World Series that year."

"I've only seen him like he is now. He sure looks healthy and in the pink of condition to me."

"Yes, getting married helped him turn his life around, Clarence. His wife, Nellie, has been a calming influence. It's made him a strong ballplayer again, too. Did you know, Clarence, he once threw a baseball 396 feet on the fly? No one on the White Stockings has thrown it farther since. Or that in 1884 he hit twenty-seven home runs? That's still the record in major league baseball, even if some unusual ground rules at West Side Park contributed a few extra home runs to his total. But, yes, Ned is a brilliant athlete when in proper form."

The rest of the conversation fades, but it strikes me this might be why Williamson shows so much interest in this new game of football.

I look out at the football game once more. The game isn't like baseball at all. More than twice as many players are on the field. I think I count twenty for each team, but it's hard to tell because the players don't stay in one place in the field like baseball players do. Instead, they move the ball, which is large and shaped like an egg, up and down the field, with almost all the men running constantly. They move the ball around from one player to another either by kicking it or by batting it with their hands. It is also a very rough game. The players on the team without the ball seem intent on tackling the player who has it until he gives the ball up.

Curious about the game, but unsure if I should try speaking with Ryan, I consider asking Williamson about it. Finally, I get up my courage to speak. "Mr. Williamson, have you ever played this game before?"

"No, Clarence, I have not, but we are supposed to play a game against one of these teams, the St. Kilda team, this afternoon. Jimmy and I agree that we want a crack at playing football, and many of our other boys do, too. It is a sport requiring exceeding manliness, don't you think, Jimmy?"

"Indeed," Ryan responds. "You can't be yellow when you go out to play football, that's certain. These are hardy lads. Still, I'll wager we'll make a good showing this afternoon."

It is easy to believe Williamson and Ryan when they say that, especially Williamson. Even though he used to be bigger, he is nearly six feet tall and still very muscular. He might not weigh 270 pounds now, but 200 seems a fair guess at what he does weigh.

"I agree," Williamson says. "Once we master the rules, we'll do fine. Our technique may be a bit raw, but we can't help that. Still, this game may have a future back in the states. What do you say to that, Jim?"

"It may. It looks especially promising as a sport for the fall and winter. Summer is when Americans play baseball. It always will be. When we finish our schedule in October, however, that might be a time for football."

"Look at that kick," Williamson breaks in. "See the accuracy. It went right to the other man. We're going to have to be on our game today, Jimmy, old boy."

"Perhaps, although those rain clouds don't bode well. Wouldn't that be just our luck; Christmas Day is so warm here you can't keep your drink cool, and now, when we get the chance to play a new sport with our hosts, rain threatens to wash out the whole thing."

"I'll bet you we play today. My two dollars against your two dollars we get in nine innings and a game of football."

"Deal. Now, let's go find someone to hold the money until this afternoon when we know the winner."

The two men walk away, leaving me to watch the footballers at play. They are all white; I don't think I've seen one other colored person since I got to Australia. I wonder why that is? I remember the newspaper article Fogarty read back in Denver mentioned Australian women having dark skin, but they must live somewhere else in Australia.

It turns out that Ryan wins the bet. The Chicagos and the All-Americas start their game but only get to play two innings before the rain sheets down. At that point, Captain Anson and Captain Ward agree to call off the game and return to the hotel.

Our horses trudge through the streets on our way back, but it's still raining hard, and it takes longer for the horses to drag the carriages as the streets get muddier. I can hear the sucking sound when each horse pulls its foot out of the slimy mud and see water dripping from their bodies. The mud has that smell of wet earth mixed with the rotting garbage and sewage puddled here and there along the side of the street.

Because the rain soaked my clothes, too, I'm huddled in our carriage, rubbing my arms and hugging my chest to try to keep warm. It isn't working very well. The whole carriage has the musty smell of wet fabric, but no one says much because they're all drenched, too. The dripping water has formed several small puddles on the floor of our carriage. It has a roof, thank goodness, so at least things aren't getting worse.

We're plodding along, the horses with their heads down, when, without warning, the coach in front of us hits a rut in the road. It must have broken one of its axles because the carriage falls over on one side, and all the men inside fall through the door into the muddy street. Ed Crane, Fred Pfeffer, Jim Fogarty, Tom Brown, and Fred Carroll all topple out into the slimy, clinging, stinking mud.

It's my bad luck to be riding with a couple of the Howling Wolves, Bob Pettit and Marty Sullivan. When they see their fellow Wolf, Fogarty, dumped into the street and struggle to regain his footing they are unhappy, and I'm a convenient target for their anger.

"What are you waiting for, Clarence?" Pettit points at me. "Go out there and help them."

"Right," Marty Sullivan says. "Tell Fogarty we have an extra seat. Yours."

Sullivan opens the door to the carriage while Pettit firmly pushes me down to the street. I guess whatever sympathy I earned for almost dying in Ballarat is gone.

Through all the rain falling against my face, I can take in a bit of what the city looks like while I slog toward the unhappy ballplayers. Where we're at, the street is broad. It looks fifty or sixty feet wide. I see trees planted near the sidewalk on each side, but because I don't know what kinds of trees Australia has, I can't identify them. Most of the buildings in this part of Melbourne are brick, and some have two stories, others three. Most have chimneys on top, but because things have been so warm until today, not all of them give off smoke. The roofs of most buildings are flat or slope gently toward the street. Today, that means rain drips steadily. One of the larger buildings has two small domes. While I approach the disabled carriage, I note that each street corner in the upcoming intersection has a lamppost made from gray iron, about the same color as today's sky. Because it's the middle of the day, they aren't lit.

I trudge over to where the five men are trying their best to wipe off the sticky, oozing mud. Ed Crane, the burly pitcher of the All-America team, is the player closest to me.

"Can I help you, Mr. Crane?" I ask. "Are you all right?"

"A little the worse for wear, Clarence, but nothing bruised, nothing broken. I'll need my uniform laundered before we play another game, but otherwise, nothing to worry over. Why are you out here in the street getting muddy with us?"

"Mr. Pettit and Mr. Sullivan said I should try to help. They say Mr. Fogarty can have my spot in their carriage."

"Those buffoons," Tom Brown, the All-American outfielder, says. "Don't they know the carriage driver won't let us in his carriage caked with mud? We're going to have to walk the rest of the way to the hotel. At least it isn't more than a couple blocks from here. I'm afraid you'll have to come with us too, Clarence, for the same reason. Pettit and Sullivan are just stupid kids. They might have half a brain between them."

I don't know much about Tom Brown except that he was born in Britain and has played ball for many years. He has been one of the quietest men on the trip. I think he is still a little flustered because of what happened to him at the gold mine the other day, because he's speaking softly, even for him, and I struggle to hear even though I'm standing just a few feet away.

Come to think of it, Brown and I have not talked much on this trip, even in passing, although he seems a decent sort. He played the outfield for the Boston Beaneaters last season. Although Brown is from Great Britain, he has been in the United States long enough that most of the players have stopped making fun of him with cricket jokes. Like Fogarty and Hanlon, he is a speedy outfielder.

He is correct about the need to walk to the hotel, it turns out. After saying as much, the driver of the damaged carriage walks off in search of a way to fix his broken axle, cursing all the while.

Mud cakes my pant legs, and a great deal of it is all over the rest of me by the time we arrive at the hotel. I'm upset at Pettit and Sullivan, of course, because I'll have to clean my pants before our parade tomorrow. When·we arrive at our lodgings, I find that, like usual, I do not receive an invitation to go to dinner and the theater with the teams, so at least I have something to do while I'm by myself at the hotel.

The rest of our time in Australia passes without major incidents involving me. The schedule does not call for the teams to play any more games until January 5, the day before we leave for Ceylon, so the men spend most of their time relaxing, shopping for souvenirs, and roaming the town. I don't go shopping. Although I have the money from my dance still, like John Tener suggested, I decide to save it until I need more clothes. It is late in the evening of January 3, and I'm almost ready to turn in for bed, but my room is on the third floor, and whoever is on the floor above me is making a great deal of noise. I'm trying to decide if it is worth trying to sleep when I hear a knock at my door. Opening it, I see Tom Brown there, along with Ed Crane and Tom Burns.

"Hi there, Clarence, may we come in a moment?" Crane speaks for the group.

"Sure, Mr. Crane, what is it?"

"We've noticed, Clarence, you have kept to yourself lately. You've been hard to find these past few days while the rest of us were out and about."

"Yes, sir, I don't really have any spare money to shop for things, or any nice luggage to store things in even if I could afford to buy them." It's also because I don't want anyone to ask me to do plantation dances and humiliate me anymore, but I don't tell him that.

15

"We thought as much," Crane says. "So, we got you something. This is to make up for you having to walk through the mud with us the other day. Here, take it."

He hands me something made of wood. Its shape is like the letter "V," but with the arms of the "V" flattened out a bit. Both the top and bottom are smooth and polished.

"It's called a boomerang," Crane says. "Yesterday, the three of us, and some of the other boys, went to the Melbourne Centennial Exhibit. While we were there, we saw a demonstration where some of the native Australian people threw them. They are wonderfully skilled at it. If you throw it right, the boomerang curves in the air and comes back to you. It is possible to catch your own throw. It's really quite amazing."

"We all bought one for ourselves," Burns chimes in. "But Tommy Brown here suggested we get you one, too, and Ed and I thought it a capital idea. So please, take the boomerang. If you can toss it as well as you toss your baton, you'll be an expert in no time."

"The Australians told us it's made from black wattle, an Australian hardwood, so it has a bit of weight to it," Crane tells me.

I carefully take the boomerang and run my hands over its smooth texture. It is about a foot and a half long, and it looks beautiful. I wonder how a person can make it curve in the air and come back to them. Maybe I can try it tomorrow and figure out how to do it. "Thank you, all of you," I tell Crane, Brown, and Burns. "It is wonderful and looks very nice. I will try to learn how to throw it."

"You're welcome, Clarence," Crane responds. "We thought you deserved to have at least one memento from Australia after sailing all this way with us—and almost getting killed to boot." The men turn to leave.

"Oh, by the way," Crane turns and says on his way out the door, "Spalding told us the name of the ship we'll take from here to Ceylon. It's a German ship, named the *Salier*. Try to remember that if you can."

"Thank you, Mr. Crane, I won't forget it," I respond.

After this wonderful surprise, I try to settle in and sleep, but I don't have much luck. I close my eyes and envision the smooth, wooden boomerang arcing through the air and coming right back to my hand, and I catch it just as surely as I catch my baton.

January 5th, the day of our last game in Australia, is a busy day. Some local cricket players try to play a game of baseball with the Chicagos but don't have much luck. After my parade duties, I end up sitting next to Harry Palmer, and we watch the game from the Chicago bench. It lasts just two innings.

He says to me, "Look, Clarence, how the Australians have already taken to baseball. In just a matter of weeks here, already they show enthusiasm that would make an American proud. I take this as proof that Mr. Spalding's mission has succeeded beyond anyone's expectations. Just look at this crowd of spectators, Clarence! There must be eleven or twelve thousand people on hand, wouldn't you say?"

"You're right, Mr. Palmer. A great many people are here today."

"Call me crazy, Clarence, but these Australians seem to love baseball almost as much as the cranks in New York, Boston, and Chicago. I have little doubt that they'll form a baseball league before long. I think that either Ward or Anson could name their price if they wanted to play ball here in Australia and captain a nine to show the Australians how to play the right way. What do you think about that?"

"I think your guess is better than mine, Mr. Palmer, but you are a smart man, so perhaps you're right. Is it true we are to see another game of football today as well?"

"You're quite right, Clarence. I believe that the teams from Port Melbourne and Carlton are to take part in the match."

"Do we have football teams in the United States?"

"We do, but they play the game by somewhat different rules. This Australian version of football more closely resembles our sport of rugby. However, the Australians have made some noted improvements on rugby, in my eyes. The game is rather less dangerous for the performers, for one thing, and allows for greater displays of skill, dash, and vim on the part of the players."

"They are quite skilled at kicking the ball."

"That they are, Clarence. Now, if only they had smarter uniforms. Do you agree?"

"I suppose so, Mr. Palmer."

"So, Clarence, who do you like in the throwing contest today?"

"I didn't know about a contest, Mr. Palmer. Who is involved?"

"After the football match, our boys will play a five-inning game for this throng of spectators. Following the game, three of our men, Crane, Williamson, and Pfeffer, aim to beat the Australian record throw for a cricket ball. The local sportswriters for the Australian newspapers tell me the Australian record is 126 yards, 3 inches. All three of our boys say they can top it. The players have any number of bets on the outcome, but most of the money is on Williamson."

The football teams play to a tie, and the Chicago team wins the baseball game, 5-0. After Palmer told me that Crane would take part in the throwing contest, I resolve to bring him good luck and don't pay that much attention to either of the games. I try everything I know to make him lucky while putting a hoodoo on Williamson and Pfeffer.

First, when Crane comes to bat, I turn a dozen circles, but not thirteen, because that's unlucky. When Pfeffer bats I make an effigy of him in the dirt, but then stomp on it and make an "X" through it with my toe. I walk toward Williamson's bat, knock it over, and leave it lying on the ground for bad luck when Tom Daly, the Chicago catcher, notices me.

"Clarence, what on earth are you doing?" he asks. From the arc of his eyebrows, he looks confused, rather than suspicious. I wonder how much he drank last night and whether he's thinking straight this morning.

"Trying to bring good luck, just like always, Mr. Daly. I must keep my mascot talents sharp. I'm trying out some new ideas today, though."

Daly shakes his head and goes back to watching the game. I think I do smell alcohol on him.

Finally, the game is over, and the players stand ready to make their throws. Williamson steps to the throwing line first while the spectators applaud. He hops forward toward the line, grunts, and makes a long, high heave. It seems to take forever for the ball to come down. The sphere arcs beautifully through the air for several seconds before finally plopping to the turf. Several men stand near where the throw lands, so they can measure the distance. One marks the spot, while some of the others measure Williamson's throw. After a few seconds to record the measurement, the word comes back: 125 yards, 8 inches. Just short! Williamson drops his head and shakes it a few times, sighs once, but the audience cheers his near miss all the same, and he remembers to tip his hat with a smile.

Pfeffer comes next. Like Williamson, he takes a running start and launches a high, graceful throw. A few seconds later, it strikes the ground. It is also a long toss, but clearly short of Williamson's. Once again, the men measure the throw, and Pfeffer's distance is 122 yards, 20 inches. The audience claps politely for Pfeffer as well, apparently believing that the Australian record throw will stand this American challenge.

If we are to see a record set today, and if any of the ballplayers want to make good on their boasts, Crane will have to be the one responsible. He, like Williamson, is a muscular, heavy man, who stands about five-foot ten and weighs near to 200 pounds. Crane is a barrel-chested man, and, if I'm not mistaken, his chest has gotten even more barrel-like on our trip. He does like to eat. When he pitches, the speed on his fastball always impresses the crowd. The speed on his ball is so great, the other players have nicknamed him "Cannonball."

"How about some good luck, Clarence?" he says to me as he approaches the throwing line.

"I've done everything I can for you, Mr. Crane," I respond. I continue to mouth some lucky sayings to myself as he steps forward. I wish I had a rabbit's foot to help, but sadly, I lost mine back in Nebraska before I got to Omaha. Part of me has always suspected that was the reason Ms. Jarbeau set me loose when she did. I should find another one here in Australia before we leave. Someone said something about how many rabbits there are in Australia, Ward, I think, so it shouldn't be hard if I can just remember to look at the right time.

Speaking of Ward, he's on one knee watching the players throw. He motions me over while Crane swings his arms a bit to prepare.

"Do you think he'll make the throw, Clarence?" Ward says to me when I wander over to him.

"I hope so, Mr. Ward. I've given him all the luck I can."

"He holds the record for longest throw of a baseball, so I like his odds."

"How far can he throw?"

"Four hundred five feet, seven inches is his best. I wonder if he's had his lucky meal lately?"

"Mr. Crane has a lucky meal?"

"Sure does. A dozen eggs in a bowl, followed by two dozen clams."

"That sure is a lot of food."

"Yes. For a man who likes sharp, tailored suits as much as Ed does, keeping his weight steady has always been a problem. His growing fondness for drink on this trip has become a larger problem, I'm afraid. You know it's best to stay clear of him in the mornings while he clears his mind, right?"

"Yes, Mr. Ward. He is a kind man when he's feeling himself, however."

"Agreed, Clarence. He's a fine companion and a great storyteller. Have you ever heard him sing? I'm most impressed with his tenor voice."

"Only once, but you are right, his voice is very powerful."

"We just need to get him to lay off the wine and beer, Clarence, and help him be himself again. Once, back in 1886, he told me he'd never had a drink in his life. Never. Now, he drinks nearly every day. It's a concern, for sure. Especially because he's my teammate on the New York Giants, and we're going to need him for the upcoming championship season. In any case, though, he's stepping up to throw now. Let's see what he can do."

Crane doffs his cap for the onlookers and gives everyone a friendly wave, smiling while he shakes his arm vigorously. He takes a deep breath, winds up, takes a few steps toward the foul line, and makes a mighty throw. It sails on and on through the air, like it might never come down. When it finally does, the crowd rises to its feet and madly applauds Crane's effort. It is clear Crane's throw surpassed the others. When the measuring crew announces the result to the crowd, another burst of clapping and cheering ensues. Crane threw the cricket ball 128 yards, 11 inches! Some of the All-America team hoist Crane upon their shoulders and carry him from the cricket grounds as the crowd continues to applaud his heroic toss.

The next day, as we get ready to board our ship and leave Australia, I find Crane to congratulate him myself. He appears sober when I approach.

"Mr. Crane," I say to him, "that was a wonderful throw yesterday. I did everything I could to give you good luck, like I said I would, and it worked. You broke the record!"

"Yes, having you along was just enough, it seems. I guess that makes up for having to slog through the mud the other day."

"That must be why people call you 'The Cannonball.'"

He smiles at the use of his nickname, but then, just for a moment, he looks down to the ground and closes his eyes. The next instant, however, he's smiling again. "Thanks, Clarence. We'll see you around, kid."

Chapter 3

January 9, 1889
Great Australian Bight

I find one big difference between the *Salier* and the *Alameda*. On the *Alameda*, there were many other first-class passengers besides us. On the *Salier*, most of the first-class people onboard are in our group. I'm thinking on what this means for my chances of avoiding Anson, Pfeffer, and a few of the Howling Wolves on the way to Ceylon when John Tener approaches.

"Clarence, Captain Thalenhorst would like to speak with you."

I wonder what chores I'll have to do on this trip to earn my way while the ballplayers lounge around. Even though I know it's pointless, I try stalling with a question. "I thought that the captain and the crew were German, Mr. Tener. How can they speak with me?"

"Yes, the captain is German, like most of the crew. He speaks English very well, however. Most of the crew only speak German, but the captain is multilingual. The bridge is right up there." Tener points, even though I'm quite aware of the bridge's location.

I wonder what my fate will be this time. Dishes again, probably. So far, I think the food is better on this ship, so perhaps I can get some extra table scraps.

When I arrive on the bridge, even before I can knock on the door, the captain sees me through the windows and waves me inside. I enter and wait for the bad news.

"So, you are Mr. Duval, the young bandleader I've heard so much about. I am Captain Thalenhorst. I'm pleased to meet you." He holds out his hand with a broad smile, and I shake it. The captain has a long, full beard and wears a white linen shirt to go with his blue captain's hat. He looks around fifty years old, with a few lines in his face and some gray hairs streaking through his dark beard. He has the slightest limp when he walks over to greet me. His grip is quite firm and steady, however.

"Yes, Captain. Mr. Tener said you wanted to speak with me?" I say it tentatively.

"Yes. I'd like to show you something, if you have a moment?"

"I think I do, Captain. We are many days from port, if what the boys tell me is true."

"They are correct. We'll be at sea for a good while. Now, I want you to look at this."

He limps over to a chair, where sits a large, roughly constructed wooden box. I'm starting to get curious, and now I'm hopeful that I won't be getting new duties after all. Considering some of the nasty surprises I've had on this trip, however, I know better than to get my hopes up too much.

While I think about these possibilities, the captain reaches into the box and pulls out a smaller wooden box. Someone has applied a clear substance to this smaller box that makes it very shiny. It has hinges on one side, so the top can open, and a crank lower down on the same side as the hinges. The captain turns the crank a few times, which makes a muffled noise of gears clicking such as you hear when you wind a clock, and hands the polished, shiny box to me.

"Here, try opening the lid, Clarence."

24

I take the wooden box carefully, sit down with my legs crossed, put it in my lap, and lift the lid as instructed. When I do, the box starts playing the most beautiful music. I don't know what the names of the songs are that it plays. Perhaps they are famous songs only in Germany, but what a delightful thing! After a few minutes, the music stops.

"Can you make it play the music again?" I ask the captain.

"Yes, Clarence, just close the lid, and then slowly wind the crank on the outside, and you can hear the music play again when you open the lid."

I do what the captain says and turn the crank several times, and when I open the box, I get to hear the music once more. Fascinating. I've never heard of or seen a device like this. The music plays again for a few minutes, and then it stops.

"I take it you like my music box," the captain says to me.

"Yes, sir, I've never seen anything like this before."

"It is a present for my son in Germany. He is about your age. I am hoping he will like it as much as you seem to. Would you like to see a picture of him?"

I nod and gently put the music box down. The captain pulls a locket of shiny, silver metal from his breast pocket and opens it up, handing it to me, so I can see inside. I see the captain, a woman I presume to be his wife, and a boy my age smiling together. The young boy has dark skin like me.

"Surprising, isn't it?" he asks me as he takes the locket back and closes it.

"That boy in the photograph is your son?"

"He is my adopted son, yes."

"I'm sorry to ask too many questions, sir, but can I ask how he came to be your adopted son?"

"About four years ago, we Germans acquired a colony in Africa we call German East Africa. Even before it became our colony, however, our merchant ships often called at the port city of Dar-es-Salaam. I was the captain of one of those merchant ships before

25

trading that position for another as the captain of passenger ships like this one. In any case, one evening some men from my crew went ashore and had too much to drink. They insulted some local officials and got into a scrape with them. Sadly, after the fight was over, they followed one of the officials to his home and shot the man and his wife. The official they shot was my son's real father. My son, who was about one year old at that time, just happened to cry from his crib as my sailors left the house. They brought him to me and, after I questioned them mercilessly and threatened them with all the authority I could muster, confessed what had happened. I decided to punish the men as severely as our rules allow, but I didn't know what to do with this child. At that point, something came over me. Call it the Grace of God, if you will, but at that moment, I decided to adopt the boy and take him home to Germany. I've raised him as my son ever since. That was eleven years ago, and he is twelve now."

"That is a very moving story, sir. You are a very kind man. I hope your son likes his music box." No better words than that come to mind, although I can think of many nice things I'd like to say to the captain because of his kindness. I start to hand the box back to him.

"You are welcome to keep it for a few hours if you want to listen some more. Just be sure to bring it back when you are done and take good care of it."

"Really? I promise to bring it back just like it is now."

"Oh, I have one more thing, Clarence."

Here comes the bad news at last, I think to myself.

Instead, the captain says, "I've instructed my sailors to show you every courtesy while on board my vessel. One member of your company, Mr. Anson I believe it was, told me how you had done chores to pay your way on the trip from America to Australia and suggested I might have you do the same. I will have none of that. The ship has plenty of qualified sailors who do these things as part of their duties. Don't worry about anything while you are on board the *Salier*, and try to enjoy yourself until we make port," he concludes with another kindly smile. The captain claps me on the shoulder, smiles again, and gives me a quick salute when I leave.

I take the music box to my cabin, guarding and watching over it like a treasure the entire way. It's hard to say how long I sit next to it, turning the crank and making it play its beautiful songs, but it must be an hour, at least. Finally, I decide to take it back to Captain Thalenhorst. I thank him again for both the music box and not having me do chores. Just as I finish, the gong rings for lunch, so I head toward the dining room.

The sailors on the *Salier* seem to go out of their way to treat us first-class—I've never seen them get upset or argue with any of the players. Even when the Howling Wolves decided to torment the crew last night, they took everything with a smile. The waiters in the dining room are just the same. They wait on all of us politely, and they always smile and bow.

Today, however, something happens that I never dreamed of. I am sitting down for my meal when two of the waiters arrive to serve me at the same moment. The first tries to put my plate in front of me, but the second waiter shoves the plate aside and tries to give me the one he carries. Both plates are identical—bread, potatoes, and chicken—so it makes no difference which one I get, but the men start talking loudly to each other. Next, they both put down their plates on the table and start gesturing wildly. Even though I don't know any German, it is clear they are arguing over who gets to serve me lunch!

A fight begins and quickly goes from shoving to actual punches. It only lasts a few moments because other waiters arrive to separate the men before either of them lands a good shot, but it's long enough for me to hear Fogarty yell out, "I have five dollars on the taller one! Who'll take the bet?"

Soon, another man shows up who appears to oversee the dining room, and he marches both waiters away, shouting what I take to be several stern remarks at them in German. Both leave with their heads bowed.

"Well, would you look at that," I hear Pfeffer drawl. "Two white men arguing over who gets to serve a nigger. I've never seen the likes of it. Something's wrong with these Germans, I tell you."

"They'll be bowing to him and addressing him as 'Your Coonship' before long, I'll wager," Ned Hanlon growls.

I try to eat and ignore what everyone is saying, although I must admit that what just happened was embarrassing for me, too. Having one person serve me food is a new experience. Having two people fight over who gets to do it, well, I'm not sure how to respond to that. I keep my head down and chew for the rest of the meal hoping to avoid any more attention and angry stares from the players.

After lunch, I decide to hide out for a bit, just in case, so I climb up on the roof of the bridge and take in the view. While I breathe in the fresh, salty, warm air, I see that one of the brawling waiters is now walking the railing of the bridge. It is a punishment, I suppose, for losing his temper in the dining hall. I start to get sleepy from the peacefulness of everything up here and decide this will be my hiding place on the ship whenever I can manage it.

While I sit, I think about what I should do when I get back to the United States. Spalding's decision to extend our trip means I don't have to decide anything as soon as I thought I would, but still, I suppose I should have a plan of some kind. Maybe the White Stockings will ask me to be their mascot again, but I'm not sure I should do that. I don't think it will take me anywhere in life, and if I'm ever to make good on my promise to Tommy, I must make a name for myself somehow.

I try to think about which of the ballplayers I could try to be like. If I could be as smart as Captain Ward, I'd be very proud of myself, but I've got a long way to go. I've had a few reading lessons from Newton MacMillan, it's true, but I'll need many more. It would feel good to be big and strong like Williamson or Crane, but I'm short, and I don't know how much taller I'll get. Being as funny as someone like Fogarty would be nice, too, although I don't want to drink as much as he or Baldwin or the other Howling Wolves.

John Tener seems like a good model. He's also smart like Ward, but at the same time, he seems friendly and easy to talk to. Or maybe George Wood. Sometimes, people tease him and call "the Dandy" because of his excellent taste in clothes, but he does look very sharp. He always seems to have a kind word for others, and he's a strong ballplayer, too. John Healy has been nice to me at times, and while he's a little more private than Ward or Tener, also seems to have a good head and a quiet seriousness about him. Tom Brown is like that, too.

I'm still thinking about which ballplayers I can try to be like when the warm air and cool breeze lull me to sleep.

I awake some time later, to the voices of Al Spalding and Cap Anson, of all people. Because I'm now officially indebted to Ward and employed by him, I listen in closely. They stand at the railing of the bridge just below me, completely unaware that I'm listening to them from above.

"How is the morale of the men, Adrian?" I hear Spalding say.

"Very good. To a man, they are thrilled to travel around the world."

"Do you think that Ward or Hanlon have any notion of our plans yet?"

"If they do, I've not heard of it."

"Has Ward said anything about missing his wife? He was the one I was most concerned would be upset by our change in itinerary."

"Not that I know of. Although he may just be keeping that to himself. You know he's too smart a man to say something publicly that would spoil the fun for everyone else."

"That is good, on both counts. Keep your eyes and ears open, however, just in case. Johnny Ward is, like you said, a smart man, plenty smart enough to cause trouble behind our backs."

"Ay, he is. Ward's been a worthy captain so far on this trip, however, wouldn't you say? You couldn't have asked for someone more organized and detailed to help you make sure everything goes smoothly."

I peer over the railing just enough that I can see the two men. They have their backs to me and face out to sea. Instead of replying right away, Spalding just leans on the railing for a while, looking straight ahead. Finally, he says, "Remember when we first started playing ball, Adrian, just after the war? So many things about the game were in a state of uncertainty. Men switched clubs every year, it seemed. Clubs came and went from their leagues almost as often. On any given day, a pitcher had to calculate which members of his club had sold themselves to the gamblers when he went into the pitcher's box and try to send in pitches so that the batter would hit the ball to the men who were playing on the level."

"Yes, I remember those days. Devlin, Craver, Nichols, and Higham got themselves expelled from the game for conspiring with gamblers but so many other players deserved the same fate, or worse. I'm sure you remember what Bob Ferguson did to Nat Hicks, right, Al?"

"Of course. Ferguson used his bat to break Nat's right arm because he thought Hicks was going to throw a game Ferguson thought he'd won. Did you ever hear about the time in New York when Ferguson challenged the men in the gamblers' box to come down and take him on one at a time before the game even started, just so they couldn't buy the outcome?"

"Sure, I remember hearing about that. That kind of courage is what makes Ferguson the best umpire in baseball today. He and John Gaffney are the only ones I can't bulldoze."

Both men laugh a bit at this joke. I've never seen Umpire Ferguson, but Umpire Gaffney comes and calls games in Chicago sometimes, and he is one of the few umpires I've ever seen whose rulings go unchallenged by the players. Captain Anson generally gets his way with the umpires when he complains, but not with

Gaffney. Anson stopped arguing against Gaffney's decisions after Gaffney fined him $100 for shouting and cursing one day. Everyone gasped because $100 is so much money, but I later overhead Anson say that Spalding paid his fine for him.

The two men continue staring out to sea for a while. Anson is the one to resume speaking. "And remember the fields we played on back in those days? There usually were no grandstands, just the spectators standing around the field of play. If you were playing on the road, sometimes the outfielders had to battle the fans for possession of the ball before they could throw it back to the infield."

"That's why the smarter outfielders kept a ball hidden inside their uniform," Spalding replies with a chuckle. "Some of the veteran players who remember those days, like Mike Kelly and Jim O'Rourke, still do."

"The games might have been a lot more interesting and uncertain in those days," Anson goes on, "but I'll take what we have today, given the choice. We have nicer parks to play the games, consistent schedules, better equipment, and standardized rules. Well, except when in Philadelphia we have standardized rules. I still don't understand why the scorers there record stolen bases the way they do."

"All good points, Adrian, for certain. That is what we are trying to preserve. This messy contract dispute with the players, their Brotherhood, the players' opposition to the reserve clause, all these things threaten to tear down what I've helped build. We've finally gotten the gambling element out of the game, or at least almost all of it out of the game, so the spectators can attend games with confidence that the outcome is in doubt. Now, we just need to get rid of some of these cities that can't fully support a ball team, like Kansas City or Indianapolis."

"You are still dreaming about forcing out the American Association and having just one major league, Al?"

"Of course. Someday the circumstances will be right, and we'll force them to close business. Imagine what that will be like, Adrian.

31

With only eight teams in baseball, no more of having two teams in one town and dividing the patronage of the city. Attendance at games will grow. And, with only eight major league teams, players will have to fight for jobs if they want to stay in major league baseball, and that will force down their salaries. We'll make them fight each other for our scraps, rather than fighting ownership. Monopoly is a virtue in sports."

"Well, I suppose that any organization containing Charles Byrne, Chris von der Ahe, and Billy Barnie is bound to make mistakes, and large ones at that."

"Yes, it is. One of these days, we'll be able to entice Cincinnati and Brooklyn to leave the American Association and join us in the National League, even if it takes providing them with a bit of boodle to convince them to move. My spies in the American Association report that Von der Ahe and Byrne are at each other's throats constantly."

"And then, Al?"

"We move to bar the drunkards and their ilk from the game. I've already vowed to do it in Chicago. You must not tell them, but on our return to the United States, I'm considering giving Daly, Pettit, Baldwin, and Sullivan their releases. They all have talent, Daly and Baldwin in particular, but I won't have them carousing around town all night and arriving at West Side Park in no condition to play the next day."

"Do we have any strategy regarding Ward and Hanlon for now?"

"No, just keep them playing ball. We got out of San Francisco in time that they know nothing about my plans. Having our tour go all the way around the world should keep it that way until it is too late for them to do anything about it. Once we are back in the states, we can put into motion my final plans for destroying Ward's Brotherhood."

"Those plans are settled, then?"

"Nearly so, yes. Delay negotiations with the Brotherhood, use the press to discredit them, and give inducements to key individual players to desert the Brotherhood."

"Like you've already done with Williamson."

"Yes. I do not know what moves the Brotherhood will make in our absence, but as long as we have Ward with us, I'll take my chances. Keep your friends close to you, Adrian, but always keep your enemies even closer. I'll see you at dinner."

With that, Spalding moves off, and Anson does as well a few moments later. That is curious news that Spalding may release some of the ballplayers on the tour. I guess the White Stockings won't miss Sullivan or Pettit that much. Sullivan is almost as big as Crane or Williamson, and when the White Stockings first signed him to the team two years ago, he had a reputation as a big hitter. His first season, 1887, wasn't bad, but last year he slumped and didn't hit well. Pettit likewise. He doesn't play all the games—he's more of a substitute who plays when another player gets hurt—and although he can clobber the ball, too, he doesn't clobber it consistently enough. Probably the strangest thing about Pettit is that he bats left-handed but throws with his right arm.

Baldwin, however, would be a loss to the White Stockings because he's one of the team's regular pitchers. Besides his high-pitched voice, speedy fastball, and full head of blond hair, he has many quirks, too. His delivery of the ball to home plate is the strangest I've seen as a mascot. He rubs his right hand across his chest, looks into his glove at the ball, puts his right hand behind his head to adjust his cap, puts his hand into his glove to grab the ball, closes his left eye, and finally fires a pitch toward home plate.

Another strange thing about Baldwin is that he almost didn't go on our tour. Although I never met them on our route, John Tener told me that Baldwin's parents journeyed with us all the way to San Francisco. They were scared he'd die if he left the United States on his own and almost refused to let him come with us.

Well, whatever Spalding has in mind for those players, it doesn't affect me today. I wait until I think it's safe, and I climb down to see if I can find Johnny Ward. While I walk around the deck, no one seems to have missed me. Even though we are at sea, we've been steaming within sight of the Australian coastline all day. MacMillan told me it was because we meant to drop anchor briefly in Adelaide's harbor, so a ship can come out to us, and we can take mail on board, but that we were not to go ashore.

Coincidentally, I run into MacMillan first while I wander around.

"Well, Clarence," he says to me, "I've considered your proposal, and I think it's a capital idea. I'm willing to help you continue to learn to read while we're at sea. We have a lot of sailing ahead of us, after all, so we might as well put our time to constructive purposes. I believe my time is better used teaching someone to read than it is watching baseball players gamble and play poker."

My first extended lesson on this leg of our trip takes place that same afternoon. I guess I'll have to find Ward a little later. Seeing how far we still have left to go, I guess I'm in no great hurry.

It turns out to be a good thing that I had a long nap in my hiding place this afternoon because the night is a short one. A bit before midnight we arrive at Adelaide's harbor and drop our anchor while we wait for the mail ship to meet us. I come on deck, partly to see the lights of the town and partly because the Howling Wolves, Fogarty and Baldwin in particular, keep an entire section of the ship awake with their howling. When I come up on deck, I see Fogarty once again. I swear that the man never sleeps.

"My good friends," Fogarty begins. "I regret that we are unable to play a game of ball for you today, but I'm afraid that certain legal restrictions prevent it. I have consulted the local authorities and concluded that a game will not take place. Although it is our fervent wish to demonstrate the great American game to you here in Honolulu, our party must follow all local laws and customs."

I wonder what he is doing, until I realize he is copying Spalding's voice and repeating a version of the speech Spalding gave in the Sandwich Islands. In addition to howling and chasing fly balls in the All-America outfield, mimicry seems another of Fogarty's talents. Except he gives this performance in pajamas, with a jockey cap on his head, no socks, patent leather shoes, and with a cane in hand. The other ballplayers laugh and guffaw at all of Fogarty's imitations, so I guess that most of the men have forgiven him for the fact they are still awake. They cackle louder when Fogarty starts dancing and ends up splitting his pajamas.

This brings hope that I'll finally be free of Fogarty's noise, but no luck. In only minutes, he is back, wearing suit pants but with the rest of his outfit unchanged. Imitations follow of Professor Bartholomew right before ascending in his balloon, as well as some of Spalding's business associates and various Australian officials who gave speeches to us. Fogarty doesn't have the Australian accent down quite right yet, but that doesn't stop him. He's still going full steam when I've had enough and start below deck again, so I can sleep. I reach the hallway leading to my room when I see Tom Daly there.

"Clarence, come over here," he says to me while motioning with his arm.

He has several brown, cylindrical things in his arms. Soon, I'm close enough to see that the cylinders are rolled up doormats. I'm trying to imagine where he got them from when he tells me, "Hold these for a moment," and dumps them into my arms and disappears through a door at the end of the hallway.

He takes me by surprise, so I drop about half of the mats. I'm just trying to get hold of them again when Daly returns, Mark Baldwin alongside. Somehow, they've acquired large pitchers of water. Each man carries two pitchers, one in each hand, and they're full.

"Okay, Clarence, stack up the mats into two piles," Baldwin says.

I do so, and when I'm done, they dump all four pitchers of water on one stack of mats. They disappear again for a moment, only to return with the pitchers refilled. They proceed to drench the other stack of mats.

"Clarence, grab a couple and follow me," Daly says.

This doesn't look good, but I go along. Baldwin is taller and bigger than Daly is, several inches taller, in fact, so he takes the entire second stack by himself. I follow behind Daly as he begins entering the rooms of various ballplayers and placing the soaking wet mats under their bed sheets.

"There's one for Old Man Anson," he says as he goes into the first room. "Here you go, John Tener," he comments after the second.

We continue, visiting the rooms of Jimmy Ryan, Ed Crane, Fred Carroll, and John Healy before we run out of mats. Baldwin, meanwhile, has done the same on the other side of the hallway. Anyone whose door was unlocked when they went on deck is in for quite a surprise when they go back to bed!

"All right," Baldwin says, "let's go up and take in the rest of Jimmy's performance. He's distracted everyone perfectly, just as he said he would. If we're lucky, we'll get there in time to avoid suspicion!"

I follow behind, but as soon as they reach the deck, I duck out of sight and head for my spot on top of the bridge. Common sense tells me I don't want to be anywhere near a bedroom when the players discover what has happened. Quite a row breaks out once they do—I can hear all the surprised shouting from where I'm sitting—so I take an entire hour before creeping back to my cabin. My idea works. Everything is quiet, and I get to sleep in a dry bed.

Chapter 4

When I get up the next morning, our boat hasn't moved. Another ship anchors alongside ours, and it's emptying something into our cargo hold. Wool, from the smell of it. If you go down to the docks of Chicago in the fall, sometimes you'll see railroad cars unloading wool into ships for transportation somewhere, so I know the smell of wool. While that happens, I notice some of the players fishing at the stern of the ship. Johnny Ward is there, but so are Ryan and Palmer, so again I postpone relaying my information to Ward. I wander to the ship's rail and look over. The water is very clear. It's hard to judge the distance, but I think I can see down at least fifteen feet.

"What kind of fish are you trying to catch?" I ask the group.

"Captain Thalenhorst tells us mackerel swim in these waters, and he provided us with poles for catching them," Ward answers. "Awfully heavy, these poles, but we've had a bit of luck with them, so I'll not complain."

"Do we need fish for dinner on the ship?" I ask.

"No, Clarence, we are merely fishing for sport. If we catch anything, we toss it back into the water."

"And have you caught anything so far?" I ask while peering again into the clear water.

"Yes, we've pulled in several, in fact," Ryan replies. "I seem to have the touch so far today. What is the count, Harry? I have four."

"Ward and I have landed two each," Palmer says. "They are a good-sized fish. Your last catch was what, nearly a yard in length, Jimmy?"

"It was. Reeling it in took some doing."

"What's that?" I shout while pointing at a much bigger shape swimming through the water. It's dark and very fast, and its fin breaks the surface of the water.

"Good eyes, Clarence," Ward exclaims. "You've found a shark. It's got to be, what, twelve or fifteen feet long, Harry?"

"I'd say fifteen at least," Palmer replies. Then he says, "Does anyone want to engage in more active sport? Perhaps we should have a test of marksmanship."

"Clarence, keep an eye on the shark. We'll be right back," Ryan says to me.

"What are you going to do?" I ask him.

"You'll see," is all he says. "Now, hurry boys. Double-time it."

While I await their return, Anson wanders over. He, too, notices the shark swimming nearby.

"What kind of shark is it, boy?" he asks me.

I jump. I'd been so busy watching the shark like Ryan told me to, I didn't notice Anson until he spoke.

Getting my composure back a little I say, "I don't know, Captain Anson. Mr. Ward, Mr. Ryan, and Mr. Palmer told me to watch it while they went to get something."

The three men return a moment later. The shark is still within sight, but quite a bit farther from the ship now. I can just barely see its fin above the calm water while the sun gleams off the tiny waves.

Ward speaks first. "Clarence, you're shaking. What's the matter? Did the shark disappear while we were gone?"

"No, Mr. Ward, it's just over there now." I point, and the men nod. I hadn't realized I was shaking, but looking at my pointing finger, I certainly am. Anson still terrifies me.

"Anson," Ward says, "you have sharp eyes. You can help us determine if we hit our mark."

"You first, Jimmy, show us what you've got," Palmer says while I continue pointing out where the shark swims now.

I'm astounded when I see that all three men have pistols and are taking aim at the shark. I had no idea some of the ballplayers brought guns with them on our trip. Ryan fires, but I can't tell if he hits. Some spray kicks up where the bullet strikes the water, but that's all I can see. Ward goes next, followed by Palmer.

"Wait, I have an idea," Anson says after all three have tried to hit the creature. "I can't tell if you've hit or not because the shark is getting farther away. Let's get everyone a closer shot by tossing Clarence over the side. We'll use him as bait to draw the shark closer."

"No!" I exclaim immediately.

"Why not?" Anson asks. "You ain't good for nothing else. You ain't even doing any work on this part of the trip. This way we can make you useful. Let's get one of those big hooks and lower you over the side. I'd like to see what a shark looks like up close."

While Anson makes his case for using me as bait, Ryan takes his second shot. I don't stick around to see any more shooting, however. Instead, I run for my cabin. I hear a couple more pistol shots while I run, so I assume that each man continues firing before the shark swims out of range.

An hour later, I creep back on deck. Ward and Palmer are still at the railing, talking to each other. Both gesture with their arms and wave them energetically. Although I think they might be arguing, it doesn't appear they're upset at each other. Both speak with raised voices, but they're also smiling, and Ward gives Palmer a pat on the shoulder as I walk within hearing. Anson and Ryan are both gone. I hear Ward and Palmer use the word "Brotherhood" when I approach, but when they see me, they turn to greet me.

"Sorry about Anson, Clarence," Ward begins. "You know we weren't going to send you over the side as bait, right?"

"That was a bit low of Adrian," Palmer adds. "It wasn't really necessary to scare you like that, but you know all about Anson's temper by now."

"I was very scared, but I shouldn't have run away," is all I can think to say. "I get frightened sometimes, though."

"You thought Anson was serious, then?" Palmer inquires.

"Do you think he was?"

Palmer opens his mouth to speak but closes it again before saying anything. Finally, he offers, "Anson just walked off without saying anything after you left. But, as for me, no, I don't think he was serious."

I'm not sure if I believe that, but to be safe, I change the subject. "Did any of you kill the shark?"

"No, we gave up hope when it swam out of range," Palmer replies. "I'm not even positive that any of us were able to hit it."

I ask Ward, "Mr. Ward, what would you have done if one of you had hit the shark square and killed it?"

"Why, nothing, of course. It would sink to the bottom of the ocean before we could do anything."

"Why were you shooting at it, if you can't do anything with it?"

"It is for sport, Clarence. Trying to hit a shark from this range is a test of steadiness and marksmanship. You don't have to do anything with what you kill; it's just a test to see whether you can hit something."

To myself, I wonder if the sharks will end up like the buffalo someday.

After a pause, Palmer finally says, "Mr. Ward, Clarence, I think I'll take my leave now. Johnny, you can keep explaining how quality marksmanship is a sign of civilization to young Clarence, if you think it will help."

Once Palmer is gone, I tell Ward everything I heard Spalding and Anson talking about the day before.

"That's my boy, Clarence. Well done." He presses a dollar coin into my hand. "There's another dollar in it for you every time you have good information for me."

By the next day, I've learned another secret. I would never have believed it until I saw it, but it is possible to make Jim Fogarty stay quiet all day. This is how it happened.

We raise anchor and sail farther from shore, and the seas have gotten rough again. I thought everyone would have their sea legs by now, but it seems it's possible to lose your sea legs, too, because many of the boys are under the weather. Instead of rushing the growler, or rushing the lunch table, today I see several ballplayers rushing to the ship's railing. The dining room is half-empty. Even Anson stays in his cabin. Otherwise, the next event might have gone very differently. However, he's not there, and neither are Hanlon, Pfeffer, or Ryan, when something unexpected happens. I am sitting alone in the dining room, minding my own business, when Ned Williamson's wife decides to sit down next to me and eat.

She has dark brown hair, about shoulder length, and is of medium height and weight. Because I've not seen her often on the trip, I don't know what she usually wears, but today she has on a bright yellow cotton shirt and a sun hat, which she takes off when she sits down.

This takes me by surprise because I almost never speak to white women. Colored people aren't supposed to. I look down, and my hands have begun shaking again. I put them under the table and hope Mrs. Williamson hasn't noticed.

Meanwhile, she takes a few bites, then says, "Good day, Clarence. You seem in fine health this afternoon."

"G-good day to you, M-Mrs. Williamson. I d-do have a knack for sailing, it seems, and keeping m-my health up."

"It is a pity we've not had much chance to talk," she tells me between bites, seeming not to notice my nervous stutter. "But because I spend much of my time with my husband or with the other ladies on our journey, the opportunity has been some time coming. Today, however, Ned is under the weather, and it looks like the other women of our party are going to pass on their midday meal as well."

"Have you had a g-good trip so far?" I ask her.

"What was that? I couldn't quite hear you, Clarence. Speak up a bit."

"I'm s-sorry, M-Mrs. Williamson. I asked if you'd had a g-good trip."

"There's no need to be so nervous, Clarence. We're just talking."

I nod.

"But, to answer your question, yes, I have, very much so. There have been so many amazing sights to see. The Rocky Mountains, the city of San Francisco, the ocean, and now Australia. So many wonderful places exist in this world, and I'm sure we'll get to see many more before we get back home. I was hoping to see some kangaroos in Australia, but I guess a woman can't have everything she wants. Tell me, Clarence, what was it like at the bottom of that gold mine? Ned wouldn't go down there with the group, and neither would any of the other ladies. I wanted to go, but Ned convinced me it wasn't a ladylike thing to do."

Should I answer? I think for a moment and then mutter, "Well, um, gee, Mrs. Williamson, it's hard to describe, really. It was very g-gray, and the light was m-murky." It's hard to find the words, but she just looks me in the face with her eyebrows raised. I think she expects me to say more, so I manage to get out, "Most of the other, um, people looked like, I don't know, ghosts, or phantoms, or something." My voice trails off, and I look out the window.

She doesn't take much notice of how scared I am. "Were there gold nuggets there in the walls, just waiting for the miners to pluck them out?"

A bead of sweat rolls down my back, then another. "I reckon not, I don't think, or, at least, there weren't any that I, um, got to see. In truth, it is very w-wet and d-damp at the bottom of a, um, of a gold mine. People slip and fall often in the m-mud and slime. It is also, well, um, it's very hot at the bottom. You sweat considerably when you go d-down there."

Without thinking, I've put my hands back on the table, and they're shaking like crazy. I put them under the table again, hoping Mrs. Williamson didn't see.

I don't know if she noticed, but Mrs. Williamson says to me again, "Why are you so nervous, Clarence? There's no reason for fright. We're just eating lunch."

She puts her head back down to focus on her plate and takes another bite of the steamed potatoes the chefs fixed. I hadn't even noticed what food she had until now, I'm so nervous. Maybe she doesn't know that when you are a colored person talking to a white woman, you have every reason for fright. I learned that lesson three years ago on the streets of Chicago, before I met Tommy. Another homeless colored boy, I think he was fourteen or fifteen, was starving, and he asked a white woman for a bit of food as she left a restaurant in one of the nicer parts of Chicago. She cursed him, and within moments, a gang of several male customers arrived and pounded the kid with fists and canes until he couldn't move. I don't know if he died or not because I ran off before they came after me, too.

While I'm thinking about how to say something to her nicely, she takes a few more bites and changes the subject without waiting any longer for me to answer. "I always enjoyed watching you at the Chicago games this year, Clarence, stacking the bats and being our mascot. I think you were very good at it. Tell me, why did you leave our team? Did the players not want you anymore?"

"No, Mrs. Williamson. I found a job in a, um, in a traveling show, so I went with them. That was a b-bad mistake, though. They didn't treat me very well. I should have, um, should have stayed with the Chicagos and remained their, their mascot. I won't walk out on the boys like that again, for sure."

"I'm glad to hear that," she says, her plate nearly empty now. "We ladies always thought you looked very sharp in your uniform with your baton, leading the players and marching."

"Thank you, Mrs. Williamson. I haven't decided if I should be the, the mascot again or not. If the ballplayers even want me back."

"I think they will. Why wouldn't you want to be our mascot for 1889?"

"I can't be the mascot forever, c-can I? I think I might need to start getting on in life."

"That's a good point, I suppose. What will you do instead?"

"I don't, um, I'm not sure. But Mr. MacMillan has been teaching me. Teaching me to read, that is."

"Really? How kind of him. I enjoy reading ever so much, Clarence. Do you think I could help with your lessons? I'd love to help you learn. What do you say?"

"That is very kind of you, Mrs. Williamson."

"It's settled, then. I'll help you learn your letters. Oh, it'll be such fun! Still, I hope you'll reconsider and be our mascot again this coming season, and I hope you have a good rest of this trip. However, if you'll excuse me now, I need to take a little food down to Ned and see if I can get him to eat something."

She walks out the door but after a moment comes back in. She says to me, "Clarence, do you see several of our players outside on their deck chairs? One of them asked for you."

"Sure, um, Mrs. Williamson, tell them I'll be right out."

I finish my last few bites and walk out to where Fogarty, Mrs. Anson, George Wood, Tom Brown, Jimmy Ryan, and Tom Burns sit. None of them looks in good health.

Fogarty motions me over with a weak wave and says faintly, "Clarence, find me a waiter. I think I'm well enough to eat a bit but going into the dining room for a full meal may be too much for me. See what you can do, Sergeant Duval." His hand shaky, Fogarty gives a feeble salute as I turn to go.

Because I just left the dining room and because all the waiters treat me extra politely, I'm back in no time.

"Thank you, Clarence," Fogarty tells me. Then, to the waiter, "I'd like a cheese sandwich, if you can manage it, my good man."

The waiter bows and walks away. With nothing better to do, I sit on a deck chair and look out at the waves. After several minutes, the waiter returns with a platter. When he hands it to Fogarty, I can see the platter holds no cheese sandwich. Instead, the German-speaking waiter has delivered sauerkraut and steamed Italian sausages to the All-America outfielder.

His face blanches, and he rolls off his chair. "No, no, take it away!" he tries to shout, but it comes out as more of a gurgle. He vomits. At the same time, Mrs. Anson faints in her chair, while the faces of all four of the other players turn a shade of green I don't think I've ever seen on a person before.

Seeing that I don't speak German, I'm trying to figure out what to do when John Tener happens to walk by. "What on earth happened to Mrs. Anson? Why is Fogarty rolling around on the deck?"

I answer, "He asked for a cheese sandwich, Mr. Tener, but the waiter brought sauerkraut and sausages instead, and everyone got sick. Mrs. Anson fainted, I think. What should we do?"

At this, Tener laughs heartily, and he takes the waiter by the wrist and leads him back to the dining room. Fogarty doesn't say another word the rest of the day.

Chapter 5

January 15, 1889
Indian Ocean

"Gather 'round, boys, and hear the strangest tale you've yet heard on our expedition."

It is Tuesday, January 15, and Jim Fogarty, healthy once more, addresses anyone in the dining room who will pay attention to him.

"I have been to strange lands and seen the heathen ways of the infidel, the lowly hut of the peasant, and the decadent nobility of the mysterious East. I've lived in the yurt of the Mongol, the pagoda of the Chinaman, the cottage of the German, and the villas of Italian princes. Listen now, while I tell you the tale of my journey to the forward deck of the steamer *Salier*."

Several laughs follow, but Fogarty continues. "You think I jest? Why, just this morning the intrepid adventurer Harry Palmer and I braved the perils of the unknown to find out what happens on the steerage deck of an ocean steamer. Listen, if you can face your fears, to what we witnessed."

"You mean you found cows, pigs, and chickens, right?" burly Ed Crane says with another laugh. "Where else do you think all the food we're served at dinner comes from? Do you think the cooks just conjure it up out of thin air?"

"Spoken by one who has not seen the depravity, the dirt and filth, or the mystic pagan rites of the steerage passengers," Fogarty responds. "Yes, it is true that animals of many kinds dwell in the ship's pens, coops, and cages, but do you know from whence these creatures came?"

Crane just rolls his eyes and shrugs his shoulders.

"I thought not," Fogarty says, grinning and going on with his tale. "Take, for instance, the lowly cow. Meek in spirit yet rich in milk, it is all the same a common and unremarkable beast. Yet, on this very ship, there exist those who believe this creature of divine status. I speak, you see, of the Hindus. Nigh on ten dozen of them dwell in the steerage compartments, and whoa to the infidel who seeks to infiltrate their sanctum. Not partaking of the ship's cooking, they slaughter a sheep of their own for their weekly sustenance. As their machetes slash through the air in graceful arcs of steely death, they carve the poor creatures up while the blood flows, the innards ooze, and their fellow Hindus gather round, chanting incantations of magical purification for both animal and man as they stomp the deck and circle the carcass, reaching a state of near-ecstasy. All the while, their weird, discordant horns and flutes play a death-dealing dirge for the bloody remains of their sacrifice. Thus purified from the evils of contamination by Europeans, they take the cuts of meat and cook them in their own pans to ward off the sinister plots of the good Christian passengers of the ship.

"This they have every reason to fear, for nearby to the Hindus, the Germans squat on their haunches, patiently smoking their large pipes while their women knit drab shawls and rough wool clothing. Nothing rattles or perturbs these stoic people, or even interrupts their pipe-puffing contemplation, save when the Hindus dance. At that time, you will see all the Germans gathered to witness the spectacle, with all its pagan idolatry and superstitious litanies, furiously genuflecting and whispering "*mein Gott*" to ward off the hellish, evil demons they believe the Hindus wish to unleash. They shout curses in German, and once, they attempted to rescue the sheep from its fate, only to be overwhelmed by the sheer numbers and fanaticism of the Mohammedan host."

By this time, Crane has his head in his hands, slowly shaking it back and forth, while John Ward gives a little whistle showing his disbelief. Many of the other men, however, can hardly contain their laughter.

Fogarty continues his story, saying, "Across the deck from the Germans and Hindus, you'll find the Italians and Turks. Unlike the stolid Germans, the Italians are an expressive lot. They gesticulate wildly to make even the slightest point, indeed, to make no point at all, for that is their nature. As evidence, I offer as proof their fondness for their gaudy-colored shawls, shirts, and trousers. Also, unlike the Germans, who pine for the strong beers and stout ales they imbibe daily in their native land, the Italians showed enough forethought to bring copious quantities of grape wine with them for their passage. They drink this wine at every meal, breakfast not excepted, which lends an always-festive air to their section of the deck. They graciously extend a goblet to their favored guests, and I can personally vouch for its potent and highly intoxicating effects. *Saluti*! Frequently, however, this leaves them in a debauched state, and the resultant noise renders them obnoxious to their neighbors. Of all the steerage passengers, however, they remain the friendliest toward outsiders.

"That leaves the Turks. These Turks are not the warriors who died so valiantly while defending Plevna or the Shipka Pass from the Russian Cossack hoards. Nay, these red-turbaned fellows are rather less noble and more avaricious than their heroic fathers and brothers. They mean to profit from their voyage by sewing silks with geometric patterns of considerable artistry, which they will sell to the other passengers. Embroidery and beadwork are their trades. Their skill is commendable but matched only by the greed with which they offer their wares to outsiders. They are a suspicious and secretive people when not engaged in commerce. The chanting of their daily prayers sometimes overlaps with the revelry of their Italian neighbors, at which time they produce the flashing scimitars so feared by their enemies in days of yore. The Italians, in their drunken fearlessness, respond with their long daggers, and now several members of the two groups bear the scars of battle."

At this point, Ward wipes his mouth, stands up, and leaves. He wears an angry scowl, and I hear him mutter something about "drunken nonsense." Some of the others, however, including Tom Daly, Mark Baldwin, and Billy Earle, encourage Fogarty to continue.

He disappoints them when he says, "I'm afraid my tale is at an end, for even a free and Christian adventurer can only withstand the foul stench and putrid airs of the steerage deck for so long before he must retire. I promise you, however, that before another sun has set I'll return to 'The Zoo' and that Palmer and I will have more adventures with which to captivate you over breakfast tomorrow."

Because everyone has finished eating by this time, they all disperse when Fogarty concludes his storytelling. I don't even have to ask Palmer to confirm that everything Fogarty says is fiction because I've been to the steerage deck myself. I know what fiction is now, too, because MacMillan taught me the difference between fiction and nonfiction.

Without having any chores to do, I have much more time to wander around and see things. Because we have no more need for the cricket tent now that we've left Australia, most of the ballplayers spend their time lounging or playing shuffleboard, quoits, or various other deck games. Today, I decide to venture around the *Salier* to see what some of the other people are doing.

When I visit the steerage deck, I'm reminded that passengers from many nations are on board. That part of Fogarty's tale is true enough, but everything else is just him making a big deal out of minor things. I think I see one or two of the German people smoking pipes, but everyone else just moves around normally. Some of them visit the Italians who, as far as I can see, did not bring much grape wine with them. Among the Turks, I meet an older man with darker skin wearing white robes and a turban who, to my shock, speaks some English. He is trying to sell raffle tickets, the prize being a finely embroidered silk pillow. He asks me if I'd like to buy a ticket, but since I'm saving the little money I have, I turn him down. I see no daggers or any other weapons, save cooking knives, in anyone's hands.

While I drift up from the steerage deck, I think a little more about Fogarty. He's the prankster of our tour. Everyone knows that. Not only was he the one who had the idea of starting the Order of the Howling Wolves, but also he's had a hand in most of the practical jokes, like the one with the door mats I helped with the other day. However, I also think he's one of the smartest of the players. Frequently, I've noticed him speaking with Ward and Hanlon, so I suspect he is helping them plan something for their Brotherhood.

Fogarty may also be the fastest of all the players on the tour. Someone, MacMillan, I think, told me he had 102 stolen bases during the 1887 season. I believe it. In one of our games in California, he stole seven times, and the defense could not throw him out.

Still, I think everyone will remember his sense of humor most of all. Fogarty even got his revenge on the German waiter who served him sauerkraut and made him vomit. The next morning at breakfast, the same waiter brought Fogarty wheat pancakes. None of the ballplayers thought they were very good because the ship's cook let them cook too long, and they were tough to chew. I overheard Newton MacMillan comment that they were "impregnable to the knife." So, Fogarty took five of the pancakes, shuffled them into his hands like he was playing poker, then tossed three pancakes on the table and said, "I'll take three cards." The waiter's face turned red, and it didn't seem very polite to me, but a lot of the boys thought it was funny.

The Italians and Turks might not have all the weapons Fogarty claimed they have, but that is not to say that none of the passengers traveling on the *Salier* carries arms. Besides the ballplayers who shot at the shark with their pistols, I learn that two Australian hunters are sailing with us. I hear them talking with Johnny Ward and Jimmy Ryan just after Fogarty's breakfast story. Although they talk about the different rifles they've brought, the only thing the two men have right now are some impressively large hunting knives strapped to their belts. The knives have handles made of ivory.

"You Americans are really traveling the world?" one of them asks Ryan in his thick accent.

"We are," Ryan confirms. "We mean to show as many people as we can the glory and manliness of American sport. Did you happen to see us play in Melbourne?"

"I did," the other hunter confirms. "Although I'm not sure I really understand all the points of the game, being brought up to play cricket, you know. Still, you Americans did show considerable skill in catching and throwing the ball. You chaps look the manly type. You'd probably make good companions on our hunt."

"You men are sportsmen?" Ward inquires.

"Ay, we are. We plan to prove it, too, and make some money besides. Bound for Africa, we are. Tommy and I, we're planning to bag as many big animals as we can. We'll sell the skins, horns, and ivory to pay for our trip. We plan to make a few shillings as compensation for our efforts, too," the second speaker finishes with a knowing grin.

This first man smiles back, then says, "For me, a rhino is the prize. A rhino or a hippo. This fool wants to go after lions, though."

"That sounds grand," Ryan puts in. "If I wasn't pledged for one trip around the world already, I might enjoy something like that."

They go on with the small talk, but now I'm confused on what being a sportsman is about. When Ward and Ryan were shooting at the shark, Ward told me you didn't do anything with what you killed—the act of killing the thing made it sporting. Now, however, these two men call themselves sportsmen, and it appears they are trying to make money out of killing things. Someday, I'll have to find out which explanation is right.

January 17 turns out to be an interesting day. For one thing, the weather clears up, and the sun shines brightly. We also pass another steamer. Apparently, when that happens, it is the duty of each passenger to crowd to the railing of the deck and yell salutes to everyone aboard the other ship. Following this chance meeting, I'm on my way to my hiding place on top of the bridge when the chief steward of the ship, Mr. Stiers, arrives on deck and informs the players that Captain Thalenhorst just ordered him to tap a keg of beer in the dining room. It's no exaggeration to say that within ten seconds, I'm the only person left standing on that part of the deck.

Knowing that I'm not likely to get any beer with so many thirsty players in line, I continue up to my little perch. I'm just sitting there daydreaming when, to my dismay, I hear Anson stomping around below.

"Where is that darky?" he mutters. "Why am I always the one sent to find the nigger?"

I swallow hard and decide to answer. I don't want to give away my hiding place, though, so I decide that once he moves away, I'll get down and run into him "on accident." After Anson stomps away, I climb down and hurry after him.

"I'm over here, Master Anson."

"Get over here. I've half a mind to put you in Professor Bartholomew's balloon again and set you free to drift over the ocean until you splash down and a shark eats you."

"What do you need me for, Captain Anson?"

"Come with me," is all he says.

Shortly, I'm standing amongst several of the players. "Duval," Anson says, "several of the men are bored, and we require some entertainment. Since you ain't had to do anything this entire trip, you owe us. You wouldn't be here if it wasn't for us, after all."

I think I know what's coming. This time, however, I have a plan.

"Boys, get your hands ready to give us a tune," Fred Pfeffer says.

"W-Wait a minute," I manage to stammer despite my fear. "If I show you boys how to play a new game, so you won't be bored anymore, will that do instead of a dance?"

Pfeffer frowns and Anson scowls, but several of the other players look curious.

"What kind of game?" Ned Hanlon asks.

"Can you gamble on it?" Baldwin says.

"Let me show you," I say as I pull my craps dice from my pocket. "This is how the game works. It's called craps. I'll show you all how to play."

"Sure," says Baldwin. A few other players shrug their shoulders as if to say, "why not?"

"Go on, Clarence," Ed Crane says. "I don't mind learning something new."

I start explaining while all the men gather around me. "The person who rolls is the shooter. Anyone can bet on the outcome, not just the shooter. Before the shooter rolls, you decide if you want to bet for or against the shooter.

"If you think the shooter will win, that's called betting the Pass Line. If you think the shooter will lose, you bet the Don't Pass. After everyone has placed their bets, the shooter roles both dice, and you add the numbers."

Several of the men nod as I start to explain. Maybe this will work!

"You call the first roll the Come Out roll. What happens next depends on your bet. If you bet on the shooter and bet the Pass Line, on a seven or eleven, your bet wins. On a two, three, or twelve, the shooter craps out, and your bet loses.

I continue. "On any other number, you call the number the point. Once you know what the point is, if the shooter rolls the point again before rolling a seven, your bet wins. If he rolls seven first, your bet loses.

"Now, if you bet Don't Pass at first, it works almost the opposite. If the Come Out roll is a two or three, your bet wins, but if it is a seven or eleven, your bet loses. If the roll is a twelve, it's a push. If the Come Out roll creates a point, if the shooter rolls seven first, your bet wins, and if he rolls the point first, your bet loses."

More nodding from the ballplayers. "The shooter remains the shooter until he rolls a point and then he rolls a seven. If he does that, he passes the dice clockwise. He can also pass voluntarily. That's it. Those are the rules of craps."

The boys show great enthusiasm for this new game, and soon, no one is talking about plantation dances anymore. Instead, a large crowd of people surround the game while the ballplayers start playing. I spend a bit of time teaching the boys the way a person talks when they play the game.

"Come seven. Come along there, eight! Whoa there, nine!"

It goes on, and soon, the game so absorbs the ballplayers that I can wander off and no one cares. My gamble paid off!

In fact, I hit the jackpot. The players take to playing craps for days at a time, and for the moment, my status among the ballplayers is as high as ever. I just need to remember to get my dice back because they're the dice Tommy gave me, and I can't lose them.

My luck doesn't last, however. Every day after I teach the boys to play craps, the temperature gets hotter and hotter. One day, there comes a knock on my cabin door. I put down the book I've been practicing reading and open the door to see Mark Baldwin and Bob Pettit.

"Sergeant Duval, you're wanted on deck. Come with us," Baldwin says as sternly as he can in his high-pitched voice.

I follow, thinking that another pretend trial is about to begin.

Most of the ballplayers are there when I arrive. Fogarty spreads out a rolled-up piece of paper and proclaims, "After the careful deliberation of the Chicago and All-America baseball teams, we declare the present temperatures unnaturally warm. We have no doubt that we must take some action to break Nature's hoodoo. In view of our bad luck and the excessively warm weather, and after a thorough consideration for the comfort and peace of mind of our entire party, the players of the Chicago and All-America baseball teams declare that Clarence Duval, the chocolate-colored person who accompanies us, must take a saltwater bath."

Take a saltwater bath? No way! I tried one of those aboard the *Alameda* and hated every second of it. I try to run away, but it's no use. Pettit and Baldwin lay hands on me before I can get anywhere. They drag me over to the location of the bath, which is really a shower that you stand under, and Pettit goes to pull the handle that releases the water. Baldwin still has hold of me, but I decide now is the time to use some of the wrestling moves that Mr. Miller taught me while aboard the *Alameda*.

I grab one of Baldwin's fingers on his right hand and twist, so he'll let go with his right arm. He yells out, "Ouch!" and does.

Next, I grab his left arm and give it a sharp jerk, twisting it again. He shouts shrilly, "Damn it, Clarence," while he hunches over to relieve the tension. When he bends over, he lets go of me with the other arm, and I run again.

I'm free! I run for the stairs that lead below deck, so I can get to my cabin and lock myself inside. Once again, however, my small size lets me down, just like it almost did at the Salt Lake City train station, and I don't get far before Tom Daly collars me.

"Where do you think you're headed to?" he says sarcastically as he yanks me back toward the shower.

I struggle mightily, kicking my legs, aiming for Daly's shins, so he'll let go of me. I only get in a glancing blow before Baldwin comes over and grabs my left leg. He and Daly hoist me off the ground. I can't punch because Daly has one arm and Baldwin the other, so I try a headbutt on Daly, but I can't quite reach. Nothing works, and before I can think of anything else, the saltwater is splashing over me, and I'm drenched, spluttering and swallowing some of it in the process.

It's awful. Both tasting and choking on the salty water, and not being able to do anything about it. "Stop it! Let me go!" I yell with as much force as I can, considering that I have a mouthful of saltwater. I continue to kick wildly, but they won't let go. The bath does not end until they've emptied the entire tank of water on me.

"Go on now, Clarence; you've done your duty," Baldwin says as he lets go of my arms. I hear many voices laughing at me, but I don't even look at who they are. I don't care.

I've had enough. Again, I run, but not to my cabin this time. I hear most of the players continue laughing at me.

Instead of my cabin, I go around the rooms of the players to see who has locked their door. Some of the boys have become more careful about that since the incident with the floor mats. Anson's remains unlocked, however, and I know that he has what I'm looking for.

I start back toward the deck, ready to get my revenge. I don't care who it is, I'm going to make someone pay. Climbing the short stairway to the door leading on deck and peering out the window, I see Baldwin nearby. He's a good person to start with.

With a yell, I open the door and burst out onto the deck. Just as Baldwin turns around, I whack him just above the left knee with one of Anson's bats. He yells out "Ayeeee!" and goes down in a heap, holding his leg.

Unfortunately, Daly sits nearby, and before I can strike again, he's up and has his hands on the bat, wrestling me for control of it. I know I'll lose because he's bigger and stronger, but I fight, yank, and pull all the same. In desperation, a thought occurs to me, and when he leans in too close, I let go of the bat but rake his eyes with my fingers. He drops the bat, which goes thunk when it hits the wooden deck planks. I pick it up again.

Now, I look up and see several other players closing in. I'm in trouble.

"Just leave me alone! I don't want any more baths, or dances, or trials, or anything else!" I shout at the top of my lungs, saltwater spraying outward from my clothes as I turn quickly back and forth, swinging the bat in the direction of anyone who gets too close.

I'm in a real pickle, for sure. The players are liable to throw me overboard if they ever catch me, Baldwin especially. So, I take another swing at him when he reaches for the bat. He jumps back, and I miss. Unfortunately, while Baldwin distracts me, Pfeffer gets his hands on me, grabbing me from behind. Daly wrenches the bat out of my hand, and they lift me off my feet. "This way," Pfeffer drawls loudly.

In a moment, I'm looking over the railing of the ship. Pfeffer yells to Daly, "One, two, three!" Over the side I go.

It looked like a long drop to the water when I was on the deck, but when you're falling, it only takes a moment, and it seems to go even faster than that. At least I go in feet-first, and don't belly flop. Only now, however, do I realize the most serious flaw in my plan for revenge. I can't swim.

I flounder around a bit, doing a dog paddle to try to keep afloat. I've been in the water before, of course. Chicago is right on Lake Michigan, and the lakefront has beaches where people can go in the water, but without anyone to teach me, I never learned to swim. Moreover, Lake Michigan is freshwater, even if the water is a funny color sometimes from what the factories dump into the lake. I flap my arms and legs around, trying to keep my head above the water, but it isn't working very well. When I try shouting for help, I end up taking a gulp of saltwater, and before long, I take another. I cough and gasp at the horrible taste, which only causes me to lose my concentration on paddling. After another salty drink, my head drops below the water for a moment.

When I resurface, kicking my legs furiously, I hear someone on the deck yell out, "Man overboard!" and, while I can barely see it because I'm fighting to stay afloat, people start running around frantically.

Although I don't realize it until later, I'm lucky. When Pfeffer and Daly tossed me over the ship's railing, we were near the front of the boat. This means that some of the sailors have time to run along the side of ship, grab Kisbee rings, and toss them into the water. When one plops down a few feet away and drifts toward me, I flail my arms and reach until I can grab hold of it. While the sailors at the railing pull me in toward the ship and then upward out of the water, I discover that the Kisbee ring is cork.

This is not the end of my troubles, however. Once some of the German sailors haul me over the railing, saltwater still streaming from my clothing, the group of angry ballplayers, led by Baldwin and Pfeffer, crowd around me again. I get into a crouch and start to swing the Kisbee ring around to protect myself.

Pure luck saves me from another drop over the railing, however, because Captain Thalenhorst, accompanied by Johnny Ward, just happens to walk by at that moment and sees the commotion. Because I'm still dripping water and soaked head to toe, Ward and the captain don't need long to figure out what happened.

"That's enough, boys!" Captain Thalenhorst shouts out, and we all look up.

"Drop the buoy now, Clarence," he says to me in a commanding tone, "and stop fighting. I won't have it on board my ship! All of you stand down and back away from each other. What on earth has happened?"

"I think I can tell you, Captain Thalenhorst," Ward says. "The boys are mighty uncomfortable in all this tropical heat, and because Clarence is our mascot, they blame Clarence for bringing it down on us. Last night I overhead some of the boys talk about giving the mascot a bath, and it appears that's what they've done."

"Is this true?" Captain Thalenhorst says to whoever among the players has guts enough to answer.

"Yes, it's true," admits Bob Pettit.

Although he is just as wild as anyone else and just as fond of strong drink, too, Pettit at least is decent and honest enough to admit his mistakes most of the time. Call it listening to the better angels of his nature, or whatever you'd like, but he'll at least admit it when he crosses the line of common decency.

"All this hot weather is unnatural," Pettit continues, "make no mistake about it, so we had to do something to bring on some cooler weather. Clarence is supposed to be our lucky mascot, so it was all we could think of."

"You men should be ashamed of yourselves, picking on a young boy like that," the captain admonishes everyone. "You are sailing in the tropics in the middle of summer! What kind of weather did you expect to find?" He shakes his head and frowns, his eyes looking from player to player with disgust.

I'm hoping that will be the end of things, and he'll order everyone away, and they'll leave me alone at last, but I'm not so lucky.

"As for you, Clarence Duval, you should not be hitting people with buoys, or threatening them. Violence only leads to more violence and a desire for revenge. I'll not allow that on my ship, no matter the circumstances. Captain Ward, please put an end to this stupidity by keeping these people away from each other until they learn some sense." With that, he stomps off, muttering under his breath.

"You heard the captain," Ward says to the group. "Now shape up. Everyone just disperse and cool your tempers for a while. Clarence, don't you touch any player again." At this point, he notices the large red spot on Baldwin's leg from where I hit him. "Unless you plan to take Baldwin's spot in the pitcher's box when we get to Colombo, we can't have you, or anyone, injuring people, whatever your reasons might be. Go on now, men. Everyone just calm down and collect your wits."

While I wander off, I just wonder why everyone picks on me so much. I know that I'm small and weak and that because I'm the mascot I'm supposed to be lucky, but no one can control the weather. The ballplayers are all big, strong, and fast. There's no way I can do what they do or be like them when I'm only twelve years old. Maybe if I were smarter and older, they'd treat me better. Well, I can't be older, but I can get smarter. I resolve to put even more efforts into my reading lessons with MacMillan and Mrs. Williamson. Maybe then, people will take me more seriously and think twice before they do things to me.

Mercifully, no one else decides to trouble me the rest of the way to Colombo. I apologize to the captain, who'd been so nice to me earlier. He accepts my apology and lets me borrow his music box one more time. I decide I'd like to have one of my own someday.

Chapter 6

January 25, 1889
Colombo, Ceylon, British Empire

"Wow! Did you see that?" Ed Crane shouts to whoever can hear him.

He's looking out over the railing of our steamer at the vast number of rowboats, canoes, and various other ships whose names I don't know surrounding the *Salier* as we steam into Colombo's harbor and drop anchor.

"What is it, Ed?" Ned Williamson asks as he trots over to get a look, joining me at the railing.

"Follow me," Crane says as he runs for the railing on the other side of our ship. "I don't believe they can do it!"

Like puppy dogs, Williamson and I dutifully follow Crane to the other side of the vessel. In a few moments, we see why he is so excited. Four dark-skinned boys, who appear to be a few years older than I am, suddenly surface with a huge gasp for air. They tread water while a school of dolphins circles them.

"Can you believe that?" Crane asks anyone in his general vicinity. "Those four boys just swam underneath our steamer."

"There's no way," Williamson says. "This ship draws twenty-two feet of water. And look how wide the deck is."

"I'm telling you, they just did it," Crane answers. "I'll bet even you couldn't do that, Ned. You're as good an athlete as we have, and I'll wager you're not foolish enough to *think* about trying it. Those four boys just did it, though."

"Let's see what else they can do," Williamson says, reaching into his hip pocket. With a flick of his wrist, he flings a couple sixpence coins from Australia into the water near the four boys. "I won't need those, anyway," he says by way of explanation.

They flash huge smiles and dive. It takes them almost a minute, but they surface again and hold up their hands, coins gleaming in the sunlight.

Williamson and Crane both applaud the boys and, not knowing what else to do, I clap, too. Crane and Williamson toss a few more coins into the water before losing interest in the divers.

Williamson speaks next. "Look at the dolphins, Ed. Now there's a sight you won't get back in Boston harbor, my friend."

"I'm less interested in the fish than in this amazing variety of people," Crane answers. "Just look at it all. You have these people over here, who I think are the natives of the island. Singhalese, I believe, is what you call them. No shirts, just those sheet-like robes they wrap around their waists. But look at their hair! It's combed straight back, tied in a knot, and held in place by those combs. The combs come from a kind of shell, don't they? Can you tell?"

"Judging from some of these people who have boarded our ship, I'd say so, yes. Just listen to them, chattering and waving their arms like a bunch of monkeys. They might not wear shirts, but how many colors do you count on their turbans?"

"Well, I see red, yellow, green, orange, and purple, each in many different shadings of color. It's impossible to count, really. Look at all these natives on the boat already. Merchants, traders, money-changers, and goodness knows who else."

The two men continue their conversation, but suddenly I see Spalding appear in front of us, striding through the diverse crowd of new people. I've barely seen him for a week, and it's been longer than that since he's spoken to me, so I'm surprised when he turns directly toward me and says, "Clarence, why don't you come ashore with me and Mr. Lynch? We could use your company for our errand."

I'm so surprised, it takes me a second to answer, but quickly I recover my senses and say, "Of course, Mr. Spalding, I'd be happy to help you if you need it."

He leads me to a small boat at the side of the ship, and once the three of us, Spalding, myself, and Lynch, take our places in the boat, Spalding gives a signal to a pair of crew members. The men lower us to the water, and we head toward the shore. Two of the German crewmen row the small boat for us.

If I'm lucky, maybe Spalding will say something interesting, and I can earn another dollar from Ward. He promised me a dollar coin every time I learn something useful from Spalding or Anson about their plot against Ward's Brotherhood. However, after getting in the boat, Spalding just sits for several minutes without saying anything. While he sits there, and I wait, I can smell the salty sea air just as clearly as ever, but there's a new smell now, too. As we row nearer the docks of Colombo, the stench of rotting fish and putrid garbage assails us. Looking over the side of our boat, I see various fish parts drift by as we approach the dock where we'll tie up.

After a few more moments, when Spalding still hasn't explained why I'm included in his shore party, I get up my nerve and ask about it.

"Oh, yes, Clarence, I was just ruminating on other matters. To answer your question, I've decided that we should secure hotel rooms for the boys tonight. After all that time at sea, I think they'll appreciate a good night's sleep on solid ground. It will cost extra, certainly, at least $100 or so, but I believe it is worth the expense to keep the men satisfied and in good spirits. Not to mention we've scheduled an exhibition at the local cricket grounds tomorrow, and we want everyone fully rested and ready to play their best."

"Why do you need me to get hotel rooms for the players? I reckon you can do that without me as easily as with me, sir."

"Oh, I didn't ask you to come along for that purpose, Clarence, my boy," Spalding says with a good-natured chuckle. "You are here to test an idea, a theory that I have."

"Can I ask what your idea is about?"

"Our companion here," Spalding gestures to the other man in out boat, "Leigh Lynch, informs me that when traveling through the city of Colombo, it is likely that beggars will accost us at every turn. It seems to be their way whenever foreigners move about in the city. Bah! I can smell the filth from here. In any case, my theory is that if you accompany me, Lynch and I can pass ourselves off as English gentlemen, with you pretending to be my servant. If my plan works, the beggars will be less likely to bother a gentleman of status than they would a mere merchant or tourist."

Lynch laughs at all this. "I think you're nuts, Al, but we'll see."

"You may well be right," Spalding answers Lynch. "But either way, I find no risk to bringing Clarence with us. My idea will work, or it won't, but Clarence must come ashore at some point, so it may as well be with us. Besides, I fear we may owe him a bit of recompense for the saltwater bath incident. A regrettable thing; I wish the boys had shown better judgment that day, Clarence."

"I think everyone is over that now, Mr. Spalding, except maybe for Mr. Baldwin. He might still be a bit sore at me, I'm afraid, because I hit him with one of Captain Anson's bats."

"It was a regrettable incident all around, as I said. In any case, Clarence, while we move through the city on our way to the hotel, I need you to do your best to appear as if you are my servant. Bow when it appears to be appropriate. If you must speak to me, do so deferentially, and only after I've spoken to you, and so forth."

I don't mention to Spalding that I do all these things already just to survive from day to day, except the bowing, so it should be easy enough for me to help. Not only was I in an acting company before getting stranded in Omaha, but a homeless colored person must know these things, or he won't last long.

I figure that I'll get my first test of my acting skill when it comes time to open the door for Spalding to the carriage taking us to our hotel. To my surprise, however, I see no carriages in Colombo. Instead of a carriage with seats mounted on four wheels and pulled by horses, Lynch directs us to a small cart that seats the three of us and has two wheels. Most strangely, I see no horses. Instead of horses, a man pulls the cart through the streets. I feel very sorry for this man. We are traveling uphill toward the hotel, it's hot, and he appears very skinny to me. Somehow, he manages to get us there. He is much stronger than he looks, apparently.

Everywhere we go in the streets, I see poor, sometimes almost skeletal, people stretch their arms toward us and cry out something that's partly in English and partly in some other language I don't understand. They must know the streets that foreigners use because they throng both sides of the busy dirt street, emerging from alleys or the stalls of street merchants when we pass by. Most of them are rather dirty looking—some have scraggly white beards and graying hair that disappears underneath their dusty turbans, and many lack one or more teeth. I can sympathize; there have been times in my life on the Chicago streets when I haven't looked much better. Except for the teeth. I still have all of mine.

"What did I tell you, Al? No one escapes from the peddlers and beggars in the city," Lynch says.

"Yes, their pathetic cries of 'master' and their constant refrain of 'baksheesh, very hungry' grow tiresome exceedingly quickly. I'm glad you have a few copper coins to fob them off."

As we continue up the hill, the chorus of the beggars not diminishing, Spalding says, "I say, Leigh, is this the way everyone travels in the Orient?"

"So it appears, Al."

"What do you call this mode of transport?"

"The local Englishmen call it a rickshaw."

"I'll admit I am most impressed with this setup. We could move a bit faster if we had horses pulling us along, certainly, and if all these poor people would get out of the street, but this driver is by no means slow."

"I believe rickshaw-pulling is a profession in these parts. I'd imagine our driver is very experienced."

"What intrigues me most, Leigh, is the potential for money that may exist here. Running an omnibus company back in the United States can be expensive because horses, along with their harnesses and other gear, cost money to upkeep. If we manufactured the seats and cart, but simply paid wages to one person to drive the passengers around, there may be the potential for a profitable business endeavor. Do you think Americans would take to this?"

"I don't know if I can say, Al. The United States isn't India or Ceylon. Besides the fact that we have streetcars in some cities, do you think Americans would tolerate hitching other people to a cart to move them from place to place?"

"I've been mistaken before, but I believe they certainly would. I never underestimate the power of money to motivate people, whether it's these street beggars or some lawyer or doctor back in the States who likes his nice two-story house but wishes it were three stories. If people could save money by having a human being personally transport them around town, I think a great many people would find a way to justify it, no matter how demeaning to the unfortunate person doing the running. Don't forget, Leigh, in the United States we tolerated slavery until just one generation ago. Within my lifetime, all over the Southern states masters worked their colored slaves like animals to squeeze profit out of them. Do you think so much has changed since 1865 that people would be above using free people in a similar way when money and profit is involved? We like to tell ourselves how advanced and civilized we are, but the Tsar of Russia, one of the most despotic rulers in the world, ended serfdom before the United States ended slavery. I'm not persuaded the moral objections would be as considerable as you might imagine."

"Well, Al, I'll let you think over the possibilities, then. While you do that, however, what do you say we make our arrangements at the hotel desk? The entrance to the Grand Oriental Hotel is straight ahead."

When we arrive at our destination, Spalding still seems very amused by the whole setup, even as he admits to Leigh Lynch that my presence doesn't save him from dealing with beggars.

Our driver pulls us underneath the covered archway right outside the front door of the Grand Oriental. We get down and Lynch pays our driver for running us to our destination.

It seems everyone's already forgotten about me pretending to be a servant, so I simply follow the two men inside. The hotel's name is a proper one, to my eyes at least, because it is rather grand. The builders used white stone all around the outside of the three-story hotel, giving it a very sturdy and solid look. It has a covered archway about twenty-five feet tall that shields the front door from sun and rain, which is where we're standing now, and each room on every floor has a very large window, taller than I am, where people can look out. The front of the hotel faces back toward the harbor and offers a fine view of it. On both sides of the hotel the second- and third-floor rooms have shaded porches where the guests can sit and take in the view of the city.

Once we get inside, the place is equally grand. I see that the ceilings in the lobby are quite high—possibly thirty feet up. Equally tall marble columns prop up the lofty ceilings. Off to the side of the lobby, I glimpse a huge hall filled with tables and chairs. I'm guessing that's where we'll dine this evening. While the three of us stand at the desk so Lynch can negotiate arrangements for our stay, a pair of local men stand nearby, one on either side of us, waving large fans to keep us cooler. They wear brightly colored cotton garments and, like many of the people who came on board our boat, have their hair held at the back of their head with a comb. I am surprised that I see no chairs in the lobby. Instead, a number of low couches line the lobby and adjacent hallways, and the couches have pillows at one end. A few guests recline upon them.

Spalding and Lynch conclude their business at the front desk, and a pair of porters show us to our lodgings. Each room, even mine, has a stone balcony from which a person can look out across the city. The rooms have no carpets, only thick, colorful plush rugs featuring geometric patterns and polished stone floors. I've never seen anything like this, even in my dreams. Usually, when I have dreams at all, I dream about being next to a warm fire in my own house. There's food on the table, and for once, I'm neither hungry or cold. Maybe now I'll have new dreams.

Spalding informs me that I am free to do what I'd like while he returns to the *Salier* and informs the rest of our party to come along. I've spent plenty of time sitting around these past few weeks, so I walk across the street from the hotel, which takes me to one of Colombo's marketplaces. Once again, I'm in a world full of things I can barely imagine. Chicago has many street markets, of course, but they don't sell these kinds of things. I see little boxes made of some wood I don't recognize, items made of shiny shells, carvings of ivory, calico shawls, embroidered curtains, and more of the rugs like I saw in my hotel room. I breathe in a host of smells I've never encountered on the streets of Chicago, either. Incense. More than one kind, too. I think I even catch a whiff of perfume from somewhere.

This market area, like the streets on the way to the Grand Oriental, has a crowd, but with different types of people. The men, and a few women, I see here have nicer clothing, look better fed, and don't smell quite so much. Some are obviously foreigners because they have light skin. A few even bring some servants with them to carry around the things they've purchased. Still, the alleys in between the stalls of the merchants are busy places where people jostle each other, and the noise of squabbling voices haggling over prices in languages I don't speak never ceases.

I don't have time to look too long, however, before more rickshaws arrive at the hotel with the ballplayers. The rickshaw drivers, all of them, are much stronger and tougher than meets the eye. The players seem to have no problem with another person towing them around, and soon the whole party is back in the lobby, ready to see the town.

It takes me aback when, for the second time, Mrs. Williamson seeks out my company. She's been very helpful in the handful of reading lessons we've had together, but she's never approached me in public before. "My, Clarence, isn't this all so strange and wonderful? It is primitive, certainly, but new and vibrant and alive at the same time."

"It is very new to me as well, Mrs. Williamson. I've never been anywhere quite like this back in Chicago."

"Well, Clarence, Ned and I want to do some shopping, and Ed Crane is coming with us. Would you like to tag along as well?"

"I visited the marketplace across the street earlier, Mrs. Williamson. Would you like to start there?"

Mrs. Williamson turns to her husband, who has just come downstairs to the lobby. His chest strains his cotton shirt a bit, I notice. Ned's always been a large, husky man with a broad chest, but I think he's been eating a little extra on our trip, and it's starting to show. "What do you say, Ned, does that sound good? You said you'd buy me something pretty when we got to Colombo, remember?"

"Yes, of course I remember. I promised you something pretty, and something pretty is what you'll get," Williamson says with a happy smile.

Crane also has a big smile on his face. "Don't forget you owe me something, too, for losing that bet on our throwing contest."

"I haven't forgotten that, either," Williamson replies. "You beat me fair and square, so I'll pay my debts. What a pity we couldn't get Pfeffer to bet along with us. Then we'd both be walking out of here with something this evening."

"Yes, that man might act crazy in the head sometimes, but he seems to have a way of being smart with his money, regardless. Well, why stand here talking when we could be out exploring, right? Let's see what we can find."

Chapter 7

January 25, 1889
Colombo, Ceylon, British Empire

We do start with the marketplace, and I point out some of the attractive things I noticed earlier.

"Oh, look, cashmere shawls," Mrs. Williamson says. "And a moonstone necklace. Over here, that is an ivory watch charm. What a pretty little box that is, don't you think, Ned?"

"Yes, these sandalwood boxes are beautiful," Crane says while he and I look at another one.

"How do you know it's made from sandalwood?" Mrs. Williamson asks him.

"My father died before I turned eight years old, so I had to do some work as a carpenter for a time before I started playing ball for a living. I learned to recognize different kinds of wood."

"How sad," she replies, but before she can say anything more to Crane, an embroidered silk shawl distracts Mrs. Williamson and she says, "That's the one! That's what I want you to get me," to her husband.

Ed Crane roll his eyes. Apparently, he's heard those words before when shopping with the Williamsons.

It is funny watching Williamson haggle over the price, since he can't speak Singhalese and the merchant knows no English. He holds up some coins, but the merchant shakes his head. The trader holds up three fingers and points to a pound note, but Williamson shakes his head vigorously and scowls, saying, "no, no." Eventually, Williamson pays one pound plus a few shillings. He seems happy enough afterward, and his wife appears even more so.

They continue shopping for a while, and it is getting on into the afternoon when we bump into some of the Howling Wolves, namely Baldwin, Daly, and Sullivan. I can see that all three have been shopping for clothes. They've donned white duck suits, each wears a light-colored silk sash around his waist, and they all sport white cork hats with hatbands made of silk that drape over the back of their necks. All of this registers instantly, and then I realize that Baldwin is among the trio. I look around for somewhere to run. With all the traffic and commotion around us, I could probably lose him in the crowd if I had to. Now, which way do I go to get back to our hotel from here?

Shortly, however, I realize that Baldwin is smiling and isn't even paying any attention to me. He looks back, gives a quick tug on a leather leash he's holding, and a monkey hops into view.

"Is that yours?" Ned Williamson asks.

"Yes, it is. I just bought it from a merchant a couple streets over. I thought he'd be a great little souvenir."

"You plan to take a monkey home with you?" Mrs. Williamson asks Baldwin.

"Sure. Why not? It's not like we don't have room aboard the ship for a little monkey."

"Do you know how to take care of a monkey?" she asks.

"I had a dog growing up. How much different can it be?"

"Are you sure about this?"

"Ned, you'd better get your woman in line," Baldwin says with a wink toward Williamson and a goofy, lopsided grin. "I hope she doesn't ask this many questions at home."

Baldwin finally notices me. I've been trying to hide behind Crane while they talk about Baldwin's monkey.

He just smiles. "Don't fret, Clarence, no more saltwater baths for you, at least not today. No hard feelings."

I relax my shoulders when he says this. I had no idea I'd hunched them up so tightly until now.

"You just forget about the bath," he continues, "and I won't tell Anson you touched one of his bats to hit me with."

"It's a deal, Mr. Baldwin."

I'd forgotten the fact I used Anson's bat to strike Baldwin. I was so angry and so scared the men would throw me overboard for the sharks that I just grabbed whatever bat I found first and didn't think enough about where it came from.

"It's good to see a fellow Wolf out and about this afternoon," Daly says to Williamson. "Perhaps you'd like to join us? We're heading back down to the harbor. There's another American ship in port, if you can believe it, and its captain has invited all the ballplayers to come aboard and meet the crew. Are you with us?"

Everyone voices their agreement, and we start toward the main street to hail a few rickshaws to take us there, when suddenly, Sullivan calls out, "Whoa there, boys, what's this?"

On our right, two Indian men play an improvised version of a familiar game. Between them they have six coconuts, which are round but cut off at one end near the bottom, so they form a cup, and two small rubber balls, and they move the balls by switching them quickly from one coconut to the next, all the while shifting the coconuts about to confuse the viewers. They are wonderfully quick at this game, and all around, people are shouting and placing bets on which coconuts truly contain the balls.

That occupies our attention for only a moment, however, because we've seen this game played before. When we walk a bit farther and glance to our left, however, we encounter a scene we would not find on the streets of Chicago. There, a pair of men, who also look Indian rather than Singhalese, sit across from each other playing flutes. Between the two of them, two large snakes sway back and forth. The smell of incense is very strong in the air.

"Are those cobras?" Daly asks Baldwin.

Baldwin just shrugs, but Crane answers, "Yeah, I think so. You can tell by the flap on either side of their head. They're very venomous, very poisonous." We all take a step or two back but, fascinated, continue watching. Almost as charmed as the snakes themselves, I sway slightly to the music while the dangerous reptiles loll their heads back and forth. Bit by bit, the snakes rise up until they are as tall as Crane, who stands almost six feet. These two snakes have black bodies with bands of gold. The flaps near their heads have gold patterns underneath, too. When the music ceases, they drop back to the ground and coil up.

While we hasten away and flag down some transportation to the harbor, Daly says to anyone who can hear, "Did you see that? I never thought any of that snake-charming stuff was real, that it was just stories for kids and nonsense. That, my friends, was the real thing. How long were those cobras?"

"Well," says Sullivan, "they were standing up as tall as we are, and I'll bet two-thirds of their bodies were still on the ground. That makes, what, about seventeen or eighteen feet?"

"What do you think, Tom, should we buy one of those and put it in Anson's bed instead of a wet floor mat?" Baldwin asks, and the group has a good laugh.

"So, it was you guys who did that," Crane says. "I thought as much but didn't have firm proof until now."

"Oops," is all Baldwin can say. He puts his head down a little, raises his eyebrows, and extends his arm with the monkey's leash toward Crane and says, "I'll give you a monkey if you keep quiet about it to Anson."

"How about you pay my entire rickshaw fare today, and we'll call it even."

"You got it."

When the rickshaws arrive, we ride down to the harbor. The crew of the USS *Essex* greets us with a hearty cheer when we approach and come aboard. None of us has much experience visiting ships in foreign ports, so we are all surprised when the captain himself, Captain Jewell, asks us to share a meal with the officers of the *Essex*. We accept, of course, because it is nearly dinnertime, and all of us are hungry. We meet the captain's lieutenants, as well as many other crewmembers.

We are just standing on deck after the meal, trying to decide what to do after touring the ship, when a sailor approaches Ed Crane. The man looks very young, even for a sailor. I'd be surprised if he was even twenty years old. He has flaming red hair that just peeks out from underneath his sailor's hat, and he shoves his hands deep in his pockets when he approaches us.

The sailor says, "Ex-excuse me, sir, you are Ed Crane, the, um, the 'Cannonball,' aren't you?"

"Yes, I am," Crane says, smiling again at the use of his nickname.

"My n-name is Hagerty, Patrick Hagerty. I-I'm from South Boston, just like you. I've followed your career ever since, ever since you joined the old Boston Reds back in '84. I even w-watched you pitch a few games t-that year."

"You don't say," Crane replies. "Well, it's a pleasure to meet a fellow son of the Emerald Isle, and a baseball fan, too, so far from the States."

Hagerty finally takes his hands from his pockets and his shoulders untense when Crane says this. "I'm honored to meet you, too, Mr. Crane. All my life growing up, I wanted to be a real crack pitcher like you, but I couldn't quite make the grade as a ballplayer, so I joined the Navy, and now here I am in Colombo. When are you going to come back from New York and pitch again at the South

End Grounds where a good Irishman belongs? I know that Arthur Soden, the Boston owner, is a bit of a miser, but it sure would be good to have you back in Boston."

Crane has a good laugh at this. "Whenever Mr. Day gives me my release, I guess."

"I just had an idea. Please, don't leave for a moment. I have something I'd like to give you, but I'll need a moment to fetch it."

"You really don't need to give me anything."

"I'll explain when I get back. Just don't leave."

While we wait, Daly wanders away and talks with some of the other sailors seeing to their duties on deck. In a few minutes, however, Hagerty is back, with a small wire cage. A little monkey squats inside.

"Here, have this monkey," he says, holding out the small cage to Crane. The creature has dark brown fur. It just looks at everyone timidly, it's small head turning back and forth frantically.

I look over at Baldwin's monkey, which is bigger and has lighter fur than this second creature. How many monkeys are we going to have by the time we get back aboard the *Salier*? Maybe I'll get a monkey somewhere, too. I've never had a pet.

"I really can't take a monkey from you," Crane tells Hagerty. "I wouldn't know what to do with it or how to take care of it."

"Please, you must take him," Hagerty says, practically begging. His eyes even begin to water. "You just have to. You see, when we made port, I wanted to get an original souvenir of traveling to the other side of the world. All the other men were buying jewelry, or fancy shawls for their mothers, or wives, or girlfriends, and I wanted to do something different. That's why I bought a pet monkey—so I'd have something no one else aboard the *Essex* had. Except, you see, when the captain found out, he said it was against Navy regulations to bring a living creature aboard our ship, and my monkey had to go. He told me I had to get rid of it by the time we leave port, which is only two days away. Because I must give away my monkey anyway, I'd like you to have it."

76

Crane's shoulder's sag and his gaze softens visibly after hearing the sailor's story. "Well, I guess that settles it. I guess I'll have to do the best I can to take care of this monkey."

"Thank you, thank you, Mr. Crane," Hagerty says, practically in tears now. "I don't want to see the monkey go because I'm very fond of it already, and it's so kind and gentle. All the other sailors love it, too. It just eats right from your hand. Watch this."

Hagerty takes out some breadcrumbs he'd hidden inside his uniform pocket. The monkey grabs them tentatively, then it chomps them down.

Next, Hagerty reaches into the cage and pets the monkey on the head. "Good boy, good monkey." He sets the cage on the deck of the ship and gets down on one knee to talk to his pet for the final time.

"Well, little monkey, I guess I'm not allowed to keep you. I wanted to bring you to my home in Boston and take care of you, but I don't get to. I found you a new home, though. This is Ed Crane, the famous baseball pitcher. He's from Boston, like me, and his family is Irish, too. He says he'll take good care of you, so you have to go with him now."

With a shaking arm, Hagerty hands the cage over to Crane and turns away, trying to return to his duties on the ship. It is a very touching scene. I almost cry because I've always liked animals. Just like the idea of the buffalo disappearing makes me sad, the thought of Hagerty losing his pet gives me a knot in my chest. If only I could take care of a pet, I'd get one myself to keep me company. Tommy told me he had a dog once, a beautiful brown lab, but I don't think he ever said what happened to it. I look over and see that Mrs. Williamson is sniffling.

This is how we ended up with two monkeys aboard the *Salier*. While Crane and Mrs. Williamson are looking over this new monkey, which Crane has already named "Patrick," Daly returns and addresses the group.

"Fellow Wolves, I know our next destination. Now that we've dined, we need to wash our food down with something. Those sailors over there told me just the place."

Our next stop, therefore, is an old building a few blocks back from the waterfront. It has a sign out front, and the words are in French, which none of us can read, but the foaming mug of beer on the sign makes it clear this is our destination.

The neighborhood looks a bit rougher than the one our hotel is in. Many people who appear to be dockworkers or sailors roam about, the streets are narrower, and the smell of saltwater and fish is very noticeable, even over the sweaty smell of men who work outside in tropical places.

"This is the place," Daly declares. "The sailors told me the proprietor is an old Frenchman, but he speaks about a dozen languages, including English, and that his beer is affordable and plentiful."

I'm not so sure about this idea. I remember the last time I went drinking with the Howling Wolves and how it almost got me run over by a train. There's no choice but to go with them, however, because I don't have the money with me to go back to the Grand Oriental by myself, so I go inside.

The pub is very warm, stuffy, smoky, and full of people, almost all of them speaking languages I don't recognize. Before long, Baldwin and Daly have chatted up the proprietor, and we have our drinks. Baldwin offers me a beer, too. "No hard feelings, right?" he says to me. Then, to the group, "Drink up, men, to our only night in Ceylon."

It looks like my earlier judgments about Baldwin's character were about right. He is just young and carefree, never taking anything too seriously for very long. I relax a bit more after my first sip of beer. Enough of the players don't like me already, so knowing that Baldwin hasn't held a grudge is a comfort. Unless he's just getting me off my guard to set me up for later. I'd better keep an eye on him after all.

Ned Williamson says, "Just one for me. You know I've eased up on the foaming amber since last year." His wife gives him an encouraging smile and a pat on his shoulder. Williamson says to Baldwin, "Why won't John Tener join us? You two are both from Pittsburgh, and he's your friend. How come he isn't one of the Howling Wolves?"

"I tried to talk him into it, but it was a bit beneath his supposed dignity, I guess," Baldwin says in response, his high-pitched voice getting a bit higher as he drinks and relaxes. "You know he has ambitions of going into politics someday. I think he finds drinking in bars like this a little undistinguished or something. He's a good man all the same, just a little too uptight at times."

"His loss," Daly says.

"Yeah, especially since he owes me for getting Old Man Anson to sign him to play on the White Stockings. You know that story, right, Ned?"

"Yeah. Wasn't he working as a bank teller or something before you got Anson to look at him pitch?"

"That's right. Heaven knows the White Stockings pay him better than the bank did, too."

We have a little break in the conversation while everyone drinks. The bar is stuffy, baking, in fact, and the air is close enough that I'm sweating rather badly, but to distract myself I decide to ask a question I've been thinking about since we sat down.

"Does anyone know what that thing in the corner is? The one mounted on the tripod, and that has the little pipes and tubes that the people around it keep putting in their mouths? I've never seen one of those back in Chicago, although I think I recognize the smell from our trip to Chinatown."

"It is curious, to be sure," Mrs. Williamson puts in. "Do you recognize it, Ned?"

"Let me ask the barkeep. We need more drinks, anyway," Baldwin says, and he's off to the bar, where he engages in some lively chatter with a man who appears to be a British sailor while he waits for his next round of drinks.

In a couple minutes, he's back with four more mugs of beer, two in each hand. "So, here's what the old barkeep told me. First, he says the contraption is a hookah, and that using it is kinda like smoking a pipe, but more potent. He doesn't like it much personally, but having one brings in the customers, and they buy more beer after smoking it. Then, when I told him we were Americans and he realized we weren't with the Navy, he asked why we were in Colombo. I mentioned we were on our way to France and asked him what the best French beers were. He told me some names—although I'll probably forget them by the time we get there, who can remember these silly French pronunciations, anyway—then mentioned that when we arrive, France has something going on called the Boulanger Affair, and we should stay out of it. He said Boulanger's supporters are idiots, and we should stay clear of them. I promised that we would."

"I think I remember reading something about Boulanger back when we were in San Francisco," Crane puts in. "If memory serves, he is, or was, a general in the French Army, and a great many of the people there adore him. Apparently, France lost some war with Germany back when we were just children, and he wants a war of revenge."

Crane's memory of world events sounds reasonable, but Daly and Baldwin simply shrug and drink some more. One hour and a couple more beers later, they are still rambling on about whatever comes to mind. I've only had one drink. It was strong stuff, but I don't think it's bothering me too badly. The bar remains so hot and the air so thick and smothering I think I've sweated out the alcohol by now, anyway. Ned Williamson has lived up to his promise, but his wife is working on her third beer and Ed Crane the same, while the other Howling Wolves are much further along than Crane. It is starting to show. Although I think that Crane still has his wits about him, Williamson remains the only person I am sure is fully sober.

"Remember that time back in Arkansas when we almost died?" Daly says to Baldwin.

"Yeah, in Hot Springs we drank just like this, and you blew out the gas light, but forgot to turn off the gas."

"How long were we unconscious that time, Mark?"

"I don't know. I was unconscious, just like you were. At least the house didn't blow up, like that tunnel in Chinatown back in San Francisco."

"I don't know about you guys," Sullivan puts in, "but I'm thinking it's time to give the hookah a try."

"I'm all for it," Daly says.

"Sure," Baldwin agrees. "Here, take my monkey for a minute." He hands Williamson the leather leash.

The rest of us pass on the hookah and continue taking in the scene. The bar remains crowded, as do the tables. Judging by the number of uniforms I see, many sailors are here for a drink. A good number of them smoke tobacco, too, which, mixed with the beer and the smell coming from the corner with the hookah, assaults my nose. I've never liked the smell of burning tobacco, and adding these other things is almost too much for me to breathe. It is a potent mix, for sure.

Our trio of Wolves have been experiencing the pleasures of the hookah for a while when I hear Williamson say, "Oh no, now they've done it."

Right as he says this, I realize the bar has indeed gotten much louder, and Daly, Baldwin, and Sullivan are part of the reason why. It appears they've engaged some Englishmen in a debate on the merits of baseball as compared to cricket, and neither side is willing to give up the argument. Now, both groups gesture wildly and shout at the other. One of the sailors gets into Sullivan's face and bumps his chest. I think a fistfight is about to start unless we do something.

Crane jumps up from his seat immediately and moves quickly and decisively, with Williamson a few steps behind because he must hand the monkey over to his wife. Striding over to the corner, Crane thrusts his body between Sullivan and his English counterpart and separates them with his arms. Now, Crane is a large man. He stands nearly six feet tall, and he's quite muscular, as well. Baldwin and Sullivan are likewise large, powerful men, and Williamson is bigger and stronger looking than anyone else I can see in the bar. I'd give any of them good odds against the Englishmen standing across from them, but fighting isn't what Crane has in mind.

"That's enough men, that's enough. It isn't worth fighting over. You, sailor, think what your commanding officer will do to you when I tell him about this," Crane bluffs, then turns to another of the men. "And you, how many hours do you want to spend cleaning the deck this week? Here, this is enough shillings for another beer." He finishes by tossing a few coins on a table to draw their attention away.

Facing our party, he continues, "Tom, Mark, Marty, let them be. You want to spend the night in an Oriental dungeon and get left in Colombo?" He hustles the men back to our table, even as they continue yelling at the Englishmen over their shoulder, trying to make a case for baseball's superiority. For the moment, Crane prevents disaster.

Crane, with a bit of help from Williamson, finally gets Baldwin, Daly, and Sullivan outside the bar, and we hail more rickshaws to take us, and our monkeys, back to the Grand Oriental. A steady rain begins falling while we wait. It is late enough that the daylight is starting to fade.

Our group finds seats in several rickshaws. I'm in one with Daly, and the Williamsons are in another. Crane boards a third to keep Sullivan from falling or jumping out because he's had the most to drink, which means Baldwin is in the fourth rickshaw, his monkey alongside. Everyone who tried the hookah acts very peculiar. They had a few beers, for sure, but not enough to appear so confused. Baldwin falls backward when he tries to get into his rickshaw the first time. Sullivan points upward and says, "Look at the pretty birds flying around." I can only see one bird, and it isn't even moving. Must be something in the hookah pipe, I guess.

"I say," Tom Daly shouts to our driver, even though the man is only a few feet away, "I'll give you an extra shilling if you get me to the hotel first." He pulls out some coins and points up the hill toward our hotel. "Grand Oriental, fast!" Turning to the other rickshaws, Daly calls out, "Let's have a race!"

Before Crane can muzzle him, Sullivan shouts back, "You're on!" He pulls some coins from his pocket and repeats Daly's instructions to his rickshaw driver.

I don't know if they understand exactly what the players mean, but when the rickshaw men start up the hill, Daly, Sullivan, and Baldwin try encouraging them by slapping the side of their rickshaw and yelling, "Faster! Faster!"

Now, I feel worse than ever for the poor rickshaw drivers. They are trying to run up the hill carrying people in their carts, and those people are trying to get them to go faster, as if they are horses. The rain has increased in intensity, as well, and is now coming down hard. We haven't gone more than a few hundred feet when I look over and see Baldwin standing up in his cart, waving at whomever we happen to pass. I hear him say, "Look at me, monkey, look at me!"

Williamson is watching, too, just like I am, so we're too late to interfere when Daly decides to go Baldwin one better. Before I can say or do anything, he jumps on top of his seat and then jumps up again so that he's standing with one leg on the front and one on the rear board of the rickshaw. He tries to balance as the driver plods forward.

"Look at this, no hands!" he yells across to Baldwin and Sullivan.

Maybe the sudden shift of weight distracted the man pulling our rickshaw, or maybe it was Daly's shouting, but he looks back at Daly for just a moment. When he does that, he misses seeing a patch of mud created by the rain, slips, and lets go of the rickshaw as he falls to one side. This unbalances the rickshaw, and it crashes over on its right side. Because I was the one sitting in the left seat, the crash propels me through the air, and I land at the side of the street, face down in the mud. Great. Another set of clothes I'll have to clean. It knocks my breath out of me, but at least the ground is softer than it was an hour ago.

Quickly, I learn that muddy clothes are the least of my problems. I've landed just a yard away from another snake charmer and king cobra! I lift my head from the mud, wiping some of it from my eyes, in time to see the creature rear up to a full six feet tall. Looking up at it from the ground, though, the snake looks twenty feet tall, at least. It extends the flap on either side of its head, sticks out its forked tongue, and hisses. The hiss is not what I expected. The sound is very low, so low that it sounds like a dog growling at me.

I remember what Crane said about cobras being venomous. What do I do? The fear takes hold of me. I'm on my hands and knees in the mud, and I can't move. My only thought is that I'm going to die halfway around the world from my home, and it's going to be a very painful death.

The snake growls again. The people gathered around are gasping and shouting, but I can't make out any of it. I've locked my gaze on the cobra, waiting for it to strike and make an end of me. I still can't move. I'm too scared.

It strikes. I try to dodge finally, but the snake is far too quick for me, and I'm bitten. I see it recoil and I recognize Mrs. Williamson's scream behind me. I feel someone grab my ankles, and I black out.

Chapter 8

Slowly, dimly at first, a gray light emerges from the blackness. Someone is slapping me gently on the cheek. Gradually, I can make out that someone is saying something to me as well. Are they calling my name? The voice sounds familiar, but distant. Now my vision is a blur of vivid colors changing rapidly. They shift and recombine before I can make out any pattern. Is it the snake venom doing this to me? Am I dying? Is this what dying feels like?

Then, I catch the trace, the dim murmur of the words again, and I try to concentrate on them. I can't tell how much time has passed, but gradually, I realize the voice is repeating my name, and in a few more moments, it gets a bit clearer and easier to hear. It takes great effort because my brain feels like it's twisting in circles still, but I force my eyes open.

"Clarence!" Ed Crane calls out, his voice louder and clear now. "You're okay my boy, you're okay."

"Am I in Heaven?" I ask. "Did the snake kill you, too?" My eyes close again, and I think I might black out once more, but Crane shakes my shoulders gently, and I come back to the light.

"You aren't dead, Clarence, you're fine. It's okay. Everything is all right. Stand up, son."

Slowly, I'm aware of feeling returning to my arms and legs, and I move my head a bit. I notice something soft and sticky clings to my cheeks when I do. My eyes focus a bit more, and I can see Crane and some of the others I was with standing in a circle around me, looking down at me. Only then do I realize I'm lying on my back in the muddy streets of Colombo. It's still raining, but softer now. Water drenches my clothes along with the mud, and they cling to my body.

"I must be dead. The snake bit me. Why are all of you here?"

"Yes, the cobra bit you. Right there on your neck. Can you feel the puncture marks?" Crane asks me.

I put my right hand on my neck. I can certainly feel them, two small bumps spaced about an inch apart with holes in the middle. I wince, although whether from the memory of being bit, or because the bite is painful and my neck is sensitive, I'm not sure.

"You're fine, though," Crane tells me. "You have no swelling, no discoloring, nothing. You're fine."

"Are you sure? That can't be true. The snake bit me, and I passed out. Why did I pass out if I'm fine?"

"It must have been the shock, I guess. I know you're fine, though, because there happened to be a British official watching the snake charmers just as your crash threw you from your rickshaw. He explained to all of us that none of the cobras has any venom at all. The snake charmers remove the glands from the snakes that store the venom, so they can train them without fear of snakebites. Can you believe that? You're not hurt, and you aren't going to die because of the snake."

I sit up, pull my mud-caked knees to my chest, and start crying, right there in the middle of the street. The smell of garbage and wet mud assaults me when I close my eyes.

"What are you crying for, Clarence? Aren't you happy that everything is okay?" Ned Williamson says to me.

"How is everything okay? I'm halfway around the world, and people drag me to wherever they want to go, and they get drunk, and smoke hookahs, and do dangerous things. I almost get killed by trains, and snakes, and angry miners, and hot air balloons, and men with pistols. People give me saltwater baths, and throw me overboard, and think I should be shark bait, and I do the dishes and sweep the deck, and I must do stupid plantation dances when I don't even know any. How is everything okay? Why should I be happy?"

No one says anything for several moments. I just sit there in the mud, rain dripping gently from my face, and I put my head down again. I go to rub my head, only to find that all my hair is muddy, too. Of all the people, Mrs. Williamson comes and sits in the mud next to me. I don't look up, so I don't even know it's her until she puts an arm around my shoulders.

"I'm so happy you are unhurt, Clarence," she says after a moment. "Whatever would we do without our mascot?"

I debate if I should say anything back but finally ask her the only thing that comes to mind. "How come you decided to sit in the mud with me? I don't think any of this is your fault, and now you're all muddy, just like me."

"Well, when that evil snake bit you, I fainted, just like you did. Watching the snake do that scared me very much. I screamed, and I saw Marty try to grab you and pull you away from the snake, things went dark, and that was the last thing I remember until I came to. When I fainted, I fell in the mud. A little more won't hurt at this point."

"No, I guess it won't. It was Mr. Sullivan who tried to help me?"

"Yes, it was. He jumped down from his rickshaw and tried to yank you away from the cobra by your ankles. That is all I saw."

"Here," she says, standing up and reaching out her hand, "let's get you back on your feet." We walk over to where Williamson, Sullivan, and Crane are waiting. The other two Howling Wolves, Daly and Baldwin, are nowhere in sight, and I could care less.

"Let's get Clarence some clean clothes on the way back to the hotel," she tells her husband. "Maybe buy him one of those duck suits. They look cool and comfortable."

"Yeah, I guess that would be the thing to do."

"I was hoping to see some ancient ruins when we got to Colombo, maybe some ancient temples, too, but I think I've had all the excitement I can take for now."

"Come on, Clarence," Crane says to me. "Let's see if we can get you cleaned up a bit, my friend."

At least I get a new set of clothes in return for the cobra almost killing me.

Chapter 9

January 26, 1889
Arabian Sea

"Well, Clarence, my boy, it sounds as if you had quite an adventure yesterday."

We are back aboard the *Salier*, steaming for the Red Sea and Egypt, and I'm sitting on a deck chair next to Harry Palmer as the setting sun highlights the clouds to our west with flashes of gold and glints of rose. We've just enjoyed another fine dinner, and after everything that happened in Colombo, I'm feeling lucky just to sit there beside him, the warm sea breeze in my face.

"Yes, Mr. Palmer, I thought that snake was going to be the end of me. I was very lucky, I reckon."

"It appears your mascotic talents have not deserted you. You still have your good luck. Was the snake really thirty-five or forty feet long like Daly claimed?"

"I really couldn't say, Mr. Palmer, because I passed out after it bit me. The fright just took hold of me, and I couldn't move, just like with the mining cart back in Ballarat. I'm rather ashamed of the fact that I always seem to panic in emergencies."

"Don't let it get you down, my lad. I know many grown men who would have fared just the same as you did, and maybe worse. You should feel no shame."

"I don't know about that. I just hope it never happens to me again. Will there be snakes when we get to Egypt?"

"I'd guess the Egyptians probably have snakes, yes. We'll just try to stay away from them. Just like Baldwin, Daly, and Sullivan should have stayed away from the hookah. I thought they would have known better, but it seems I overestimated the quality of their judgment. Not that I rated it highly to begin with, mind you, but even still, they continue forcing me to reconsider almost weekly."

Palmer turns to Tom Brown, who sits on the other side of him. "Say, Tommy, I've been working on my description of our ballgame this morning for my letter to *The Sporting Life*. Let me read it to you, and you tell me if this sounds about right."

"Okay, Harry, go ahead and read it."

Palmer clears his throat, and begins his account. "The native Singhalese gazed in wonder at the teams when they jumped upon the pier in their uniforms half an hour after docking, and followed in crowds to the doors of the Oriental Hotel, where we took, not carriages drawn by gaily plumed horses, as we did in America and Australia, but bullock carts and rickshaws, and such a scene as the road from the hotel to the cricket grounds presented was one never to be forgotten. Hundreds of howling, chattering, grotesquely arrayed natives; a dazzling blending of red, white, green, blue, and orange turbans, sashes, and jackets; scores of black, shining skins; odd-looking, heavy wheeled carts, drawn by ambling, hump-backed little bulls not bigger than our calves at home; bare-legged Singhalese darting among the carts with their rickshaws; peddlers and beggars until you could not rest, and, in fact, a state of wild confusion that was simply laughable to our party. I wondered would we ever get there. It looked questionable, but we finally pulled up at the gates of the cricket grounds and entered. Mr. Lynch had laid out a diamond in the center of the cricket field, and around the big lawn, forming a hollow square, stood 5,000 people—the most picturesquely attired crowd, without a doubt, that ever assembled to witness a baseball game. The officers and crew of the *Essex* took up a position in front of the clubhouse and yelled themselves hoarse over the plays in the five-inning game that followed our arrival at the grounds. The Englishmen seemed to enjoy the sport, but the Singhalese and Hindus broke into wild enthusiasm over the batting and baserunning. It was laughable to see their desperate efforts to get out of the way when a ball was thrown or batted among them. They flew in all directions, tumbling over each other and chattering like a lot of magpies."

"Not bad," Brown says. "The trip there and back was a strange one, no doubt about it."

"I tried to fit in a bit of praise for the manners of the English, just for you."

"I noticed that. You didn't write anything about my home run during the game, however. That was the best ball I've struck so far on the trip."

"Right. I shall work that into my account of the game itself if I can. You did your part to turn the natives into magpies," Palmer says with a smile.

"Also, you might mention the British military band and the Scottish Highlanders who came to watch with their bagpipes. I know we missed their performance because we had to make it back to the ship, but I'm sure it was quite a sight."

"How did that sound to you, Clarence?" Palmer turns back to me and asks.

"It's all fine, I guess, Mr. Palmer," I say. "I spent most of the time watching out for more snakes, to tell you the truth."

We all laugh, and I decide to return to my cabin. I don't know how well I'll sleep, but I decide to try.

I sit up with a start. More nightmares. Snakes this time. I feel better when I realize I'm in my cabin, and it contains no snakes.

91

Looking around my cabin, it's far too big for me, but because none of the ballplayers will share a cabin, I get my own. A bunk bed is up against one wall. I always sleep on the bottom. The cabin also contains a dresser for clothes, but because I have so few, I don't bother with that. The full-length mirror is nice, however. Two of the books I've been reading lie on the writing desk that sits across from the dresser. The ceiling of the cabin isn't tall, I'd guess about six-and-a-half feet, but that's plenty for me. It's not a lot of space for a grown person, but because I'm twelve, I can move around easily.

It is light outside, and I lie back down. A bead of sweat stings my eyes, and I see that some parts of the sheets are damp with sweat, too. I think I'll try to sleep some more because what sleep I've had was so troubled. I've just closed my eyes when I'm startled fully awake again. That was gunfire! Big guns. It sounded like cannons. What's happening now? I open the door and poke my head outside my cabin to see what's going on.

Looking to the end of the hallway, Jim Fogarty pops into view. He runs down the hallway and back, yelling at the top of his lungs. "Pirates! Pirates! My God, boys, the Chinese pirates are upon us!" Another burst of cannon fire follows Fogarty's declaration.

Chaos ensues as other ballplayers open their doors and step into the hallway. A few, like Daly and Sullivan, have pajamas on. Ned Williamson is bare-chested, and I can see his gut bounce a bit when he scrambles out of his door. Once several more doors have opened, Fogarty repeats his warning and adds, "Grab your bats, men, we'll defend the ship to the last man. Don't let them take you alive! You'll be slaves for life in Hong Kong." He already has a bat and runs toward the door to the main deck, yelling at the rest of us to follow. His bat points forward, like he's giving us the signal to charge.

I look up and down the hallway and see John Tener. His face is ashen. Tener is the treasurer for our trip and keeps track of our money. He yells out, "I've got to hide our cash!" He backs into his cabin and disappears.

Ed Crane, clad only in his nightshirt, runs down the hallway in the other direction from Fogarty. "I've got to get my monkey! I can't let the pirates take Patrick!" he says as he, too, disappears from sight.

I look a few doors down and see Anson. In the excitement, he has donned one of his wife's dresses and has her diamonds in his mouth. His eyes dart back and forth like a startled, frightened animal.

Ned Hanlon, meanwhile, stumbles into the hallway with his baseball hat on, a pair of trousers around his ankles, and nothing else. Some of the other players, including Sullivan, Williamson, and Baldwin, really do grab bats and run down the hallway after Fogarty.

What do I do? Billy Earle happens to have the cabin next door to mine. "Save me, Mr. Earle!" I cry. "I don't want to be a pirate slave! Help me hide!" I try to crowd into his cabin.

"Get out of here, Clarence!" he shouts hysterically. "See to yourself, boy." He slams the door in my face. I hear the lock click.

I'm too scared to go up on deck, so I go back to my cabin and try to fold myself underneath the bottom bunk. I don't move—I'm almost too scared to breathe at first. My jaw starts shaking, so I try as hard as I can to prevent my teeth from rattling.

Probably, it's only a couple minutes, but it seems like an hour that I wait, breathing through my mouth because it's quieter that way. It seems like I wait forever. Suddenly, I have an idea. If I stay here and wait, the pirates will probably find me. However, if I can get up to my secret perch on top of the bridge, perhaps the pirates won't see me, and I won't have to be a slave. I don't hear any sound in the hallway yet, so I decide to chance it.

I open my cabin door and creep down the hallway toward the door to the deck as silently as I can. In the drama, I forgot to put on my one pair of shoes, but that's okay, my bare feet make less noise while I tiptoe toward the window and look out at the deck. I haven't heard any more cannons. I get to the door and, ever so slowly, crack it open and peek around the corner.

I thought I would see men with thick beards wearing long coats and waving pistols, and probably see a dead ballplayer or two somewhere on deck along with other dead passengers. That's how pirates act in the stories I read with MacMillan and Mrs. Williamson. Instead of pirates, however, I find that, once again, the joke is on us.

Jim Fogarty lies on the deck of the ship, but he's not dead. Instead, he's laughing so hard I think he's liable to split open at any minute. Williamson, Sullivan, and Baldwin are laughing, too, but everyone else is frowning. Hanlon's scowling and fuming so much I think he's about to punch Fogarty, but instead, he pulls the All-America outfielder to his feet by his shirt and shakes him vigorously.

"What do you mean, there aren't any pirates?" he yells in Fogarty's face.

"Got you!" Fogarty practically giggles as Hanlon shakes him harder. "It's all a joke. Today is the Kaiser's birthday!"

"Birthday? What do you mean, birthday?"

"I talked to Captain Thalenhorst this morning, and he happened to mention it was the Kaiser's thirtieth birthday today, and he planned to order a salute. That's what all the noise was." Fogarty breaks into another round of hysterical laughter.

Now Hanlon just looks at Fogarty with a blank stare. Jimmy Ryan, standing nearby, is more upset than ever, though. He's clenched his fist so tightly and the veins on his neck stand out so much, he looks like he could burst from the pressure. The crimson hue of his cheeks grows darker by the second. He also brought his bat on deck, and now he winds up to clobber Fogarty. Luckily, Fogarty's fellow Howling Wolves notice just in time, and Williamson and Sullivan grab the big Chicago outfielder by the arm just before he breaks several of Fogarty's ribs.

"Whoa there, Jimmy, ease up, old boy. Can't you take a joke?" Sullivan says with a huge grin.

Sullivan's comments do not appease the rest of the crowd, however. Hanlon grabs Fogarty with both hands and shakes him again.

"Throw him overboard!" George Wood shouts out, and he and Tom Brown charge Fogarty. With Hanlon's help, they manhandle Fogarty toward the ship's railing, and soon he is dangling over the side while Wood and Brown hold him by a leg each.

"Where are your pirates now?" Wood yells at him.

"Maybe a pirate ship will pick you up after we drop you," Brown taunts.

Finally, Ward and a properly dressed Anson arrive on the scene and restore calm. They order the ballplayers to different sides of the deck until everyone cools down. Finally, I heave a sigh of relief.

Crane is also on deck by now, and fully clothed, after hiding his monkey. He simply shakes his head at everything. "Those Wolves went too far this time, I reckon."

"I don't know too much about pirates," I say to him, "but I decided I didn't want to let them do me in."

The big pitcher just smiles. "Well, Clarence, I guess we're safe for now. I'm going to go and retrieve Patrick. Would you like to come with me? I know you like that monkey, too."

"Sure, Mr. Crane. Patrick is a very good monkey. Let's go and get him."

On the way, we stop off at Crane's cabin. He goes inside for a moment and momentarily returns with some beer he'd acquired in Colombo and stashed somewhere in his berth. "Let's drink to escaping from Chinese pirates," he says with a smile. "What do you say? It might not be very cold, but it's beer."

He leads me onward, down toward the deck of the ship where the colliers feed coal into the ship's boilers. "I took Patrick down here because I hoped the pirates would know nothing valuable is in the boiler room," he says by way of explanation as we descend farther into the ship's bowels.

We are about to round a corner when Crane says, "I stashed Patrick just up ahead, I think."

However, when we turn the corner, we find a young Singhalese, maybe in his middle or late teens, sitting on the floor and crying.

Crane says to me, "I'd ask him what's the matter, but I don't know that he'd understand me." Instead of asking the boy, Crane hands over his beer, smiles, and opens a nearby door to retrieve Patrick. The Singhalese boy stops crying and gives Crane a tentative smile.

We duck into the room for just a few moments. Crane fumbles for Patrick's cage in the half-light and eventually finds it and pulls the little monkey out into the hallway.

"Can I hold Patrick for a moment, Mr. Crane?" I ask the pitcher.

"Sure, Clarence, he isn't that heavy yet." Crane hands me the cage. "Wait, what's this?" he asks as angry voices start shouting behind us.

I turn to see several dirty, sweating coal stokers confronting the young Singhalese boy. They must have come out of the boiler room while we retrieved Patrick. The men are several feet away, but I can smell their stale perspiration from where I stand, along with the smell of burning coal coming out of the boiler room behind them. One of them steps forward and grabs Crane's beer from the lad. They are speaking loudly to the boy and making menacing gestures, pointing and grunting at him.

"Hold here a minute, Clarence," Crane says to me, and he sticks his chest out and strides over and inserts himself into the argument, roughly bumping one of the colliers in the shoulder in the process.

"You speak English?" he says loudly to the man who appears to be the leader of the stoking crew. "Who told you that you could take this kid's beer?"

Surprisingly, the man does speak English, at least a little bit. He replies, "Captain hire boy in Colombo to shovel coal. We not like him. He not shovel coal with us now. He not part of crew. He not deserve beer." The stoker gives the boy a kick. The others laugh.

Crane strikes as quickly as the cobra that bit me. In a flash, he has his right hand around the throat of the abusive coal stoker.

"Listen, friend," he snarls while also giving a squeeze, "you watch yourself."

Crane pushes the man backward until he is up against the wall in the hallway. "You will give the boy his beer back, you will apologize to him, and you will let him do his job without bothering him again. Am I understood?" For emphasis, Crane thumps his opponent's head into the metal wall of the hallway, all without letting go of his throat. The man winces in pain and gasps for air. Crane hasn't quite lifted him off the ground, but he's on the tips of his toes.

"Am I understood?" Crane asks again. His knuckles whiten as he squeezes a little harder.

"Yes, sir," the man finally splutters out.

Crane eases his grip, ever so slightly. "Apologize. Now."

"Here, boy," the coal stoker says, extending his arm to return the beer. "We sorry. We not bother you now. You do job with us." Crane eases up a little more, then finally releases his grip, and the man, still gasping, bows as well.

Crane backs up a step as the man inhales a lungful of air. Before the stoker leaves, however, Crane points his right index finger in the man's face. "You tell the rest of your cowardly crew that if I hear anything more about you abusing this lad, I'm going to break the back of every one of you. Then, and only then, I'm going to tell your captain how you abused a fellow crewmember whom he just hired. Understood?"

"Yes, understood," the stoker manages to pant. He turns and says something in German to the other stokers. Their eyes, already as large as saucers, get bigger, and they back away from Crane. One of them pats the Singhalese boy on his shoulder and motions for him to come along. The boy simply stares in wide-eyed wonder at Crane. I believe he's found a new hero.

Maybe I have, too. I know that Crane might be unreliable because he likes beer too much, but it isn't often I see someone stick up for a helpless boy like Crane just did. I'm so used to people picking on me that I admire it when someone does the opposite.

Now, I'm happier than ever that I brought Crane good luck in the throwing contest.

"Come on, Clarence," Crane says to me. "Now that that is over, let's take Patrick on deck for some fresh air. We'll drink to escaping the pirates the next time we make port."

Crane and I decide to return to the main deck by way of the steerage deck. "I need some time to calm down after all that," he says to me.

We haven't been there long when Baldwin, Daly, and Pettit turn up. Baldwin leads his monkey, which is much bigger than Crane's, by the creature's leather leash. Now, I thought that after the pirate prank they just pulled, the Order of Howling Wolves might decide to lay low for a day or two, but they have other plans. Daly decides to inspect a cage full of colorful birds.

The man who keeps the birds is middle-aged and appears to be Hindu. He smiles a gap-toothed smile through his gray beard and says, "Cockatoo."

Cockatoo appears to be the name of these types of birds. They have white feathers on their bodies but an unusual crown of feathers ranging in color from bright yellow to shiny gold on top of their head. They are a rather large bird, as well. From beak to tail, these measure about one foot. They sing shrilly as Daly approaches.

To my surprise, the bird keeper opens the cage, and one of the cockatoos flutters onto the Hindu's arm when Daly gets near. When Daly shows interests in the birds, the man motions for him to open the cage and do the same. The Chicago catcher hands the Hindu a coin, puts his arm into the cage, and one of the cockatoos flies to him. Daly draws his arm out and stands there for a moment, admiring the colorful creature.

Baldwin, meanwhile, is also admiring the brilliant coloring of the cockatoos when his monkey decides to climb the cockatoo cage. Unfortunately, Baldwin is too distracted to notice until the monkey has hold of the side of the cage. It starts shrieking at the birds. Next, Baldwin's monkey grabs the cage door, which no one thought to lock, and pulls it open. By now, all the cockatoos flutter around in their cage, bumping and cawing at each other, because of the monkey's shrieking, and before long they fly out of the cage, through an open window, and out of sight.

The Hindu scrambles unsuccessfully after his birds for a moment, and then locks eyes on the ballplayers and decides to chase them, instead. Rather than face the now-wrathful Hindu man, Baldwin grabs his monkey, and he, Daly, and Pettit run for the main deck. When Pettit turns to escape, he happens to slam into a man who is struggling to get a pig into its pen. The man falls, loses hold of the pig's rope leash, and the pig takes off as well. The pursuing Hindu tries to dodge it, but the pig is large, and it succeeds in knocking the Hindu man off his feet, buying the Howling Wolves the time they need to get away.

The pig does not stop there, however. Thrilled at this short burst of freedom, it runs straight into a group of four German women seated on crates and knitting. Scattering them in all directions, the pig looks around wildly for a new place to run, but this brief hesitation gives its leaping owner a chance to grasp its rope leash once again. The owner then resumes the difficult task of dragging the unwilling pig back to its pen. Crane and I just laugh.

I must admit that wandering the steerage deck is a lot more fun than doing my reading lessons with MacMillan. That reminds me, however, that I have another one of my lessons planned right after lunch, which is almost here. I've been true to my word, and so has MacMillan, and we've practiced almost every day that we've been at sea. Learning to read takes a lot of time, but I am getting better, and I know more words than I used to.

Thinking ahead to my next lesson, but still chuckling at all the fun down on the steerage deck, I walk back up to the main deck, Crane alongside. Upon arrival, we learn the fate of the cockatoos. Fortunately, they have not flown off, but they might as well have because now they've perched themselves in the rigging of the ship, and no amount of calling on the Hindu man's part will get them to come down.

Soon, we discover that the Howling Wolves have taken refuge on the other side of the main deck. They have a plate of cheese sandwiches and several mugs of beer. Baldwin takes a drink of the foaming amber and offers his monkey a drink. The creature takes a swig in imitation of its master and munches hungrily on the piece of cheese sandwich Baldwin offers. Before long, it has downed a whole sandwich and about half a mug of brew.

"Let's just sit here and watch a moment," Crane says to me in a quiet whisper. "This could be interesting." Then, out of nowhere, Crane says, "Good day, Mr. Spalding. How are you this fine afternoon?"

"I'm doing well, Ed. Splendid, actually. I've spent most of the past few days reconsidering our route upon making port in Egypt. I've been hoping, as you know, that we might have the chance to play a game of ball not only in Egypt but also in the Holy Land. I've been unable to learn, however, whether Jerusalem has suitable grounds to play a game of ball. After all the calculating and figuring, however, it's nice to just stroll along the deck and enjoy this exceptionally pleasant weather."

"I take it you remain unsure of the precise route we'll take after leaving Egypt?" Crane asks him.

"That is true. I know many of you boys would like to see Jerusalem, as would I."

"Yes, Mr. Spalding, I very much would, and I know several others among the men who feel likewise. Still, we know you're doing your best, and we have confidence in whatever you decide to do."

"How is Patrick today?" Spalding asks, gesturing toward the monkey, whose cage I'm still holding.

"Patrick is doing just fine, I think," Crane replies. "He has adjusted to life at sea admirably thus far."

"What is happening here, if I dare ask?" Spalding says as he becomes aware of the cockatoos above and points toward Baldwin and his increasingly tipsy monkey.

"Well, Mr. Spalding, they had a dramatic escape down in the steerage deck when the monkey accidentally freed some of these fine birds from their cage. I think they are calming down with some sandwiches and ale."

Spalding just puts his head in his hands and rubs his forehead with his eyes closed. While he muses on this news, Crane speaks again.

"I say, sir, who is this young man at your side?" he says, pointing to a Singhalese boy of about my age standing next to Spalding. He's dressed in a white duck suit and has a straw hat, just like some of the players purchased while we were in Colombo. The boy is a little taller than me, however.

"Oh, yes," Spalding says, "this young man is going to be my personal valet for the remainder of the trip. Captain Thalenhorst took him on board to haul dishes in the dining room, but with the captain's permission, I've signed him to a five-year contract to be my personal servant. I will teach him English, of course. He appears to be an intelligent lad. The captain tells me his true name is William, of all things, but I've named him Akbar. It seems more appropriate for someone we picked up in Ceylon."

Crane is about to comment when, suddenly, Baldwin's monkey gives a shriek and Baldwin yelps. For the moment, everyone forgets about Akbar.

Before Spalding can say anything more, Baldwin yelps again. We all turn from Akbar to see what's happened now.

Baldwin's monkey bites Baldwin on his leg. The big pitcher tries to backhand his monkey as he screams in a high-pitched wail again. Baldwin connects, but only partially, and before he can ready himself for another blow, the creature jumps on Baldwin's shoulders and slaps Baldwin in the face several times.

Now enraged, Baldwin shoves the creature to the floor. It runs off, the leather leash trailing behind it. Pettit and Daly have been laughing hysterically the whole time, of course, and only Baldwin's storming around, curses, and threats of a thorough beating get them to calm down a bit.

"I say, how's the monk doing, Baldy?" Pettit chortles.

"Here, have some more beer. That'll help it feel better," Daly adds.

I can't see any bloodstains on Baldwin's pants. It appears that the wound isn't bad, and the bite did not break his skin. Baldwin remains enraged, however, and limps off cursing the monkey and promising it a long and painful death should he ever catch it.

"What am I going to do with that man?" Spalding says with disgust to whoever happens to hear him. He turns to Crane and says, "Ed, as the one reliable person here, if Baldwin ever calms down, will you check and see if he needs any medical attention?"

"I'll try, Mr. Spalding."

"Come on, Akbar," Spalding says to his valet, motioning him to follow. "Let's seek the company of some adults, if we can find them." I don't know if Akbar understands what Spalding says to him, but he smiles and follows obediently, hands folded behind his back.

"Well, Clarence, you don't see that every day, do you?" Crane says to me.

"No, sir, I guess not," I reply, still trying to take in everything that I've seen so far.

"I'll catch up to you later, after I see what I can do about Baldwin and his drunken monkey. Would you mind taking Patrick to my cabin? I don't know if Baldy can stand the sight of another monkey right now."

I do as Crane asks and place Patrick on the floor of Crane's cabin. Not knowing what else to do but sure I don't want to see Baldwin right now, I wander to the other side of the ship and up to my perch above the bridge to kill the last bit of time before my reading lesson. When I get there, I just stare at the beautiful cockatoos perched above me.

Chapter 10

February 7, 1889
Cairo, Egypt, Ottoman Empire

This morning, I have another first in life. Besides getting my first ten-dollar coin, my first drink of whiskey, my first trip into a gold mine, my first sea voyage, and my first Christmas present on this trip, today I have my first donkey ride. I guess it isn't that big of a deal, but I've never done it before. After the *Salier* docks at Suez on the Red Sea, we ride donkeys to the railroad station, so we can get to Cairo.

While we ride along, the donkey drivers trailing behind us and urging the beasts to greater speed, Newton MacMillan declares to the group, "Not exactly Christ arriving in Jerusalem for Palm Sunday, is it?"

Harry Palmer rides alongside his fellow newspaperman. "Speaking of palms, of all the tumbled-down, dilapidated-looking places we've seen on this trip, Suez takes the palm, wouldn't you say?"

MacMillan laughs as he agrees. "If dirt, decay, and general shiftlessness are evidence of antiquity, then surely Suez and its people are the most thoroughly antique of all the antiquated antiquities of the nineteenth century. Although I must admit, the brass bangles and colored ribbons on the donkey bridles are an interesting touch on the part of our Arab friends."

A short time later, after we've boarded the train for Cairo, I'm sitting near the two reporters, and they are still talking while I look out the window with wonder at the land of Egypt. When we left Suez, all I could see was desert everywhere, in every direction. Now, however, we travel alongside an irrigation canal, and wherever the canal goes, green plants blossom. I see vast fields of grains and clover, stands of tall palm trees, and herds of sheep and goats, while here and there, camels dot the landscape. I also see a very large, dark gray beast with enormous horns that I don't recognize.

"Mr. MacMillan, do you know what the creatures with the big horns are?" I ask him.

"I believe you are looking at water buffalo, Clarence."

"Are they like our buffalo in the United States? In the photographs, our buffalo are shaggy, and their horns are not nearly as big."

"I do not know the precise difference between the two species, Clarence; I just know that water buffalo is what people call them."

Turning to MacMillan, Palmer says, "Why do you suppose that all these Egyptians live in mud huts amongst their fields?"

MacMillan shrugs. "I would suppose that either they are too poor, or too attached to their traditions, to live in more modern surroundings."

"These fields seem exceptionally lush, Newton. I suspect your second idea might be the correct one. Look here, for example. That is an ox turning a water wheel. The wheel has earthenware buckets to move the water into the irrigation canals. A manufacturing pump back in the United States would do the same work in half the time. Perhaps well less than half."

"Quite true, and yet, they must have some intelligence to construct such a vast and successful system of canals to move the water."

"Or perhaps that is part of tradition as well. They might line the canals with stones to prevent seepage, but because that is not the way their fathers moved water or irrigated their fields, it will not suit the Egyptians of this generation."

"Perhaps when our train stops we can ask them?" I volunteer hopefully.

"I'd like to pass on that experience, Clarence," Palmer responds. "I'd rather not repeat what happened at Port Aden a few days ago, when another horde of beggars accosted us, and we had to shoo them away with our canes."

"Yes, that was a disappointing stop," MacMillan concurs. "I'm not sure if the ostrich feathers I bargained for justified the inconvenience."

"Well, I did get a nice set of Indian curtains for my trouble," Palmer says. "But overall, I'd have to say that nothing I saw or heard in Arabia tempted me to remain there or want to have such an experience again."

"I think that Crane's monkey got the best deal of any of us. Ed found it that little scarlet jacket with the gold braids and trim, and now Patrick looks quite the miniature Oriental potentate."

Speaking of Crane's monkey, by the afternoon we are at a train station, twenty miles from Cairo, waiting for the train that will complete our journey to that city, and Patrick is making faces at the travelers from his perch atop Crane's shoulder. We've been sitting and waiting for a considerable time now. Captain Anson paces the platform like he's stalking something. Fred Pfeffer mutters something to Fred Carroll over on one side, his finger digging in his ear. John Tener dozes off while sitting on a bench. Fogarty can't sit still. He tosses a ball to himself for a while, then gets two baseballs and tries juggling them, but without much success. Ned Williamson yawns while his wife rests her head on his shoulder. Crane seems engrossed in monitoring his monkey's behavior while the little animal bounces up and down and squawks at the people. Usually, Patrick is very quiet, so I suspect that the large crowd bothers him.

I just stand there and watch Patrick until, before I know what's happened, Jimmy Ryan and Mark Baldwin are right behind me. "This way, Clarence," Ryan says as he and Baldwin clap their hands on my shoulders. "We need some entertainment."

"How much *heqet* beer did we just drink?" Baldwin asks Ryan while the two pull me over to where some luggage sits on the platform.

"I'm not sure," the Chicago outfielder replies. "But it was enough to know how much fun this is going to be. Almost as much fun as pounding the beer was."

Daly is waiting for us, and he has my scarlet drum major uniform in his hands. "Put this on, Clarence. It's time for some fun."

Seeing no other choice, I do as they say. I'm not sure what they have in mind, but I'm looking around to see if any of my friends are nearby to save me, just in case.

Once the drum major jacket is on, Ryan says, "Now try this." Daly puts his catcher's mask over my face. At the same time, Baldwin loops a rope around me and cinches it at my waist.

"What are you doing? I don't like this," I stammer in surprise.

"Shut up, Clarence," Baldwin says. "Now, look at you. A big monkey that looks just like Crane's little monkey."

"Whatever you do, I'm not going to dance."

"Oh, yes, you are," says Baldwin.

"No, I'm not."

Just then, Ryan pulls me toward the middle of the platform by the rope. I try to grab onto something or drag my heels to prevent it, but I fail because I find nothing to grab. People, both ballplayers and the Egyptians on the train platform, start to notice.

Once he thinks he has the attention of most of the onlookers, Baldwin shouts out, "Behold, the missing link between ape and mankind! It's the monkey-boy himself, Clarence. Dance, monkey, dance!"

Ryan gives me another tug with the rope, and I lurch to the side. "Dance, boy! Show us how the animals do it!"

Tears forming, I run toward Ryan, intent on hitting him even though he is nearly twice my size. At least I have a mask to protect me. Unfortunately, he just leans back on the rope and swings me around. I lose my balance and crash into the crowd of watching Egyptians, all of them shouting and scrambling to avoid a collision. A few women on the platform scream, and the men fall over each other trying to get out of the way. Soon, a big pile-up of bodies, most of the people clad in white cotton robes, rests on that part of the platform. As quickly as I can, I climb out and make another run at Ryan. As I charge, I scream in rage.

This time, I only get halfway before Daly shoves me from the side. Because I was so mad, I could only focus on Ryan, so I did not see Daly. Again, I crash into the crowd, and bodies fly. Someone spills a drink on my pants, but I'm not sure what kind and don't bother to check.

"See how the monkey becomes angry and loses control!" Daly shouts to the crowd, arms upraised. "See the animal instincts take over as it lashes out in rage!"

I go after Daly as soon as I can free myself from the tangle of bodies. I leap at him but come up short when Ryan yanks the rope. Landing on my stomach, hard, all the breath goes out of my body. I can barely raise my head to see it, but the platform is now in general chaos as the people try to move away from me. Men shout, more women scream, and people of both sexes run away from the madness.

Before I can regain my wind and sit up, I realize that Ryan and Baldwin are dragging me toward a carriage just off the rear of the platform. Once again, Daly addresses the crowd, as if they could understand him, yelling "Behold, good people of Cairo, the Missing Link between humanity and the apes!"

I try to get to my hands and knees before we reach the carriage, but Baldwin and Ryan get hold of me first and toss me inside, and shut the door. It is a very nice carriage, with padded leather seats and glass windows, although I have no idea who owns it.

"Stay in the cage where you belong," Ryan says sternly as he and Baldwin walk away.

Banging at the door with my palm, I scream, "Let me out! Let me out! Open the door!" I shout more pleas, but they continue walking away. My panic increases when, through the window, I see the train we've been waiting for arrive at the station.

"Don't leave me here!" I half shout, half cry through the window. I bang on the carriage door again. Many of the Egyptians have crowded around for a look at me. They jump back when I slam the window with my palm. They point and chatter to each other, but I can't tell what they are saying through the carriage walls and my own sobs.

I get an idea. I'm still wearing the catcher's mask! I can use it to break the window and get out! I remove the mask and draw back my arm to smash the window.

Just then, the door flies open. John Healy and John Tener have come to my rescue. "We are sorry, Clarence," Healy tells me, "but because of all the commotion on the platform, it took us a moment to get you out."

Tener extends his hand to help me out of the carriage, and with tears streaking my dusty cheeks, I climb down and walk numbly back onto the platform where my knapsack still sits. At least no one stepped on or crushed it during the commotion. I slowly take off my bandleader uniform and stash it back in my pack.

"I'll find a home for the mask, Clarence," Healy tells me. I just let it drop to the deck of the platform.

"Right over here, Clarence. Get on board and find a seat, lad," Tener says as he ushers me onto one of the train cars.

"Clarence, how come you didn't use the door handle and just let yourself out?" Healy asks me after a while.

I should have thought of that, it's true, but I'm too angry to say anything.

"Maybe best to just let it go, John," Tener says to Healy.

I just sit down and stare out the window. I don't even bother to ask the air why I decided to come on this trip. It won't be able to answer me, anyway.

It doesn't seem like we are on the train for long because the remainder of the trip to Cairo is only twenty miles, but I just stare out the window and don't bother with anything else. The sun has almost set by the time we get to Cairo's train station. The sparse clouds in the sky have the golden hue of sunset. Some of the other players bound down onto the platform, but I just sit at the window and watch for several minutes before getting out. It's a lucky move, too, because immediately, a host of people in colored turbans and long, ankle-length white and gray robes crowd around the ballplayers and attempt to grab both the players and their luggage. I assume the men are porters trying to get fares, but the ballplayers are not taking this treatment kindly.

Through the glass, I see one man try to pull the arm of Ed Crane, but Crane grabs his neck right under his chin and pushes the man away. He flies four or five feet. Anson, meanwhile, shoves the nearest man who is trying to pick up his luggage, and the shove sends another four or five porters onto their backsides.

Jim Fogarty has an inspiration. "Their feet, boys, give them a good stomping! They have no shoes; they can't take that!"

Several of the men do exactly as Fogarty recommends, and before another minute has passed, the porters of the Cairo station are in full retreat. Once the commotion ends, I shoulder my knapsack of clothes and step down onto the platform. I'm still too numb to notice that Tener and Healy are right behind me.

We don't ride donkeys in the city of Cairo, thankfully. It's not that they are bad for riding; they just aren't very fast, and all I want to do is get to our hotel and lock myself away in my room. Instead, we take carriages to our hotel, the Hotel d'Orient. For once, I don't even bother to take notice of what the hotel looks like because I just want to get to my room and get away from everyone. Once I do, from the balcony of my room, I can see outside to one of the main squares of the city. Although it's called a square, in fact, the street makes a huge circle, with almost a dozen side streets branching out from the center. It has a public garden in the center of the circle where people stroll. From this distance, it all looks so peaceful. Around the edge of the circle, I see booths, cafés, and various other types of street amusements, just like I would see if I were back in Chicago. I hear music as well, faintly drifting up to me on the balcony, although the tunes sound strange. The Egyptians must have instruments you don't find in bands back in America.

However, I don't care about any of these things for long. I just sit and watch the people without focusing on any of them. They blur into a whirl of motion and color as the tears come again. I just cradle my head in my hands and wonder what I'm doing here. I've seen so many amazing things on this trip, and I'm sure I'll see many more just as amazing, but tonight, it doesn't matter.

Somewhere, a gong sounds. That is the signal for dinner, I think, but I don't move. I don't care. I'm so sad and humiliated that I break my rule about meals without even thinking about the fact that I'm breaking it. Then I hear a knock. Tener's muffled voice comes through the heavy wooden door. "Clarence, are you coming to dinner?" he calls.

I don't answer. Instead, I continue staring at the square below. If I wandered off, would anyone care enough to come and look for me? It wouldn't be much different than if I were back in Chicago, except that I can't speak the language here. I guess that would be a bad idea. Begging for food is hard enough even when you speak the same language as everyone around you. Still, maybe I should sneak off for just a while tonight. It is a very tempting thought. I decide I'm going to try. Besides, I've already noticed that it is quite warm in Egypt. Hot, in fact. I don't know if I could sleep even if I wanted to after everything that's happened to me today.

Briefly, I considered opening the door when Tener knocked. On our voyage from Australia to Colombo, I spoke with him a few times, and I learned that I have one thing in common with him. Tener was born in Ireland, but his parents decided to immigrate to the United States. John's father, George, died before they could but his mother Susan wanted to come anyway, and did, bringing John with her. They hadn't been in the United States long, however, before she died as well, leaving John in the care of his older brother, George Jr. So, he's gone through most of his life without his parents, just like I have.

The difference is that he had more family to help raise him, and I don't have any. Tener also has an education and worked in a bank before becoming a baseball pitcher. He's even the treasurer on our tour, which is quite a job considering how many different places we've been, and that most places have their own type of money.

What I like best about him is that he seems to get along with everyone on the tour. Tener doesn't raise his voice very often or joke with other people in a way that makes them feel bad. He'll laugh and have a good time with the boys but not at someone else's expense. Plus, he doesn't gamble or do crazy things for attention. Even though he's friends with some of the Howling Wolves, Baldwin especially, he hasn't joined their group, and no one expects him to.

Although I almost opened the door when Tener knocked, instead I stay with my plan to sneak away tonight. Staying up late waiting for everyone to sleep seems to take forever, but after I think it's safe, I creep downstairs, my feet making little sound on the plush red carpet covering the marble staircase. When I reach the lobby of the hotel, I find a message in English posted on the bulletin board. I decide to test my new reading skills and walk under the gas light and look. It's from Spalding, and it reads,

> Baseball at the Pyramids. On Saturday, February 9, the Chicago and All-America teams, comprising the Spalding

American Baseball party, will report to the hotel office in uniform promptly at 10 o'clock. The party will leave the hotel at that hour, camels having been provided for the All-America players, and donkeys for the Chicago players, with carriages for the balance of the party. The Pyramids will be inspected, the Sphinx visited, and a game played upon the desert nearby, beginning at 2 o'clock.

A. G. Spalding

I can read some of the notice, thanks to MacMillan and Mrs. Williamson, but not all of it. I can, however, understand the part about playing on February 9. That is two days away, meaning we'll have tomorrow to check out the city of Cairo. I can sneak off for an entire day before anyone will miss me. I walk out of the Hotel d'Orient, wondering which way I should go to lose myself first.

Chapter 11

February 7, 1889
Cairo, Egypt, Ottoman Empire

Almost all the booths on the main square remain lit at night. The merchants and street entertainers of Cairo use paper lanterns that give off a reddish glow, so a soft light illuminates parts of the square, even at this late hour. I wander into a booth where people play a game of chance. It looks like roulette, or some version of roulette. The ball bounces around a wheel for a while, and I listen to the players and audience cheer, shout, and clap, but I soon tire of watching a game I can't afford to play, so I wander along a few hundred feet farther.

I pass a tall, rectangular building with white sandstone walls. At each corner of the building, a skinny tower, like a spike, pokes high into the air, capped with a small, pointed dome. I've never seen something like this back in Chicago. No one appears to be in the building right now, so I wonder what people do inside as I continue along.

As I walk farther, I pass street jugglers, more of the donkeys that some people ride on to move about the city, and booth after booth of shops. Because I want to get truly lost, I meander down one of the many streets running outward from the main square. To make sure I can get back when I want to, I follow the same pattern I use when I go in an unfamiliar neighborhood back in Chicago: turn right, turn left, turn right, turn left.

After a while, the streets get narrower, and the buildings on either side seem to almost lean out over the street. Some are two stories, some are three, and most have second floor balconies with railings overhanging the street. Some of the houses have arched doorways instead of the square ones I'm used to. For a few of the nicer houses, the stones creating the archways alternate in color, usually between sandy red and crisp white. Probably a residential neighborhood. I stay in the middle of the street as best I can. Mud isn't a problem here on the dusty, sandy streets of Cairo, but my nose tells me people emptying chamber pots by dumping them out their windows can be. I might be halfway around the world from my home, but that smell of human waste never goes away no matter what city I'm in.

It's late enough that the streets are mostly empty, and only a few lights show in the open windows. Everyone's windows are open; in fact, most people have no glass in their windows, just curtains. A few pigs brush by me while I walk down the street, grunting while they nose their way through the trash on either side of the avenue.

With so little happening here, I decide to retrace my steps toward the square. Soon, I'm almost there and back in the area with the street vendors and merchants. Do these people ever sleep? Perhaps they figure it's so hot this evening, they couldn't sleep even if they tried, so they might as well keep their businesses open. I don't know if it's always this warm in Egypt in February, but tonight it is.

I see something interesting from the corner of my eye. One of the vendors I'm approaching sells fruit—dates and lemons, it looks like—and a young man who appears about twenty years old is in a fierce argument with the older merchant running the booth, getting in his face and shouting while waving his arms around. While they argue, two young boys of about my age creep around each edge of the booth and attempt to steal some of the fruit.

Just about the time I pass by, the merchant realizes people are robbing him and makes a call that sounds like an alarm. The man arguing with the merchant, seeing that the game is up, runs off in one direction while the two young boys scatter, each going their own way. Next, I realize that instead of chasing the real culprits, the merchant starts pointing at me! He must think that because I'm about the same age as the thieves, that I'm working with them. I run, too.

Luckily, this isn't the first time I've done this. A few times back in Chicago, when I just was so hungry I couldn't help myself, I've tried stealing food from street vendors, so I have a plan of what to do in case they see me. When I run, I reverse my pattern. Left turn, then right turn, then left, then right.

The man who owns the fruit stand tries to chase me. Even though I'm small, he's fat, bald, and old, so I think I can outrun him. I turn left, but I can hear him panting after me. Next, I go right, and I think I'm a little farther ahead. After turning the next left, I look back to see where he is. The man comes into view but, suddenly, he stops and runs the other direction.

I turn my gaze ahead to see what's scared him. Oh no. No more than thirty or forty feet ahead, two groups of young men face each other in the street, and it's a standoff. I don't know if they have street gangs in Egypt like in Chicago, or what people call gangs in Egypt, but that looks like what these people are. I see knives, chains, clubs, metal pipes, and any number of other improvised weapons before I duck down behind the wheel of an empty oxcart and hope they haven't seen me yet.

If they have, they don't care. Some men on each side yell angrily at each other, but no one will back down, so soon, the fight begins. It's a real fight, too. People suffer cuts and stab wounds. Blood flows into the street. One young man chokes another with his metal chain. In just a couple minutes, several of the combatants are already down, holding their head, or chest, or whatever other body part the blood comes from.

I decide now would be the proper time to backtrack and leave, so I start to creep away. Just when I'm ready to turn and run for it, however, a bunch of men in uniforms turn the corner and charge down the street where I'm hiding. The one in front blows a whistle. I freeze in place under the cart again. The last thing I want is for these people to arrest me and end up in a dungeon where they'll cut off my fingers and toes one by one until I talk!

As soon as the police run past me, I turn and run the other way while their backs are to me. I turn the corner to head back the way I came, but almost as soon as I do, I hear another group of men, more police it looks like, running down the street, probably to help the first group. Again, not wanting them to catch me, I duck into a side alley and scamper around a corner and up another street to lose them.

My heart thumping in my chest, I turn and look back. No one's followed me. That's good. I take a deep breath and relax a moment. What isn't so good is that now, I'm not sure exactly where I am because I had to change from my pattern. Plus, all the police are back the way I came, and an angry street vendor, too, who's probably still on the lookout for me, so I decide to head back to the city square and the hotel by another way.

Once the excitement of the chase starts wearing off, I realize I'm now extremely tired. My eyelids are quite heavy, but I know I can't close them here, so I walk off in the direction I think I need to go. Listening for a moment, I turn in the direction where I can hear the most noise and walk that way. I wonder what time it is by now?

I wander around for a while and pass more people as I go, so I figure I'm probably going the right way. The street noise picks up again, too, another good sign. Finally, I hear something. Something beautiful.

A voice, full and powerful, draws me toward an outdoor theater. A woman sings in a language I don't understand, but her voice sure sounds pretty, so I just sit down on the edge of the street and listen.

The song doesn't sound like it's in the same language I've heard most people using tonight, but it isn't English, for sure.

Because I'm homeless back in Chicago, I know that when wandering the streets of a city late at night, a person should watch out for robbery. My experiences of the past hour are a good reminder of that fact. However, my things are still in the hotel, so I have nothing of value anyone can take. I just close my eyes for a few minutes and listen.

It's only a little while before a familiar voice calls me back.

"I didn't know you liked to partake of French opera, Clarence," a voice says with a British accent.

I open my eyes, and who is there but Tom Brown, the slugging outfielder for the All-America team, along with Harry Palmer. I close my eyes and put my head back down. "Go away. Leave me alone."

"Cheer up, my boy," Brown says. "You can't let your bad luck today on the train platform ruin your evening, or should I say, your nighttime, too. You are our mascot, so you know your luck is about to turn."

"We noticed you weren't at dinner, Clarence," Palmer adds. "An understandable decision, certainly, but you must be very hungry by now. Come with us, and let's get something for the palate, my boy."

Palmer is wrong. I'm not hungry. At least, when you are homeless like I am, you learn to go a long time without food. What someone like Palmer calls hungry, I call normal. I tell them, "No. I'm leaving. I'll be back on Saturday, but until then, I don't want to see anyone." I rise to go.

"Come now, Clarence, we are in a strange land," Palmer offers. "You don't know anything about this city. Westerners like us must be careful when traveling in less-civilized places such as this."

"I have a lot more practice wandering city streets than you do, I'll wager, Mr. Palmer. I don't see many colored people here, but I don't attract stares from the Egyptians like you do. Besides, tonight

I've already seen roulette players, people stealing from street vendors, and a big street brawl, and here I am, as good as ever."

Palmer looks down and shuffles his feet, giving silent confirmation of the truth of my statement.

Brown takes up the effort to persuade me. "You probably do, Clarence. More experience than either of us have. Still, we must watch out for each other in a heathen place such as this."

"He's right," Palmer says, returning to his efforts at consolation. "In these streets, you will hear people speaking Arabic, Hindustani, Greek, German, Egyptian, French, Italian, and English. Sometimes you'll hear several of them at once. It's best that you don't just wander off again."

"I don't care about that. If no one speaks my language, they can't ask me to do any stupid dances or call me a monkey. I won't take it anymore. I won't."

Just like on the train platform, something snaps in me, and I try to run away. I don't get far, however, because Tom Brown is one of the fastest runners on the All-America team, and he catches up to me right away.

"That won't do, Clarence," he says to me as he grabs my arm. "We've got to stick together here."

"Why do you even care? Why are you out here instead of sleeping at the hotel, anyway?" I ask Brown and Palmer, who has trotted up as quickly as a middle-aged man with an expanding waistline can trot.

"Part of my contract with *The Sporting Life* calls for me to report on all aspects of our journey, Clarence," a slightly winded Palmer tells me. "Few of our readers have ever been to Cairo, or Colombo, or most of the places we are going. If I'm going to let them know what the world is like, I must get out and experience it. Even if that means wandering the streets of Cairo past two in the morning. Like we've been telling you, however, it is unwise for good Christians to wander alone in such heathen places, so Tommy here agreed to accompany me on my adventures."

"Let's go inside here," Brown suggests, pointing to a small shop across the street. I'd rather go back and listen to the opera, but he herds me toward the door.

I know that I can't get away from him, so instead I ask, "What does this shop sell? I can't read any of the signs."

"It's a drinking establishment, apparently," Palmer says, "judging from the tables and mugs."

"What would you like, Clarence, coffee or hot chocolate?" Brown asks me.

"How do you know what drinks they serve, Tommy?" Palmer asks. "I know you don't speak the local language."

"No, I don't. However, I grew up in Liverpool, which is a seaport on the west coast of Great Britain. You still remember your British geography, Harry?" Brown asks with a smile as Palmer nods. "In any case, with India being part of the British Empire and all, the docks of Liverpool simply thronged with all kinds of people, and as a boy I visited many of the shops and tea houses down by the docks. I know what these various drinks are, even if I can't ask for one in Arabic."

At this point, Brown catches the eye of one of the men serving drinks and waves him over. This man, like many Egyptians, wears a brightly colored turban and long, flowing gray robes that reach to his ankles. His turban happens to be bright orange. Brown points to a large, steaming teapot, holds up one finger, and the man pours some hot tea for him. "So, Clarence, what will you have to drink, coffee or hot chocolate?"

"I've never had hot chocolate."

"Here, let me order you one. It is supposed to be useful in calming the nerves after one has had too much excitement."

He points again, and the server pours a drink from another vessel and hands it to Brown, who hands it to me. "Careful, Clarence, it's a bit hot. What about you, Harry?" Brown inquires.

"Coffee for me."

Brown pays the server, and soon we all have our drinks. It doesn't take long for me to declare hot chocolate the best thing I've ever had to drink.

Brown smiles at my announcement. "This is better than walking the streets of Cairo alone, isn't it, Clarence?"

"I suppose so, Mr. Brown. Can a person get hot chocolate in America?"

"You can, although it might be harder to find in some neighborhoods than others. Most coffee shops offer it, although I suppose that, given your circumstances, you don't get to spend too much time in coffee shops."

I look around the café while I sip my drink and see a device like the one that the Howling Wolves smoked from right before our rickshaw adventures in Colombo. "Is that another hookah, Mr. Palmer?"

"Yes, Clarence, although I believe here it is called a *narghile*. I don't know who came up with the invention first, but it seems a popular one in this part of the world."

"I don't want to smoke it," I say. "Last time someone smoked one, a snake bit me, and I nearly died from fright."

When they recall the rickshaw incident, which Daly, Sullivan, and Baldwin never tire of talking about, my companions smile and nod. "Okay, Clarence, no hookahs or narghiles tonight," Palmer says.

I finish drinking while Palmer and Brown talk further about the exotic surroundings in Cairo. "How many palaces does the Khedive of Egypt have, I wonder?" Brown muses.

"More than the Khedive can visit, I'd guess," is Palmer's reply. "None of them lack for beauty, however. Between the Oriental architecture and the magnificent gardens we saw on our way to the hotel, I'd say they are about as picturesque as nature and art can make them."

"And what about these bazaars? Did you buy any tapestries or other pieces of art?"

"Not today. Perhaps I will tomorrow. I must pace myself a bit, however. *The Sporting Life* and *Chicago Daily Tribune* both gave me a travel stipend for this journey, but the amount is not so great that I can afford to enrich every cloth merchant we come across."

He doesn't mention the extra money I've seen him accept twice already on our travels. I wonder how many more things Palmer's purchased with his money from making up stories. But I don't say that aloud.

"I see," Brown says. "But you'll still have time and money enough to watch the Algerian dancers at the Byzantio tomorrow evening, right? It is just across the square from our hotel."

Palmer smiles as he says, "I had a feeling that was your destination tomorrow, Tommy. You seem to know exactly where to go in this town for a good time."

"What are the large white buildings with the four towers in the corners?" I blurt out. "I could not tell what they are for."

"Those, I believe, are places of worship for the local population," Palmer states. "The buildings are where the Mohammedans worship. Their leaders use the towers, which they call minarets, to call the faithful to prayer. You'll probably hear them tomorrow morning. Or, should I say, later this morning."

"It sounds like you spent more time in the library on board the *Salier* than I gave you credit for, Harry," Brown says. "You've done your research well."

"Part of my duty to my readers."

"Now, Clarence," Brown says after a short pause, "can we persuade you to return to the hotel with us? We can't keep guard over you all night to make sure you don't leave again, of course, but certain members of our party would be most sad to lose our mascot in Egypt. Besides, people tell me that the Great Pyramids of Egypt are a sight one should not miss for any money. What do you say?"

I think it over for a while, and I nod my head.

Chapter 12

Our magical day to visit the wonders of Egypt begins on a down note. When the players, in uniform and ready to play, gather in the lobby of the Hotel d'Orient for their donkey and camel trek to the Great Pyramids, Spalding addresses them.

"Men, I have unfortunate news for all of us. I've received word from my advanced agent in Europe, Mr. Parry, who informs me that to keep all of our European engagements we must proceed to Brindisi in Italy immediately after our sojourn here in Egypt is complete."

Almost all the players sigh at the news, their gazes downcast. I can see that many of them wanted to visit Palestine and Jerusalem very badly.

"I know this is a disappointment. I wish it were otherwise, believe me," Spalding continues. "I, too, wanted to see some of the famous sites of the Holy Land, but I'm afraid it is not to be. Again, I am sorry. However, let us prove our manliness by bracing up today and giving the Egyptians as good a game of ball as we know how."

A few of the men continue muttering for a bit, but because the trip to Palestine was never certain to begin with, most of the ballplayers recover from the bad news quickly. Pfeffer kicks the floor and stands with his hands on his hips, staring into the distance with his jaw set, but I don't have much sympathy for him.

As for me, I've never been in a church, and so all this talk of visiting sacred religious sites doesn't carry much meaning. After what happened two days ago, the quicker and straighter our route back to the United States, the happier I am.

Once all the men have had a chance to hear Spalding's news, it is time to board our transportation to the Pyramids. When we step into the hotel courtyard, I can see this will not be a normal day. The person in charge of securing the camels, whom people call the dragoman, has a dozen of the hairy beasts of the desert ready to go. They wait passively. When it comes to the donkeys, however, there must be at least one hundred of them outside the Hotel d'Orient.

"Great," says John Tener. "It appears someone spread the word that we need donkey transportation, and every boy with a spare donkey is here now, trying to secure a fare."

One boy a little older than me, who appears to be a donkey driver, tries to come forward. Another driver, slightly older and bigger, steps in his path and confronts him. They shout at each other. A third, who also seems to be a teenager but is sadly overweight, barges in, leading a pair of donkeys by their bridles. The second boy pushes the third, who returns the shove with his meaty forearm. The second boy stumbles backward, knocking over still another donkey driver, who joins the fray. Soon, fists fly, and a major fight breaks out. Scores of Egyptian boys engage each other in a battle to secure the money for transporting us to Giza.

The fight scene is already comical, but the circumstances make it even more so. For one thing, surrounding the donkeys and camels, dozens of street vendors have moved their wares to the hotel courtyard. Perhaps someone told them we were American tourists, and they think we'll buy something. I see booths selling tapestries, earthenware, and piles of fruit. Dates, oranges, and figs are all for sale, just to name a few of the choices. I'd say that between the donkey drivers, the donkeys, the camels, the street merchants, and the ballplayers, two or three hundred living things vie for space in the Hotel d'Orient courtyard.

When the fight begins, it immediately spreads amongst these booths. One of the first boys I saw start the argument, the youngest one, gets elbowed into a fruit stand selling oranges, with the predictable amount of destruction. Piles of fruit spill to the ground, and the oranges roll every which way. The owners of the fruit spring wildly about, collecting their goods back into wicker baskets while shooing away a pair of pigs who've wandered into the courtyard and want to eat the fruit. The brawl also knocks over a stand offering tapestries; several get a coating of dust as a result. Another well-timed punch sends a boy sprawling into a booth nearby where I watch, causing other items to spill from wooden storage boxes. I think they are fancy stones of some kind, or maybe just imitations of fancy stones. One Arab man even has a camera set up to take photographs of our party, but he wisely retreats from the scene rather than risk damage to his equipment.

The ballplayers, of course, find the entire scene comical in the extreme. Several members of the All-America team, perched on the backs of their camels, have nearly fallen out of their saddles in laughter.

Luckily, several members of the Cairo police are also at the scene. Maybe they wanted a look at the American tourists, too. They look just like the men I saw at the street gang brawl, so my guess that those men were Egyptian police was a good one. In any case, before long, these men wade into the fight to restore order. They do not wield billy clubs, like the police in Chicago do, or carry firearms. Instead, these men have canes made of tough bamboo which they use to whack arms, legs, and any other target below the head and neck that presents itself. They prove quite skilled at using these canes to tame the donkey boys, and within fifteen minutes or so, most of the extras retreat. The poor merchants pack up their goods as well once the party begins to move.

Thus begins our solemn, reverent procession to one of the ancient world's greatest monuments.

The trip itself proves uneventful once we start out, other than navigating the busy streets of the city on beasts with which we are not familiar. We cross the Kasr el Nil Bridge over the Nile River, passing from the east bank to the west. An enormous pair of stone lions guard the walkway of the bridge, one to either side. They dwarf everyone in our party from their pedestals.

Once we cross the bridge, we follow the road to Giza. For several miles, it runs southward along the west bank of the Nile, so I get an extended view of one of the world's greatest rivers. I've been over the Mississippi River back in America a couple times, and I think the Nile looks bigger. Small boats skitter here and there on its waters, sails aloft to catch the slight breeze in the air today. Irrigated fields surround us as we plod toward our destination. When we reach the outskirts of the city, we pass through a gate in the city's wall. I didn't even know cities had walls. I've never seen city walls back in the United States.

By chance, my donkey is close enough to the head of our party that I can hear our Egyptian guide describing what some of the buildings are. The man appears to be a government official of some kind. He speaks English with a British accent.

"On your left, this grand edifice is another of the Khedive's palaces. Currently, His Eminence, Tewfik I, attends to affairs of state, although he has expressed a wish to see a game of American baseball once he has concluded the pressing needs of government."

I look over at the building. Palace is the right word for it. This one is rectangular, the color of sandstone, and three stories tall. It has a railed, covered walkway on the second and third floors. I see a handful of people in white robes walking around, talking to each other. The walls on the first and second floors have curved arches to support the floor above them. The curve of each arch is a perfect half circle, and between each arch is a circular window. The third floor also has arches to support the roof of the palace, but these arches are smaller, and I see two of them, side by side, instead of just one. Shading the first floor of the palace are palm trees of exceptional size.

"We would certainly like to show the Khedive our great American game," Spalding says to the man. "When will he complete these affairs of state?"

"The business of government, as you know, is the Khedive's highest duty. His ministers have informed me that he will send word to you once he has a timetable. His Eminence also asked me to bid you welcome to his land, and to tell you that he is always pleased to host American visitors."

"Forgive me for asking, and I hope this is not a touchy subject for you, but I am rather perplexed as to the structure of government of Egypt. Your land remains attached to the Ottoman Empire, does it not?"

"It does, in a way. Although we remain part of the Sultan's empire, Egypt holds considerable autonomy in terms of government and running our own affairs locally."

"What of the British and French? As I recall, they exert some influence here as well."

"Indeed. I won't burden you with the details, but the essentials are as follows. More than a decade ago, in the 1870s, our reigning khedive, Ismail Pasha, was on the verge of securing full independence from the Ottomans. In 1876, however, the reigning sultan in Istanbul, Abdul Aziz I, fell from power and died five days later. Whether his death was suicide or murder, no one knows with certainty, although most of the populace suspected murder, naturally. After three months, his successor, Mehmed Murad V, also fell from power after he attempted democratic reforms of which various governmental ministers disapproved. In his place, the current sultan, Abdul Hamid II, ascended to the throne.

"All these political changes threw our relationship with the Ottomans into turmoil. The Khedive's worst fears came true when Abdul Hamid entered into an agreement with the British and French ten years ago, in 1879. Working together, these nations helped Abdul Hamid depose Ismail in favor of our current leader, Tewfik. A rather nasty revolt against Tewfik's leadership occurred in 1882, at which time British forces landed here. These British troops did help end the uprising, but at the cost of a permanent British presence in Egypt. At present, the British Consul General, the first Earl of Cromer, advises our Khedive, and together, they govern Egypt."

"Thank you. I hope I've not caused you any discomfort. I simply want to know the diplomatic situation, so I can avoid accidentally offending anyone," Spalding says in his best diplomatic tone.

"It is no problem. Like I stated earlier, Khedive Tewfik wishes you a pleasant stay and hopes you will remember your time in Egypt fondly once you return to the United States. It is his dream to make Cairo the Paris of the Nile."

The two men continue discussing things, but I'm more interested in our surroundings than I am in the finer points of Egyptian politics. We pass another enormous and fancy building, which our guide identifies as the governor's residence.

What impresses me the most about the journey, however, are the huge trees standing guard on both sides of the road all the way to Giza. MacMillan replies that the trees are acacias when I ask him what kind of tree they are. Their branches intertwine above our heads to form a leafy tunnel leading all the way to the hills of sand where the giant pyramids loom. I hear John Tener say the distance is about seven miles.

When our party follows a turn in the road to the west, the pyramids themselves appear in full sight. We take a meal in the shadow of one of them, which our guide identifies as the tomb of the ancient pharaoh Cheops, and then we gather around the Sphinx. With dogged determination, the Arab photographer from outside our hotel has followed us to our destination, and Spalding agrees to have our photograph taken grouped around the ancient stone creature.

"Okay, men," Spalding directs. "Find a position that suits you somewhere on the Sphinx. Let's have Ward and Anson in the center by themselves, as the captains of the teams. Everyone else, pick a spot you like."

"This way, Clarence," Newton MacMillan says to me. "Let's find a spot near the top where we'll be easy to recognize."

It takes some effort, but the weathering on the front of the Sphinx has left plenty of handholds, so MacMillan and I clamber up and take spots by ourselves underneath the creature's right ear. We are easy to find in the photograph because we are off by ourselves. Several of the players sit or stand underneath the other ear.

"How come the Sphinx doesn't have a nose?" I ask MacMillan.

"I suppose you didn't hear our guide as we approached, Clarence, but he told us how, almost a century ago, the French army landed in Egypt under the leadership of the famous general Napoleon Bonaparte. Some of the French soldiers contrived to blow the nose off with explosives."

"That is a shame. Why did they damage something so old and original, and just leave the rest?"

"That I cannot answer, but you are quite correct. It is indeed a tragedy. I've also noticed that your speech is improving from our lessons, Clarence. You've learned to use some of the words we've practiced."

"Yes, Mr. MacMillan. Reading is hard sometimes, but I like it, all the same. I am very thankful you've been nice enough to help me get better at it."

After the photographer takes a few pictures of us, we scramble down from our perch on the Sphinx's shoulder just in time to hear Tom Daly announce, "Who wants to get into our pool? It's only ten dollars to enter! The first man to hit the eye of the Sphinx with a thrown baseball takes the prize!" Who is manly enough to put their money on the line?"

Meanwhile, Tener pays the photographer. I hear him say, "Thank you, Mr. Sebah, for your troubles. I am sorry things became so boisterous back at the Hotel d'Orient, but as you know, it was not of our doing. Certainly, you are welcome to stay for our game this afternoon." The man smiles politely, bows, and gathers his equipment. I have no idea if he understands English.

I turn to look at the Sphinx again, and several of the players are now drawing lots to see who gets the first throw at the eye of the Sphinx with a baseball.

Williamson wins the draw and takes his aim. The throwing contest in Australia demonstrated that he and Crane have the strongest arms in our party, so many of the players think he'll hit the Sphinx's eye, for sure.

Anson and Hanlon differ, however. "I give odds of five to one he will miss," Anson says to anyone willing to take the bet, while Ned Hanlon offers six to one.

Williamson lets the baseball fly, but his aim is low, and the ball merely strikes the cheek of the stone beast. I see several dollar bills change hands.

Tom Burns has the next shot. He gets a running start and heaves a baseball high and hard. His aim is worse than Williamson's was, however, and he misses the massive creature altogether, throwing low and to the right of its cheek. Billy Earle, Mark Baldwin, and Marty Sullivan try after Burns' miss, but all fail to throw the ball high enough in the air to gain the prize money. The side bets continue, and the players wager freely while the cash changes hands at a furious pace.

Jim Fogarty is next. "Come over here, Clarence."

Having nowhere to run to or hide, I comply.

"I need some luck," Fogarty says as he starts rubbing my head with his palm. "No one has hit the target yet, but this might help break the hoodoo."

His superstitions satisfied, Fogarty turns back to the Sphinx. As a member of the Howling Wolves, he lets forth a mighty

"Awooooo!" He lets the ball go. Everyone's eyes track the throw, and a roar of applause follows as it pings right off the center of the mythical beast's right eyeball. The other Howling Wolves mob Fogarty in congratulations.

"Clarence, you did it!" Fogarty says to me after freeing himself from the celebration. "Here's a share of the prize money for bringing me luck." He hands me a five-dollar bill!

Ever the generous sportsman, Fogarty immediately agrees to a suggestion that anyone else who paid money into the pool at least gets a shot at the Sphinx's eyeball, for a lesser share of the prize money. However, even after Anson, Crane, Pfeffer, Brown, Hanlon, Ryan, Pettit, and Daly have all tested their accuracy, Fogarty remains the only ballplayer who can claim success. All come up short with their throws except for Crane, whose toss misses high and to the left of the target.

While the rest of the contest unfolds, I'm standing next to MacMillan once again, looking at the money. When he finishes scribbling down things in his reporter's notebook, I hear him mutter with disgust, "When Napoleon was in Egypt he stood in awed silence before the solemn majesty of the forty-century-old Sphinx. The members of the Spalding Party, when brought into the presence of the impassive mystery of the desert, threw baseballs at it and hit it in the eye. The Sphinx has seen and suffered much, but never has she been hit in the eye by an American ballplayer."

"Is this throwing contest a bad thing, Mr. MacMillan?"

"Well, Clarence," he says after thinking for a moment and scribbling down a couple more words in his notebook, "I don't know if I'd call it good or bad, but it seems to me it is in poor taste. This massive sculpture has stood on this spot since time immemorial, weathering the sands of the desert for centuries. Not just for centuries, but for four millennia, in fact. I feel as if a bit more respect for its history is in order. Our hosts may not take kindly to this exhibition of American bluster, I fear. I hope the men can tone things down before we get to Europe, with its great arches, statues, cathedrals, and all else. Otherwise, I fear we may have to invoke the kindly offices of the American Secretary of State, so we can rescue some of our ballplayers from a French or English jail, should they choose to try pelting the images of Napoleon, Wellington, or Admiral Nelson."

This makes sense to me. Although I do not know all the fancy rules of behavior a person is supposed to follow when they visit another country, it does seem rather rude to me to throw things at their famous buildings and bet on it, too.

Finally, the two clubs get around to playing a game of baseball. Underneath the Pyramid of Cheops, they lay out a diamond and take their positions in the historic sands of Egypt. The teams play for five innings, at which point the All-America team leads the Chicagos, 10-6.

The game is almost as comic as the scene outside the Hotel d'Orient. Although the sand is firm, no one manages to send a ground ball rolling through the infield all game long. As a result, the fielders move up closer to the batter, hoping to get to the ball on the fly or before it plops to a complete stop in the sand.

Ned Hanlon tries to steal second base at one point and slides into the base, but skids to a stop well short of his goal. He only succeeds in kicking up a spray of golden dust. This blinds shortstop Ned Williamson, however, to the point that he misses Tom Daly's throw, and Hanlon scampers to third base before Jimmy Ryan retrieves the ball and returns it to the infield.

Speaking of Ryan, neither he, nor any of the other outfielders, has much luck catching fly balls because tracking the flight of the ball while running over sand dunes requires more coordination than any of the ballplayers can claim. As a result, Fogarty, Sullivan, and Pfeffer all hit triples. Each hit would have been a home run, except the ball doesn't roll far in the sand, so the fielders can retrieve it before the men can run all the way home.

All of this pales in color and flavor when compared to the crowd, however. Some of the white-robed observers take in the action while seated on horseback or camelback. They surround the diamond in a large circle. Others climb the side of Cheops' pyramid to get an elevated view of the action.

Once, when Tom Daly launches a ball over the head of the outfield, some of these spectators yell, jump up and down, and fire their rifles into the air in their excitement. The players scatter at the report of the rifles, including the ones attempting to chase down Daly's hit, so the young catcher, apparently not scared, circles the bases for a home run while everyone else looks for cover.

The problem for the players is that the only cover available is behind sand dunes, the camels, or other people. They are still running around frantically, looking for somewhere to hide, when our guide runs over to Spalding, who is the umpire, waving his arms. "Please, please, you are in no danger. They are merely showing their appreciation. Please, tell your players they may continue."

"Gladly," a slightly ashen Spalding replies as he rises from the desert sand. "But would you please send word to them to hold their fire from now on?"

After Spalding talks to the official, the official mounts his camel and goes and talks to the armed spectators, and things calm down a bit. John Ward, who ran in from the field when he heard the gunshots, picks himself up from the sand and says to Anson, who also rises, brushing off his uniform, "Have you ever had to play ball amidst gunfire before, Cap?"

"No, but there's a first time for everything, it seems, especially in this benighted land. How about you, Johnny?"

"Me neither, but I've got a good story for you that Erastus Wiman told me one day. When he owned the Metropolitans and they still played in New York, back in '86, they played an exhibition game with Newark. Remember the Tom Burns who played for Newark then, the one they call 'Oyster?'"

"Yeah, I've played him in exhibitions. He's a big guy with a temper, right? Not like our Tom Burns, who is a normal guy."

"Right, that's the one, Cap. Anyway, in this game in '86 he gets into a fight with Elmer Foster, who was playing second base for the Mets."

"Foster's a decent-sized man himself. Should have been a good match for Burns. Didn't Foster play with you on the Giants last year?"

"Yeah, I'm sorry to say. We played him in about forty games, and he didn't hit at all."

"He couldn't hit with the Mets, either. Anyway, what caused the fight?"

"Dave Pierson's umpiring, according to Wiman."

"I remember Pierson. He played for the old Cincinnati club way back in '76, I think. That was my first year with the White Stockings after coming over from Philadelphia. Maybe I'll tell you that story sometime between now and New York. Anyway, you were saying about Burns and Foster?"

"Well, Cap, according to Wiman, three or four hundred people come out of the stands and onto the field to take part in the fight, and the police wade into the crowd and try to restore order and get the game resumed. One of the spectators had a pistol, and he fired a couple shots into the air before some of his friends finally intervened and disarmed him."

"Yeah, I remember that story now, Johnny. The entire American Association decided to boycott playing Newark after that. I can't say that I blame them."

"It looks like our guide has finished telling the Bedouins to hold their fire. I think the game is about to resume. I do want to hear how you got to Chicago someday, though. That year, 1876, was a couple of seasons before I got into the National League with Providence. Does the story involve some shady work by Spalding and Hulbert like I think it does?"

Anson just smiles at this last line, and Ward jogs back to his position at shortstop.

No more shooting occurs during the game. In the last inning, when Williamson makes a poor throw that Tener cannot catch at first base, the spectators swarm after the ball, and Anson gets a bit rough with some of them, so he can retrieve it for further play. The afternoon heat is extreme, and soon the players' uniforms have soaked through with sweat, so they give up the effort after five innings.

"Do you think the Egyptians liked baseball?" I ask MacMillan.

He just laughs. "I don't know if they understood a particle of what was going on, but I'll wager neither of us will ever see another game of ball like that one as long as we live! How can I describe it to my readers back in Chicago, Clarence? Where does one even begin when describing our entire day? Should I start with the hotel scene, the ride here, the palaces, the game itself, the Sphinx, or with the Pyramid of Cheops?"

"Well, Mr. MacMillan, words just don't do justice to the pyramids, do they?"

"They don't, but these tombs are quite a lot of trouble for one dead person, wouldn't you say?"

"I suppose so. I imagine it took a long time to build them."

"It did. Years, in fact. But come, let's practice your vocabulary. How would you describe them?"

"They have four sides, and as far as I can see, all the sides are the same length. That makes the pyramids perfect squares at the bottom, doesn't it?"

"Yes, Clarence, very good. How else would you describe them?"

"The huge, sand-colored stone blocks used to build them fit together exactly. I see no cracks, no spaces, and no crumbling blocks to ruin their perfection. Each pyramid is just so enormous, so massive, and so solid looking and immovable, surely nothing else on earth is like them. I saw a photograph of them once, back in Chicago. Only now, however, when I see them in person, does their greatness strike me the way it should. Tom Brown was right when he said I should not miss seeing them for any money."

While we talk, MacMillan and I walk toward the Pyramid of Cheops because the ballplayers are gathering there.

"Wait, what is happening now?"

It's Harry Palmer speaking to me this time. I almost bumped into Palmer while looking up and trying to understand just how tall the pyramids are.

"Oh, I'm sorry about that, Mr. Palmer. Did you know dead people rest inside these things?"

"Not people. Just one person lies entombed in each. Well, one king rests in each one, anyway, and many servants who perished along with him."

"My goodness, Harry, you really did put your time in the *Salier*'s library to good use," MacMillan says to him. "I note no end to your knowledge of facts and native folkways."

"It calls to mind the same question we discussed earlier, doesn't it, Newton?" Palmer continues. "Why does a people capable of such wonders, or to be more precise, capable of such wonders as far back as 4,000 years ago, live in such squalor today? What is it about the Oriental mindset that allows them to sacrifice so much for the dead that they forget or refuse to attend to the needs of the living?"

"It is a bit of a stretch to link the ways and attitudes of an entire people to a few buildings constructed millennia ago, isn't it, Harry?"

"Well, the point I am trying to get at is, why don't we see the same thing now? Just look around here at all the complexes that go with each of the pyramids, at all the artwork carved into stone. Clearly, these people must possess considerable knowledge and craftsmanship, or, at the least, some of them do. Why, then, all the poverty we've seen in the city, the desperate beggars lining every commercial street, and the donkey drivers fighting for our fares? That is the question of the hour, is it not?"

"Well," MacMillan says with a smile, glancing over Palmer's shoulder toward the ballplayers, "that may be your question, but as for me, my question of the hour is, what are Ward, Fogarty, and Manning doing?"

"Oh, that's right; you and Clarence were speaking with each other off on your own when Anson and Hanlon offered their latest bet. They bet ten dollars that no one in the party could climb to the top of one of the pyramids and get back down in less than ten minutes. Fogarty, Ward, and Manning accepted. I believe everyone in the party wants to climb to the top eventually, but those three were the only ones who believed ten minutes sufficient to both ascend and descend these amazing monuments to morbid hubris. I am the timekeeper for the bet."

"I'm fascinated to see whether any of the triumvirate possesses the muscular prowess to make good on their wager. Those three men are fine athletes, however. They just might succeed."

It would not surprise me if they do, although it seems somewhat unlikely, looking upward at the pyramids from the bottom. However, if anyone can make it, these men can. All of them are young, in the pink of condition, and confident in their abilities.

While the reporters discuss the climbers' odds of success, Daly gets another of his brilliant ideas and exclaims, "Who thinks they can throw a ball over the pyramid?"

Even as many of the men express their doubts about the odds of success, Anson says, "I think I could. Why don't you go to the other side, so you can retrieve the ball if anyone succeeds?"

Daly agrees to this plan, and off he goes. "What a rube," Anson laughs once Daly runs off. "No one is going to toss a ball over something that big. Daly deserves his extra run for being such a chump."

"I'm sure you're right, Cap," Williamson offers. "But what do you say we give it a try anyway, just to see how high we can get?"

"It's a deal. Let's get the baseballs. Just wait another minute or two before you throw, or else Ward, Fogarty, and Manning might think we are throwing at them. Let's just hope these heathen Bedouins don't try to shoot us again."

Soon, everyone has a baseball, and each tries to heave it over the massive tomb. No one comes close. Unsurprisingly, Crane and

Williamson make the highest throws, but they strike the side of the pyramid less than one-quarter of the way up before the balls bound downward harmlessly.

By now, the three climbers are descending, so the men cease throwing while Baldwin goes and retrieves Daly.

"I think they just might make it," says Harry Palmer while he times the men. "They are halfway down, with still two minutes to go."

In the end, all three make it. Fogarty is first, followed by Ward, and finally Manning, who touches the ground with fewer than five seconds to spare. More money changes hands while the exhausted athletes regain their wind.

A thought nags me. All the ballplayers, or almost all of them, continue betting and passing money around as if it were nothing. Ward, Fogarty, and Manning were confident enough to wager ten dollars on whether they could climb a building in ten minutes or less. Ten dollars! With that much money, I could eat for a week, maybe more. Yet, some of the players win or lose bets of that size or more almost daily on this trip. It doesn't seem quite right to me that some people can be so free with money while others must beg just to get scraps of food most nights.

"All right, men, let's all head up to the top now," Spalding announces, breaking my silent thoughts. "We can't go all the way to Egypt without climbing the pyramids, can we?"

It is a hard climb for me because I am not very tall, and my arms are weak. Ed Crane and Healy give me a little help, and I'm one of the last ones to reach the summit, but I get there. I must say that the view is worth it, and then some. I can see all of Cairo, or very nearly all of it, stretching away on both sides of the Nile. When I look any other direction, however, it is just sand and hills extending endlessly. I see no trees, or water, or anything living, just a golden-brown sea stretching toward the horizon. Wait, to the south, I can just make out more buildings. They look like they are far away, so they must be very large.

"What are those buildings, Mr. MacMillan, which we can just barely see to our south?" I ask.

"More pyramids, Clarence, at a place named Saqqara. Not quite as large and grand as where we are now, but our government guide told us that one of them is over 60 meters tall and is the tomb of a pharaoh named Djoser. It is a step pyramid, which is a little different from what you see here. This pyramid has nearly straight sides, as you know from climbing them just now, but a step pyramid has several squares stacked on top of each other, each level a little smaller than the one below it. Think of it as a layered birthday cake, but larger, I suppose."

"I've never had a birthday cake, Mr. MacMillan, so I don't exactly know what that looks like."

"I am sorry about that, Clarence," is all MacMillan says before looking out into the distance again.

Soon, we descend, and having exhausted the opportunities for fun, we return to the Hotel d'Orient. When we arrive, the bulletin board updates us on our travel plans. It reads, "Trunks must be packed and in the office by three o'clock tomorrow afternoon for shipment to Ismalia. The party will leave Cairo Monday at 11:15 for Port Said, where we take the North German Lloyd steamer *Stettin* for Brindisi, Italy."

"Why are we shipping our baggage to Ismalia when we are going to Port Said?" Billy Earle asks anyone who can hear him. "Shouldn't we be going to the same place as our luggage?"

John Tener answers the question. "Ismalia is a port on the Suez Canal. From there, we steam through the canal to Port Said, a city on the Mediterranean, and then on to Italy. Everything will end up where it is supposed to."

"Well, that learns me," Earle says to Tener good-naturedly. "You can call me a chump if you'd like."

"Don't worry, Billy," Tener replies with a smile and a pat on the shoulder. "Even a little globetrotter like you can't be expected to know all the details. Everything will be fine, trust me."

We are almost to Italy! I'm one country closer to getting home.

Chapter 13

February 16, 1889
Naples, Italy

The players swarm like hornets after someone's disturbed their nest. They crowd around the poor postal carrier as if they are deathly ill and he is the only one on earth with a cure. None of the players has seen any mail since we left San Francisco back in November, and boy, are they anxious. We thought we'd receive mail while in Australia but didn't because of delays. All the men are eager for news from friends and family, and they are almost as eager for news of what has happened in baseball back in America. After they finish mobbing the mail carrier, most sit down outside of the customs office of Brindisi to find out all they've missed.

Harry Palmer has a huge stack of mail. "Guess what, boys?" he calls out to anyone who can hear him. "I've got issues of *The Sporting Life* here for us to read!"

Several of the players leap up and surround Palmer almost as aggressively as they did the mailman just a few moments ago. Johnny Ward is foremost among them, and Palmer immediately supplies him with a stack of sporting newspapers as if they'd arranged the deal ahead of time.

Just then, Anson stomps out of the customs office, spittle and curses leaving his mouth with equal frequency. "The scoundrels!" he yells. It's the only thing both coherent and fit for printing that comes out of his mouth for quite some time.

"What's the matter, Cap?" Tener asks him once Anson's had the chance to calm down a bit.

"It's these damn thieving Italian officials. A little man, couldn't have been more than five feet tall and about seventy years old, insisted on an extra fare for our bats because they were above standard weight."

"What did you do?"

"I paid because we can't very well continue without our bats. But it cost me a box of candy for my wife and the dozen Turkish hats I bought in Cairo."

"You bought a dozen fezzes in Cairo? Why did you buy so many?"

"I thought it would be good luck for our boys to wear them in the field this season. Not to mention they would be a curiosity that might attract more cranks to West Side Park."

"You'll have to rely on Clarence for good luck instead, I suppose," Tener offers, then winces when he remembers to whom he's speaking.

I worry that this will send Anson into another rage of cursing, and his face does redden, but instead, he sits down, pounds the bench with his fist, swears a few more times under his breath, and reluctantly sifts through his pile of mail.

The rest of the group, even the Howling Wolves, reads quietly outside the customs house. Soon, we'll board a train for Naples. No one except me notices that I'm the only one who doesn't get any mail.

The trip to Naples, which is on the western side of Italy, takes a good part of the day. I'm sitting in a train compartment with John Healy, John Ward, Tom Burns, Tom Brown, and Billy Earle, whom everyone has taken to calling "The Little Globetrotter" after Tener's comments in Cairo. With no Howling Wolves present, I feel as safe as I ever have on this trip. I wonder if Healy will ever tell me more about our plans to free Ireland before we get there. If he has plans, however, he isn't talking about them today. Instead, like most of the rest of us, he just looks out the window, staring in fascination at everything we see.

"Is that a real castle?" Earle asks, pointing out the window.

"It isn't a mirage, if that's what you're asking," Brown playfully responds.

"I know the building is real, but do people live in them still?"

No one seems to know with certainty. Ward, the person in the train car most likely to know the answer, doesn't even look up. Already, he has buried his head in the sporting newspapers and continues reading all the way to Naples. I've noticed that he hasn't even asked me for more news about Spalding and his plans for quite some time. This is good because I haven't learned anything new. I assume it is because either he's lost interest in what I can tell him or because he already knows everything he needs to know to make his plans. Probably the second.

After our train rounds yet another hill, of which Italy has many, suddenly, we see it. The mountain. It towers over the city of Naples wreathed in a dull, red-gray halo. Every few moments, red flames clear the edge of its crater. Even during a mostly sunny afternoon like today, the dark clouds surrounding the mountain reflect the light of the flames in unearthly shades of reddish colors. The view captures our attention and holds it fast until we pull into the Naples train station. No one speaks for a good long time. We just stare and watch.

"Do you know the story of Mount Vesuvius, Clarence?" Tom Brown asks me once we are inside the station and the mountain is out of sight.

"Is that the fiery mountain we saw just now?"

"It is. Almost 2,000 years ago, in AD 79, it erupted, and the lava flows buried an entire town named Pompeii. We'll probably get to visit Pompeii while we are here. I hope we will, at least."

"How can we visit a town that is buried? Are there tunnels, like in Chinatown?"

"No. People called archaeologists have dug up part of the town so that all of it isn't buried anymore. We'll get to see the uncovered part, I hope."

"Will the mountain erupt again while we are here Mr. Brown? Those flames look frightening."

"It isn't likely, but you never know, I suppose. The flames in the crater are fascinating, aren't they?"

"Yes, they are. Very fascinating. Are there very many volcanoes in Italy?"

"I don't know for certain, but I don't think Italy has too many others. Certainly, none are as famous as Mount Vesuvius."

We debark from the train and prepare to take carriages to our hotel. I think all the ballplayers are happy to be back riding in carriages again, rather than in rickshaws or on donkeys. I manage to end up in the same carriage as Harry Palmer, which is good, because he appears to have quite a bit of knowledge about the various buildings we pass on our way.

"Quite a scene, isn't it, men?" he asks our small party, which consists of me, Jim Manning, Jim Fogarty, and Tom Burns. I half expect some new prank from Fogarty, but he is so busy watching the ashes from the cone of the volcano rise into the sky that I decide I'm probably in the clear, for today at least.

"Harry, you spent a lot of time reading on our sea voyage. Do you know what all these buildings are?" Burns asks him.

"I know many of them, yes. The important street we passed a little while back was the Strada Roma. It is famous for its fashionable shops and equally fashionable people. The immense building we can see just ahead is the San Carlos Theater, one of the most famous opera houses in the world. While on the train coming here from Brindisi, I learned that the theater will host the opera *Lucrezia Borgia* while we are here. You love the opera, right, Fogarty?" Palmer asks the outfielder with a smile.

"What?" Fogarty responds as if slowly awakening from a dream, distracted from his view of the mountain by Palmer's question.

"Opera. You plan to go to one while we are in Naples, right?" Palmer says with another wide grin.

"I think not. I have other ideas in mind for our time here," Fogarty says as he directs his gaze toward Mount Vesuvius once again. His eyes just watch the mountain with intent curiosity. I don't know if I could ever describe Fogarty's face as looking thoughtful, but this is about as close as he gets.

"Yes, that's right, I'd forgotten," Palmer continues after a moment. "Being the religious type, you plan to spend most of your time at the Church of Saint Francis, which is just up ahead over there."

Laughs abound at Palmer's latest comment, and our eyes follow his finger when he points out the church.

Suddenly, Fogarty gets the old look back in his eye. He drops to one knee as best he can in the jostling, crowded carriage, folds his hands, closes both eyes, and says, "Father, forgive them, for they know not what they do." The carriage crackles with laughter once again.

We pass another huge building. It has three stories, the top two of which have about twenty windows each, all the height of a person. At street level, I see various human-sized sculptures set within shallow hollows in the facing of the building. Burns says, "What's that one, Harry? It looks palatial."

"That's because it is a palace. That building is the royal palace of the King of Naples."

"I thought Rome was the capital of Italy. Naples is in Italy. How can Naples have its own king?" Burns asks.

"Italy was, for centuries, I believe, divided into many kingdoms and other political units, of which Naples was one. Only recently, within my lifetime, have all the kingdoms united as part of Italy. Naples joined in 1858 or so, as I recall. This palace is where the King of Naples lived before that happened."

"Harry, you are a veritable factotum," Burns jokes. "Did you read every book in the *Salier*'s library?"

Palmer smiles again at the compliment and bows.

Finally, our trip ends, and we reach the hotel. Its name is the Hotel Vesuve, naturally. Palmer can't resist the opportunity to show off a bit more knowledge as we climb out of our carriage. "My goodness! We can see the Castle Ova, the Bay of Naples, Vesuvius, and the island of Capri, all from the hotel!"

I turn around and see that Palmer is correct. The city of Naples stretches outward from its harbor and waterfront, and the hill leading down to the harbor is steep enough that one can see a good way out into the bay, even though several of the streets of Naples have tall buildings, four or five stories, that might block the view otherwise. The streets are a bit wider than in Cairo, but still very crowded with people here in the evening, and I see several close calls when the carriages nearly run over people in the streets. The city has paved some of the streets with paving stones, at least, so the ride is not as bumpy or dusty as usual. The dominant feature of the city, however, is Mount Vesuvius. It towers over everything from its location due east of town.

Shouldering my knapsack, I descend from the carriage to the hotel courtyard. Fogarty takes one more look at the mountain and motions me over, along with Burns and Manning, and says, "Clarence, Tommy, Jimmy, listen to me. I have a plan. We don't play a game or do anything else official tomorrow. Let's climb the mountain."

Jim Manning, who hasn't said much on the trip but takes pride in his athletic abilities, simply says, "Sure, I'm in. If I can handle a pyramid, I can handle a mountain."

"Are you sure about this idea, Fogarty?" Burns asks him doubtfully. "I mean, the volcano is *active*. I don't know how safe it is."

"You don't see anyone here in the city running away in fear, do you? It's probably safe. Besides, how many chances at climbing an active volcano will we ever get back in the United States?"

Burns wears a deep frown and furrows his brow.

"You aren't getting soft on me, are you Tommy?" Fogarty says to the Chicago infielder. "You've had a few too many state dinners on this trip, I think. I saw you were one of the last ones to get to the top of the Great Pyramid, and you were out of wind when you did."

"I'm not getting soft, just pacing myself. I'm in the pink of condition, like always."

Fogarty shakes his head. "You can't fool me. You probably couldn't even make it to the top of the mountain anymore."

"I could, too."

"Ten dollars says you can't."

"You're on, Fogarty."

"Okay, Jimmy and Clarence, you are our witnesses for our bet. We'll get up and leave early tomorrow morning. We'll be the only ones on this trip who can say they climbed a volcano!"

"Excuse me, Mr. Fogarty," I say, wondering if my eyes look as terrified as I feel. "I don't think I can climb a mountain. I'm only twelve years old, and I needed my share of help to get to the top of the pyramid in Egypt. Do you really want me to come, too?"

"Of course, you're coming with us, Clarence. You don't think we'd be so crazy as to try to climb a volcano without our mascot for good luck, do you? You proved yourself once again when you helped me hit the eye of the Sphinx with the ball. I wouldn't think of going without you after that."

"I'm scared. It looks really risky to me."

"We'll watch out for you and help you if you need it. Don't worry. This will be something we'll never forget."

I guess that means I'm climbing a volcano tomorrow. While I ponder this new plan, I shuffle toward my room at the Hotel Vesuve. It's on the second floor. I'm almost up the stairs when Ward and Hanlon come bounding up the steps and overtake me.

"Clarence, this way, quick now!" Ward says, patting me on the shoulder as he hurries past.

I follow him to his room and go inside, followed by Hanlon. "John, what's the nigger doing here?" Hanlon says gruffly.

"Ned, Clarence here has been in my employ ever since the Sandwich Islands. He's uncovered details of Spalding's plot that we never could have learned on our own, at least not until we got our hands on those." Ward points to the stack of sporting newspapers he acquired from Harry Palmer this morning.

"You trusted him?" Hanlon asks skeptically.

"Yes, and Clarence has come through for us in fine form. We owe him our thanks."

"I'll be damned. Well, Johnny, if you're satisfied with him, then I'm satisfied with him. Clarence," Hanlon says to me while extending his right hand, "I apologize for being a bit rough toward you on this trip. I've never known a colored person who I could trust where I grew up in Connecticut, and I figured you'd be no different, but if you've done right by Johnny, then, by God, I'll admit I was wrong about you."

I shake his hand cautiously. "Thank you, Mr. Hanlon, I've tried to do my best for Mr. Ward and your Brotherhood."

"Speaking of," Ward puts in, "these issues of *The Sporting Life* have plenty of details on the plans of the National League against the Brotherhood of Professional Baseball Players. That means we probably won't need you to do any more spying for us, Clarence, because we know everything we need to know at this point. Ned, these things I've shared with you from the newspapers corroborate what Clarence has told me all along on our trip. Our Brotherhood is in for its biggest test so far when we get back to America."

"Those scoundrels. Spalding is a damned liar, just like a nig—" Hanlon stops himself short and glances at me. "Like a fox," he finishes with a rueful smile. "Sorry, Clarence, old habits and all." He turns back to Ward and continues, "He's used us, you and me, the whole time we've been on this trip."

"Yes, he has. Although, thanks to Clarence and the information he's provided me, I've put quite a bit of thought into how we can use him right back. One thing I've decided is that I'm leaving the tour as soon as we get to France and I can book passage to New York. Ned, you'll take over for me as captain of the All-Americas."

"Should I order Crane to bean Anson the next time he comes to bat, too? And do it again the next time after that?" Hanlon says. I never noticed before how deep his voice is. Maybe it only gets that way when he's angry.

"No, we're going to handle this like professionals, so calm down a bit. You and I still have a few days to plan before we get to Paris. I want you to pretend like nothing's changed. That includes," and here Ward looks at me, "treating everyone the same way we have the entire trip. You'll have to continue being rude to Clarence, just to make sure no one can piece together who we got some of our information from."

"I'll do it, but no hard feelings from now on, okay, Clarence? Whenever you come to Detroit next season, or better yet, whenever Detroit comes to Chicago for a game, I'll try to do something to make it up to you for my bad behavior. Deal?"

"Okay, Mr. Hanlon" I tell him as I shake his hand once more.

"Oh, and Ned?" Ward says.

"What else?"

"About playing for Detroit next year . . . I just read that your owner, Fred Stearns, disbanded the team."

"What?"

"Yes. The Wolverines are no more. Stearns has begun selling players to the highest bidder."

"Another scoundrel. This is the type of thing our Brotherhood must put a stop to, John. This buying and selling players like cattle."

"You know I agree. It's all wrong. Cleveland will take Detroit's spot in the National League."

"Cleveland. Isn't Cleveland in the American Association?"

"Not anymore, apparently. Oh, but there's more fun going on in baseball."

"More fun than seeing your team disappear, John?"

"Stearns tried to sell Deacon White and Jack Rowe to Pittsburgh, but they won't go. They decided to buy the Buffalo team in the International League and play for Buffalo, instead. The National League owners blacklisted them in response, saying they had to play in Pittsburgh and can't even play for the team they own."

"That is sheer nonsense. You see, Clarence," Hanlon says, nearly shouting as his face colors in anger, "events like this are why we formed a Brotherhood. Buying and selling players. Telling players they can't play for the team they want to, even when the players own the team they want to play for, these sorts of things must stop."

I nod agreement.

Hanlon sits down, and some of the color leaves his face after a little while. "Well," he says to me, quieter now, "I'm glad you're on our side. We need all the help we can get. Ward and me, and our Brotherhood, are a little like St. George, I suppose."

"Who is St. George?" I ask.

"He's the Catholic saint who slew a dragon. The story's metaphorical, of course, but it describes what we're doing well enough. The National League owners are like dragons, and we're fighting for the rights of the ballplayers against long odds."

Even though I don't know what metaphorical means, the part about fighting against long odds sounds a lot like my life. I'm glad I chose the right side.

Chapter 14

February 17, 1889
Naples, Italy

"Come on, Clarence, you're almost up." The voice belongs to an ash-dusted and sweaty Tom Burns, but I'm exhausted as I try to climb a little higher.

I can't believe I've even made it this far, but Jim Manning, his face also streaked by ash and sweat, extends his hand and helps me onto the ledge.

"Well, men," Fogarty informs us, "the volcano is about 4,000 feet tall, and we still have a few hundred left to go. We'll take a minute to rest here and then see how high we can get."

He says this almost as a shout because the activity in the volcano's cone is extremely loud, and it's hard to hear him.

While we regain our breath, we all take out some bread that Fogarty and Burns purchased at a market before we left Naples. We sit there chewing slowly while fine particles of ash rain down on us. I look up. The sky around the top of the mountain is still the same mix of angry-looking, brooding gray clouds and reflected eerie red light that we saw yesterday on the train. I run my dirt-streaked hand over my head a few times. Gray dust silently drifts down onto my chest and shoulders.

"What is that smell?" Manning asks Burns.

"Burning sulfur, I think," Burns replies. "I don't know how it works, but I think that the volcano gives it off when it releases gases into the air."

"What do you think?" Fogarty asks our group. "If we go this way, it looks like we can get close to the edge of the cone right up there." He points upward toward the smoking crater at the summit of the mountain.

"Let's go, then," Burns says. It looks like he might win his ten-dollar wager. He's panting a bit and his green linen shirt is almost as gray as his boots by now, but Burns has kept up with Fogarty and Manning to this point, and he doesn't look beat quite yet.

"Are you ready, Clarence?" Manning asks while he chews down a last mouthful of Italian bread.

"Just a moment, sir, I'm afraid my arms and legs are not as strong as yours are. I'll be ready in a bit." I drink a little more from my canteen.

"See, what did I say?" Fogarty says as he spreads his arms, gesturing toward the city that is now a couple thousand feet below us. "Look at this view. We'll be the only ones who can say they climbed a volcano in Italy when we get back to America. First, we climbed the pyramids and now this. The whole city spread out below us, the bay, the warm air, just take it all in. No one can say we haven't lived a full life on this trip. Just wait until Palmer and MacMillan hear our story this evening. Awooooooo!"

"I think I can go again now," I tell the group. Partly it's true, and partly I don't want to hear Fogarty howl again.

My legs ache badly, my arms bleed from a few scrapes I got after I rolled up my sleeves, and my hands are raw, but I can't deny that the view is amazing. We are almost up to the top, so I might as well go on.

I am worried, however. More scared than ever. A person could probably hear my heart beating if the rumbling noises weren't so loud. I just need my luck to hold for a couple more hours.

We begin climbing once again, although climbing isn't exactly the word for it. Most of the time we just walk up whatever slope seems easiest and doesn't have too many rocks or loose dirt. Lower down on the mountain there were quite a few trees, but now, at this height, it is mostly barren rock covered in gray ash. A few times, however, we must find handholds and hoist ourselves up. These are an enormous struggle for me because of my lack of strength. In these places, the ballplayers, true to their word, stop to help, and each time we climb a little higher. The minutes go by, and we inch closer and closer to the lip of the volcano.

"What is this?" Burns says, pointing at an unusual rock formation in our path. "Most of the rocks have sharp edges and a sandy brown color. The ones not coated in ash, anyway. These ones are much grayer and smoother."

"I don't know for sure," Manning says, "but the color of these rocks looks an awful lot like the clouds and the ash in the sky, doesn't it?"

"What is that sound?" Burns yells this because it is clear the noise of the volcano is getting louder.

A deep, rumbling boom comes from inside the mountain. Everyone hears it; it drowns out all other sound. The ground vibrates, and small rockslides begin all around us. The sulfur smell is stronger than ever. I almost stumble and fall over because of the tremors but barely keep my balance.

Next, the rumbling sound turns into an explosion.

"It's an eruption!" Manning yells.

"Run!" Fogarty shouts. Even though Fogarty is only five or six feet away, I can't hear him over the rumble. I can read his lips easily enough, though.

In moments, we learn the source of the gray rock formations. Cracks in the mountainside, that we couldn't see because they were above us, start belching out red, flaming lava, which runs downhill toward us. As the lava travels over the gray, ashy mountainside, it acquires a gray coating on top.

Unfortunately, a couple lava vents open below us, too, and one of them already has sent its deadly contents streaming across the path we took to ascend this far.

Fogarty recovers his wits first. He shouts something, but I still can't hear it because a second explosion drowns out his words. The tremors knock me down to one knee. However, Fogarty also points to what appears to be a clear route downward, so again, I can guess what he said. It's time to run for it.

Fogarty takes the lead but doesn't go far before he comes to a large drop—ten or twelve feet at least. He leaps, with Manning following. They land on their feet. I'm next, but I hesitate. For some reason, I can't make myself jump. Paralyzed with fear, again, I don't know what to do. I look back as Burns catches up with me, pleading with my eyes for help. A torrent of lava speeds toward us. I reckon we have a minute or so until it catches up to us, maybe less than that.

"Get ready, Clarence," Burns screams, so I can hear him. He grabs me by the arm and whips me over the edge of the drop—right into Manning's waiting arms. He leaps down.

Our escape is not yet certain, however. The lava flow is close behind and gaining on us. Fogarty points again, and we follow him once more.

Even though the sheet of lava flowing down behind us is getting nearer, we must choose our route carefully. If a stream in front of us cuts us off, it will trap us, and we won't escape from the fiery death coming from behind.

Fogarty pauses just a moment so that we can catch up. "I see a way clear," he shouts, "we just have to . . ."

He's cut off by a third explosive boom, the loudest and longest yet. A part of the mountainside shifts, the rocks and dirt we're standing on give way, and all of us lose our footing and slide downward.

I have some luck. While I slide, I manage to grab onto a scrawny tree that somehow survives the rockslide and holds its position. Although my poor arms scream out in pain and exhaustion, I hold tight until the slide is over.

The slide was not major, and we don't slide far, fortunately. The slide doesn't cause any serious injuries, and it does not bury any of us alive. When things settle, I see Burns and Manning jump up from the piles of rocks, dirt, and gravel. They ended up nearby each other, and while bruised, caked in ash, and bleeding from some scrapes, they seem unhurt. Then I see Fogarty. He'd been in the lead and has slid down farther, and the slide almost sent him over the edge of a rock outcropping. He clings to the lip, his feet desperately trying to find footing in the rock face, so he can pull himself up, but the rock overhangs the ground below, and he can't do it. The drop is thirty or forty feet, at least.

I hear a loud hissing sound behind me. The rockslide and the last explosion opened a new lava vent right near where we'd been standing, and now fiery lava spurts out of it! It is already flowing between the members of our party, separating us. Fogarty and I are to the right of the flaming river while Burns and Manning are to the left.

"Help me, Clarence," Fogarty shouts. "I can't get any footing, and my hands are slipping!"

It's true, and I'm the only one who can help. "I'm coming," I shout as I slip and slide down the mountainside. Behind me, I hear a crackle when the poor tree that saved me ignites and begins burning. It goes up in flame like a matchstick.

I reach the edge and try to pull on Fogarty's right arm and get him up, but it isn't working. I'm exhausted, and I'm just not strong enough. A quick look back shows that the lava is closer. Maybe fifty, maybe sixty feet.

"Brace with your legs and pull," Fogarty screams at me desperately. "Pull!"

I close my eyes, set my feet, and give it all I have. Fogarty yells with effort, swings his legs, and manages a toehold! I gather myself, pull again, and he's up!

The lava bears down on us. It is less than twenty feet away, and it's coming fast. We run to the right of the rock outcropping, even as we hear Burns and Manning cheer our escape. Sometimes we run and jump down the slope, and at other times, we just slide through the loose stones and dirt in terror.

After a few minutes of this, Fogarty turns and looks back and falls to his knees. I look back, too, and I can see that we are safe. What we thought was an eruption really wasn't an eruption after all, just powerful tremors. The flow from the lava vents has eased off already, the fiery rivers are behind us, and before long, we stand alongside Burns and Manning. By now, we all look like we have gray skin, gray clothes, gray everything. Only our eyes, and several bloody scrapes, give away that we aren't some ancient statue come to life.

Once we are all back together again, Fogarty turns to me and gives me a bear hug, lifting me off the ground.

"The luckiest and best mascot ever born," he says to me. "May your luck never run out."

To the group, he says, "What did I tell you? I said this would be something we'd never forget, right?" His broad smile reveals glittering white teeth.

Several hours later, we return to the hotel and find MacMillan, Palmer, and several of the ballplayers freshening up after a day of touring the city. We must look a sight because their eyebrows rise about halfway up their foreheads when they see us. "What on earth happened to you?" Marty Sullivan asks.

"You wouldn't believe it even if I told you," Fogarty informs him. "Just let me say that we now have a new member in the Order of the Howling Wolves."

Chapter 15

February 18, 1889
Pompeii, Italy

February 18th is a Monday. Most of our party, me included, decide to go to the ruined city of Pompeii. After my escape from Mount Vesuvius yesterday, it seems only fitting. I'm all set to see the ruins in the new suit of clothes Jim Fogarty just bought for me. He and Burns agreed to cancel their bet about climbing the mountain and pool the bet money to get me new clothes instead. All I can say about my new Italian clothes is that they are rather more stylish and expensive than the ones I got in Hastings, Nebraska. The tailors even took my measurements for my new white shirt and dark green vest, while my new leather shoes gleam in the Italian sunshine.

Pompeii is about two miles from Naples, and I join a touring party consisting of Palmer, MacMillan, Ward, Tener, Fogarty, Wood, and Hanlon. Other than our quick meeting with Hanlon at the Hotel Vesuve, I've barely seen Ward since we got to Italy, much less heard him speak to anyone, but today he emerges from his solitude and joins our group, as chipper and upbeat as he used to be. Fogarty pays my admission fee.

"It looks like, Clarence, the tour guide literature is in Italian, and I can't read that to you because I don't know any Italian," Fogarty tells me. "However, I think they must get a fair number of American tourists here because our guide speaks English. So, if you have any questions for him, just let me know, and I'll make sure you get answers."

The ruined city fascinates me. The guide describes how, because the burning hot ash buried so many people alive almost immediately after the volcano's eruption, the ruins provide us with a photograph of life in the Roman Empire almost 2,000 years ago. He tells us that the ruins show how regular people lived and how rich people lived. They also demonstrate where each class of people lived and what kinds of things they tended to keep inside their homes.

While we tour the city, we visit the private homes of both rich and poor Romans. The homes of the wealthy still have marble statues and fountains that the burning ash buried but did not destroy. We also look at the wall paintings and mosaics inside the homes. Many of them survived as well, and the vibrant colors are beautiful. I see images of animals like fish, peacocks, and birds, as well as people, gods, and goddesses. It's hard to believe such beauty could survive the town's destruction, but some of it did.

A little more disturbing to me are the mosaics of people killing things. I see ones of men with weapons stabbing animals. Streams of blood pour from the wounds. In others, large animals like bears and tigers leap on people and eat them. The worst are the mosaics showing people with weapons killing other people.

Johnny Ward is the player closest to me when we get to the rooms with the mosaics. "Mr. Ward," I ask, "what are these scenes of people killing animals and other people all about?"

"The ancient Romans had a group of people called gladiators, Clarence. They fought in public, in big arenas, some of them even bigger than our baseball parks back in America. The most famous arena is the Colosseum, and you can still go and see it when you get to Rome. I hope we'll get to go there when we reach Rome. People say nothing exists today even remotely like it in all the world, and it was built almost 2,000 years ago."

"The Romans killed each other in front of the public?"

"Yes. Sometimes the gladiators fought other gladiators. At other times, they fought wild animals or killed criminals in the arenas. A bit barbarous by our modern standards, perhaps, but in ancient Rome, it was a favorite pastime for rich and poor alike. Look at these mosaics. Some of the gladiators were so famous that the artists who made the mosaics even put the names of the gladiators next to them, so everyone would know who the best fighters were."

I get very quiet after Ward tells me this. It makes me think back on the day I saw two homeless men fight over a few pieces of bread in an alley in Chicago. One had a knife and used it to stab the other man in his eye. I'd seen fights before, of course, and a couple times, I've come across people who froze to death sleeping on the streets during the winter in Chicago. Something was different about this fight, however. The look on the man's face when he tore out the other man's eyeball and stomped on it over and over still haunts me. It was a look of anger, hate, rage, and triumph mixed together so frightening that even now it scares me when I remember it. As soon as he looked at me and knew I'd seen him do it, I ran.

I've never told anyone, but that was the real reason I left my job as the Chicago mascot and decided to go with Miss Jarbeau instead. I was too scared of ever seeing that desperate, murderous man again, so I decided to leave Chicago. When our tour gets back to Chicago in the spring, I'm not sure what I should do, stay there or move along to a new city.

"Clarence? Are you coming with us, Clarence?" It's Ward's voice. I must have been staring off and not paying attention.

"I'm sorry, Mr. Ward. I'm coming."

Other interesting places are on the tour, including the forum of the city where public activities took place, a public theater, and temples dedicated to various Roman gods. We also go in the museum the Italian government built on the site to see more artifacts that the archaeologists have uncovered when excavating the city.

"Look, men, at these plaster casts," Palmer says to our group. "When the ash and lava buried these people alive, their skin turned to dust over time, but the shapes remained, like the molds used by ironworkers. The excavators poured plaster into the shapes, and now we have exact replicas of what the people were doing at the time of their death. Some of the plaster casts still have the bones of the deceased inside of them."

"Oh, look," I say to everyone. "How sad."

I'm looking at the cast of a dog. Its cast reveals straining muscles, and I note a bronze collar around its neck. The poor thing must have been trying to get away when the burning ashes overtook it. Seeing this cast saddens me as much as the mosaics of the gladiators did because I love animals. Maybe coming here wasn't the best idea, after all.

I'm just getting over the depressing fate of this ancient pet when an unfamiliar voice calls out my name.

"Clarence Duval?" the voice says. "Mr. Spalding has sent me to find and bring back Clarence Duval. Where is he?"

"I am here," I say, stepping forward.

"Clarence," the stranger says to me, "I am Stamford Parry, Mr. Spalding's European agent. Mr. Spalding wants you to return to our hotel with me at once and gather your baggage. We want you to accompany us on a most important trip. We plan to leave for the city of Rome this evening, and Mr. Spalding wants you on the train with us."

"I need to go right now?" I say in surprise. I had no idea I might be important enough to go on any special trips with Spalding. Hopefully, it isn't just to pretend to be his servant again. He has Akbar for that purpose now, anyway.

"Yes," Parry responds. "We'll explain everything to you once we've boarded the train, but we have no time to waste. Come along now."

By evening, I'm on the train with Parry and Spalding, heading north toward Rome. No ballplayers are on board the train with us. I still can't guess why they need me, so I wait for an explanation. Did Spalding learn I've been spying on him somehow?

After ordering drinks for themselves, wine for Parry and ice water for Spalding, the two men call me over for a talk. Spalding begins. "First of all, Clarence, I hear that the All-America team still has one of its outfielders because of your efforts and that this new and, I must say, very crisp-looking suit of clothes is a reward for your help. That red and white striped tie, especially."

"Yes, Mr. Spalding, that is true. It was a crazy day. One of the most dramatic of my life. I don't believe I'll ever forget it so long as I live."

"Nor will Fogarty, I'm sure. From everything that has happened to you recently, I'd say your mascotic talents remain as potent as ever."

"Since when did you start believing in luck?" Parry asks.

"Oh, I believe we make our own luck, just as I always have. But, given all that Clarence has been through and survived since we left America, perhaps there may be something to the mascot idea, as well." He says this with a kindly smile toward me. "In any case, it won't hurt to have him with us, both for good luck and for other reasons."

Other reasons. Oh no. Sounds like the servant idea all over again. I brace myself for the worst.

Instead, Spalding continues, saying to Parry, "I plan to make one last effort at persuading the Italian government to let us use the Roman Colosseum to play a game of baseball. I realize that you didn't have any luck in securing that venue for us to play, but I plan to make one more try at it with the officials in Rome all the same."

"How can I help with that?" I blurt out, forgetting that I'm not supposed to ask questions or speak unless spoken to. The thought of being a servant again made me nervous. Sheepishly, I add, "I don't know that I can persuade any Italian officials when I can't speak any Italian. I guess I can try to bring you good luck, though."

Spalding smiles again, apparently taking no offense. "You can do more than give us luck, Clarence. You see, the American consul here in Italy is a man named Camphausen. His family has lived in the Philadelphia area for generations. Not only is he a Quaker, but his family was also prominent in the cause of abolitionism before the Civil War. They wrote letters to Abraham Lincoln, encouraging him to free the slaves during the war, and now they are active in the cause of Negro uplift in the United States. The Camphausen family contributed money to help found Howard University back in 1867, among other efforts along those lines. He's been quite helpful and supportive of our cause up to this point, and I'm hoping that if he sees you with us, your presence might make him even better disposed toward us."

"Goodness, Al, you really know your man," Parry says. "How do you know so much about our Italian consul?"

"He told me all those things himself in his letter of introduction I received upon our arrival in Brindisi. His good qualities include humanitarianism and a love of baseball, but not humility, it would seem."

Parry just laughs.

"Oh, I have one more thing," Spalding says to both of us. "I also hope to persuade His Holiness, the Pope, to watch a game of ball before we leave Rome. Again, it may be a long shot, but I'd like to attempt it, all the same."

"The longest of long shots, I'd say. What makes you think you can succeed?" Parry asks Spalding.

"I have no illusions about my chances. It is a hope and nothing more. However, just think, Stamford, what it would mean if I did succeed. If the Pope were to endorse baseball, it might encourage all the good Catholics in the United States to embrace our national game more fully than they already do. The financial benefits could be immense."

"Who is the Pope?" I ask. "I haven't heard of him before."

"The Pope is the leader of the Catholic Church all around the world. He is one of the most important religious people in the world," Spalding replies.

"How does little Clarence fit into this plot, if I may ask?" Parry puts in.

"He probably doesn't, but you never know. You are a Catholic yourself, correct?" Spalding asks Parry.

"I am."

"I want you to teach Clarence to pretend to be one, just in case. The better show of faithful devotion we can put on, the better our chances. Are you religious at all, Clarence? Are you a churchgoer?"

"No, Mr. Spalding, I'm not a part of any religion. I've gotten food from their soup kitchens sometimes, but I've never gone to services in a church. I guess my clothes aren't quite good enough to go in a real church most of the time. And I can't afford to give an offering, if you follow me."

"Well, chances are you won't have to this time either, Clarence, but we'll make sure you have a few coins in your pocket, just in case. Like I've told Stamford here, I don't expect much to come of this, but we'll give it our best try and hope that you still have a little bit of luck left that you can share with us."

"I do my best, Mr. Spalding; you know I always do. I don't suppose I'll be doing any marching for the Pope, will I?

"Not likely, Clarence," Spalding laughs. "I think you can leave your uniform and marching baton at the hotel this time."

"That just about covers our business for tomorrow, doesn't it?" Parry asks.

"It does," Spalding responds. "I think that is all for this evening, gentlemen."

Chapter 16

"Let's go over it again, okay, Clarence?"

"Here? In the lobby of our hotel?"

"I know it's crowded, but it'll be more crowded still when we get to St. Peter's Square, so we may as well practice here."

Parry is right. It's busy in the hotel lobby, but if anyone takes special notice of a grown white man and twelve-year-old colored boy, they keep it to themselves.

"I suppose we can practice one more time," I say.

"If we're called on to recite the Lord's Prayer, when do you pause, so the priest can speak?"

"After the words, 'deliver us from evil.'"

"Very good. Now, let me see you genuflect."

I cross myself the way he taught me.

"Not bad, not bad. It could look a little more natural, but I'd say we're okay there."

"I'm still not sure all the times I'm supposed to stand or kneel," I tell Parry. "There seem to be a lot of them."

"Just follow what I do. That shouldn't be a problem. How did you do in terms of memorizing some of those Latin responses I wrote out for you last night on the train?"

"Not so well, I'm afraid. I can speak some of them, sort of, but I'm still confused on when to say all of them."

"Yes, that is what I was afraid of. I guess just mumble through them quietly, and if anyone asks you why you can't say them properly, tell them you're a recent convert to the faith and you're just learning. Well, you've done about as well as anyone could hope, Clarence. You learn quickly. If you ever decide to become a Catholic, I'd say you will do well at the formal parts of it."

"Will I really have to do any of these things, Mr. Parry? If we are just going to meetings, why do I have to know about all of them?"

"It is unlikely you'll have to do anything, actually," he tells me while he helps me straighten the striped tie Fogarty purchased for me. "Still, it doesn't hurt to prepare for any possibility. Like Mr. Spalding said, the more Catholic we appear to be, the better our chances. My guess is that we'll just sit there while he speaks to one of the Curia's diplomats, but who knows what could happen? I know Mr. Spalding isn't so sure about the whole idea of mascots and luck, but I'll feel better with someone as lucky as you on our side."

"Is Mr. Spalding a Catholic, too?"

"No, Clarence, he isn't, and I suspect that is why he asked me to come with him on this diplomatic mission."

"Does he have a religion, if it is okay for me to ask?"

"Mr. Spalding is a Theosophist. It is a faith rather different from Christianity, be it Catholic, Protestant, or Orthodox. I do not claim to know much about the beliefs of Theosophy, however, so I can't say much more than that. Again, I think that is why he asked me to be here. Still, we'll let him do the talking unless he asks for our help."

An hour after this little talk on how to be a Catholic, we stand outside one of the many stunning buildings in St. Peter's Square in

Rome. I see quite a crowd of people around us. Some of them are pointing, or staring in wonder just like I am, probably because they are tourists like me. Even though the square is busy, I like it here. It's a sunny day, and although throngs of people fill the square, I don't see street merchants pressing around me, and the smell of sewage and decaying garbage doesn't assault my senses like it does in other parts of the city.

Parry, dressed in a black suit jacket, black tie, and black top hat, turns to say something when a passerby backs into him and bumps him.

"*Perdono*," the person says, bowing politely.

"*Non e niente*," Parry replies with a smile. He says it quietly and without much conviction, however. Maybe he's more nervous than he looks.

"Which one does the Pope live in?" I ask, staring around in wonder. "Is it that one?" I point to the largest building. It has a huge dome on top. If the Pope is so important, he probably has an enormous house.

"No, he doesn't live in that one," Parry responds with a little laugh while sidestepping another sightseer. "That is St. Peter's Basilica, one of the most famous churches in the whole world. I think Pope Leo XIII lives over there, in that building with all the stone columns in front. That is the Vatican Palace, also known as the Apostolic Palace."

"We are going in there to talk with him, then?"

"No, it doesn't quite work that way," he tells me with another friendly laugh. "The Pope is a hugely important person with many big responsibilities; you can't just walk into his house and see if he's home and has time to visit with you. Instead, you must arrange a meeting with one of the Pope's secretaries, whom you call a monsignor, I believe, and if that person decides you are important enough, then you can meet the Pope. That is what Mr. Spalding is inside trying to do right now. If he succeeds, we may get to accompany him to see His Holiness. It would be a great honor for a Catholic like me."

Next, I turn and point to something I'd been admiring. "What is that stone spike in the middle of the square?"

"We call that an obelisk. If the stories are true, it comes from Egypt."

"It used to be somewhere *else*? It looks 200 feet tall. How do people move something so big and heavy without breaking it? How did they get it here when you have to load it on a boat from Egypt?"

"God only knows."

Another tourist bumps my shoulder while walking by but doesn't even notice and says nothing.

"I'm sorry for asking so many questions. I just never imagined that a church could be so big. Back in the United States, I thought Chicago was a big city with lots of modern things to see, but on this trip, I've seen so many unexpected things. I've never seen a church like that in Chicago. Or anywhere else I've ever been."

"Don't worry about it, Clarence. I rather like talking about religious things. In the United States, a great many people don't like Catholics very much, so it feels good just to talk about all these spectacular buildings without anyone getting upset and questioning my loyalty to the Republic. Oh, look, here comes Mr. Spalding. Let's see if he's had any success."

We walk up a short flight of steps to meet the president of the Chicago Club and hear the news. For a moment, the crowd around us thins out a bit.

"Well, this certainly has been a tough day. It has been tougher than getting Baldwin or Daly to abstain from alcohol, in fact," Spalding says.

"You didn't have any luck?" Parry replies.

"No. It appears that His Holiness is ill and is not making any public appearances for the time being."

"Do you believe he's really sick?"

"Perhaps he is, or perhaps he isn't, and it's all an excuse. It makes little difference. There will be no game with the Pope in attendance. I tried to persuade His Holiness's secretary that America has many Catholics who love baseball and that an endorsement of our game would be wildly popular with them, but to no avail. I'm not convinced he has much sporting blood in him."

"I guess offering them money, like you did with the Italian government earlier this morning, was out of the question as well," Parry suggests.

"Correct. I doubt that trying to buy the Pope's support would go over well in diplomatic circles."

"I'm still a little disappointed that the Italian government turned down your offer to play a game of ball in the Roman Colosseum. How much did you offer them again?"

Spalding replies, "I opened the bidding at $2,000 for the privilege, but they claimed that playing ball amongst the echoes of the ancient gladiators would be sacrilege."

"What a shame. I thought the memorial of the Caesars would make a splendid backstop for a game of baseball."

"I did as well. I would have bid higher, gladly, if I thought I had any chance of persuading them, but they seemed fixed in their intent to preserve the historic sanctity of the Colosseum. The Italian authorities also claimed the galleries were unsafe for spectators."

"I'll admit I am quite disappointed in the lack of sporting spirit and promotional flair among the Italians we've met so far. Well, if Harry Palmer or Newton MacMillan asks me about it, I'll tell them you opened the bidding at $5,000 for the opportunity and tried to go higher. That will sound much more adventuresome to our reading audience back in the United States."

Spalding's face, downcast after his rejections, brightens at this suggestion. "That's a capital idea. A bid of $5,000 does sound much better than the truth. Certainly, tell Palmer and MacMillan that. Oh, and add that I also offered to give half of the gate receipts to charity. That will make even better reading. Just like all the inflated attendance figures we've reported at our games to this point and the bogus accounts we've planted of how baseball is already flowering in our wake."

"Or like the letter you told me you sent to Henry Chadwick back in January claiming that all of the boys had completely abstained from liquor while abroad."

"Yes, Stamford, just like that. If the sporting pubic knew the truth about Fogarty, Daly, Baldwin, and the rest, it would cast us in a poor light, and I won't have that happen if I can help it."

"Okay, that's settled. If I can ask you one more thing, Al, I received a cable this morning from your man, Van Kirk, in Vienna. I didn't want to bring it up until you'd concluded your business for the morning."

"What does he say about conditions in Vienna and Berlin?"

"That they remain cold and much snow remains on the ground."

"That is a shame, indeed. The people of Vienna impressed me most favorably. I enjoyed their communication about forming a committee to look after us when we arrived there."

"In their telegraph, they write that they've secured a large public building just off the Ringstrasse, so we can play a game of baseball indoors. What do you think, Al?"

"People in America have tried playing baseball indoors, Stamford, but I've never heard that the results were very satisfactory. The height of the ceiling is never great enough to handle fly balls. Besides, where would we put the spectators?"

"You'd like me to decline their offer, then?"

"I'm afraid so. Tell them that Mr. Spalding sends his deepest regrets, but due to the unfavorable weather, we must decline their gracious invitation."

It would be easy to forget I am even there while the two men talk about business matters I only vaguely understand, but for a moment they remember my presence and turn to me. Parry says, "I wonder how the game in Naples today went without Clarence to lead the parade?"

"I hope we got a decent turnout," Spalding replies. "I decided not to charge admission for the outfield spectators."

"That doesn't sound like you, Al."

"The common people of southern Italy are not renowned for their great wealth, so I decided that only grandstand spectators must pay admission. The poverty of Italy is part of the reason we Americans have witnessed such an unfortunate upswing in immigration from the southern parts of Italy in the present decade. So many of the Italians are so poor; they just want a better chance at life. I heard that many members of the local Neapolitan government, military officials, and other assorted dignitaries planned to be there, however, so we should realize a bit of cash, at least."

"I am sorry I couldn't be there to lead the parade," I put in. "You know that I really like to lead the boys onto the field."

"Well, Clarence," Spalding tells me, "when you consider that the Campo del Marte Cricket Grounds are about five miles from our hotel, it would have been a long parade. I thought your services better used here with us, even if your luck was not quite enough to overcome the obstacles we faced."

"Five miles!" I exclaim. "That is rather far. I think you are right."

"Still," Parry puts in, "it must be quite an experience to play a game of baseball with a live volcano in the backdrop."

A couple of days ago, I might have agreed with Parry, but I believe I've had my fill of volcanoes for now.

Chapter 17

February 22, 1889
Rome, Italy

"Can it be? Is it really Clarence Duval, the mascot of the Chicago White Stockings?"

I am standing with Spalding, Harry Palmer, several of the ballplayers, and Dr. O'Connell, the president of the American College in Rome. We're in the garden of the college, surrounded by rose bushes and a few other plants and shrubs I'm not familiar with, and O'Connell has just finished describing how the American College trains young men as future priests of the Catholic Church in the United States. Even though the roses aren't in bloom today, the garden has a fresh smell to it, very different from the rest of Rome. A great number of the students, 60 or 70, have gathered around our party to get a chance to speak to their favorite American baseball players. I can't believe it, but it appears that they even know who I am.

While most of the young men talk with the ballplayers, a few of the students walk over to me and shake my hand. Most look like they are in their early 20s. I'm surprised they know me, so it takes me a moment to respond to their question.

"Y-yes, I'm Clarence," I manage to stammer out, a bit nervous at getting attention. "I'm pleased to meet all of you."

"We've been following your journey in the pages of *The Sporting Life*, of course," one of them says to me. He is tall and has dark hair. "It does take some time for the paper to get to us here in Rome. Still, late news is better than no news, and we've been waiting for your party's arrival in Rome for weeks."

"You get American newspapers here?" I ask him.

"We sure do. We know all the writers for *The Sporting Life*. We read Joe Pritchard, Henry Chadwick, O. P. Caylor, Ren Mulford, Mugwump, Albert Mott, and all the rest. We have to keep that quiet while we're here, of course, because we're supposed to be preparing for the priesthood, but we love baseball almost as much as we love God."

"That's right," says another of the students to me. "We are as fond of baseball as we are the priesthood, and I try to tell Dr. O'Connell that we'll make good, faithful priests if our worst sin is to harbor a love for baseball and sports." Several of the students laugh at this. "We have several teams here at the college," he continues, "and we hope to be at the ballgame tomorrow, so we can see your baton act."

Another of the students steps forward to shake my hand. "We've read all of Harry Palmer's accounts of the trip, naturally, including when he mentions you. He writes about how excellent you are with your baton, how you lead all the parades, how you met the king of the Sandwich Islands, and how much you love doing your plantation dances for everyone. Do you think we could see one before you go? I'm from Brooklyn, and I've never seen one."

It takes me a moment before I can answer. "I'm sorry," I say, "but I think you may be mistaken."

"Mistaken? Mistaken about what, if I may ask?"

"It is true that I lead the parades and twirl my baton," I reply nervously, my eyes darting back and forth to see if anyone from our group will overhear me, "but I've never liked doing plantation dances. I don't even know how, in fact, so I just make things up as I go. I hate doing them, and I've vowed never to do another."

This takes the students by surprise. One of them, a slim young man with glasses, stammers, "But in the papers, it says how much you love doing plantation shakedowns. You mean to tell us you don't do them by choice and that the reports of how much you enjoy performing your dances are falsehoods?"

"I'm afraid the reports are false. I'm ashamed and humiliated every time I do one."

Even as I say this, I start to wonder what else Palmer, or anyone else, has written about me that I don't know about or understand. Perhaps it is time I learned how to read for real, instead of only partly, like I can right now. I'd better work even harder at my lessons with MacMillan.

"We are very sorry to hear that," the first student, the tall one, tells me. "We are sorry for you that your treatment has not been what we've been led to believe by the newspapers. God loves all his people, of course, but especially the children, as He reminds us in Matthew eighteen, verses two through six. We are also sorry for the souls of those who write falsely of others, for that also goes against our faith."

"We will not ask you for a plantation dance again," says the student from Brooklyn, "but could you, perhaps, show us your baton act? I know many of the other students would like to see your talents."

"I did not bring my baton with me today. But, if you can attend our game tomorrow like you say you will, I'll give you a great show. The best one I can." Given the importance of this information I've just learned, I owe them a good show.

"Deal!" the Brooklyn student says. "God bless you, Clarence."

The students move off in search of some ballplayers they can talk to.

After we visit the students, we continue to tour some of the famous sites of Rome. The city has a never-ending supply of huge and ancient buildings that simply astonish me. We return to St. Peter's Square first. Everyone calls it a square, even though it is circular, or maybe oval, in shape. Tener tries to explain why people call it a square, but I'm not sure I get it. This time, we have a chance to go into the giant church. All of it is breathtaking, the Sistine Chapel doubly so. I just stare up at the beautiful art.

"Do you like it, Clarence?" John Healy says to me while we stand motionless looking up, craning our necks backward to see the ceiling until they start getting sore.

"It is wonderful, Mr. Healy. Can you remind me what all the paintings are about? I've never read the Bible because I can't read very well, so I don't know all the stories, I'm afraid."

"Well, it might take a minute. See the painting where the man has a white cloud in his left arm and a dark one in his right? That is God, creating light and darkness on the first day of the world. Then, you see Him creating the sun and the moon. Over there," I keep following Healy's finger while he points to new things, "God creates Adam, and from Adam, creates Eve, the first two humans."

Because all the people in the paintings seem to be white, this makes me curious where colored people came from, but instead of interrupting Healy to ask him, I just listen while he keeps going.

"That creature that looks like a snake is Satan, tempting Adam and Eve in the Garden of Eden and causing mankind to sin for the first time."

"Who are all the men with books and scrolls that we can see?" I ask Healy. I've been thinking a lot about books ever since my talk with the students at the American College.

"I believe those are various prophets who wrote books in the Bible, such as Joel, Zechariah, Daniel, Ezekiel, Isaiah, and Jeremiah."

"What about the back wall of the chapel? It looks like a lot is going on."

"Those are scenes from the Last Judgment when the world comes to an end and the righteous ascend to Heaven, where the Irish will be, while sinners like the English meet everlasting torment in Hell. See the people with the trumpets just under Jesus? They are announcing Christ's judgment while He comes in glory."

The painting does look rather scary in places, especially at the bottom, where evil-looking creatures are pulling people down and snakes coil around them, but I decide I've asked enough questions for now. Besides, the paintings are so beautiful I think I should just look at them for a while.

After St. Peter's, we visit the Forum, the Palace of the Caesars, the Appian Way, and several other churches that the players tell me are famous. I see many of them genuflect while inside the churches, so I do as well, just to show off that I learned how. Once, I notice that John Healy nods with approval when I do so.

We manage all this above ground and in daylight, but late in the afternoon, the players decide to go underground into the famous Roman catacombs. I'm not sure if I should go in at first because I remember how panicky I got in the mines in Australia, but I decide to face my fear and go anyway. Hopefully, if I can survive a volcano almost erupting, I can survive some underground passages. The escape from Mount Vesuvius gives me the courage to try, at least. We've been underground for about fifteen or twenty minutes, and so far, I've avoided panicking. I feel my hands quivering at times but try to ignore them.

It is very dry down here. The air smells dusty and stale, even old, if air can smell old. Things are also quiet, especially compared to all the noise in the streets above ground. A few times, when our guide stops talking and people just look at things, you can hear other people breathe. That's how quiet and still it is.

About half of the players are along for the tour, including Anson and Pfeffer, but also Ward, Tener, and my new best friend, Fogarty. I expected some joke from Anson about how they should throw me in with the dead people and leave me in the catacombs, but for once, he hasn't said much since we went underground. Maybe that's because he's at the front of the group and I'm hanging in the back. Just as our party starts down another tunnel to look at more of the tombs, Tom Daly tugs on my sleeve and Fogarty whispers to me, "Psst, Clarence, let's go this way."

Daly and Fogarty lead me in the opposite direction from everyone else. Fogarty has one of the oil lamps the Italian tour guide distributed when the tour began, so we aren't in the dark, but still, I'm worried. "Mr. Fogarty, Mr. Daly, shouldn't we stay with the others? We don't have a map. How will we know where to go?"

"Don't worry, Clarence, we have a lamp, we'll be fine. How many tombs can there be, anyway?" Fogarty says to me.

"You aren't scared, are you, Clarence?" Daly adds. "You climbed a volcano, after all; you shouldn't be frightened of this."

"But . . ." I start to object again.

"Come on, Clarence, no need to get scared or nervous," Daly tells me. "Have we ever let you down?"

In the lantern light, Daly is just far enough away that I can't tell if he says this with a straight face.

We turn left, then right, then left again before coming to an area where the tombs are fancier and the corridor is a little wider.

"Look at all that artwork," Fogarty says. "It covers the walls, the ceiling, everything."

"Those are peacocks, right?" I say. Once, I sneaked into the Chicago Zoo at Lincoln Park, so I know what a peacock looks like.

"Yeah, funny they put peacocks on the walls of their tombs. Why not a noble bird, like an eagle or a hawk or something?" Daly wonders.

We just stand and stare at all the angels and animals painted around the tomb. Besides the peacocks, I also see many doves and lambs. Finally, Fogarty says, "I don't hear anyone nearby. What do you say we open the tomb and see what's inside? Maybe take home a finger bone or something, just for a souvenir."

"I think that would be bad luck, don't you, Mr. Fogarty?" I say.

"I'd say we should listen to Clarence this time, Jimmy," Daly says. "If anyone knows about what's lucky and what isn't, it's him."

"Okay, if you're scared, we won't open it. Look at this, though. The tomb has something, a type of seal, maybe, on it."

We all move in for a closer look.

The seal is a lump of glass, it appears, but someone placed an image inside the glass. The image is of a person with robes, and I see a pedestal with a bird on each side of the person.

"What is that around the person's head? Is that a kind of funny hat? Who knows what hats were in style back when these people were alive," Daly says.

"It looks more like a halo to me," Fogarty says. "I think I see some letters, too, but I can't quite make out what they say."

"How would you read them anyway, Jimmy? They aren't in English, and I know you didn't spend your time at sea studying Italian," Daly asks. After looking a few more moments, he says, "This seal is pretty, for sure, but what else is around that we can look at? The passage continues over here. Let's see what's down this way."

We wander down the corridor, passing more tombs cut into the walls. Most of them have no identification of who rests there, and most in this new hallway lack decoration, too, so we don't spend much time looking at them. Occasionally, we pass a big tomb with more artwork. Those must be for the richer people, I suppose.

After a while, I have a thought. "Mr. Fogarty, when the tour guide gave out the lamps, did he mention how long the light would last?"

"Hmm, good question, Clarence. I don't remember that he told us how long they would burn, one way or the other. Anson just handed me one when the guide passed out the lamps to everyone. Let's see how much fuel we have left."

Fogarty squints while he holds up the lantern, shielding his eyes with one hand so he can see better. His mouth twitches, he frowns, and his mouth twitches again. "Umm, boys, I don't know how fast this thing burns, but I don't think we have much time left. I'd say we ought to head back and find everyone else."

We hurry back, and we find the spot where we first left the group. They are long gone, of course, and the corridor is silent as a tomb. Which makes sense, I guess, because we're in a tomb. Oops, I probably shouldn't think about it with those words—might be bad luck. At this point, Fogarty frowns again. He bites his lips together for a moment, sighs loud enough we can hear him, and says, "Tom, Clarence, do either of you know the way out from here?"

"I have no idea," Daly responds. "I was just following the group, not paying attention to our route."

"Me neither," I say.

As soon as I finish speaking, the lamp flickers.

"Well, let's use our brains here, small as they may be," Daly puts in. "We're underground, so we should be able to find the way out by going uphill, right? Which way is that?"

None of us can say for sure. The passage seems flat where we are standing. Fogarty thinks it's to our right. Daly and I both think it's to the left.

"Well, that settles it," Fogarty says. "It's two against one, and Clarence is our lucky mascot, so let's go left." Our lamp sputters fitfully.

We hurry down the left passage. I'd forgotten about it for a little while because looking at the tombs and their artwork distracted me, but now my fear of being underground starts coming back. My body shakes, and I feel my breathing get faster, even though we haven't gone far and I'm not tired. The ceiling is about seven feet high in the tunnel, but it feels like it's only an inch or two above my head. I resist the urge to duck down while I shuffle forward.

We've only gone a short way, however, when our lamp sputters once more and goes out. The darkness surrounding us is complete.

So is the silence. Another shudder wracks my body, and I can feel my shirt sticking to my back from all the nervous sweat.

Even though it is probably only a few moments, it seems like we stand there for an hour before someone gets up the nerve to speak.

"N-now w-what do we do?" Daly says in a whisper. "Do we j-just wait here until someone comes and f-finds us?"

"I don't know," Fogarty replies in his own hoarse, quavering whisper. "Do you think someone will hear us if we shout?" I think he is nervous, too, even though it's totally black and I can't see him to tell for sure.

No one speaks again for some time. I'm about to say something when everyone hears a high-pitched, squeaky sound.

"What's that?" I say, also whispering. "Do you think the roof might collapse on us, like in Chinatown?" I suck in a big gasp of air. Even that takes a big effort.

No one else has the nerve to answer at first, but after a few silent seconds that seem to take minutes, Fogarty says, with a little more confidence in his voice, "No, I don't think there'll be a cave-in. These tombs have been here for about ten thousand years, right? Why would there be a cave-in now? And that noise didn't sound like the rock creaking."

"What was it, then?" Daly asks quietly, his voice still shaking. "I h-hate to say it, but we're in a tomb. Maybe the g-ghosts got mad at us for t-talking about opening one of the coffins!"

"Ghosts!" Fogarty says indignantly. "Ghosts? Are you for real? There's no such thing. Do you . . ." Fogarty is about to say something more when the squeaky sound cuts him off, and he stops mid-sentence. I shiver again. Even though I don't say so, I believe there might be ghosts, and I'm very scared. I attempt to say so, but the words stick in my throat.

"Yes, ghosts are real," Daly counters, still whispering. "What do you think that was? The ghosts are angry with us for being here. You see, back where I grew up in Philadelphia, we had this old house down the road, and everyone knew it was haunted. But this is worse. Now we're surrounded, and we can't get out!" I can hear the panic rising in his voice.

"What do we do now?" I finally manage to say something, but just as nervously as Daly. "Should we keep going or stay here?"

I feel something. The slightest breath of air moving on the back of my neck. "Aaay!" I squeal. I shudder again and cower down on my knees.

"What is it, Clarence?" Fogarty whispers loudly.

"T-the ghost just t-touched me," I stammer back. "But maybe it's gone. I d-don't feel it now." Sweat drips into my eyes, stinging them. I shut them for a moment, only to realize that everything looks the same whether my eyes are open or shut.

"Our plan was to go down the left passage, so let's keep to our plan and keep going," Fogarty finally suggests. I don't know if he's worried about ghosts or not, but as soon as we get ready to go, the squeaking noise pierces the air again.

We agree to get moving. Fogarty has a burst of inspiration and says, with a bit more confidence than before, "I'll go first. Tom, you follow, and put your hand on my back, so we don't lose each other in the dark. We don't want anything to separate us down here. Clarence, you go last, with your hand on Tom's back. I'll go slowly."

We travel like this for a short way, walking in silence except, every few steps, the shrill squeak returns. The sound isn't getting quieter as we go, either. I think the ghosts are following us! Either that, or we are walking toward them, which is just as bad. We haven't gone too far when, from the front of our line, I hear Fogarty yell, "Aieee!"

I hear a dull thud, followed immediately by the sound of shattering glass because Fogarty drops the lantern.

"Jim!" Daly yells. It echoes for several seconds.

"Mr. Fogarty, did the ghosts get you?" I shout forward, the pitch of my voice rising with my fear. Several seconds of more echoes. I try to take a big gasp of air but only get a little into my lungs. I'm panting badly now.

In a moment, Fogarty responds. "I'm okay, men, the ghosts didn't get me. I stepped in some water across our path, it was slimy, and I lost my footing, that's all. I'm afraid I broke our lantern, though. I guess it wasn't helping much anymore, anyway."

"The ghosts are laying traps for us," Daly says. "Just like back home in Philadelphia."

"Would you stop with the ghosts? Let's just keep going," Fogarty says.

When we continue, I put my right hand out to feel the stone wall of the catacombs while keeping my left on Daly's back.

"Clarence, don't pull so hard. You're choking me," Daly whispers back to me.

He's right. In my fear, I'd grabbed his shirt so tightly that my fingers are cramping. I try to relax them. Another shudder wracks my body.

"Sorry, sir. I'm scared, that's all."

We continue, and I put my right hand out again to feel the wall. I want to count if the passage has any side openings in case the way we are going has a dead end. After just a few steps of this, however, I feel something soft and sticky on my arm. Spider webs!

"Aaiih!" I squeal as I take my left arm off Daly's back and frantically start trying to wipe away the webs, hopping up and down.

"Clarence, what's wrong?" Fogarty says.

"Spiders! I'm trying to get them off before they can poison me!"

"How many are there? How big are they?" Daly says with alarm. As if I could tell in the blackness.

"I don't know! I put my hand through a web, and now I'm wiping it away."

Daly's doing something, but of course I can't see what. I just hear an unfamiliar sound. With no warning, something large but soft collides with my face.

"The ghosts, they're getting me!" I try to yell, but it comes out a high-pitched whine.

"That was me, Clarence," Daly says. "I'm using my vest to wipe the spiders off you." Another rush of air while Daly's vest slaps me again. I'm still hopping from one leg to the other, wiping my arms furiously.

Eventually, Daly stops swinging his vest around, and I stop to see if I've gotten all the spiders. I stand still for a moment and try to feel if any are crawling on my skin. I can't feel anything. Maybe I got them all.

"Are you okay now, Clarence?" Fogarty asks after a few moments.

"I think so, sir. I don't feel any spiders, at least. Hopefully, they are gone."

"Well, boys, what are we going to do?" Fogarty says after another moment. "We aren't getting anywhere, we don't know where we are, and every little thing that happens sends us into a panic."

"I'm hungry," Daly says as we stand and think about what Fogarty said.

"You're hungry?" Fogarty replies. "You ate enough breakfast this morning for a grizzly bear, and now you're hungry?"

"Yeah, I'm hungry. I don't even know what time it is. What if it's tomorrow already and we've been down here an entire day and night?"

That doesn't seem right to me, and I'm about to say so when I notice the squeaking noise hasn't happened for a while. I mention this to Daly and Fogarty instead.

"Maybe the ghosts just wanted to scare us away, after all," Daly says. "Now that we've left their territory, they'll leave us alone."

I think about what Daly said, but I'm panting so loudly everyone can hear me in the dark stillness.

"Clarence, what's wrong now?" Daly says.

"I'm just scared of more ghosts and spiders," I say, barely getting any words out. More sweat stings my eyes. I try to wipe them. My heart thumps so loudly in my chest, I wonder if Fogarty and Daly can hear it.

Fogarty sighs, and seems about to say something, when we hear a long, low howl. It sounds like it's coming from far away. The sound lingers for a few seconds, and then the echoes fade. It's another moment before any of us are brave enough to speak.

"More ghosts!" Daly finally says in a shrill whisper. "They're back to finish us off! Now what?"

Daly starts mumbling something to himself. I can just make out the words, "Hail Mary, full of grace" when the howling comes back, louder this time.

"That sounds like wolves," Fogarty says to us.

"How did wolves get down here?" I ask. Maybe we are near the exit after all, but now we must get past wolves!

"Awooooo!" The sound is very loud now and very close. Suddenly, I'm blinded by a brilliant light!

"The ghosts!" Daly shouts. "Run for it!"

"Yeah, run for it, Daly!"

It's Anson's voice, and instantly, insane laughter fills the corridor.

It takes some time after being in total darkness for so long, but eventually, my eyes adjust to being able to see once again. Anson stands there, doubled over in laughter, along with Pfeffer, Williamson, Ryan, Burns, Pettit, and Sullivan, who laugh at us almost as hard as Anson does.

After spending some time blinking dumbly into the light, Fogarty asks, hand shielding his eyes, "What are you guys doing here? Why didn't you help us when the light went out?"

Eventually, Anson calms down enough to explain. "You didn't think that after all the pranks you've pulled the rest of us would just let you get away with everything, did you? When I saw you planned to come down here with us, I sneaked away and dumped out most of the fuel in your lantern before I gave it to you. I hoped it would just inconvenience you by making you carry the dead weight of the lantern the whole time on the tour and you'd miss getting a good look at things. But, when you decided to take your little detour, I realized that things were going to work out better than I could ever have dreamed, especially when you decided to take a couple rubes like Tom and Clarence with you." Anson is grinning broadly while he says all of this to us.

"A set-up?" Daly asks.

"Exactly. We've been sitting here, just around this corner, with our lanterns turned down and covered for more than an hour, just listening to the three of you panic and talk about ghosts. We were lucky you decided to walk toward us, rather than away from us, so you played right into our hands. I'm surprised we managed to avoid laughing at you until the very end and didn't give the whole game away. The exit to the catacombs is right over here, by the way."

"Well done, Cap, well done," Fogarty says, reaching out to shake Anson's hand. The big first baseman extends his hand in response, but, before he can do anything else, Fogarty's fingers ball into a fist and he strikes Anson right in the stomach.

I'm worried we'll have a fight, and maybe someone else will end up in the tombs before we're done, but Anson just breaks out laughing again, satisfied that he's gotten his revenge on Fogarty. Besides, he's so large I don't think one punch could hurt him too badly, anyway.

We hear the squeaking sound again. "Here's your ghosts, boys," Sullivan says to us while he swings his lantern back and forth. Only then do we realize that the squeak of the metal handle of the lantern was what had spooked us all along. Daly stares dumbly at the lantern then looks down at the ground, his face expressionless but his cheeks turning very red. He doesn't say anything again for quite some time.

While all this takes place, I sneak around everyone toward the exit. I just want to get out in case the real ghosts do show up. When I finally reach daylight, I sit down and spend several minutes just breathing normally.

Chapter 18

February 23, 1889
Rome, Italy

Stamford Parry relays us directions in English while the Italian photographer talks to him in Italian.

"All right, let's get ready for the photograph. The All-America team can stand on my left, Chicago on the right. Mr. Spalding, you're good right there in the middle."

I'm sitting inside the Colosseum in Rome for a photograph with the teams. This place is incredible. The arches of the walls rise around me, ring after ring, three arches stacked on top of each other and supporting a fourth ring with no arches. Half of the upper ring is gone, and the bricks have weathered some over the years, but they keep their sandy-gray color. I can't tell how tall it is, but several stories, for sure. The floor of the Colosseum looks large enough that we could have played a passable game of ball here, had the Italian authorities given their approval. Looking around at everything makes me feel very small.

While the players find their spots for the photograph, Akbar, Spalding's servant, sits immediately to my right, and Spalding himself stands right behind me.

"The Romans held battles here where they fought to the death?" Anson asks the group.

"Yes, sometimes Roman gladiators fought to the death," Harry Palmer says. "They also held public executions of criminals here or organized hunts of exotic animals."

"Then why don't we have Clarence and Akbar fight to see who gets to be the Chicago mascot next season?" Pfeffer twangs.

"Sure!" Anson replies loudly. "We'll give each of them a bat for a weapon and a catcher's mask for protection and let them fight it out like the ancient gladiators. It would be baseball's version of survival of the fittest. Or, we could just hold another animal hunt and see which animal lasts longer."

"That is enough Herbert Spencer talk," Spalding says. "We're due at the Villa Borghese soon, so we need to finish the photograph and be on our way. Several American tourists in the city have delayed their travels to see us play, and if that is not motivation enough, the King of Italy himself will be there, so we'd best not disappoint His Majesty and show up tardy."

Eventually, everyone is in place, and the photographer works his camera a couple times. Then the men begin jumping down from the galleries to exit this enormous building. Newton MacMillan helps me to get down.

"Thank you, Mr. MacMillan," I say to him. Admiring the Colosseum for a few more moments, I ask, "Do you know how many people can fit in here? It is bigger than any baseball park in the United States by quite a sight."

"I can't say for certain, but tens of thousands, without doubt. Probably that is why people call it the Colosseum, because of its colossal size."

"How come we couldn't play ball here?"

"The Italian authorities said the galleries were unsafe for spectators. I'm not sure I believe that, however. The walls have stood this long; why would they collapse now? Just look at these stone arches that support everything. They don't appear on the brink of falling to me."

"How old is the Colosseum again?"

"The Romans built their arenas larger over time, but this one is nearly 2,000 years old. It stood here on this ground just about as long ago as Christianity became a religion. If you want to think of it that way."

I can't really fathom how long ago that is, but it sounds impressive, so I nod. We've been to so many grand and extremely old buildings since I got to Rome that I couldn't even begin comparing them. Maybe that is why some of the ballplayers refer to Rome as the Eternal City; one can spend an eternity looking at the famous old buildings and still not see everything.

Before we board coaches to travel to the Villa Borghese, Jim Fogarty walks over to me and hands me a small piece of stone. "I got this for you, as one last 'thank you' for helping me."

It just looks like a small chunk of stone to me and weighs just a few ounces, so I ask him, "What is it, Mr. Fogarty? Is it a special chip of stone?"

"It is. Yesterday, on our visit to St. Peter's, several of the boys and I were walking along when we came upon some workmen repairing the masonry of part of the church. We asked them if we could have chips of the marble to make into paperweights as souvenirs from our visit to Rome. They didn't know what we were talking about at first because they were Italian, but we made them understand we just wanted pieces of the floor they were trying to get rid of anyway. The masons nodded their approval, and we each grabbed a chunk. Healy told me you might be a Catholic, so I grabbed an extra one for you. Now you can walk around with a piece of sacred marble in your pocket. What do you think?"

"It is very kind of you, Mr. Fogarty. I will certainly treasure a piece of marble from St. Peter's Basilica. It is quite lovely stone, just like the church is."

"It might not be as special as a finger bone from the Roman Catacombs, but now you'll have a lucky talisman you can carry with you all the time."

"That's a good point, Mr. Fogarty. I lost my last lucky rabbit's foot some months ago, and I forgot to get a new one in Australia. This should help just as much."

With his best smile, Fogarty turns from serious back to the carefree spirit he usually displays. "I hope it will help you stay lucky, Clarence, because I could use just a bit more. Harry Palmer told me today that I rank second to last among the All-Americas in batting average on this trip. Only Healy is hitting the ball worse than I am on my team, and most of the Chicago players are getting more hits than I am, too. Do you think you could say some prayers or do something lucky, so I can get more hits? I have bets with Sullivan and Pettit of the Chicagos that I'll have a higher batting average than they do by the end of the trip. I have the lead on Pettit for now, but Sullivan is ahead of me, and I need some good luck to break into the lead over him."

"I'll try my best, Mr. Fogarty. I'm sure the piece of marble will help."

"Thanks, Clarence. I know I can count on you for good luck."

Once we near the Villa Borghese, we form up ranks and parade the rest of the way. The villa is not one single building, I learn, but the name of the entire piece of land surrounding the home of the Prince of Borghese. I also learn that the villa is a private park, although the Prince opens it to the public for several hours every week. The actual grounds for the game are at the Piazza de Sienna, which is near the middle of the park. I am in front with my baton, like usual, but instead of city streets, I'm marching through a beautiful park. Stately, tall trees line the stone path. In some places, hedges line the walkway instead of trees, and at others, little stone walls about two or three feet tall. I see statues here and there, plus a few fountains, but I can't make out too much detail about the fountains, trees, or hedges because I'm twirling my baton and must concentrate on that.

Marching in the park is easy. It has broad, gently curving paths with no potholes to watch out for and no obstacles at the side of the street. I hear birds singing in the trees and smell fresh air for the first time in several days. And it's quiet, other than us marching. A few people stroll by on occasion, but it's easy for me to avoid them.

Finally, we reach the Piazza de Sienna, and I get a hearty cheer from the American College students, who are present just as they promised. However, I stop a bit early because so many handsome carriages block the end of the route. Many have servants in livery standing nearby, so I assume they belong to very important people. Most of the servants have crests of some kind on their clothing. You don't see those too often in America, but I think it's a symbol of status.

It turns out my guess is correct. Once we get inside the grounds and the ballplayers take the field to warm up, I decide to ask MacMillan if he knows who all the important and wealthy people are.

"Well, I've been introduced to many of them because I arrived before your parade. Let me see if I can recall them all and have their names and titles straight for my newspaper article. Let's see," he says, looking up from his notebook and pointing at various people seated to watch the game. "That man is the guest of greatest honor, King Humbert of Italy."

"Is he the one in the suit there?"

"Yes, that is he."

Again, this reminds me that everything I learned in stories about kings was way off. The King of Italy looks just like a regular person. He wears no robes, has no scepter or crown, and does not even wear a military uniform today. Maybe, once I learn to read and write better, I should write my own stories about kings just to tell the world what they really look like. While I think about this, MacMillan continues.

"That man standing beside him is his son, the Prince of Naples. Next to the prince is Prime Minister Crispi, along with the minister's daughter. Flanking them, according to my notes, we have the Prince of Borghese, owner of this great park, and his daughter. Then I see Prince Colonna, Prince Corsini, Count Giannotti, Prince Torlonia, Count Ferrare, and the princesses Odescalchi, Ruspoli, Palavicini, Doria, and Rospigliochi. I wrote down who they are during my introduction to them, so hopefully I have their names correct. Over there, those men in suits are from both the British Embassy and the American Legation here in Rome. The boys from the American College you've already met, I hear."

"Yes, sir, they gave me a fine cheer when I arrived." I do not mention what else they told me back at the college.

"Although the officials of the American College try to keep the young ecclesiastics focused on their religious studies, I see that some of those same officials, Bishop McQuade included, are here, so perhaps they've recognized that having some sporting blood is not too grave a sin. I can think of at least seven more deadly ones, at any rate." He punctuates this last remark with a smile and a laugh, although I don't understand why it's funny.

The game turns out to be one of the best of the entire trip. The Chicago team wins it, 3-2, and the fielding of the boys today is spectacular. Fred Carroll of the All-America team hits a home run, but it is not enough to overcome doubles hit by Tom Daly and Fred Pfeffer, plus a triple by Tom Burns, for the Chicago nine. I'm afraid my efforts to bring good luck to Jim Fogarty have finally run out, though, because today he gets no hits in three times at bat.

Soon, we'll be on our way northward from Rome. After a short pause in the city of Florence, our next country to visit is France.

Chapter 19

Jim Fogarty didn't get any hits during the game in Rome, and he does even worse in his next game in Florence. Once again, he gets no hits even though he goes to bat five times. I wonder if he is losing confidence in me. When we get off our train in the French city of Nice, he approaches me while we wait for transportation to our hotel.

"Well, Clarence, no hits again in Florence. I wonder what's wrong with me. You said you'd bring me luck."

"I know I said it. I can't figure out why my luck doesn't work anymore. Maybe I used all of it on Mount Vesuvius."

"That could be true. I can't think of any other way to explain it, except that, maybe, just being in Italy doesn't agree with you when it comes to mascoting at baseball games. Maybe, when it comes to baseball, Italy is your Jonah."

"What do you mean, my Jonah?"

"When someone or something is bad luck, we ballplayers say it's a Jonah. It's just an expression we use."

"Can you get rid of your Jonah?"

"Sure, you can. I'm hoping that, now that we've crossed over the border and arrived in France, you'll have your old luck again. You'd better because when the players go to gamble at Monte Carlo tonight, I'm going to need all of it I can get."

"Where is Monte Carlo? I thought we were in Nice."

"We are in Nice, but right by this city is a place named Monte Carlo. It has some of the fanciest gambling casinos in the world, and tonight I plan to try my luck."

"Well, here, why don't you take my piece of marble from St. Peter's for some luck? If it doesn't work, you can give it back, and we'll try something else."

"I don't know if that's a good idea, Clarence, mixing religion and gambling, although, maybe that is just what I need to change my luck. Maybe I need to try some things that no one would expect. Sure, let's give it a shot."

I hand over the marble chip of stone, and Fogarty takes it as he walks toward a carriage. I think about the fact that an entire place nearby exists dedicated to gambling. Knowing how reckless some of our boys can be, I'm not sure that it is a very good idea for them to go there.

Sometime after midnight, I awaken to a pounding on my hotel door. "Clarence, open the door! It's Jim! We did it!"

It takes me a minute to get my wits about me, but once I wake up I walk to the door and open it.

"Look at this, Clarence! I won 400 francs! Your luck is back!"

From the smell of it, I'd say that in addition to gambling, Fogarty has had more than his share of wine this evening. Whatever he did, however, it worked, because he is waving several coins in my face as the spoils of victory.

"How many dollars is that worth?"

"They tell me it's about $80. Not bad for an evening at the roulette table, is it? I've got a few francs for you, for getting your luck back and sharing it with me."

He hands me some coins. Tomorrow I'll have to find out from Tener or someone how much they are worth, but for now, it makes the interruption to my sleep a great deal easier to accept.

"Thank you very much, Mr. Fogarty! How did the other boys do?"

"Oh, you know, some of them came away winners, some did not. George Wood is in a celebrating mood, I hear, and so are Anson, his wife, and Spalding. Say, Clarence, care to join us for a victory drink? The hotel bar is still open."

Remembering my last time drinking with Fogarty, I say, "No thank you, sir, but that is very generous of you. Good night, and I'm glad your luck is back."

"Where are we going again, Mr. Crane?" I ask the big pitcher while we take up spots along a crowded street the next morning.

"We're at the carnival, Clarence."

"This doesn't look like a carnival in Chicago. It just looks like a parade to me."

"It is a parade, but with a twist. You've got your flowers, right?"

"Yes, Mr. Crane."

"Well, in this parade, the point is to hit the marchers with flowers when they go by. They might throw some back at you, so be ready."

"So, throwing flowers makes it a carnival?"

"In this case, it does. If you can believe it, the French call this festival 'The Battle of the Flowers.'"

"It sounds like a funny thing to do if you ask me."

"I agree, Clarence, but we're in France now. This appears to be a strange land. They don't even have a cricket grounds or any other kind of grounds large enough to play a game of ball here. I must throw something if I'm to keep my pitching arm in shape until we get to Paris. That's why I'm throwing flowers along with everyone else today. I hope the Parisians are a little more sporting than these folks are."

Looking down the hill at Nice's waterfront and the white sand beaches I can see from the parade route, I say, "Maybe they like to spend their time at the beach instead." Even though today is a bit on the cool side for going to the beach, I do see a few people walking through the sand here and there. A fresh breeze wafts our way, coming off the water. It's a mixture of saltwater and the crisp, clean smell that comes after a recent rain.

"That might explain a few things," Crane tells me. "The people here appear the slothful, lazy type who might prefer a day in the sand to the manly exercise of a sport like baseball. Well, whatever the case, at least the rain is gone. Yesterday it came down in sheets."

"Welcome, Ed Crane and Clarence Duval, to the French Riviera!" Mark Baldwin exclaims in his high-pitched voice while making a mocking bow. As he does, we take our position on the edge of the street overlooking the beautifully blue and peaceful French Mediterranean. "Take your places, gentlemen. I see you are both liberally supplied with weapons for today's duel."

Crane turns to John Healy, who stands next to Baldwin. "Has Baldy been drinking already today, John?"

"Does the Sun rise in the East? You know the answer to that even without asking, I hope."

"It is a little early for rushing the growler, or the wine bottle, isn't it?" Crane says to Baldwin.

"We are at a celebration, are we not?" Baldwin says in his own defense. "Why not celebrate in style?" He turns to wave to some French women in fancy light-blue lace dresses. He even blows them kisses.

"He hasn't been quite the same since his pet monkey bit him," I hear Healy say to Crane. "Not that he was a picture of maturity before, but do you think he's contracted some kind of exotic disease?"

196

Crane answers, "I don't know, but it's true he's been crooking his elbow and lifting the wine glass almost nonstop since we reached Italy. Does he still have the monkey?"

"No. I believe it ran away from him on the *Salier*, and he never recaptured it. Speaking of monkeys, Ed, how is yours?"

"Patrick is doing just fine. He walked around in my hotel room last night when I let him out for a while, and he's just the kindest, tamest creature. I have no idea what to do with him when I get back to America, but he deserves a good home. I'll do my best to take care of him, but when we go on road trips, I'm not sure what to do with him. Maybe we can bring him along for luck."

"You'll figure something out, I suppose, if the monkey makes it back to America alive. In the meantime, however, look at this array of flowers I've picked out." Healy extends his bushel of flowers for Crane's inspection.

"What is special about them? The whole point is to throw them at the people in the parade, isn't it?"

"Yes, but I selected mine purely for weight and balance. I don't even know what kind they are, but we want all these French to know what American ballplayers can do, don't we? Pitchers such as you and I should be more accurate than these society dudes are when throwing flowers. We are professionals, after all."

"You might be taking this a little too seriously," Crane says dubiously while scanning the crowd. "If you and Baldwin had split the wine fifty-fifty this morning, it might have come out about right."

Healy smiles at this ribbing and says, "Perhaps you are right. With Clarence here beside us to bring us luck, we're sure to hit whatever we're aiming at. It worked for Fogarty, anyway."

Now it's my turn to smile. I know I'm not really a member of the teams, but at least these players tolerate my presence without wanting me to be shark bait or a gladiator. Soon, I hear an excited babble coming from the streets. The parade, and The Battle of the Flowers, has begun.

It turns out to be more entertaining than I'd imagined it would be. I'm a little surprised that both men and women ride by in carriages as part of the festival. This, however, only encourages the men to throw more flowers at the women they find most charming. Things have been going on for a while when a handsome coach, drawn by four jet-black horses, comes trotting slowly down the street. Healy and Crane still stand next to me, although they spend about as much time keeping Baldwin from wandering onto the parade route as they do throwing their flowers.

"Ed, is that who I think it is?" Healy says.

"That depends. Who do you think it is?" Crane replies.

I look at the man riding in the open carriage. He is not very tall, and somewhat overweight. The man sports a red beard, pointed at the bottom, and a dark suit, and he is enjoying the fun immensely, flinging flowers left and right.

Healy scowls and gets a twitch in his cheek I've never seen before. "It looks like the Prince of Wales," he says, almost growling the words.

"I think you're right," Crane replies.

"Are you thinking what I'm thinking, Ed?"

"Absolutely."

The two pitchers take aim, and, to my surprise, their flowers hit the Prince dead in the face. They give an excited cheer. Maybe picking flower bouquets for their weight and balance was a good idea, after all.

The Prince scowls briefly at their exaggerated show of excitement, but quickly recovers his composure, smiles, and fires back a bouquet of violets at the two pitchers before proceeding on with the parade. His aim is not as precise, however, and he misses. The Prince is out of range before Crane or Healy can think of responding with another volley. Besides, they are too busy chasing down the errant violets. Healy gets to them first and gathers them up.

They return to their places next to me. "Mr. Healy," I ask, "why did you shout so loud when you hit the Prince? You didn't do that for any of the other carriages in the parade."

"No, lad, I didn't. You don't know who the Prince of Wales is, do you?"

"If he's a prince, isn't he next in line to be King of Wales?"

"Not exactly, although that is a reasonable conclusion. The Prince of Wales is next in line for the throne of Great Britain."

Then it dawns on me why Healy is so excited. He still wants to free Ireland from Great Britain, and the Prince of Wales is part of the British royal family. After telling me this, he looks away, just staring into the distance.

Before I can say anything else, however, Baldwin wanders off again and is on one knee speaking to some French damsel who, I'm sure, only speaks French and has no idea what Baldwin is trying to tell her. Crane notices it, too, and heads over to retrieve the drunken Chicago pitcher before the woman slaps his face.

While Crane does that, Healy steps backward from the line of flower throwers so that a little distance separates him from everyone else in the line. He gets down on one knee and motions me in close, so he can speak into my ear. "I'm going to keep this bouquet of violets as a symbol that someday Ireland will be free."

"That sounds good, Mr. Healy. They will make a fine souvenir, I suppose. I take it you still have plans to free Ireland on this trip, like we talked about?"

"You bet I have a plan. According to what people tell me about this parade, the carriages go down the street one way, and then they come back again before the parade is over."

"So, you are keeping the flowers to throw at him the next time? How can you do that and keep them as a symbol, too?"

"No, lad, that isn't what they're for, not by a long shot. Clarence, have you told anyone of our partnership to free Ireland?"

"No, Mr. Healy."

"You promise?"

"Yes, I promise. I haven't told anyone because you told me not to."

"That is good because now I have a plan to free Ireland. You still promise to help me?"

"I always try to keep my promises."

"Excellent." Healy's face takes on a new look I've never seen before, and he stares right into my eyes with more intensity than I've ever seen him show on the ball field. His stare almost burns through me. He says to me, quietly but clearly, "Clarence, we are going to kill the Prince of Wales." Healy pats his side, and I see the outline of a pistol underneath his jacket.

It is probably only a few seconds, but I stare at Healy's face for what seems like an hour. I can't believe what he just told me, so I stare at him blankly. Finally, I manage to stammer, "Y-you want me to help you kill s-someone?"

"Yes. We are going to do it here, today."

"Why right now? How will that free Ireland?"

"It is the deed that will provide a spark, igniting the masses of Ireland to rise against their foreign oppressors. All they need is something—a great deed, a heroic action—to ignite their passions and rouse them to throw off their shackles."

"I can't do that! I've never killed anyone."

"You don't have to kill anyone. This is all you need to do. When the prince's carriage comes back up the street, grab some flowers and run toward his carriage like you are going to hand them to him. He'll stand and face you when you approach, and I'll have a clear shot when he turns toward you. No one will even suspect you were part of a plot."

"What will happen to you, Mr. Healy? I see police every fifty feet or so on the parade route."

"I don't know what might happen, but I'm willing to let the hide fall with the hair. My plan is to escape in the commotion."

"Please don't ask me to help you, Mr. Healy. It isn't right!"

"You promised, Clarence!"

"I did promise, but I didn't think this was what you meant! I just can't do it."

"You'll do it. Just walk onto the parade route with your flowers when you see the Prince on his way. Here, take this bouquet. Now, get yourself in position."

This is the wrong thing to do, and I know it. I gave a promise, though. If I break it, I'll be just like all the other people on our trip who say one thing but do something else. But, I can't be part of killing someone. Even if the French police don't catch me, my conscience will. I don't know what I should do!

Healy has moved about ten or fifteen feet to my left, probably so it won't appear that we are working together. He glances at me with that strange look of focus and determination. His right hand moves to his side.

I see the carriage approach, its shiny black horses out in front. It comes into view, moving from my right to my left, coming closer and closer. Soon, it is almost even with me. My heart pounding and my ears ringing, I step into the street.

I take three quick steps toward the carriage before anyone can grab me and pull me back. Without warning, I step in a muddy spot left over from all the rain yesterday. While my feet slide forward out from under me, I wave my arms frantically for balance, but I lose my footing anyway and land on my backside, flowers falling all around me. Sitting up so that I can look forward, I can see the Prince stand up to get a view of what's happened. I also hear the spectators lining the street laughing at me. Frantically, I look back over my left shoulder to see what Healy does. He reaches for his pistol and takes two steps forward.

Before he can even grab the weapon or raise his arm, however, the drunken Mark Baldwin slams into him, and they crash down in a heap. Baldwin lands on top of Healy, and because he's drunk and lacks coordination, needs a minute to regain his feet.

"Oh, ssorry, John," Baldwin manages to say as he finally stands up. He offers his hand to Healy and pulls him up, too. "I wass jusst going to help Clarencse, and you got in the way. Can't have the masscot of our nine lying in the mud in front of the Princse of Waless now, can we? That might look bad for all of thesse fine French ladiess."

I look back to the street and see that the Prince's carriage has already resumed its course, the Prince tossing more flowers as it goes. It appears that the danger is over. I look over at Healy again while I stand up myself.

He stares at the carriage while it passes down the street, slowly dwindling in size. "It's okay, Baldy, it's nothing." Baldwin is too drunk to notice that Healy says this in a flat monotone, almost as if the words came from someone else.

I take a quick look around. Most of the people have stopped laughing and resumed watching the parade. I see one man on the other side of the street, dressed in the rough clothes of a dockworker, looking at our group for a moment, but after a quick glance he, too, goes back to watching what's happening in the street. The drama passes. My shoulders slump, and I give a huge sigh.

The parade ends soon after that. We return to our hotel to prepare to travel to our next destination, which is Paris. My pants are muddy, of course, but I get them as clean as I can. On my way downstairs to the carriages that will take us to the train station, I walk past Healy's room. I stop for a moment outside his door, considering whether I should knock. Unsure of what I should do, I put my ear to the door to try to discover if he's still inside. I hear him crying.

I decide not to knock. I've also decided that, even though I always try to be honest, I won't ever tell anyone how I slipped in the mud on purpose.

Chapter 20

March 5, 1889
Paris, France

I haven't spoken much with John Healy since the parade in Nice. This evening, however, he joins most of the ballplayers in the lobby of our Paris hotel, the Hotel St. Petersburg. All the boys are anxious to play a game of ball for the Parisians, but Leigh Lynch has been unable to find a suitable place to play, and so once again, the boys are taking in the sights of the city. I'm standing by Healy trying to think of what to say because he's barely said a word since boarding the train from Nice. He sits apart from the rest of the group while they decide where they each want to go.

Before I can decide what to tell Healy, Johnny Ward comes over to us. Unlike Healy, Ward's smiling and talking with everyone he meets. He's practically bouncing around the hotel lobby. I haven't seen him look this happy and excited in quite some time. "John," Ward says to Healy, "aren't you going to join us for the evening? Today is Shrove Tuesday, the conclusion of the carnival season here in Paris. That means that people throughout the whole city will dress up in masks and costumes and party all night long. Our group's plan is to start with the Comedie Francaise, which is the home of the dramatic arts in Paris. Then, we're going to the Jardin Bullier, where they have a ball for the students of the city. People tell me that the ball features nearly 5,000 dancers in a gigantic pavilion hall. Students in black tights hold hands and run through the crowd in lines even while you're trying to dance, knocking people down in every direction. It'll be wild fun! Next, at midnight, we plan to attend the great ball at the Eden Theater. It's going to be full dress, with an orchestra, dance floor, ballet dancers, everything first class, all lit by gas lighting. There'll be Parisian beauties everywhere. Finally, when all the formal events conclude, we plan to walk the boulevards and visit the cafés of the city until the sun comes up. Are you with us?"

Healy just sits and thinks for several moments before answering. "It sounds great, Johnny, but I don't think it's for me. I'm still very tired from our travels and from last night, and I don't know if I can handle all that again tonight. I think I'll try something a little tamer."

Ward's brow furrows. "Are you all right, John? You've been real quiet the last couple days."

"I'm fine, Johnny. Really, I'm fine. I'm just tired, and my head hurts. It sounds like a great adventure, but I just don't know if I can handle it tonight."

"Are you sure? You know we'll never get another chance at being part of a Paris carnival, don't you?"

"You go on, Johnny, and have yourself a time. I'm just not up for it tonight, okay?"

"Well, I suppose you know your own business best, but now that you know where we'll be, you can find us if you change your mind."

When Ward departs, a spring in his step, the rest of the ballplayers begin filing out of the lobby themselves, equally anxious for whatever awaits them and anticipating an evening full of memories, if their excited chatter is any indication. Ward never asked me if I wanted to go anywhere. No one else does, either, not even Fogarty. I imagine he's too distracted to worry about me tonight.

The two of us just sit there for a while in silence. Healy looks at me for a moment before dropping his head to look at the table while his shoulders droop lower than ever. "Come on, Clarence," he mumbles to me quietly, chin cupped in his hands, "let's go for a little walk."

We meander along a main street named the Rue de la Paix, Healy walking slowly and me alongside. He hasn't said anything more since we left the hotel, and I'm starting to wonder if he's upset with me about what happened in Nice. The streets still have large crowds because of the festival, and several times someone jostles us as we walk along. Streetlights brighten things here and there, but the illumination is modest, at best.

Healy just walks along with his head down, hands in his pockets, only looking up now and then to avoid colliding with oncoming people. Finally, he turns and looks at me, his face expressionless other than a glint of a tear in one eye. "Our chance is gone, Clarence. We missed our chance."

I continue walking next to him, sidestepping another person on the sidewalk. "I guess we did. I'm sorry, Mr. Healy. I tried to do my part, even though I was scared, but I just slipped. And then Mr. Baldwin ran into you."

"It isn't your fault, Clarence. If Baldwin hadn't have gotten himself drunk, the plan might still have worked, but I don't think I'll ever get another chance now."

"You said that the Prince of Wales was heir to the throne of Britain, right? Aren't we going to Britain after we leave France?"

I say this to cheer him up, but I realize I should probably shut up about the matter before Healy comes up with another plan requiring my help. We part momentarily to get around another group of people standing in our path, their animated faces gazing at the buildings that line the street. I smell wine and cigarettes. After doing so, I'm next to Healy again, and he continues.

"Yes, we are, but things will be different there. We might meet the Prince again, but the circumstances will not be the same. The anonymity of the parade was our best chance to pull it off, but it's over now."

"I know it's not really my place, Mr. Healy, but can you explain again how this was going to help us free Ireland?"

"Have you ever heard anything about the philosophy of anarchism, Clarence?"

"I'm afraid not, sir, but then again, I'm only twelve."

"I'm a little surprised, seeing that you are from Chicago, where the Haymarket Square murders happened back in '86, but I guess your age is probably the reason."

"I was at Haymarket Square when the killings happened, Mr. Healy. But, no one told me anything about anarchism. I was too busy crying after the police killed my friend Tommy."

"Yes, I remember that now, Clarence. You told me about it once, early on in our adventure. Let me tell you a bit more of the story, so you'll understand better. Anarchists like me believe that government and authority are among the most important sources of evil and suffering in the world. It is because of government using its power on the side of the wealthy that workers and regular people lead miserable lives so much of the time. Do you want to hear the rest of the story of what happened at Haymarket Square?"

"I suppose so," I say as I walk along, thinking whether I should try to change the subject.

"It began in May of 1886 when the city police murdered two workers at the McCormick plant in Chicago. Shot them in cold blood. They were marching for an eight-hour workday. Many people were striking in the city that month, about 40,000 of them, because their working conditions were so miserable. The evening of the murders, one of the working-class newspapers in Chicago called for a meeting in Haymarket Square the next day to come up with a response to these foul deeds. That was on May 4. It was a peaceful meeting. When it was almost over, it started raining, and things were starting to break up when the Chicago police showed up again. Before anything else could happen, a bomb went off and killed some of the police. No one knows who threw the bomb, although I suspect someone in the police force planted it to discredit the anarchist cause.

"The mayor of the city, Carter Harrison, got scared after that and started taking away even more of the rights of working people. He suspended public meetings and processions and had the authorities destroy printing presses that were loyal to the labor movement, completely ignoring the First Amendment to the U.S. Constitution. The regular press tried to scapegoat foreigners and anyone involved in the labor movement. The worst part is that the authorities put eight anarchists on trial for murder, even though seven of them weren't even at Haymarket Square that day and the eighth one was the speaker on the platform, and hundreds of eyewitnesses could prove he didn't do it."

"What happened at their trial?"

Very animated at last, Healy waves his arms and gestures wildly as he continues, nearly smacking some passersby. "Some newspapers offered money to the jury to come back with a guilty verdict. The judge, Joseph Gary, curse his name, didn't even pretend to uphold the law at their trial. The jury found all eight men guilty and Judge Gary sentenced them all to death. The state of Illinois hanged four of them already, and a fifth committed suicide before the law could hang him, too. The other three are still in prison. Or, at least, they were still in prison when we left San Francisco last year."

"That doesn't sound very fair at all."

"No, Clarence, it isn't. The law, the authorities, and the government aren't about being fair. They are about protecting the wealthy while the wealthy steal from the poor, miserable working people of the world. I'm sure you've met plenty of miserable people on the streets of Chicago, right?"

"I see a lot of them, yes. I know lots of people like me who must beg for meals or beg to get work every day, so they can feed themselves. Some days I get a bit of food, and I'm not too hungry, but not every day."

"According to what anarchists believe, government and the leaders of industry are to blame. People today are one hundred times more productive than our ancestors were, but many of us have lives that are just as wretched, poor, filthy, and hungry as people who lived in caves thousands of years ago. The reason why is that governments and the capitalist class governments support have mismanaged the wealth everyone produces and stolen most of it for themselves."

I'm a little confused at this point. I'm not sure exactly what a capitalist is, except that they are allies of governments, but I'm even more confused about what all of this has to do with Ireland, so, after ducking under the arms of a drunk person singing in the street, I ask Healy the question that seems most important to me. "Mr. Healy, may I ask how this relates to freeing Ireland from the British?"

"I apologize, Clarence, for taking some time to explain anarchism, but the answer to your question follows from what I've told you. If we get rid of national governments and the capitalists, workers and regular people will run things for themselves and won't have the profits of their labor stolen from them anymore. The idea is to get rid of government. If that happens, the British government won't control Ireland, and the Irish people will be free at last."

"But, I don't get it. How does killing a prince help get rid of government? If he dies, there's probably another prince to take his place, right?"

"Well, Clarence, anarchists believe that to get rid of government, people need a spark, a valiant deed, a dramatic event, a transcendent act, something to rouse their passions and channel their anger toward their oppressors. My belief is that if I had managed to shoot the Prince of Wales, the British authorities would crack down on people. This would push the people over the edge and give them cause to rise against the oppression of the British."

I know very little about how governments work, and I have no idea if Healy's plans are good ones with any chance of success, so I just nod my head while he speaks. In any case, he's already admitted that his plans failed, so hopefully, I won't need to join him in any more plots. Helping him free Ireland sounded like a good idea when he first mentioned it, but perhaps I need to be more careful about what I agree to do in the future.

Because I'm listening to what Healy says, I don't notice too much about our surroundings. I keep dodging the people moving through the streets. Sometimes other people come up behind us and pass around us because I don't walk that fast, but it happens often enough that I barely notice them.

Healy, who doesn't take much notice, either, finishes speaking and gets quiet again. We turn onto a new street, the Rue Rivoli. After walking a bit farther in silence, we come to a part of the street lined with stalls of street merchants. Healy points ahead of us. "See that building there, Clarence?"

"Yes, Mr. Healy."

"That is the Louvre. It is a museum with many pieces of famous artwork, one of the most famous museums in the world."

I look around at the stalls of the merchants while he speaks to me. "Is that where all the paintings in these booths come from? Are they copies of the paintings in the museum? Several of these merchants appear to have the same paintings."

"I believe you're right."

Suddenly, we both feel a firm hand clasp each of our shoulders. "Excuse me, friends, might I have a word with you?" a voice says.

We both jump at this surprise, but the hand does not let go of me. I turn to see it's the rough, calloused hand of someone who works for a living.

The voice, which, although in English, features an Italian accent, comes from a man of modest height, wearing a light-brown workers' jacket with a patch on the left elbow, who has slightly messy brown hair and a full, dark mustache. A dark scar mars his right cheek.

"Please," the man says, "I would like to speak to the two of you, if I may. I apologize if I've taken you by surprise, but I believe we may have some common interests we might discuss. Let me introduce myself. My name is Errico Malatesta."

The man lets go of us and backs up one step, and Healy looks him up and down for several seconds. Healy looks suspicious of Malatesta. His hand drifts to his side.

"Please, sir, you have no need to reach for your concealed pistol. Might we find a nearby café and have a talk?"

"How did you know I'm armed?"

"I know you carry a pistol because I saw you at The Battle of the Flowers in Nice. I know you're armed and apparently unafraid to use your weapon. You are one of the American baseball players, are you not?"

"I am," Healy says, speaking slowly and carefully, "but I'm not so sure you are really Errico Malatesta. How do we know you aren't part of the French police in disguise? Or someone else entirely?"

"Do you see any of my fellow deputies running in to arrest you?" the man counters. "For that matter, do you think the French police would have let you board a train from Nice to Paris and check into your hotel unmolested if they really planned to arrest you for trying to kill the Prince of Wales?"

"Perhaps not, but Malatesta is supposed to be in Argentina."

"Indeed, I was. I've spent the past four years living in Buenos Aires, trying to educate the workers there. I also spent time prospecting for gold, so I could contribute more money to our cause. My friends and I found some, too, but the Argentine government confiscated our claim once it discovered my identity. As a result, this winter I returned to Europe, although not to Italy. Right now, I live in Nice. I'm trying to inspire the revolutionary potential of the dockworkers there. If you do not believe I am truly Errico Malatesta, allow me to present you a complimentary copy of my newest publication, *L'Associazione*." He unfolds a four-page newspaper from inside his jacket and hands it to Healy.

Healy accepts the paper and resumes examining the man. "Perhaps you are Errico Malatesta. But even if you are, why follow us all the way to Paris from Nice?"

"Well, the carnival in Paris is something to behold, is it not?" Malatesta says with a smile, holding up his arms, palms to the night sky, and turning in a circle, as if to take in the entire city with his gesture. "Encouraging revolution is a difficult calling, and it helps to relieve the tension now and then with a bit of fun. I am happy to tell you more. However, shall we find a location a bit more private than the open street? I know a man who owns a café nearby where we can speak without concern of someone overhearing us who shouldn't."

Soon, we sit across from Malatesta at a back table of a Paris coffee house. The place itself is rather quiet because most of the people are outdoors at the carnival this evening. After saying something to the waiter in French and handing him a few coins, Malatesta turns to us and begins speaking in a quiet but firm voice. The waiter returns shortly with three glasses of wine, sets them down, and departs silently.

Malatesta begins. "First, allow me to explain how we came to meet in Paris this evening. Like I said, I am currently living in Nice, which your party of ballplayers just passed through on your way to this fine city. I had no idea who any of you were when you arrived; I'm afraid being a revolutionary leaves little time for leisure and sport. As pure luck would have it, I happened to be standing directly across from you during The Battle of the Flowers, although you probably never noticed me, given your, shall we say, other preoccupations."

"Go on," Healy says to him.

"You drew my attention when you and your teammate first succeeded in hitting the Prince in the face with your bouquets. Your little demonstration of excitement was rather out of tune with the

211

behavior of the other people watching the parade, so I decided to observe more closely. Next, you took your young companion here aside for a little talk, during which he started looking rather excited and nervous."

"My name is Clarence," I say to the man, whom I'm still not sure I like. Although, there does seem to be something about him, an earnestness, maybe, a quiet charisma, that I don't see in many other people.

"Clarence, then," he says with a smile. "During your chat, Clarence appeared uncertain and very agitated about whatever you told him. When I saw that the Prince was nearly even with us, I looked over to see what you were doing—and saw that your face was notably tenser and more serious than before. When the Prince passed by and Clarence had his unfortunate slip in the mud, I saw you reach for your side, I assume to draw the same concealed pistol you have with you right now. If that drunken buffoon of a teammate had not blundered into you at exactly that moment, you might have changed the course of history considerably."

"You seem awfully interested in our doings for a chance meeting like you say," Healy says to Malatesta.

"What can I say? The authorities have hounded me from my home so many times that I've lost count. When you live the life I've chosen, you become very observant of every small detail and unexpected movement in the people around you. The only reason I dared go to the parade in the first place was that I haven't lived in Nice long enough for all of the local police to know who I am yet."

"So why did you follow us here, then? You know that we failed in our mission if you were there."

"You failed, yes, but it would have been a beautiful deed. You have my compliments." At this point, Malatesta raises his wine glass and toasts us silently. Healy tentatively returns the gesture, although he does smile a bit.

Malatesta continues. "Although it appeared to me that you intended to do away with the Prince, I was still unsure of the motive

212

behind your intent, of course. Again, as luck would have it, the brother of a dockworker I know well is a porter at your hotel in Nice. I inquired of the man who you were, and he told me your party consisted of American baseball players on their way to Paris. It wasn't until I followed you this evening, however, and overheard your conversation about anarchism that I realized we are brothers in our cause. At that point, I decided to reveal my identity to you. And here we are."

With that, Malatesta folds his hands on the table and smiles calmly, waiting for Healy's reaction. Finally, the pitcher decides to speak.

"You are sure we can speak freely here?"

"Quite sure. Our waiter is a friend of mine. I did some work for his father when I first came to Paris almost a decade ago, after the Italian authorities expelled me from my home country for the first time. He will warn us should any of the French police come near. The back door is down yonder hallway." He points to a dark passage near our table. "Simply turn left, then right, and you can escape into the crowded streets unnoticed through the alleyway."

"We don't get much anarchist literature in America, Errico," Healy says in a more relaxed tone, a bit of enthusiasm in his voice once again, "so I've read only a few issues of *La Questione Sociale*, but it's an inspiration to those of us exiled in America who would see Ireland free of British rule."

"Thank you for the compliment. It has been some years now since those heady days in Florence when I worked on that paper while staying underground to evade the Florentine police."

"But as you know if you saw The Battle of the Flowers, my efforts failed. I've missed my only chance to perform the propaganda of the deed and spark my people into action."

"Don't feel badly, Mr. Healy. When you become a revolutionary, you discover that failure is normal, and success is exceptional. Perhaps it is not that way in baseball, but I've tried to ignite revolution many times and failed without exception. You may

213

recall that I went to Egypt to fight against the British in the Anglo-Egyptian War back in 1882. I don't think I killed any Brits, but it was the act of trying to fight that mattered. My scar that I acquired in Egypt reminds me of the fact daily."

Although the man speaks quietly, he has an air of honesty and sincerity surrounding him. I like him better the more I listen. Maybe I'm wrong, but I get the feeling he is a man who truly believes what he says, and he's told us a great deal about himself, trusting that we won't reveal his identity to anyone. Beyond that, he just has a way of speaking that's hard to describe—a friendly smile at just the right time, a clap of the hands or a slap of the table at a crucial point in his story, or a pause to sip his wine while a point sinks in—that makes me wish he could succeed, just once. I have the impression he is not a man who would say one thing to my face and write something else in the newspapers.

While Healy and I listen, he continues speaking. "Yet, despite all my failures, I still believe in the cause, and I will fight for it as long as I have the strength to fight. You cannot let the failure burden you too deeply, my friend. I still love my friends in the struggle, and I still refuse to hate my enemies. We will triumph in the end, however long the fight."

"Thank you," Healy says, then adds, "that was my first attempt at revolution, but I don't see how I will ever get another try."

At this statement, Malatesta's eyes brighten. "What if I told you we might?"

Healy straightens up. "I'm listening."

I put my quivering hands under the table and bite my lip to try to hide how scared I am at this news.

"My friend in Nice, the porter at your hotel, overheard some member of your party mention the fact that the French president, Sadi Carnot, is invited to your game in Paris. If he accepts the invitation, we may get another opportunity."

"I'll be on the field playing ball, though. How can I help? There will be no place to hide, like I had on the parade route. And how will this help free Ireland?"

"Our goal is to free all the working class, all the people everywhere, isn't it?"

"Yes, that is true," Healy concedes.

"You might not be able to hide in the crowd, but I can. If your game takes place in a cricket oval, I'll arrange to hide in the standing crowd. What if, for example, President Carnot leaves himself out in the open and gets up from his seat? What if he decides to shake the hands of all the ballplayers and goes onto the field? I might get a clear shot at him when he finishes and returns to his seat."

"I still don't see how I can assist you while I'm on the field. You could do any of those things without me."

I'm relieved when Healy uses the word "me" instead of "us."

"What I need you to do is to cause as much confusion as possible after the deed is done. Perhaps you can fake that I've shot you as well, to draw peoples' eyes away from Carnot. You could also call attention to the wrong part of the crowd or misidentify the shooter, or 'accidentally' run into any pursuers while claiming to be chasing me down. I'm sure you can think of some reasonable distraction, between you and your partner Clarence."

At the mention of my name in another plot, I feel I'd better say something. "Please don't ask me to do this again, Mr. Healy," I plead nervously. "You know I didn't want to do it the first time, and I'm too scared to try again."

"But Clarence, you are one of us now," Healy tells me. "You have to help. You still want to free Ireland, don't you?"

"Yes, but I don't want to do it by killing any people. I told you that before, and I can't bring myself to do it again."

"How old are you, my young friend?" Malatesta asks me.

"I'm only twelve."

"I suspected as much. Perhaps the lad is too young. I mean no criticism of your methods, but can I ask why you involved the young man in your plans to begin with, Mr. Healy?"

"I asked Clarence to help because none of the other players understand our cause. Some hate the Irish. Many don't care about politics. Most of them just want to play ball on this trip and enjoy themselves. They simply want to eat, drink, and go to fancy ceremonies where they can hobnob with the local bourgeoisie and royalty, the very leaders who oppress the people of the world. I had no one else to turn to. Besides, Clarence knows, all too well, what it's like to have people push you around and take advantage of you, just like the Irish do. Just like the working class does," he adds quickly.

"Ah, yes, the plight of the Negro in the United States is known to some of us here in Europe. Their exploitation is yet another wrong that we anarchists will undo when our moment comes," Malatesta says to me.

"That sounds like a very good idea, sir," I answer him. "But please tell Mr. Healy not to make me take part in this new plan. If you two work together, you don't need my help, right? I promise I'll never say a word no matter what happens. Most people think I'm stupid, so they probably won't even think to ask me about it, anyway."

"Let me think on things and plan out our actions in more detail," Malatesta says. "The morning of your game here in Paris, I'll pass through the smoking room of your hotel at nine o'clock. Wait ten minutes and follow me out into the street. I'll let you know what we plan to do and if we'll need your help, Clarence."

With that, Malatesta drains his wine glass, wishes us good health, and leaves by the back door.

A few minutes later, we do the same. All the way back to our hotel, I plead with Healy to leave me out of this new plan, but he has that strangely intense look on his face again.

Chapter 21

March 6, 1889
Paris, France

It is after eleven o'clock the next morning when the ballplayers start trickling downstairs after their night on the town. If I'm not mistaken, Healy and I were the only ones to rest our heads before midnight. Even Palmer and MacMillan, usually among the more sober members of our party, don't appear until eleven, and when they do, they spend lots of time rubbing their foreheads and scowling as if they are in pain. The two men sit down next to George Wood, who must have been with them last night because they begin going over what they did almost immediately. Although I finished my breakfast long ago, I sit near enough to overhear them.

Wood speaks first. "You two look a little the worse for wear this morning, if we can even call it morning at this point. What time did we finally get back to the hotel? I went straight to sleep without even checking a clock."

"Half past five, or thereabouts, I believe," MacMillan answers him. "That is a night I'll never forget. I wasn't sure anything would top the luau and hula dancing in Honolulu for me, but I think last night did it."

"And to think, we were far from the last members of our party to turn in," Palmer adds. "Did either of you ever learn what became of Ed Crane or Ned Hanlon?"

"I don't know," MacMillan answers. "I was with you when we saw them disappear from the Eden with those French damsels on their arms. Do you know, George?"

"I've no idea," Wood replies. "For all I know, they've been challenged to a duel by some jealous French aristocrat. However, since I beat you gentlemen downstairs by a few minutes, I've learned that Leigh Lynch has arranged for us to play a game in Paris at last."

"Where?" both men ask in unison.

"We will play at Park Aerostatique two days from today, on the eighth. My geography of Paris is a bit sketchy, but I believe the park is on the banks of the Seine."

"No game for two days?" Palmer says.

"That's what I heard."

"You know what that means?" Palmer inquires, looking at his two companions, the pain in his forehead temporarily forgotten.

"We're going out again tonight to paint the town, aren't we?" MacMillan says with a grin.

"You bet we are," Palmer tells him. "The carnival might be over, officially speaking, but Paris has plenty of theaters, cafés, and historic sights to visit. We won't lack for things to do, you can bet on that."

"Getting back to our game," MacMillan says, "I know that Spalding and Lynch invited France's president, Sadi Carnot, to come watch. Will he accept, do you think? We are batting .500 so far when it comes to monarchs but .000 when it comes to religious leaders."

Palmer replies, "True. We were a hit with the King of Italy but swung and missed with the Khedive of Egypt and the Pope."

I nearly jump when I hear MacMillan mention Carnot's name. It rattles my table a bit. MacMillan, Palmer, and Wood glance over at me, but I just say "oops," bend over to "pick up" my knife that I never dropped on the floor in the first place, and they turn back toward each other and forget about me. I strain to hear what they say, just so I won't miss any details.

"I bet he turns us down," Palmer says. "Anyone beg to differ?"

"I'll bet a five that he's there," Wood replies.

"You heard him, Newton," Palmer exclaims. "It's official."

"My friends," MacMillan says, "Leigh Lynch just came in. Let's ask him for some news. The bet may get resolved without any wait."

"Where is Spalding?" Wood says. "Shouldn't he be here, too?"

"He left to cross the English Channel and go to London yesterday," Palmer says.

"Strange that he'd invite the president of France to our game but not attend himself," Wood opines. "I wonder what that means?"

"It's hard to say," Palmer replies. "But I have faith that what Mr. Spalding doesn't know about diplomacy isn't worth knowing, so I'm sure he has a good reason."

Several people have crowded around Leigh Lynch by now, anxious to hear any news they can get. Although I hang toward the back of the crowd like always, no one is more interested in what he has to say than I am. Just out of curiosity, I look around for Crane and Hanlon. I see no sign of them.

"What can you tell us, Leigh?" John Ward is the first to pose a question. "Will there be a game in Paris for certain?"

"Yes, there will be a game in Paris. I've confirmed that we'll play a game of ball at the Park Aerostatique in two days. It is a very picturesque spot located on the banks of the Seine, right here in the city. It should be a wonderful location to show the people of Paris what baseball is all about."

A small cheer goes up from the players. Several of them pat Lynch on the shoulder for a job well done.

"And what about President Carnot, will he be there?" Anson asks.

"I've just received a communication from President Carnot's representative, General Brugere. Let me open the envelope and read it to you all."

It's a good thing I'm in the back of the group because I don't want anyone to see how badly I'm shaking while Lynch takes out the one-page letter and begins to read.

> *Sir, I have the honor to inform you that the President of the Republic is warmly appreciative of the invitation extended him to attend the baseball match at Park Aerostatique.*
>
> *He, however, regrets that because of his numerous occupations he will be unable to be present, as he attaches much interest to the development of physical exercise in the education of our youths. He will, however, be represented by officers of his military staff.*
>
> *Accept, sir, every assurance of my distinguished consideration.*
>
> *General of the Brigade, Secretary General to the President,*
>
> *General Brugere*

Palmer looks toward Wood and extends his hand with a smile. Wood digs into his pocket for his wallet.

"Hmpf," Anson declares. "President Carnot is a no-show. The French have no spirit."

"I'd guess," Lynch puts in, "that Carnot is preoccupied with General Boulanger just now. We might cut him a bit of slack. It was only one month ago that many feared Boulanger might try to seize control of the French government, after all."

"I could furnish President Carnot with a cabinet that would knock Boulanger out the box in the first inning, if they'd ask me," Anson says, to general laughter all around. Turning toward Jimmy Ryan, Anson says, "You'd take care of him right quick, wouldn't you Jimmy?"

"You got it, Captain," Ryan replies.

The banter about Carnot and Boulanger goes on for a while, but I've heard all I need to hear. I look to find John Healy. He just stares off into the distance out the window.

I look down at my hands. They've finally stopped shaking.

Healy never talks about what happens at his meeting with Malatesta. I assume that nothing comes from it, however, because I never hear Healy mention the Italian's name again. Healy is learning the hard way what Malatesta meant when he talked about his revolutions failing all the time, I guess.

Chapter 22

March 12, 1889
London, Great Britain

The channel crossing from Dieppe in France to New Haven in Great Britain will go down as one of my least favorite parts of the trip. When the players forced me to dance was worse, but nothing else. I finally learn what it feels like to get seasick. When I tried leaving my stuffy and cramped cabin in the hope that fresher air might help me, I didn't even mind seeing Mark Baldwin and Fred Pfeffer doing the same thing. That evening, at any rate, both were far too sickly to say anything to me, let alone try to make me even more miserable. On the way, I passed by Healy's cabin. I considered knocking, but through the door, I heard him alternate between pathetic moaning and praying to St. Patrick and the Virgin Mary to save him from a watery grave. It didn't sound like we could help each other much, so I left him in misery. The next morning, after docking in New Haven, the locals said the storm was the worst they'd seen in several years. I hope my luck works better the rest of my time in Great Britain.

That was two days ago. Our group has spent the last two days in London, seeing the various sights the city has to offer. Some of them, at least. We walked up the Strand, which takes only a few minutes to reach from the First Avenue Hotel where we sleep. The Strand took us to Trafalgar Square, past other famous hotels like the Victoria Hotel and the Hotel Metropole, past the British Parliament building, and to various other well-known London landmarks. All of them are fascinating for their size and historic importance, like these famous buildings always are, but I'm not afraid to admit that by this point, I've seen about as many historic places as I want to see. A month ago, I wanted to get back to America just to get away from the ballplayers who didn't like me and treated me badly. That is still true, but now, I'm also just tired from traveling for so long. The life I have back in Chicago might not be a good one, but at least it's familiar.

That's why, after we got to Trafalgar Square and I learned who Lord Nelson was from MacMillan, and how he helped save Great Britain from Napoleon, I didn't ask any further questions about why this or that building or person is famous while we were in London. I was just content to enjoy seeing new things.

The other reason I didn't say much while touring the vast city is that I was just trying to keep warm. It's a lot colder—and foggier—in London than anywhere else we've visited. Just a few weeks back, I was in Egypt watching a baseball game in the desert, and now I'm shivering through the streets of London. Maybe the change was just too sudden for my body to handle, or maybe it's because I don't own a warm coat, but whatever the reason, a cold chill has gotten into me, and I just can't seem to get warm. It puts a damper on my desire to enjoy the city.

When it comes to the fog of London, it coats the city almost all the time, not only in the early morning or the evening, like you'd expect to find in America. The fog isn't quite as dim and murky as being at the bottom of the gold mine in Ballarat, but sometimes it gives the whole city the same ghostly appearance. Occasionally, the air clears up, and I can see some of the old churches and landmarks clearly, but at other times, I can't even see things one block away, and the smokestacks of the city's factories appear and disappear as the mists drift about. I don't know if it has anything to do with the fog, but Ed Crane appears to have picked up a cough that he just can't shake.

Today we are at Kennington Oval, home of the Surrey County Cricket Club, for our first game in Britain. The cricket grounds are quite nice—very flat and green, with a grandstand and clubhouses, just like in Australia. Once again, however, it is foggy. Even though we didn't plan to begin play until one o'clock in the afternoon, the fog stalls our attempt to play ball, and Spalding thinks about canceling the game. He decides to play, but the vapors still drift through the Oval even as the game begins. If things don't improve, I don't know how the outfielders will see the ball when someone hits it to them in the air or how they will even know that someone's hit the ball in the air. While I'm stacking the bats on the Chicago bench, Johnny Ward comes over to consult with Spalding about the playing conditions.

"What are we going to do, Al? The fog has thinned a little, maybe, but I'm not sure everyone in the field can see what's going on when the pitcher makes his pitch."

"That's true, Johnny, but the same problem will apply to both sides, so at least it will be fair."

"Yes, it will, but if we're to show the British all the merits of the American game, we need to have decent playing conditions. How will the spectators even know what's happening if they can't see the field?"

"Look around, John, and see all the people in the stands. We can't cancel the game and disappoint them."

"Or lose their admission fee?" Ward asks with a wink.

"Yes, that is also a consideration. However, I have word that a special guest may join us today, one the boys won't want to miss seeing. That's why, barring an unexpected downpour, the game must go on today, despite whatever minor inconveniences Mother Nature strews in our path. To buy a little time for the weather to improve, however, I've arranged for a photographer to take our picture. You go and let the boys know, so we can get that out of the way."

"There will be another special guest? I see plenty of nobility here already."

"Yes, our American diplomats have done a thorough job in turning out some of Britain's finest to see our game today. I have confirmed that the Duke of Buccleuch; the earls of Bessborough, Sheffield, and Londesborough; Viscount Oxenbridge; and the lords Beresford, Churchill, Kinnard, Hawke, and Littleton will all be here, along with the Mayor of London and various American diplomats."

"Well, if you have another guest who tops that list, my hat is off to you, Al. I'll go and gather the players."

Noticing me sitting nearby, Spalding turns to me and says, "Sorry, Clarence, players only for this photograph."

The fact that I won't be in another photograph isn't that big a disappointment to me. I'm curious, however, as to the identity of this mystery guest, but it isn't too long before I find out. During the third inning of the game, the noise coming from the crowd changes suddenly, so I turn to see who's creating such a commotion. To my shock and horror, like some phantom that won't stop haunting me, the Prince of Wales appears on the grounds.

Immediately, all my old fears of plots to free Ireland, or the working class, flood back to me. However, most of the players are pleased. They raise three ringing cheers for the Prince, which in turn draws cheers from the spectators. I don't get a chance to observe how Healy reacts very closely, however, because he is on the All-America team, and I'm sitting on the Chicago bench like I always do, and the fog hides him from my sight. If he's made any plans, it seems I'm not a part of them. Thank goodness.

The game goes forward as planned until the middle of the fifth inning, when Spalding halts the action and calls the players in from the field.

"Men," he begins, "the Prince has asked to meet all of the American ballplayers. The ushers here will inform the spectators that we'll resume the game after a brief respite."

We go underneath the grandstand and into one of the clubhouses where stands a reception table. The Prince stands next to it, dressed in a finely tailored black suit, complete with black top hat and sparkling white gloves. I see some of the ballplayers looking at their own hands, which are dirty and muddy from playing ball in the soggy conditions outside. The Prince, however, shakes everyone's hand in turn, regardless of whether it is dirty or clean, with a smile.

I hold my breath as Healy moves through the line. What will he do? I can't imagine he brought his pistol with him to the game today, did he?

When his turn comes, however, he gives a smile and shakes the hand of the Prince, just like everyone else. I'm surprised, but grateful, that their meeting passes without anything going wrong. Anyone could have heard my sigh of relief, had they been paying attention to me. I'm trying to hide near the back of the clubhouse, however, hoping that no one notices me. Normally, at these events, no one pays me any attention, so I think I'm safe. It turns out, I'm wrong.

After all the boys have taken a turn greeting him, the Prince says to Spalding, "Tell me, Mr. Spalding, who is the young colored chap in your party? If he's toured the world with you, I'd like to shake his hand as well." My heart sinks. I hope it doesn't show too clearly on my face.

"Why, that is Clarence Duval. He is our mascot for the trip."

"Mascot? What role does a mascot play on a baseball team, pray tell?"

"The mascot's job is to bring luck to his team. He does other jobs as well, such as taking care of the playing equipment on the bench during the game, but the main purpose of the mascot is to bring good luck. Many American baseball teams have a person or animal as their mascot, in fact."

"I find it a rather strange, superstitious practice, but I think I understand. Does the mascot do anything else?"

My hands begin trembling again. One of the players might have told the Prince to ask me for a plantation dance when they walked through the line and shook his hand. I couldn't possibly turn down a request from the heir to the throne of Great Britain, but I've promised myself never to do another dance.

Feet feeling like lead, I walk slowly toward the Prince. Besides my fear that he'll ask to see a dance, I'm scared he'll remember how I slipped in the mud during The Battle of the Flowers and ask me for an explanation, as well.

I breathe another sigh of relief when Spalding answers the Prince by saying, "Clarence also leads our men onto the field before each game. You see, we often hold parades on our way to the grounds to let the public know that a game is about to take place and draw attention to ourselves in that fashion. Clarence is second to none as a bandleader."

"How fascinating," the Prince responds, and I begin to feel a little better. Spalding said nothing about a dance, and the Prince probably would have asked to see one by now if that was his plan.

I finally reach the Prince, and he extends his right hand to me. I take it. His grip is firm but not crushing. As we shake, recognition suddenly dawns in his face. "I remember you now, Clarence. Toward the end of The Battle of the Flowers, you were going to bring a handful to me, but slipped in the muddy street. I am sorry the spectators laughed at you; it was a noble gesture on your part."

I can't hide my relief when he says that. If he could have guessed my true purpose back in Nice, well, I think that would be the end of me. He notices my nervousness, however.

227

"Why, Clarence, what is the matter? Is our spring here in Britain a bit cold for you? Is this your first time among royalty? I assure you, you have nothing to fear."

"I am sorry, sir," I manage to stammer after a moment's hesitation. "But you are right. I don't think I've ever met a real prince before. I am pleased to meet you, sir."

After concluding that exchange, I manage to retreat to a corner of the spacious clubhouse while the Prince mingles with some of the players for brief conversations. I sit down in a plush, cushioned armchair, close my eyes, and try to breathe deeply to regain my composure. Soon, I realize that not all the ballplayers are happy.

"Would you just look at that," I hear Pfeffer say. "We just saw the prince of the second greatest country on earth stooping to shake hands with a nigger."

"I can't explain it, Fred," Ned Hanlon answers. "I expect His Coonship is mighty pleased with himself right now. Look at him, over in the corner away from everyone, like he's too good to mingle with us now. Maybe it's time we teach him another lesson."

Hanlon is secretly my friend now, and I know that he's just acting to keep up appearances like Ward told him to, but I wish he would have thought of something different to say. No one needs to give Pfeffer any new ideas about how to treat me.

Eventually, we return to finish the game, which the Chicago club wins 7 to 4, but all through the remainder of the game, my only thought is: Why can't London be Chicago? All the tension that happens whenever we meet someone important is just too much for me.

Chapter 23

March 14, 1889
London, Great Britain

"Captain Ward is leaving."

Those are the words on everyone's lips when I come to the hotel's dining room for breakfast this morning. It occupies everyone's thoughts so completely that I hear very little about how the players visited the House of Commons and House of Lords yesterday, which, in the few moments he could spare, MacMillan explained to me is a rare honor for foreign visitors of any kind. Nor does anyone speak of the game played yesterday at Lords' Grounds in London, a beautifully kept athletic field, which the All-America team won 7 to 6 with a rally in the ninth inning. Not a word about our game this afternoon, either, which is to take place at the Crystal Palace Grounds at Sydenham. Instead, all anyone will speak of this morning is that Johnny Ward, captain of the All-America team, is leaving today and steaming back to the United States immediately.

When Ward himself reaches the lobby, a porter toting his luggage, Palmer and MacMillan want to get the scoop, naturally, and so they ask him the reason for his departure. I tag along behind them, so I can get the story, too. "Johnny, why are you leaving us now?" Palmer asks the shortstop.

"I am called home upon matters of a purely private nature, and, as I have assured President Spalding, nothing but the most urgent reasons could induce me to leave him at this time."

"Does that mean that Mr. Spalding has agreed to allow you to go, despite the contract you signed?" MacMillan asks next.

"Yes. I assure you, the separation is an amicable one. I will rejoin the All-America team when it reaches New York to complete our exhibition schedule there."

Palmer is next. "Who will captain the All-America team in your absence?"

"Ned Hanlon will take my place as captain. Now, gentlemen, I am sorry to run off on you, but I must make haste if I'm to make my berth on the steamer *Saale* as planned. I'll see you again in New York!"

Having said that, Ward departs. Not satisfied with such meager news, both the reporters immediately rush toward Ned Hanlon for more information. MacMillan gets to him first while Palmer shuffles up behind. "Ned, what news do you have regarding Captain Ward's departure?"

"Ward knows that our Brotherhood wants him at home, and he is going there. That is all there is to the matter."

Palmer's turn. "Are there any complications in the Brotherhood's affairs?"

"No. The Brotherhood is as solid as it ever was, and had it not been for the action of the National League clubs in undertaking to put a new yoke upon the necks of the ballplayers, Ward would not be going home at present, in my opinion."

"To what do you refer when you say, 'a new yoke upon the necks of the ballplayers'?" MacMillan inquires.

"I mean the classification scheme. You know that every one of the ballplayers in this party is exempt from the operation of the classification rule until fifteen days after we have returned to New

York. There are those among us whom the League moguls have not the nerve to classify like so many sheep in the stockyard pen. They knew the president of the Brotherhood was with us, and they thought to pacify us with this exemption snap. But it won't work."

The classification scheme. I remember Spalding talking to Anson and Palmer about the classification scheme, back in the hotel in San Francisco in November. That was where the National League owners were going to place the players into certain categories and pay them based on what category the player found himself. It was Spalding's plan all along, but he got everyone to believe it was the plan of John Brush in Indianapolis instead. Meanwhile, the conversation continues between the writers and Hanlon.

"What will John Ward do upon reaching New York?" Palmer asks Hanlon.

"I do not know for certain, but you can rest assured he will act promptly. The League has made a mistake, and the moguls have got to correct it before any man of this party not already signed puts his name to a contract for the coming season."

"Just one more question, Ned," MacMillan says. "Do you believe that the acting career of Mrs. Ward has anything to do with John's departure?"

"That is a private question best answered by John himself. However, I think it is general knowledge that he opposes her resuming her career and going back upon the stage. I cannot say any more regarding that question, however."

At this moment, Spalding himself appears, giving MacMillan and Palmer a new person to pepper with questions. This time, Palmer is first. "Mr. Spalding, what information do you have regarding John Ward's departure?"

"All I can tell you is that I deeply regret it. Ward tells me that nothing can alter his determination, that matters of a private nature of vital importance demand his presence in New York, and with this explanation, he leaves me."

Palmer continues, "Do you know the nature of the business that calls him there?"

"No. He has not chosen to tell me more than I have told you, and I have naturally refrained from asking him."

I think back once again on the conversation I overheard in the San Francisco hotel, and all the work I've done spying for Ward. I know that it is the affairs of the Brotherhood and the salary plan the National League wants to place upon its players that calls Ward home. Now I understand why Ward buried his head in the sporting newspapers upon reaching Italy and why I barely saw him for days at a time. He needed to know what was going on back in the United States, and, apparently, this new salary plan that I overheard Spalding, Palmer, and Anson discussing that night in San Francisco has upset him enough that he's leaving our party.

Maybe I should have told Ward about it back in San Francisco instead of waiting until we reached the Sandwich Islands. Did I make a mistake when I decided not to? I'm not sure. If I had told Ward at that time, Spalding probably would have figured out it was me who squealed. After all, I was the only other member of our group in the hotel that evening. He probably would have left me in San Francisco, contract or no contract, and I don't know how I would have survived the winter in a new city more than one thousand miles from my home.

However, now that I know how Spalding just makes things up that suit him, and Palmer helps him by printing false things in the papers, maybe I should have taken my chances and said something to Ward when I first found out. I've never liked Anson anyway because he's never liked me, so if I'd have known then what I know now, maybe I would have done differently. It's a little late to try to change things, however, so I guess I must live with my decision.

I'm not surprised at Harry Palmer's questions, however. Now that I know how he does one thing while someone is are around but later writes other things in the newspapers, it doesn't shock me that he asks questions when he already knows what the answer is going to be. For all I know, he planned the questions with Spalding ahead of time, too.

In any case, the rest of our time in London isn't as exciting to me as is Ward's departure. The teams play in the afternoon and again on March 16, before we wrap up the London part of our tour. Each team wins once. The second game features an interesting incident, however. The Chicago Club is batting Ed Crane without mercy, and his ball lacks its usual speed. Chicago has eight runs against him by the fourth inning. Ned Hanlon, the new captain of the All-America team, runs in all the way from center field to talk to his pitcher. Hanlon is so angry with Crane that I can hear what he's saying from my spot on the Chicago bench.

"Crane, brace up and pitch some real ball. You aren't pitching like yourself. What are you doing?"

"I'm doing my best, Captain Hanlon."

"No, you aren't. You're pitching lazy ball today. You didn't go drinking with Fogarty and Baldwin last night, did you?"

"No, Captain, I'm fine. Go back to the outfield and let me pitch."

"I know you're saving your strength for the throwing contest today, but you're going to play real ball in the meantime."

"I'll be fine for the contest. I'm not tired."

"You might not be, but the outfielders sure are from chasing down all these long hits. Now pitch real ball."

Hanlon's pep talk works, to some extent. I think Crane tries harder from that point onward, but the Chicago team gets four more runs later in the game and wins, 12 to 6. Before it's all over, Pfeffer has connected for both a double and a triple, Marty Sullivan hits two triples for Chicago as well, and both Jimmy Ryan and Tom Daly hit home runs against Crane.

When the players come off the field at the end of the game, Hanlon remains steaming mad at Crane. He gets in Crane's face again, neck strained and face red, and I think they might start fighting as they enter the clubhouse. Then Spalding comes in.

"Ed, I've got news. Bonner, the man you were to throw against today, is not present. It doesn't look like we're going to have a contest, after all."

The glare that Hanlon gives Crane at this point seems likely to melt the big pitcher, but Crane simply says, "What are we going to do, Mr. Spalding? I think the crowd expects a throwing match."

"Indeed, it does. We have men searching the more respectable sections of the crowd to see if anyone would like to participate, but I don't believe we're going to find anyone to pose a credible challenge."

"Blast that cowardly Australian," Crane says. "I've been waiting to defend America's superiority at ball throwing ever since I set the record back in Australia. Now, he isn't even man enough to show up so that I can beat him."

"Perhaps we can still satisfy the crowd if you go out and throw anyway. What do you say, Ed?"

"Sure thing, Mr. Spalding. You know I'm ready to do what it takes to uphold our American honor and show these Brits what Americans can do."

With that decision made, Crane exits the clubhouse, and we all follow him to the field to watch him throw. The crowd applauds politely. Crane waves to them.

Seeing that no one else stands at home plate, I conclude the effort to find a challenger for Crane failed. Despite this fact, he tips his cap to the spectators, takes up a cricket ball, and lets it fly. Just like back in Australia, it soars through the air, onward and onward, before finally striking the turf. It looks like a very long throw to me, but Crane shakes his head and gives the ground a gentle kick. The people measuring announce the results to the crowd: 124 yards, 11 inches. It is less than his record, but, not knowing that, the spectators give him a lengthy round of applause for his effort. Crane doffs his cap once more in thanks, and we all return to the clubhouse. Crane remains the champion of distance throwing in the United States, Australia, and Great Britain.

Chapter 24

March 23, 1889
Liverpool, Great Britain

Since we left London, we've toured many of the large cities of England and Scotland, including Bristol, Manchester, Sheffield (where we saw six inches of snow the night after our game), Bradford, and Glasgow. Thankfully, there have not been many scenes or incidents along the way. The All-America team misses Johnny Ward, of course, but the games go on, with both teams winning some of the contests.

At each stop, the ballplayers do similar things, almost as if they've established a routine. They debark from their train amidst the large crowds that have come out to see them. Next, they walk the main thoroughfares of whatever city they visit, seeing the sights and doing some shopping for souvenirs or clothing. Usually, the ballgame comes next, followed by another banquet I don't get to attend featuring good food, fine wine, and the same by now all-too-familiar-sounding speeches.

Most of the men have set their hearts on the journey home, just like me, I'm starting to think. Although they continue to give a full effort during the games, at times, it seems like they just go through the motions of being tourists. If Hanlon and Pfeffer really have a plan to put me back in my place, even they seem to have forgotten about it, but I've tried to stay close to either Tener, Crane, or Fogarty, just in case. Hopefully, Hanlon talked Pfeffer down from whatever he had in mind, since he's secretly on my side now.

I note only one unusual thing about our trip at this point: our train. Stamford Perry and Spalding seem to have used some of their diplomatic abilities to arrange a special train just to take us from place to place. It has nine cars: two for dining, two for smoking and relaxing, and five sleeping cars. All are first-class, even by the high standards Spalding has treated us to on this expedition. On the outside, the train features white paint along with gold and seal-brown trimmings, and the door of each car bears a royal coat of arms, painted in gold and scarlet. Each car also bears the words, "The American Baseball Clubs" done up in brown lettering. Whenever we pull into any train station in Great Britain or Scotland, crowds throng the platform to greet us and see the special train.

We've also had good crowds at our ball games, weather conditions considered. Most of the other cities of Britain don't have quite as much fog as London does, but they are just as rainy and cold this time of the year. Despite that, the people come out to watch us in good numbers. They cheer the boys and me when we march onto the field in uniform, and even though they probably don't know much about the finer points of baseball, they cheer for the long hits, the sparkling defense, and the aggressive base running. By now, I'm sure that whatever Harry Palmer writes for *The Sporting Life* probably exaggerates the true number of people. However, no matter the numbers he gives, the crowds are rather large, considering the season, weather, and strangeness of baseball to the people of Great Britain.

Today we are in Liverpool, and I'm expecting the same routine to play out, but it doesn't happen that way. I lead the parade from the train station to the playing field, like always, but after that, things get a little strange.

"Is this place really named the Police Athletic Club Grounds?" Billy Earle, the Little Globetrotter, asks the group when we arrive.

"Police? Are Healy, Sullivan, Carroll, and I safe here?" Ryan follows up nervously.

"Why would Ryan be worried about that?" I whisper to Tom Brown, who happens to be standing nearby. Brown was born in England, Liverpool, in fact, so he seems like a good person to ask. "It seems like Mr. Ryan should be joking, but the frown on his face says he's not."

"Because, historically, the English and Irish have not gotten along well," Brown answers.

That makes sense to me. John Healy has explained some of the reasons why ever since our unsuccessful attempt to free Ireland.

Brown goes on. "Have you ever heard people in Chicago use the expression 'paddy wagon,' Clarence?"

"Yes, Mr. Brown, I have, although I think it just means that someone got arrested."

"Well, that is part of it, but not all. Calling someone 'Paddy' is an inconsiderate way of calling them Irish because Patrick is a common name for Irish people."

"Like the sailor who gave Ed Crane his monkey?"

"Indeed. I've heard that the police vehicles got the nickname 'paddy wagon' because police often accuse the Irish of being prone to crime and drunkenness. Although there may be other explanations for the name as well, it shows that a great deal of hostility exists toward the Irish in America. Ryan, Carroll, Healy, and Sullivan all have Irish last names, so it appears they are a bit worried."

While Brown tells me this, Spalding also reassures the men. "You have nothing to be nervous about," he says, facing Ryan. "The local police help keep the grounds and grandstand in order, that is all, and so the local cricket association decided to recognize the fact by putting their name on the grounds. Now, let's get ready for a game of ball."

The teams play for five innings, and the game is a tie, 2 runs each. I expect everyone to take his position for the sixth inning, like normal, especially since Baldwin is pitching beautiful baseball for Chicago, allowing just one hit so far. He can still toss the sphere with great speed when he bothers to stay sober for a little while. Instead of starting the sixth inning, however, the men clear the field, and in place of the four bases, some of the British people watching the game pound four iron stakes into the ground, each sticking up about three feet.

"What is going on?" I ask Palmer, who is on the bench next to me, keeping score of the game like he always does.

"We are going to see a special event, Clarence. Instead of finishing the ball game today, eleven of our boys have accepted a challenge to play a game of rounders with a picked English eleven."

"What is rounders, and what does it mean to have a picked eleven?"

"Rounders is a game bearing some resemblance to baseball. In fact, some Englishmen claim that baseball is simply a derivative of rounders, although I put little stock in that claim. Like most Americans, of course, I believe that baseball is a purely American invention with no roots in any foreign game, but I'll not let that spoil the fun today. I've never seen the game played myself, so let's watch and see how experienced rounders players perform.

"Oh, and to answer your other question, a picked eleven just means that the opponents are not all from the same team. These men are a combination of players from the Crescent, Union, Cranmer, Crown, and Derby clubs, according to the local British sportswriters to whom I've spoken. They've picked their best men to play in the game."

We watch, and Palmer is correct; rounders has quite a few similarities to baseball. Eleven people take the field, and most of them stand where baseball players stand, except that a tenth man stands in back of the catcher, called the long stop, and another extra man lurks behind the third baseman. The game features a pitcher and batter, like baseball, although the batter can only swing at the ball with one arm. The ball is a little smaller than a baseball, and the rounders bat is also smaller than a baseball bat, and its shape is somewhat like a paddle. The stakes, or bases, are a little closer together compared to baseball as well. To my eyes, the biggest differences are that to put a man out, the fielders must hit him by throwing the ball at him while he runs the bases and that the pitcher must keep his arm straight when delivering the ball to the batter.

The eleven men of our party who play in the game are Spalding, Earle, Tener, Anson, Wood, Fogarty, Brown, Hanlon, Pfeffer, Manning, and Ryan. Those who aren't playing immediately place bets on which team will win the game and by how much. Their opponents, dubbed the Rounders Association of Liverpool, win the game by a score of 16 to 14 after two innings.

"Okay, now time for another game of baseball," Spalding says once the rounders match is over. "Bring the bases back out."

The stakes disappear, the bases reappear, and the rounders team sends their men up to bat against the pitching of Mark Baldwin. Every baseball fan in the United States knows that Baldwin has some of the fastest pitches in baseball. Well, he is using all his speed now. The first batter swings at the ball weakly but is far too late for Baldwin's speedy pitching and strikes out. The second batter up for the Rounders Association also fans the air, and Baldwin strikes him out, too. Their third batter suffers the same fate.

The ballplayers come up to bat. Even though the rain is coming down hard and steady now, evidently the crowd wants to see how their boys stack up to ours because many of them are still here. Their pitcher sends the ball to home plate. It takes him a bit to get his accuracy down, so that our boys can hit the ball, but when they do, the fielders really must scramble after it. The American team scores thirteen runs in the first inning. Having seen them play as often on this trip as I have, I think they might have eased up a bit after scoring eight or nine.

Palmer observes the same thing. "Wouldn't you say, Newton," I overhear him saying to MacMillan, "that the boys are going easy on the Rounders Association now?"

"It may be so," MacMillan replies. "Although I'm not sure eight runs with only one man out counts as going easy."

"I think our men are just getting tired of running the bases and want to play one more inning to get things over with," Palmer says in return.

They do play one more inning, and by that time, the score is eighteen runs for the American baseball players, zero runs for the Rounders Association.

"Do you still think the boys were giving it their all that second inning?" Palmer says to MacMillan.

"Well, Baldwin certainly eased up. I have no doubt of that. He merely lobbed the ball in to the batters in the second inning, just so they could hit it, and they still made three consecutive outs."

"I say, enough of rounders," Palmer opines. "It is childish and brings out no strong qualities in batting, fielding, or running. I suppose we've just proven the American game the superior game in every respect. Dollars to doughnuts that soon, Englishmen will say the same thing about baseball compared to cricket. We just need to give the game time to grow here. This tour may be the event that begins it all, the stone that starts the avalanche, if you will."

"Easy there, old boy," MacMillan says with a smile. "Remember that a great deal of novelty is involved with our tour. Do you think we'd see this many people come stand in the rain to watch any sport, day in and day out, like Americans do for baseball? Why, you couldn't get fifty Americans to come watch a game with weather like this back in the United States, and I'll wager you wouldn't get fifty Englishmen, either, if they had to withstand this kind of rain just to witness a game between the teams in seventh and eighth place in the standings on a Wednesday afternoon."

"What you say is good sense, Newton; it's true. Still, I believe the English are the most sporting people we've met on our journey, save only the Australians. It does not surprise me that the Australians come from English stock, for the most part. The English and Australians are manly, sporting peoples, second only to Americans in that regard."

MacMillan gives a big sigh, wiping water from his hair and forehead and closing his notebook with a snap. "In any event, it looks as if things have concluded here. Let's go find someplace dry, so we can prepare for tonight's round of banquets." Clearly, MacMillan has seen enough for today.

"Do I note a hint of fatigue, Newton?"

"I don't know if fatigue is what I'd call it, Harry, but the repetition has become a bit monotonous, wouldn't you say? Every time the teams play ball, the result is new and different, I'll grant you, but the banquets, the plays, the speeches, and all the rest have started blending for me. If I weren't a newspaperman who wrote everything down just to keep it all straight for my readers, I don't think I could keep any of it straight at this point. Do you agree?"

"I don't know about that, Newton. I don't know if I'd say I'm fresh as a daisy, but I still enjoy the food, the toasts, seeing the sights, and all the rest."

"Well, suit yourself. I'm glad you are holding up a bit better than I am," MacMillan tells him. "One thing we can probably agree on, however," he says, looking down at his waist, "is that we might need to enter the gymnasium for some training when we get back to the United States. All of this rich food and wine is soothing to the palate but not the belly."

"You've hit a home run there, my friend. Especially since we reached Europe, I've found my pants and shirts wearing just a bit tighter than I'm used to," Palmer says with a chuckle.

"Will I see you at tonight's performance? I hear we have a choice between the Royal Theater and the Shakespeare Theater here in Liverpool. I think I'll try the Royal. What do you think?"

241

"I was thinking the same, actually. The Royal it is. I'll see you in a few hours."

I'm happy that at least one other person is starting to wish for home as much as I am. I suspect some of the others would admit as much in private, too, but maybe not aloud. Not, at any rate, when Spalding is around, because no one will deny he's put together a first-class trip for us.

I've seen much more of Spalding on this trip than I ever did as the Chicago mascot, of course, but I'm still trying to decide exactly what to make of him. On the one hand, I know he isn't always honest. He's said so himself. I know that one reason he invited Johnny Ward to go on this trip was so that the other owners in the National League could try their salary plan without Ward around to help his Brotherhood. He also tried bribing the Italian government so that we might play a game in the Roman Colosseum, which makes me wonder if any of the other opportunities we've had were the result of bribes, too. In addition, he knows how much several of our players have been drinking, but he's planted false stories of everyone's good behavior. Spalding tricked everyone on this trip when he got the players to sign contracts that did not specify the route of our return, so he could choose whatever course he wanted when returning home. Although no one that I know of complained when he decided to extend our trip and it has been a lot of fun for the players, it was sneaky.

On the other hand, I must admit that I've probably gained as much as anyone from coming along. Even with all the hard knocks and humiliations and even though I'm ready to be home now, this trip beats trying to find food and warm places to sleep in Chicago all winter long. I've had my own cabin and bed to sleep in, although that is mainly because none of the players would share with a colored person. The food is much better than what I usually get, and there always seems to be plenty of it. I don't know if I've become friends with any of the players, except maybe for Healy, and Fogarty since the episode on Mount Vesuvius, but several of them are polite toward me now and treat me nicely. I am an honorary member of the Order of the Howling Wolves, too, even if we haven't done much howling since they let me join. Finally, I can't ignore that I've had the chance to see and do more things than a poor, homeless kid from Chicago could ever expect. All of this is true because Spalding allowed me to go on the trip. The accommodations have been first class the entire way, and it's doubtful that anyone on the trip will spend another five months of their lives in such an interesting and carefree way ever again. Plus, I'm learning to read better all the time, thanks to MacMillan's generosity and Mrs. Williamson's help.

Despite all these good things about Spalding, I've overheard other things during the past week or two that trouble me. Before our game in Glasgow, I was cleaning things up on the bench, stacking bats for the players, when I overheard Spalding and Harry Palmer hold an interesting conversation. I don't know if they know I overheard them, or if they even cared, but it went something like this:

Palmer says to Spalding, "I say, Al, what do you plan to do with Akbar once we get back to America? I know you said you've hired him as your personal valet, but what on earth will you do with him for the next five years?"

"I will make sure he learns English because I have plans for him. Do you know why Captain Thalenhorst hired him and let him come with us on the *Salier*?"

"Seeing that the boy can't speak a word of English right now, no, I don't know."

"The boy ran away from his family because all the grown men in his family are rickshaw drivers, and he didn't want that life. The captain took pity on him and hired him to work in the kitchen."

"I knew that Captain Thalenhorst was a good man, but it seems I underestimated his charity."

"Yes, he is quite an interesting specimen, without doubt. Once I discovered this from the captain, I decided to acquire Akbar's services. You see, Harry, when we return to the United States, I am considering founding the American Rickshaw Company."

"I thought Akbar ran away because he didn't want to drive rickshaws."

"I never said I wanted him to drive them. I want to acquire his knowledge and expertise about the business. If his family has been driving rickshaws for generations, surely he knows something of how to build them properly and maintain them. My plan is, once he learns English, to put him to work with American engineers to build rickshaws efficiently. I'll open a new division of Spalding Sporting Goods to manufacture the carriages, and once those are ready, I'll hire people to run them through the streets of Chicago and other cities."

"Al, I don't know about that. Do you think Americans will take to riding in rickshaws? Will they, perhaps, reject the practice as an example of barbaric oriental despotism?"

"We shall see, Harry. Our nation is a mere generation from abolishing slavery, and we both know the attitudes of white Americans toward Negroes, Indians, and certain immigrant groups. You may find them more willing to let drivers run them about than you'd think. I had this same conversation with Leigh Lynch one day, back when we were in Colombo. I believe hiring people will be much cheaper and require much less upkeep than maintaining a stable of horses."

"I still don't know about that, Al. They are a bit on the pricey side right now, but it seems to me that the bicycle might prove more attractive to people than the rickshaw. Especially now, after the safety bicycle came out a few years back. Now that the wheels are the same size, instead of the front wheel being as large as it is on the high-wheelers, they are much safer. The practice of bicycling has yet to catch on generally, but it might be the coming thing."

"Either way, my company will be in good shape because we certainly manufacture our share of bicycles at our factory in Chicopee Falls, Massachusetts. I can initiate rickshaw production there as well, or perhaps start production alongside the boats we build at our Ogdensburg factory in New York State. It seems wise to give it a trial, in case the rickshaw does catch on with Americans."

"If I might venture an even more forward-looking prediction, what of the automobile?"

"What of it, Harry? The automobile's future is as a toy for the rich, not a means of transport for the public."

"I'm not convinced of that. The first working model, the Benz motorwagon, just came out back in, what was it, 1886, right? I'm no mechanic, but a few friends of mine who dabble in such things tell me that Otto's engine, the internal combustion engine, as they call it, has great possibilities, given enough time and experimentation."

"That may be the case, Harry, but my company is a sporting goods company above all. Rickshaws appeal to me because they would be cheap and easy to manufacture in large quantities. It would take major new investments to open a new division that manufactures complex machine engines and automobiles. It may be worth a thought, however, just like you've suggested. I'll take the idea under consideration."

The fact that Spalding wanted to hire a person for five years just to get his knowledge about rickshaws doesn't seem right to me. If the rickshaw really does catch on in the United States, I doubt very much that Akbar will get too much money for helping. As for automobiles or motorwagons, I don't even know what those are. Names like Benz and Otto don't mean anything to me.

Speaking of names, though, when Spalding and Palmer finish their conversation, Spalding says again that Akbar's real name isn't Akbar. Spalding just decided to call him that because he liked the name and thought that the boy looked like his name ought to be Akbar. That doesn't seem right to me, either.

Chapter 25

March 26, 1889
Dublin, Ireland, British Empire

"Hawf pawst foive! Wud ye be gettin' up, sirs? It's hawf pawst foive."

The booming voice of the Irish hotel porter wakes each of us from slumber at half past five on March 26. The man continues down the hallway, repeating his call of "hawf pawst foive" every ten seconds or so until he reaches the stairway and moves to the next floor of the Imperial Hotel where we stay in Belfast. The reason we all must wake up at half past five is to catch the train taking us to Dublin this morning. The ballplayers, however, are not about to let this pass without having some fun.

As soon as the porter moves upstairs, I hear some commotion in the hallway, so I walk to my door and open it. When I do, I see Ned Hanlon roll through the doorway of his hotel room and into the hall, doubled over and laughing like a schoolgirl. Another dozen or so heads have poked out into the hallway as well, most of them saying something like, "Did you hear that?"

I'm not sure why the thickness of the porter's brogue is so funny. People talk like that all the time in the neighborhoods of Chicago where I live. The players love it, though. Maybe they don't have too many Irish people in their neighborhoods. For the next several days, at random times some ballplayer will yell out, "hawf pawst foive," and everyone nearby breaks out in laughter. I'm not surprised that Jim Fogarty proves especially good at imitating the porter's voice.

Lately, most of the nights have been pleasant ones for me. I've had few dreams and no nightmares like I often had earlier in the trip. I've never understood why I have such awful nightmares sometimes, but they've troubled my sleep from time to time for as long as I can remember. Sometimes I dream about Tommy and me, and those remind me of how much I miss my friend. Other nights, my dreams are repeats of scary things that happened to me during the day. It feels good to be free of them for a while. Maybe it's because I've finally gotten used to traveling.

Our party reaches Dublin by 11:00 in the morning, and we go to stay at the Morrison Hotel. It does not look quite as grand as some of the hotels where we've stayed, but it has four floors, and each room has a large window with twelve square panes of glass overlooking the street. Streetlights flank the entrance to the lobby from the street, and a wrought-iron fence rising to chest height surrounds the hotel.

Once we've all arrived in the hotel lobby, Spalding holds a quick meeting.

"Men, I've arranged a game here in Dublin for tomorrow. I know our trip is nearly over, and many of you are ready to see your homes again." At this, many of the players nod.

Spalding continues after a short pause. "I also know this will be your last chance for sightseeing. Let's make sure we finish our tour the way we started it, representing our nation and flag with honor. Although the reputation of the pubs of Dublin needs no embellishment from me," he says while looking directly at some of the Howling Wolves, "I trust all of you to be in top condition for our last game. I hope that by tomorrow you'll all be well rested and ready to play good ball, but for today, take some time to see what Dublin has to offer."

Ned Hanlon moves to the front of the group. "And don't forget, boys, your curfew this evening is at hawf pawst foive." Laughter from the entire group follows.

While the group breaks up, I overhear MacMillan ask Palmer, "This is the Morrison Hotel. Isn't this where the British arrested Parnell back in '81? Or was it '82?"

"I believe it was in '81," Palmer answers.

Before I can learn who Parnell is or why the British arrested him, Healy strides over to me, a spring in his step. I swallow, not knowing if this will be good or bad. He is almost bouncing up and down, however, so I suspect it will be bad. "Clarence, stow your things in your room, and get ready to come with me today!"

"Where are we going, Mr. Healy?" I ask, more than a little scared on the inside. My left hand starts twitching, just a bit.

"You'll see. Just get ready and wear your best clothes. The ones Fogarty bought you in Italy."

Seeing that no one else volunteers to share my company, about fifteen minutes later, Healy and I are together again down in the lobby. I still don't know what he has in mind, but he whistles an upbeat tune when I approach. Various players trickle downstairs before going on their way. I really hope we don't meet any more anarchists here in Ireland. Even though I'd still like to help free Ireland, I've had enough of secret plots for now.

"This way, Clarence, I'll hire a carriage," Healy says, and soon we're on our way. He doesn't say where we're headed, so I'm surprised when we leave Dublin and travel into the Irish countryside. Mostly, I just watch the scenery go by, staring at the quiet green fields with their walls of stone or green turf. Healy has a strange look of anticipation on his face again, staring straight ahead and not saying much, but it's different from the look I saw in Nice. He relaxes his jaw, and he doesn't look nearly as intense or serious. Although he's smiling, I think I see wetness in one corner of his eye. Finally, I decide to ask him a question.

"Mr. Healy, back at the hotel, I heard Mr. MacMillan ask Mr. Palmer if our hotel was the place where a person named Parnell was arrested. Do you know who that is?"

"Of course I do, Clarence. Every Irish patriot knows the name Charles Stewart Parnell."

"What is he famous for?"

"Back in 1881, Parnell was the leader of the Irish Parliamentary Party in the British Parliament. He led the group advocating Irish Home Rule within the British Empire. He also was the president of the Irish National Land League."

"You mean the British arrested a member of their own government?"

"Yes, they did."

"How can they do that?"

"Governments will arrest anyone they think is a threat to them, even if it's one of their own politicians. That's why anarchists like me believe we must destroy national governments. They deny people their freedom."

Finally, I ask the question that I've wanted to ask ever since we started. Might as well get the drama of waiting over with. "Are we going to meet more anarchists today, so we can free Ireland, Mr. Healy?"

"No, my lad. I have something rather different in mind for today. If you're worried about more plots, you needn't be."

Sensing that I'm not going to get a direct answer right now, I fall silent again and watch the fields of Ireland creep by. Whatever will happen will happen, I guess. I've managed to escape all my adventures so far, so I trust in my luck that today will be the same.

Eventually, we come to a stop on a dirt lane. Healy leans forward in his seat and looks around, clearly anticipating something. All I see is a modest farmhouse nearby where an older woman sweeps dirt out the front door.

"Are you sure this is the place?" Healy asks the carriage driver as the older woman looks up from her chores.

The man nods and simply says, "Aye, it is."

"Wait here a moment, Clarence," Healy says as he steps down from the carriage and goes to speak with the woman. Presently, a man also appears at the farmhouse door and speaks to Healy.

I can't hear what they are saying, but after a few moments, I see that everyone is happy and exchanging hugs. Healy waves for me to come over to the house.

He has a big smile on his face, and he's bouncing on his toes again. "Uncle, Aunt, this is our mascot, Clarence Duval. Clarence, this is my Aunt and Uncle Healy. Uncle Fergus is my father's brother, and his wife is named Roisin."

The man looks me over thoroughly and gives a little whistle when he sees me. "Are you sure about this, Johnny?" he asks Healy.

"Yes, Uncle, don't worry. Clarence is a good lad. Don't let his skin color fool you. He is one of us. Once we can sit down, I'll explain how he's tried to help me free Ireland on our trip."

Uncle Fergus looks at me a few seconds longer, motionless other than biting his lips together, but after a moment he claps a hand on my shoulder and leads me inside. "Will you boys take some bread and coffee?" Roisin asks us. We nod as we take seats near the gray, stone fireplace, where a small fire burns on this cool spring day.

John Healy turns to me and says, "You see, Clarence, this is the first time I've ever met anyone in my family who stayed in Ireland rather than coming to the United States. I wasn't sure if I'd ever get to see them, but thanks to this trip, I have." Healy smiles again as the brown bread and coffee appear in front of us.

"Thank you, Aunt Roisin," he says.

Uncle Fergus speaks next. "Well, Johnny, I suppose you should tell us about this trip you're on and how young Clarence here came to be with you. We've got the letter you sent us from London, telling us you were coming to visit, but your letter forgot one or two details, it seems."

Healy tells them many of the tales of our adventures, including finding me in Omaha, the ocean voyages, playing ball in the sand in front of the Sphinx, and everything else. He goes into extra detail when he gets to the part about The Battle of the Flowers in Nice and how Mark Baldwin prevented us from carrying out Healy's plan to kill the Prince of Wales.

"A shame, that," Uncle Fergus says when he hears about Nice. "You know, Johnny, I don't share your belief in anarchism, but I've no love for the royal family, make no mistake about that."

He turns to me. "You really meant to go through with that crazy plan and help our nephew?"

I nod, hoping that Uncle Fergus won't ask me too many questions about it, so I won't have to stretch the truth any further than I already have.

Suddenly, Uncle Fergus breaks into an enormous smile and gives me a hearty slap on the shoulder. "Well, in that case, you're welcome in my home any time. We don't see many of the colored here in Ireland, Clarence, so I don't know much about them as a people, but if they are all like you, perhaps having a few around wouldn't be so bad."

"Thank you, Uncle Fergus," I respond. "Mr. Healy has been a good friend to me on our trip. I think he should tell you more about how brave he was to save me in the mine in Australia."

"Can I get you some more?" Aunt Roisin asks. We both nod yes, and soon, more slices of buttered bread and black coffee sit in front of us. I still don't like coffee, but I drink to show my appreciation for the hospitality.

"May I ask you a question, sir?" I say to Uncle Fergus.

"Go ahead, m'boy."

"If Ireland used to be its own country, like Mr. Healy has told me, how come the people speak English? Doesn't Ireland have its own language?"

"It does. It's called Gaelic. However, because the English have had control of our country for so long, most of us learn English. I

251

can speak the old tongue just fine, as can my wife, but my children do not know it very well, I'm afraid."

"To finish my story, Uncle," Healy interjects, "we had a really stormy trip across the Irish Channel. I'm afraid I got a little seasick, but I arrived here in the home country all the same."

"Oh, don't worry about that, Johnny," Aunt Roisin puts in. "You just had to get all the England out of you before you got to Ireland." We all laugh.

"So, you boys got to see Rome. What was St. Peter's like?" Uncle Fergus asks us.

"Well, Uncle, the church is as big and grand as anything I've seen. I'm not sure how to describe it. The artwork was so beautiful, just paintings all around us everywhere we went. We didn't get to play ball for the Pope, though. We tried to arrange it, but Our Holy Father was ill when we arrived."

"Another shame," Uncle Fergus says. "At least you got to see the Pope's palace with your own eyes. That is more than I'll ever be able to say, it seems."

Suddenly, Healy has an idea. "You might be able to see it after all, Uncle, after a fashion. Let me see if I have it with me. Yes, here it is. Take this, Uncle." Healy hands over the small piece of marble he acquired from the stonemasons in Rome.

"It's just a hunk of stone. What does this have to do with anything?"

"That is a piece of marble from St. Peter's. While we were there, some masons just happened to be replacing a section of the floor. We convinced them to let us have pieces of the old floor. I was going to make that into a little good luck charm, but now I think you should have it. I got one for Clarence, too."

"I'm afraid I left mine back at the hotel, however," I say to everyone.

"Well, we'll certainly treasure it, both because it's from Rome and because it's from you," Aunt Roisin says to John as she gives him a kiss on the forehead.

After we've talked a bit longer, Uncle Fergus decides we should meet his neighbors, some of whom turn out to be John Healy's cousins, nieces, and nephews. While we walk across the fields to meet the people in nearby cottages, Healy looks as happy as I've seen anyone on the entire trip, sharing hugs, kisses, and handshakes with everyone around. It appears most of the people in the village don't know much about baseball, so several times he must explain to them how he makes a living. They also are a bit suspicious of me at first, but once Healy explains how I'm his friend, most of them take me in, as well, and I get hugs and handshakes, too.

It doesn't take long to get dark in Ireland in March, but that doesn't stop anyone. Before long, a village bonfire blazes, fiddles create festive music, alcohol flows, and a dance is on. The party looks like it will go on and on into the night. While everyone is setting up and getting ready, and while a little light remains, I manage to get close enough to Healy to ask him a question.

"How are we going to get back to Dublin?" I ask between musical numbers. "I think our carriage driver left a long time ago."

"I told him to come back in the morning. This party will go on for several hours yet, but we aren't expected back in Dublin until our game tomorrow afternoon."

"Are the other players visiting their families, too?"

"Some of them are, yes. John Tener told me he was going to visit the place he was born, in Donaghmore, while Tom Daly is off to Kildare and Jim Manning to the town of Callon in Kilkenny."

A few minutes later, I notice a young girl looking at me curiously. Healy sees it, too. He walks over to her, takes her hand, and walks her over to me.

"Hello, Clarence," she says to me very quietly. She takes a step back and looks like she's going to turn away, but then faces me again and says, "I'm Clara."

"Hi, Clara, I'm Clarence." I'm shocked this girl wants to talk to me, and I can't think of anything else to say. She looks like she is probably nine or ten years old, with long, reddish-gold hair and dainty hands and fingers.

"Clara is one of my nieces," Healy explains to me. "I told her you were the leader of our parades, and she said she wanted to see you march. She loves parades."

At that, Clara gives me a sweet smile, folds her fingers over her chest, and says, "Please?"

"I'd like to, but I don't have my baton with me, Mr. Healy. What should I do? I'd look silly just marching in place."

"We'll find you a replacement, Clarence, don't worry," Healy says, and immediately he goes off in search of one.

"Thank you, Clarence, thank you!" Clara says to me, and out of nowhere, gives me a hug.

I blush. A lot. I can't help it. I just hope that not too many people notice in the twilight. I'm not exactly sure how to act when the people around me like me and want me around.

It takes five minutes or so before Healy comes back with something that looks like a broomstick. When the next musical number ends, he claps his hands to get everyone's attention.

"Friends, family, everyone. Thank you all for this warm welcome. It truly is a blessing to be home in Ireland." Everyone cheers. Most raise their mugs in salute, too.

Healy continues. "As you know by now, I've brought the mascot for our journey, Clarence Duval, with me today. He's been a good companion to me while we've traveled the world, and he loves Ireland." More applause, and a few more mugs rise into the air. I blush again in the twilight.

"Clarence is also the leader of our parades. Whenever we play a game of baseball, he leads us onto the field. He doesn't have his uniform or his baton with him this evening, but he said he'd try his best to perform his march if we can give him some music. What do you say?" On cue, the fiddles start up again, and I start marching.

I go around the bonfire in a large circle three times, twirling and tossing my broomstick as I go. Twice, it hits the ground because I'm not used to the weight compared to my baton and also because it is mostly dark by now, so I can't see it very well when I toss it in the air, but I smile, pick it up, and keep going. After my third circle, I stop and bow to everyone.

By chance, I end up only a short distance away from Clara, who claps her tiny hands together excitedly and jumps up and down in little hops, her curly red hair bouncing on her shoulders.

"Thank you, Clarence, thank you!" she says to me. The music keeps going, but I figure I've done my performance for the evening, and I can relax now.

Healy is also nearby. "Clara? Clara? Do you think you could show Clarence how to do a jig like people do in Ireland?"

"Sure!" she says as she turns toward me. "Do you want to learn, Clarence?"

I nod.

She takes my hand, and soon I am dancing with Clara. For the first time on the entire trip, I'm dancing because I want to.

When I finally go to sleep late that evening in front of Uncle Healy's fire, in my heart I know that this has been one of the best days of my life.

Chapter 26

"Why are we here again?" Billy Earle says, so the whole group can hear him. "Today is the day we steam home to America, and we're visiting still another castle? Haven't we seen enough of them by now?"

He says this while we walk up a staircase inside an Irish castle known as Blarney Castle.

"We've seen castles aplenty, for certain," Tener says to Earle. "But none of the other castles has the Blarney Stone."

"What's so special about the Blarney Stone? Do you rub it for good luck or something?" Earle replies.

"Not quite. If you kiss it, it gives you the gift of eloquence."

"Magic rocks? Well, why not? We've done just about everything else on this trip, might as well look at a magic rock, too."

George Wood chimes in. "Let me get this straight. You kiss a rock, and all of a sudden, you're another Shakespeare?"

"I'd prefer to say you're another Oliver Goldsmith or Jonathan Swift," Tener replies with a smile, "but, yes, that is what the legend says."

"Does that mean that Johnny Ward was born in Blarney Castle?" Anson asks, getting a few laughs. "From the way he talks, you'd think so, anyway."

Fogarty says, "I hear it only works if you kiss the stone before hawf pawst foive." More laughs.

The castle, unlike the kings we've met on our tour, looks about like the stories say a castle should look. The tower with the Blarney Stone is several stories tall, and it's constructed from gray stone that's a little worn down from the weather over the years. We walk up some stone stairs to get to the Blarney Stone, and when we get to the top of the castle wall, a walkway takes us to the stone itself. I notice a short wall on the top floor of the castle, too, like a railing, so visitors don't fall over the side. Someone says this lower wall is the parapet.

Soon, we reach the section of the castle wall where the famous stone is. To the amazement of several of us, anyone kissing the stone must have people hold their legs while they dangle from the wall of the castle. A hole opens at the base of the parapet, and a person must stick their upper body into the hole while someone holds them in place.

"You've got to be joking," Billy Earle says when he sees this.

"I'm first," Fred Carroll calls out, relishing the moment. "Who'll help me?"

Carroll leans out, with several of the men assisting, until he is dangling down far enough to touch his lips to the stone. John Healy follows Carroll, and Daly, Ryan, Fogarty, Manning, Spalding, and Hanlon all take a turn. Even Earle decides to try it eventually.

"What about you, Clarence?" Fogarty says once he is back on his feet and leaning against the castle parapet.

"No thank you, sir. I don't know if I would reach, anyway."

"I guess you don't need luck. You're the mascot, so maybe the Blarney Stone won't help you that much."

"No way," Anson says. "No Ethiopian is going to kiss that stone while I'm here. Would you want to put your mouth on it after he's done?"

"Just give it a rest, Anson," Fogarty says. "You know how many thousand people have kissed that rock already?"

Tener breaks into the conversation. "Stop it, men. It's pointless, anyway. Clarence already said he'd pass. Now let's get moving, so we don't miss our ship."

"I don't know about this," Fred Carroll says while we walk down the stairs from the parapet. "Are you sure there aren't any more magic rocks around here that will put sense into the head of a pitcher who can't field a bunt and throw to first base properly?" He nudges John Healy, who is right behind him, with his elbow as he says this.

I'm behind both, so I see Healy twirl his mustache a bit before replying, "Or any other magic stones with enough luck in them to make a ballplayer of a man who couldn't catch a football if it was thrown to him?"

The banter continues all the way to the ship. I decide that the magic of the Blarney Stone must take a while before it starts working because what the ballplayers say sounds no different than it ever did. One thing I've learned on our tour, however, is that most of the players have a lot of faith in luck, so I guess having faith in a magic rock isn't too much of a stretch for them.

The final steamer on our voyage, the one taking us home, is the *Adriatic*. It is quite a large ship. Tener tells me over 1,000 passengers are on board, and we should be back in the United States within six days. He also tells me that by the time we reach New York, we'll have traveled more than 27,000 miles. We leave Ireland at 2:00 in the afternoon of March 28. I am ready to see New York again, and I'm not the only one.

I have my last few lessons with MacMillan while we travel across the Atlantic Ocean. Mrs. Williamson isn't with us for our lesson anymore, though. Sadly, Ned injured his leg while playing ball in Paris. He's still in France right now, recuperating, and she's with him instead of sailing with us. I miss her.

It's a pity because I enjoyed her helping with the lessons. Sometimes, recent events distracted her attention, and she wanted to talk about them instead of reading, but most of the time Mrs. Williamson was a patient teacher and very helpful. She told me she would buy me some more books when we got to New York, so I could practice on the way to Chicago, but because she's still in France, I don't think that will happen now. Mrs. Williamson even tried to make me call her by her first name, Nellie, but I didn't have the nerve to do that.

MacMillan tells me I am a good pupil, but I'm not sure. I've learned a lot about spelling and grammar and practiced how to read and pronounce the words in the books we have on hand to study but learning to read takes a long time and lots of practice. Sometimes, I get very discouraged, but he always tells me to keep going. I always keep at it, even though it's hard, because I know that if I'm ever going to do better than living on the streets of Chicago, this will help me.

Chapter 27

April 6, 1889
New York City, New York, United States

Because of unfavorable weather, it takes us more than six days to get to New York, but now we are here, steaming proudly into the harbor. A tugboat named the *George Wood*, of all names, steams out to meet us with a reception party. How George Wood got the honor of having a tugboat named after him excites a bit of jealousy in some of the other players, but only a bit. Most are happy just to be home. A German band plays us a greeting from the tug.

When the welcoming tug gets close enough, I can see faces. John Ward is one of them whom I recognize.

"Quite a scene, isn't it, Clarence? Lots of famous people have come out to greet us," MacMillan says to me as he takes up a spot on the front rail of the *Adriatic*. He just leans over the ship's railing to take everything in. Today the weather is calm, so he's in no danger of losing his top hat.

I tell him, "I see Mr. Ward, but who are the others? The only other person I recognize is George Gore, the famous outfielder who used to be with Chicago but plays for New York now."

"Yes, he is there, along with a few other ballplayers. Do you recognize Charley Jones over there, Clarence?"

"No, I'm not familiar with him."

"That isn't too surprising. Charley Jones has been an American Association player for several years now, but once, he was among the king home run hitters in baseball. He once hit ten of them in a single season! Charley lives in Queens. I wonder if he's found a team to play for this season. Kansas City let him go after just a few games last year. He's never been the same since his wife got angry with him and tossed cayenne pepper into his eyes one evening."

"His wife hurt him? Was it on purpose?"

"If the stories I've heard are correct, yes. Jones was not exactly a paragon of virtue during his younger years. It was an exceptional evening when he would retire before two or three in the morning, and I think his wife suspected infidelity. I've never heard if her suspicion proved justified. Still, he's always carried a reputation for being a jolly, convivial fellow. In any case, let's see who else is here to meet us. Do you recognize that gentleman?" MacMillan points to a man who is about the same age as Spalding.

"He looks a bit like Mr. Spalding, wouldn't you say?"

"That's because it is Mr. Spalding's brother, Walter, who is the co-owner of their sporting goods business. Standing nearby to him is Cap Anson's father."

"And is he like his son?"

"I do not know, Clarence. Oh, yes, that is DeWolf Hopper and Digby Bell."

"Who are they? They don't look like ballplayers."

"Hopper and Bell are among the most famous actors on the New York stage, Clarence. Just like Johnny Ward's wife, Helen Dauvray Ward. They are also tremendous fans of baseball, all three of them. I should probably recognize a few more of these people," MacMillan continues, pushing himself back from the ship's railing and adjusting his top hat, "but I am a Chicago newspaperman, not a New York newspaperman. Welcome home, Clarence."

With that, he tips his hat and takes his leave of me and goes to speak with some of the other men. I hear several of the players yell things like, "It does my heart good to see some Yankees again," but MacMillan's last comment, about being home, gets me thinking. What am I going to do now? I'm back in the United States, yes, but I don't have a home. I suppose I should go back to Chicago where I'm from, but Chicago is a long way from New York, and I'm not sure how I'll get there. Hitch a ride on a train, perhaps. I guess I don't have to worry about it until Spalding tells me my contract is complete. Until then, I might as well hope for more parades to lead and see what my luck brings.

That's not a very good plan, though. I've been putting off making a real plan for months, but I can't do that much longer. I need to do something different, so maybe Chicago isn't the answer. Maybe the White Stockings will want me for their mascot again next year, maybe they won't, but either way, what future do I have leading parades and watching baseball games during the summer?

Perhaps I should do something unexpected and see what my luck brings me. I bite my lips while I look down at the blue-green water splashing against the ship's hull.

When we get closer to docking, several more ships come out to greet us, including one full of New York newspapermen anxious to get the story of the returning ballplayers. They've gathered on the deck of the *Adriatic* in semicircles around various members of our party. I wander from one group to the next to hear what the boys have to say about our trip, since none of the writers want to talk to me.

The largest group goes to Spalding, of course. "We had a glorious trip," I hear him tell the assemblage, "and were treated royally everywhere. I am glad to get back, however, for we have the greatest country in the world. Australia is a nice place, so is England and the other countries we visited, but there is only room for one United States on this globe."

"What is the best thing about being home?" one reporter asks.

"The chance to get a piece of pie," Spalding wittily responds while everyone laughs.

"Tell us, Al, how America stacks up to some of the other countries you visited. Honest, now," another reporter asks.

"Well," Spalding says, "we've supped with royalty in Australia, eaten curry in Ceylon, gazed on the ruined palaces of the ancient Romans, looked into the siren eyes of Parisian beauties, grasped the hands of men who are in line for kingly thrones, and wept at the scenes of poverty in Ireland. Despite all of that, I never fully appreciated anything nor experienced such keen delights in all my travels as that which swelled my breast this morning when I saw New York. I am proud to be called an American."

Next, one of the reporters asks Spalding about Akbar, who happens to stand nearby. While Spalding rattles on about his plans for a rickshaw company, I drift over to where big Ed Crane fields questions. It appears he's stayed sober for the occasion. Like Palmer and a few others, he's put on some pounds during our trip, and it seems the reporters have noticed, too. "Is it true, Ed, that you received sunstroke while crossing the equator and that you haven't been the same in the pitcher's box since then?"

"No, boys, that is nonsense," Crane tells them. "I am in splendid condition and weigh nearly 210 pounds, just what I weighed last season. I'll be just fine, believe me. I'd also like you boys to meet my newest pet, Patrick. This hairy son of Ceylon will serve as mascot for the New York nine this year." Crane holds up Patrick in his cage for all to see and gives them the details of how he acquired the monkey. The story about Patrick is no exaggeration, even if Crane's description of his weight is.

Ward, meanwhile, goes directly to where Ned Hanlon stands, and the two engage in close conversation for quite some time. I guess they are probably talking about the affairs of their Brotherhood.

Another group speaks to Tom Burns. "Where is the fourth member of the Stone Wall Infield? Where is Ned Williamson?"

"Williamson remains in Paris with his wife, Nellie. He will recuperate from his injury in due time but is not ready to return to the United States just yet."

The talking continues for quite some time. After about half an hour, still no one wants to interview the mascot, so I just wait around until it's time to go to our New York lodgings, the Fifth Avenue Hotel.

Chapter 28

April 8, 1889
New York City, New York, United States

The teams resume playing once they are back in America, although I don't know how much their hearts are in the games anymore. On April 8, they play a game at Washington Park in Brooklyn before a couple thousand spectators. Once again, we line up for a photograph before the game, and this time, I sit for the picture with the Chicago Club. The photographer tells us the image will appear on cards sold with packages of cigarettes. I see the photograph some time later. It identifies all the Chicago players by their last name. Underneath my picture, it simply reads "mascot."

The evening of April 8 is a special one, however. After our exhibition, I learn that the leading figures of New York decided to arrange a special dinner for the ballplayers at Delmonico's, which MacMillan says is the most famous restaurant in Manhattan. All the players put on their best suits when we load up in carriages to go to dinner. No one tells me I can't go, so I get into a carriage and ride to the restaurant with some of the players. I have on my Italian suit.

It's fraying a bit at the sleeves by now because I wear it most of the time, but it's still the best clothes I have.

Only after we arrive does the usual rejection happen. "What are you doing here, Clarence?" Anson asks angrily when he sees me. "Who told the nigger he could come to dinner at Delmonico's?"

"Did they hire you to wait tables, Clarence? Or open the doors for your betters?" Pfeffer drawls. At least he's shaved his mustache back to a normal length since arriving in New York, even if the words coming from his mouth are no nicer than ever.

Ryan can't resist taunting me, either. "No boys, it's his job to bring hay for the horses while the carriages wait, I think."

Some of the other players, Healy and Tener included, speak with Spalding some distance away while I take the abuse. Soon, Healy comes over, his gaze downcast and voice quiet. "I am sorry, Clarence, but it appears someone made a mistake. No one reserved a seat for you, and no extras are available now. Here, take this money, so you can return to our hotel."

I had hoped that once, just once, I'd get to go to one of the fancy dinners on the tour, but that is not my luck. I shuffle away, head down, while the ballplayers file inside the restaurant doors. Tener, Ward, and Crane go in last. I see them say something to the doorman but turn my back to the door while I walk slowly toward a waiting carriage.

Just when I reach into my pocket and I'm about to hand the omnibus driver my fare, I hear the doorman call out, "Psst, Clarence. Come over here, lad."

I turn to look, and the doorman waves me over with his right arm while putting something in his pocket with his left hand. He has on a dress suit just like everyone else I've seen this evening, complete with pearl-white gloves. "Wait here just a moment," he says to me. "I've got someone coming who'll get you in."

"Really? No tricks?"

"No tricks, son. I read the sporting papers, and I know what's happening here tonight. I also know who you are, and anyone who

266

travels the world as you've done at least deserves to see what happens at this dinner. Look," he says, pointing to another restaurant employee in a suit walking toward us, "this is my friend Anderson. He'll find a place where you can watch dinner and get a little to eat for yourself."

I'm still not sure about this, and the fact must show on my face, because next the doorman says, "Don't worry, we do this all the time, right, Anderson?"

"That we do. This way, Clarence, I know just the place."

Once we go inside, I see why people consider Delmonico's such a stylish restaurant. It has huge silver chandeliers, ice sculptures, a fountain with flowers, artwork on the ceiling, huge illustrations on the walls of us posing at the Sphinx and in the Roman Colosseum, and waiters in tuxedos. Everything is first-class. The main dining room looks almost as much a ballroom as a dining room. The roof is thirty or forty feet up, and a second-floor balcony surrounds the dining room.

After leading me up a stairway, Anderson tells me to sit in a chair near the back wall of the second-floor balcony. It is behind an enormous plant, just like in the Sandwich Islands. He assures me the waiters won't take any notice of me or complain of my presence. "Like I said, we do this all the time," he tells me with a wink as he departs. He even hands me a program before leaving, along with one of the souvenirs that everyone at the banquet receives. It is an illustrated book containing scenes from our trip.

When we first set out, back in Omaha, this illustrated book would have done me little good. I would have flipped through the pictures, then put it down. Now, however, I can read a good deal of the print that goes with the pictures. Not all of it, yet, but I'm getting there. Just for a moment, this gives me a feeling of pride that cuts through the humiliation of nearly being sent away at the door once again. I've finally done something that will help me keep my word I gave to Tommy when he died. Someday, I'll be able to read everything printed in them, I vow to myself.

Soon after sitting down, I notice a woman sitting nearby. Her peach-colored evening gown appears very attractive, with a fur shawl and lots of glittering jewelry, but she is by herself. She sits gazing down toward the ballplayers as if she can think of nothing else in the world. I decide I'll listen up next time a waiter comes to serve her.

It doesn't take long before a tuxedoed man comes to refill her champagne glass. The woman thanks him, and he says, "You're welcome, Mrs. Ward."

This must be Johnny Ward's wife, the one who meant to travel the world with us but could not go because of her acting career. I don't think she's noticed me at all because I'm peering at her between the fronds of a fern. For a moment, I wonder why she is up here in the balcony while her husband sits in the dining room, but I notice that Spalding's mother, Anson's wife, and various other ladies sit near to Mrs. Ward, so I figure that all the women must have to sit in the balcony. All the women, that is, and me.

For the briefest moment, my memory flashes back to Honolulu and finding Ward with the woman at the hula dance, but I do my best to banish those thoughts. He was one of my best friends on the trip, he bought me clothes in Hastings, and he's probably the main reason I got to come inside the restaurant tonight, too. Plus, I promised not to tell anyone what I found out about Ward, and so far, I've kept that promise. I don't plan to break it now. Why would she believe me, anyway?

The dinner takes a long time because it comes in nine courses, one for each inning of a baseball game. On a couple occasions, waiters hand me plates with extra food on them, so, as promised, I don't go hungry waiting to see what happens afterward. Once dinner is over, the speeches begin. Right at 10:00, a middle-aged man whom I do not recognize ascends the speaker's platform first.

"Friends and honored guests, thank you for coming to our banquet to celebrate the great achievements of Albert Goodwill Spalding and the American baseball teams. As most of you know, I am Abraham Mills, and for many years, I have had the honor of calling Al Spalding my friend and associate. For the last six months, he and these ballplayers have been abroad, delighting foreigners with exhibitions of our National Game of baseball. We have many great and dignified men here tonight, ready to toast our returning heroes. First, however, it seems only fitting that Mr. Spalding himself say the first words regarding this momentous achievement."

Spalding moves to the podium.

"Friends of baseball," he begins, speaking loudly so all 300 or so guests can hear him, "two days ago, we returned to our native land after more than five months abroad. Before we left, we proclaimed it our mission to display the manly virtues of American sport before the nobility, crowned heads, and peasantry of the Old World. In this, we succeeded. If members of the British royal family honored us with their presence, which I am willing to concede, we repaid it by a splendid exhibition of our National Game." Plenty of applause follows.

"These representatives of American enterprise and citizenship," Spalding says, extending his right arm and waving it over the crowd such that it covers all the ballplayers, "return as victorious gladiators, covered in the glory of American manhood." More applause.

"Not only have we represented our nation in fine style in Australia, Europe, and everywhere in between, these players have shown the world the greatest game yet created. No matter if the audience consisted of the civilized nobility of Britain or the benighted hordes of Egypt, they did their utmost. If, incidentally, we have paved the way for greater American commercial relations abroad, we've done the world a yet greater favor by creating more devotees of manly sport. I hope I do not exceed the bounds of modesty when I state that these bold and plucky young men did in six short months what as many years would have failed to accomplish under ordinary circumstances."

Spalding speaks for a while longer before giving way to the next speaker on the program, whom Mills introduces as DeWolf Hopper. I only recognize him because MacMillan pointed him out to me two days ago in New York's harbor. Because his name includes the word "wolf," I'm worried that the Howling Wolves might decide to put on a performance of their own, but the men keep quiet tonight. I guess Baldwin hasn't had enough to drink just yet. Hopper recites a poem that, he informs the audience, appeared for the first time the previous June. Written by Ernest Lawrence Thayer, its title is "Casey at the Bat." I'd never heard the poem before, although most of the audience seems familiar with it. I am surprised when I hear Hopper read that mighty Casey strikes out at the end of the poem.

"I am told," Hopper announces after finishing his reading, "that Casey is modeled on Captain Anson." The assembly laughs, even Anson. Normally, this type of thing sends him into a spluttering rage, but tonight, even he can take things in good humor. Anson simply raises his glass to Hopper before draining it with a smile. I notice his glass contains water, not wine. Anson didn't drink liquor on our tour, either, now that I think about it. He is a man of principle, even if I don't like what all his principles are.

Following Hopper, Mills announces a speaker whose name I do not recognize: Theodore Roosevelt. It is a good thing that Mills stays on the speaker's platform to announce each new speaker in turn. This is helpful for me because I can test what I think the program says against what Mills says out loud. Mills identifies Roosevelt as the author of the book *The Naval War of 1812*, a New York assemblyman, and a founding member of the Boone and Crockett Club. I don't know what the Boone and Crockett Club does, but most of the people in the room nod when they hear the name, so I suppose it's an important thing. Like Spalding before him, Roosevelt gives warm praise to the ballplayers for their manly example and strenuous lifestyle.

"I've met President Harrison in the White House, and I can confirm the stories that the president proudly displays a baseball scorecard on the mantle of his private study. With the future of baseball in the hands of such men as these gentlemen assembled here tonight, America will long remain at the forefront of the world in push, drive, and manliness, so long as such a sport as baseball leads the way. I believe that a country that holds liberty dear must have men of athletic spirit who make a race fit for peace and war. This generation is breeding men with the athletic spirit needed for the future defense of the country against foreign foes. These men have that spirit." The audience greets these remarks with loud and hearty applause.

"I glory in the triumphs of the scholar, yet gladly admit the body has its honors as well as the brain. Open-air sports are conducive to health and hardihood. They give vigor to the arm, fleetness to the limbs, alertness to the eye, and nerve to the heart. Sports ignite the fires of emulation. They create a thirst for distinction and encourage the longing desire to win a name that will mark them among their fellows.

"I bid you all Godspeed, for an institution that teaches a boy that nothing but honesty and manliness can succeed, must be doing a missionary work every day of its existence. It will not only make a high standard of baseball men, it will make the world better for its presence."

"Next," Mills informs the audience as Roosevelt sits down, "we will hear from the captains of each team, Mr. Ward and Mr. Anson. I'd like to introduce Captain Anson first, the man we all know as the greatest general of the ball field."

Anson stumbles a bit getting up from his chair, then walks up to the podium and slowly unfolds a piece of paper to read from. None of the other guests so far read from a paper. I see his right arm twitch just a little. He clears his throat. Twice. He adjusts his tie and gives each arm of his suit jacket a little tug.

"They say I have pretty good qualities for arguing," Anson begins, his voice a little quiet and shaky, "and if I could argue out of making any remarks here, I would do so. Still, I believe this is the proudest moment of my life. I am proud of having been captain of one of the teams, and I am proud of the manner in which people abroad have received us, and the kind patronage we have received. My only regret is that Ned Williamson, whom we all regard as a brother, is not with us tonight. We were obliged to leave him abroad, but we all wish him a speedy recovery. You may bet you will all find Ned in his accustomed place at shortstop for the Chicago Club this coming season. Thank you."

Anson shuffles back to his seat, wipes his brow, and sits down quickly.

Next, Johnny Ward steps to the platform. Unlike Anson, he strides confidently, smiles at the audience, uses no notes, and is all ready to speak by the time Mills finishes his introduction.

Of Ward, Mills says, "I now call on Captain John Montgomery Ward to address our gathering. You all know Mr. Ward as a skillful ballplayer, an accomplished writer and author, and a man who adds great dignity to the profession."

Ward looks as comfortable speaking to the audience as Anson did awkward, and I expect he'll speak for some time because he delights in showing off his knowledge of the English language. To my surprise, however, and probably the surprise of everyone, his remarks are short and terse.

"We are about to complete a delightful trip and a delightful experience, and I assure you we have seen it in first-class style. In Honolulu, in Australia, in France and England, and, in fact, in every country we have visited, we have received cordial hospitality. I offer a toast to the American baseball teams." With that, Ward walks away from the podium and sits down.

It seems his short speech takes Mills by surprise as well because it takes Mills a moment to realize that Ward has finished and to move to the podium and introduce the next guest. After he does, an older gentleman with white hair and white whiskers takes the speaker's platform. Although I am unfamiliar with this new speaker, Mills shakes his hand respectfully, even reverently, almost as if he feels small in comparison. I recognize this look because I do the same myself whenever someone introduces me to a white person.

"It is now my great pleasure," Mills says with solemn seriousness, "to introduce the guest who requires no introduction. I know that all of you recognize him, and all of you know him. What Mr. Spalding and these players have done for American sport on their tour, this man has done for American literature internationally many times over. Allow me to introduce Mr. Samuel Clements, whom you all know best as Mark Twain."

Twain gives a rambling speech. He speaks for quite some time, and the audience laughs frequently, but one part of his oration sticks out to me. He says, "Although not a native, I have visited, a great many years ago, the Sandwich Islands—that peaceful land, that beautiful land, that far off home of profound repose, and soft indolence, and dreamy solitude, where life is one long, slumberless Sabbath, the climate one long, delicious summer day, and the good that die experience no change, for they but fall asleep in one heaven, and wake up in another. These boys have played baseball there! Baseball, which is the very symbol, the outward and visible expression of the drive, push, rush, and struggle of the raging, tearing, booming nineteenth century! One cannot realize it, the place and the fact are so incongruous; it's like interrupting a funeral with a circus. Why, there's no legitimate point of contact, no possible kinship between baseball and the Sandwich Islands; baseball is all fact, the islands all sentiment. In baseball, you have to do everything just right or you don't get there; in the islands, you have to do everything just wrong, or you can't stay there. You do it wrong to get it right, for if you do it right, you get it wrong; there isn't any way to get it right but to do it wrong, and the wronger you do it the righter it is."

None of this makes much sense to me, but everyone else seems to think it is excellent, if the amount of applause Twain gets is any indication. The audience doesn't seem to care that we didn't actually play a game of baseball in Honolulu. Once again, I vow to myself that I will learn how to read and write even better, so these things will make sense to me, too.

Meanwhile, the speeches continue. The next man to rise and talk is bald on top of his head but has bushy white sideburns. Mills says of him, "This gentleman is well-known to those in our audience from the great state of New York. His many services to the public include serving in the New York Assembly and as New York's Secretary of State during the War Between the States. President Andrew Johnson appointed him as the United States minister to Japan, and he was a colonel in the New York National Guard for nine years. Right now, he is the president of the New York Central Hudson River Railroad Company. I'd like to welcome Chauncey Depew to the podium."

"Thank you, Mr. Mills," Depew begins. "I am often fond of saying that I get my exercise acting as pallbearer to my friends who exercise, but tonight, among such distinguished athletes, I feel such remarks are out of place. You see, if there was anything that ever kept the cockles of my heart beating with pride for my country, it was the story of your progress around the globe. I read of you in the Sandwich Islands, where, without any clothes, the king and the people greeted you. We read of you on the plains of Egypt, where the pyramids, that have looked down on forty centuries and have seen their peoples disappear, greeted you until the applause rattled the bones of the pharaohs, and the Sphinx bowed its head and handed the box to the captain of the team. Recently Mr. Gladstone of Britain said to me, 'What is the difference between your press and ours?' I replied, 'Yours gives ten columns of Parliamentary reports and a half-column of cricket; ours gives ten columns of baseball and a half a column of speeches.' Mr. Gladstone asked me, 'What is the reason?' I replied, 'The reason is that you have to work out the scheme of your liberty. It is your most important duty, and play with you is an excrescence. We have worked out our liberties and we have time to play. We have 65 million people in this country differing in everything else, but who stand united on baseball. The wonder of it is that only about 6,000 people understand the game, and there is danger that they will become the aristocracy.'"

The last speaker on the program is Abraham Mills himself. He is the former president of the National League according to Spalding, who returns to the podium to introduce Mills. All the people present seem to expect something important, and polite silence greets Mills when he grips the podium and begins speaking. After the usual round of toasts, he says, "When I look out before me, I see such worthy examples of American manhood and citizenship, it does my heart proud to address all of you tonight. And who shall say that this tour of our baseball players—bearing no diplomatic mission—unversed though they be in the arts of statecraft—a tour devised to display in foreign lands a manly sport developed by Americans—who shall say it has not also been a useful contribution toward that universal peace and goodwill among the nations of the earth that we as a people are ever foremost in promoting? All honor, then, to Mr. Spalding and to every man in his party. They have reflected credit alike upon our National Game, our enterprise, our manhood, and our citizenship."

After the roar of cheers dies down, Mills adjusts his tie and grips the podium a bit tighter. "However, friends, I have not been called on here this evening merely to express my admiration for Mr. Spalding, Mr. Ward, Mr. Anson, and the rest of these exemplars of manly virtue, great though that admiration is. Rather, some time ago I agreed to take the task upon myself of investigating the origins of baseball in America. Tonight, I am ready to share my findings."

I was not aware that the origins of baseball were a matter of great concern, but apparently, they are, because no one says a word while Mills pauses for effect. Every person in the dining room stares at him expectantly. "As our National Game gains in popularity, both here in the United States and abroad," and here he nods toward Spalding, "many have tried to claim credit for its origination. Here, tonight, we can finally put those various claims to rest. Without regaling you with all the hours of toil spent in investigation, the false leads, and the excitement of my various discoveries, I have reached a conclusion which is beyond reasonable doubt."

Again, Mills pauses for effect while the audience hangs on each word. Finally, he smiles and continues.

"Baseball is a game that quickens all the senses, stirs the blood, brings into play every muscle in the body, and usually develops the lungs of the spectators. In short, it embodies all the characteristics of American society that each of us holds so dear. I can therefore say, by virtue of patriotism and research, that baseball is a distinctly American game, that it has no antecedents in any other game, sport, or country, and that these American origins are beyond dispute."

With this statement, the audience erupts in applause. The ballplayers pound on their tables, and a chant develops: "No rounders! No rounders! No rounders!" This goes on for at least a minute, and the people give Mills a standing ovation lasting at least a minute more.

After this patriotic flourish, the guests start filing out of Delmonico's. Mr. Anderson returns and ushers me toward the staircase. "That is our cue, Clarence. The dinner is over, and if I'm going to sneak you out of here, you'd better come with me now."

I do as he says and descend the staircase. Anderson shows me out through the back door of the kitchen. I still have the money Healy gave me, so I plan to hire a carriage and return to the hotel. Even as I'm leaving the restaurant, I hear the chant of "No rounders!" start up once again.

I've had a great deal of luck on this trip; however, that luck deserts me at the end of the evening. While I'm looking around to find a carriage, I see that Pfeffer and Ryan are coming toward me, also looking for transportation. Suddenly, they see me.

"The nigger is still here," Pfeffer says to Ryan. Pfeffer looks a bit unsteady on his feet, and twice he stops moving, blinks his eyes several times, and lurches forward again. Ryan doesn't look much better. He's swerving a bit while he walks toward me. As they approach, the smell of wine on their breath becomes obvious.

"He's got a program from tonight," Ryan adds, pointing at what's in my hand. "That means he snuck in, the little thief!"

"Get him, Jimmy, we've got to teach him a lesson!"

I jump into the street, so I can try to dodge them and run away. They appear drunk enough I might be able to. Unfortunately, because it is only April, the streets are wet and muddy, and in my excitement, I slip, just like in Nice. I land on my backside, drop both my program and my illustrated book into the mud, and the two men grab me by the shoulders and haul me up.

"What should we do with the little coon, Fred?" Ryan asks his companion.

"Let's do just what you said when we first went in, Jimmy. Send him to the horse stalls so he can feed them hay."

"Good idea, they're over here."

I struggle and squirm. I almost get away once because I'm muddy and slippery, but after one near-escape, Pfeffer has me by the arms and Ryan by the legs, so it's hopeless. My wrestling moves are useless without having an arm free.

We reach the horse stalls. "One, two, three!" Pfeffer shouts, and they toss me in. I land on my side, which isn't too bad, except that my side happens to land in horse dung. Next, Pfeffer and Ryan douse me with a pail of water sitting near the horses' trough. Laughing and patting each other on the back, the two men walk away.

I just lie there for a good long time, trying to decide if it's okay to cry. I do, a little. Then I sit up and look around. I stink. Badly. I'm soaked, too, and my other clothes are back at the hotel. These ones, the nicest I have, look so bad, I think they're ruined. I wonder if the hotel will even let me in, looking and smelling like this. Standing, I wipe away another tear. Next, I look for another pail of water, hoping I can find a clean one to rinse off the horse dung on my right side. I find one in the next stall, and do the best I can, but I'm in sorry shape when I wander back to the street.

On the way, I see my program and book, lying right where I dropped them. A carriage has run over my program, tearing it and staining it with mud. I leave it. Somehow, the book escaped damage, so I wipe a little mud off the back cover and pick it up to take with me.

Next, I try to hail a carriage to take me back to the hotel. None of them will accept me as a passenger because of the smell and sogginess of my clothes. I'll walk back to the Fifth Avenue Hotel on my own, I guess. Part of me worries that someone will meet me on the way and try to steal my book, but no one does, mercifully. Perhaps I look so hopeless that even thieves aren't interested in me.

Finally, I arrive at the front entrance of the hotel and get the predicted response when I try to convince the doorman I'm a guest. He won't let me pass, no matter how much I beg. I even offer the money Healy gave me as a bribe, but he only scoffs at me and tells me to move along before he summons a policeman. In the morning, I'll try to find one of the players as they leave the hotel, so they can go to my room and fetch my belongings. I shuffle to the alley behind the hotel to sleep there. I sleep in alleys most nights in Chicago, so I know what to do, even if I haven't had to do it for a while.

I try to settle in, but it's only April, and because the dousing soaked my clothes, and I have no way to get them dry or warm myself up, I can't sleep. So, I wander the streets near the hotel until dawn. I meet one policeman while I walk and try to tell him my story, but he doesn't believe me and tells me to move along.

The night goes on forever. I pace, or I sit, but the chills seep in when I sit, and I get up to pace some more. No matter how tightly I grip my chest with my arms, I still shake and can't warm up.

After realizing I'll never get to sleep, I think while I stumble around. Finally, I reach some conclusions.

I'm tired of the humiliations. It doesn't matter what their source is—whether it's my skin color, or the fact that I'm only twelve, or that I'm puny and weak, or that I'm just learning to read and write. I can't take any more humiliation. I won't be entertainment for other people anymore.

That settles my mind on something else I've been thinking about. No more parades and no more being a mascot.

Although I'm still not sure what else I should do instead, my mind's made up that Chicago won't be my final destination. Chicago is the city I know best, but I'll adapt wherever I end up. Maybe I should go west. I'm not sure where, but I need to make a new start.

I have a little luck, if you can call it that, when Tener is the first person I recognize to exit the hotel in the morning.

"Clarence, what are you doing out here? What's happened?"

I explain everything from last night, from sneaking into Delmonico's, to Pfeffer and Ryan catching me and tossing me into the horse stall, and about having to stay outside and stay awake all night when no one would let me in.

"Well, I'll go and grab your things," he tells me. "Just wait here, I guess. We're boarding a train for Chicago in a couple of hours; just tag along with me, and we'll make sure you're on the train. You can change your clothes then."

I do as Tener says and board the train to Chicago, our tour's last stop. I also know now it will be my last stop as the mascot of a baseball team. Forever.

Chapter 29

April 20, 1889
Chicago, Illinois, United States

After almost six months and thirty thousand miles, I'm in Chicago again. In my excitement to be here and depression after everything that happened in New York, I'd quite forgotten that the tour schedule called for playing more baseball games in America on our way back to Chicago. Nothing has changed my resolve to quit being a mascot, however, so when we reach Chicago, it's my turn to lead our parade for the final time.

At each stop between New York and Chicago, there have been more parades, more banquets, and more speeches. The one here in Chicago even features Roman candles and other fireworks, but it all feels familiar by now.

When we line up to march, one last time, to the field at West Side Park, I go through my routine. "Dress ranks there," I say to the players like I always do, but it comes out flat and without much zest, and I don't think they are listening in any case. My heart isn't in it, either, so I just turn around and toss my baton a few times while I walk onto the field. I sit down on the Chicago bench just like always and watch the game.

It is one of the strangest games on our trip. Mark Baldwin pitches for Chicago, but he just lobs the ball toward home plate, so the batters hit his pitches all around the park. The final score is 22 to 9 in favor of the All-America team.

After the game, when the players prepare to depart for their real homes, be they in Chicago or elsewhere around the country, a few of them, plus me, wait outside Spalding's office. After the game, he came around to speak with me, but also with Daly, Baldwin, Pettit, and Sullivan, asking them to come to his office once the game was over. Now, I wait outside while the four of them go in to see Spalding.

A few minutes later, they emerge from Spalding's office, looking very gloomy and muttering under their breaths. After they file out, Spalding says, "Clarence, please come in."

Spalding sits behind a large desk made of very expensive, polished wood. I'm not sure what kind of wood it is, but the desk only holds my attention for a moment. I see many cabinets and shelves in the office, most of them containing books or papers of one kind or another. Behind Spalding are framed photographs that I recognize from our trip. One is the photograph at the Sphinx, and next to it the one in the Roman Colosseum and a few others that he must have had taken on his own because they don't have any of the players in them.

Since I didn't have a chance to ask the players, I decide to ask Spalding what has happened and why the boys looked so sad. "Mr. Spalding, sir, why did the boys look so down when they came out of your office just now?"

"The Chicago Club decided it could do without their services for the 1889 championship season, Clarence."

"You mean that Daly, Baldwin, Pettit, and Sullivan won't be playing on the Chicago nine this year?"

"That is correct. All are excellent ballplayers, but we have men enough under contract. Too many men, in fact, and I preferred to let these players go rather than the others."

"That is sad, I suppose," I say. "I know it's not my business, Mr. Spalding, but what will they do after traveling all around the world with us?"

"Oh, I'm sure they'll find a team to play for somewhere. Like I said, all are good players, and someone will want them. The Chicago Club, however, has decided to play with men of a more sober disposition this year. You have firsthand experience, I believe, with what happens to ballplayers when they imbibe of alcohol too freely."

"Yes, Mr. Spalding, I suppose I do."

"As for you, however, as far as I'm concerned you have fulfilled the contract you signed back in Hastings last October. You've done your duty, Clarence, well and faithfully, so I am pleased to say thank you for a job well done."

"Thank you, Mr. Spalding. I've always tried my best."

"I know you have, Clarence, which is why I'm also pleased to say that you are welcome to take this." He hands me a little cloth pouch; it jingles with the sound of coins inside. "Before our game today, several of the men passed the hat for you. Tommy Burns made the greatest contribution. I believe he still feels bad over what happened in the Sandwich Islands. Fogarty, Ward, Tener, and a few others also made liberal donations. It surprised me a bit, but even Ned Hanlon chipped in. Whether you know it or not, you've made some good friends among the boys, Clarence, and several of the ballplayers wish you well. I'm sure you know which ones by now."

"That is very kind of them, Mr. Spalding. Will you please tell them thank you for me?"

"You can tell them yourself, Clarence. The same players also asked me if I'd bring you back as the White Stockings' mascot for the 1889 championship season. I thought it a terrific idea. What do you say? Will we see you on the field leading our parades again in 1889?"

"That is a fine compliment, Mr. Spalding. I don't know if I'm worthy, but I am glad that the players think so. I appreciate your offer to be the mascot, too."

"Our first home game is on Wednesday, May 8, Clarence, so you have a few weeks before we'll need your services. Are you with us?"

I pause for a long moment. Here is my last chance to change my mind and fall back on what I'm familiar with.

"I am sorry, Mr. Spalding, but I don't think so. Your tour showed me I need to learn how to read and write better if I'm ever going to get on in the world. I want to go to school and learn."

"That is a very worthy goal, Clarence. I congratulate you on your resolve. Will you be here in Chicago?"

"No, sir, I think I'll head west once I've learned my letters. Mr. MacMillan has been kind enough to offer me a few more lessons in the meantime."

"Will you go back to Omaha afterward?"

"No, not Omaha. I was thinking I might see what Montana Territory is like, to tell you the truth. I've never been there, but I want to see a buffalo someday. I hope maybe I'll find one there."

"You don't say, Clarence. Montana Territory. I hear rumors that Montana may become a state before the year is out. You'll get to experience the excitement first hand. Well, that certainly is a change from Chicago, no doubt about it. What will you do there?"

"I'm not sure, to be honest, Mr. Spalding, as long as it isn't mining. I don't do very well underground. I'll see what turns up."

He smiles when I mention mining, remembering what happened way back in Ballarat. "Well, my boy, I wish you luck." Spalding extends his hand, and I shake it.

"Thank you again, Mr. Spalding, for allowing me to come on your trip," I say to him as I turn to leave. "I'll never forget it as long as I live."

"None of us will, Clarence, none of us will. I don't know if my business will ever take me to Montana Territory but until then, farewell."

I leave Spalding's office and walk downstairs toward the doors to the street. I thought all the ballplayers had left for their homes, or for their teams to get ready to play their 1889 season, but to my surprise, Fogarty and Healy wait in the lobby.

Fogarty speaks first, of course. "Clarence Duval. The luckiest and best mascot ever born." He gives me a big hug. "You didn't think you could just sneak away from us, did you? Even you aren't that lucky." Fogarty releases me from his hug and says, "I found out we play our first game with Chicago on May 13 this year. Game time is hawf pawst foive."

We all laugh at his imitation of the Irish porter in Dublin. He really has it down now. "I thought it would be quite a reunion for the Order of the Howling Wolves, but I just found out what happened to Daly, Sullivan, Pettit, and Baldwin. Still, at least you'll be there, along with Williamson. See you again, then?" He offers his hand.

I look down for a moment before answering, "No, Mr. Fogarty, I'm afraid not. I think I'm done with mascoting for baseball teams."

His eyes widen, and his eyebrows perk up. "What will you do? Where are you going to go?"

"I don't know for certain, but I want to learn how to read better. Then I think I'm going to head west and see what my luck brings me. I'll try Montana Territory first, I think. I've always wanted to see a real buffalo. Maybe in Montana I can."

Healy is next. "I'm sorry to hear you won't be on the diamond this season, Clarence. I was looking forward to our next meeting. I'll never forget our adventures together. Someday, Ireland will be free, and when it is, I'll think of you." His voice cracks a little at the end, and he shakes my hand sadly.

Suddenly, I have an inspiration. "Here, take this, Mr. Healy." I hand him my most treasured possession, my marching baton. "I don't suppose I'll need it anymore, so I want you to have it. It looks a little beat up after going all the way around the world, but I guess it has done its duty."

"I'm honored, Clarence. I'll keep it safe at my house in St. Louis in case you ever need it again." A small tear forms in his left eye.

"And you can have this, Mr. Fogarty." I open my knapsack and pull out my bandleader's hat, handing it to him. "I don't think I'll need that again, either. I think I've led my last parade."

"That is very generous of you, Clarence, thank you. I'll treasure your hat, I promise you."

"Well, Clarence, if you think you are going to Montana Territory, let me give you something in return," Healy says to me. "Give me just a moment to find a piece of paper. I'll be right back."

He heads up the stairs to Spalding's office. It takes a few minutes, but he returns before long with a piece of paper that he folds and places in an envelope before handing the envelope to me. "I've written a letter of introduction for you because one of my brothers lives in Butte, Montana. It's a mining town in the Rocky Mountains. If you need somewhere to stay while getting situated in Montana, he'll take you in, I'm sure of it. I'll also write him a letter myself, just so he knows you might try to find him. Don't worry. He won't care about your color. His wife is an Indian, if you can believe that."

"Thank you so much, Mr. Healy. That is very kind. Perhaps I'll meet your brother someday."

The two men look at each other, and then they look at me. "Well, I suppose it's time to go our separate ways," Fogarty says. "I wish I had you around to bring me more luck, Clarence, but I guess I'll have to live by my own merits now. And stay away from volcanoes. John, I'll see you on the field."

"That you will, Jim, that you will. Take good care of yourself, Clarence, my boy. May your luck never run out."

With that, Healy opens the door to the street, and Fogarty walks outside. I follow him out to the living, pulsing streets of Chicago.

I didn't know it at the time, but I wouldn't see those streets again for a decade. Instead, a new series of adventures awaited me a thousand miles to the west in the soon-to-be state of Montana.

Clarence's adventures continue in book three of the Clarence Duval series, The Buffalo Soldier.

If you enjoyed this book, you can find other books in this series, as well as my works of historical research in baseball history, at my website:

robbauerbooks.com

You can also sign up for my Readers Club mailing list to receive notifications about future books and promotions. If you enjoyed reading the book, I would be grateful if you'd leave a short review on whatever website you purchased it from. Favorable reader reviews are very important to authors like me. They help tremendously in attracting new readers and spreading the word about existing books you think others will enjoy. Finally, if you like the book, please consider recommending it to fellow readers of new and original historical fiction.

Thank you!

About the Author

I hold a PhD in history from the University of Arkansas, where I attended school as a Distinguished Doctoral Fellow, as well as Masters degrees in history and education. In addition to my writing and publishing business, I am the History Department Chair at Flathead Valley Community College in Kalispell, Montana, where I teach United States History, Western Civilization, Montana History, Environmental History, Civil Rights Movement History, and the occasional Honors class.

In my historical novels, I attempt to bring to light some historical events that are not general knowledge. The stories are fictionalized, of course, but based on real events that I find important, interesting, and worth spending time researching and writing about. I hope my books spur people to try to learn more about the real events featured in them.

When I'm not writing, researching, or teaching, I spend time with my sweetheart of a dog, Ally, and enjoy the outdoors in Western Montana. Besides my love for history, I grew up a sports fan, especially baseball. I also like strategy games, fitness activities, and, of course, reading. I still hope to run that marathon someday.

Acknowledgments

I also want to thank the people who helped make this book possible, especially Jim Soular for his help with editing. Ali Holst gets the credit for the cover art and design. Thank you to Jennifer Lodine-Chaffey and Mary Asplund for reading and making suggestions on various chapters.

Made in the USA
Coppell, TX
16 November 2019

11467697R00173